Praise for Anne Perry's William Monk mysteries

DEFEND AND BETRAY

"Engaging and sharply observed . . . The climactic trial, and its ugly disclosures, are well wrought."
—*The New York Times Book Review*

A DANGEROUS MOURNING

"The strong-willed pair persists in pressing the case to its chilling conclusion."
—*Publishers Weekly*

THE FACE OF A STRANGER

"Richly textured with the sights and sounds of London and its countryside; the rigid social structures of the well-born; the abysmal misery of the poor and haunting echoes of the slaughterhouse that was Crimea. Solidly absorbing and Perry's best to date."
—*Kirkus Reviews*

Also by Anne Perry
Published by Fawcett Books:

The Thomas and Charlotte Pitt Mysteries
THE CATER STREET HANGMAN
CALLANDER SQUARE
PARAGON WALK
RESURRECTION ROW
BLUEGATE FIELDS
RUTLAND PLACE
DEATH IN THE DEVIL'S ACRE
CARDINGTON CRESCENT
SILENCE IN HANOVER CLOSE
BETHLEHEM ROAD
HIGHGATE RISE
BELGRAVE SQUARE
FARRIERS' LANE
THE HYDE PARK HEADSMAN

Published by Ivy Books:

The William Monk Mysteries
THE FACE OF A STRANGER
A DANGEROUS MOURNING
DEFEND AND BETRAY

A
SUDDEN,
FEARFUL
DEATH

Anne Perry

IVY BOOKS • NEW YORK

Ivy Books
Published by Ballantine Books
Copyright © 1993 by Anne Perry

All rights reserved under International and Pan-American Copyright Conventions. Published in the United States by Ballantine Books, a division of Random House, Inc., New York, and simultaneously in Canada by Random House of Canada Limited, Toronto.

Library of Congress Catalog Card Number: 93-70006

ISBN 0-8041-1283-5

Manufactured in the United States of America

First Hardcover Edition: October 1993
First Mass Market Edition: October 1994

10 9 8 7 6 5 4 3 2 1

To Elizabeth Sweeney, for her friendship, and patience
in reading my handwriting

1

WHEN SHE FIRST CAME into the room, Monk thought it would simply be another case of domestic petty theft, or investigating the character and prospects of some suitor. Not that he would have refused such a task; he could not afford to. Lady Callandra Daviot, his benefactress, would provide sufficient means to see that he kept his lodgings and ate at least two meals a day, but both honor and pride necessitated that he take every opportunity that offered itself to earn his own way.

This new client was well dressed, her bonnet neat and pretty. Her wide crinoline skirts accentuated her waist and slender shoulders, and made her look fragile and very young, although she was close to thirty. Of course the current fashion tended to do that for all women, but the illusion was powerful, and it still woke in most men a desire to protect and a certain rather satisfying feeling of gallantry.

"Mr. Monk?" she inquired tentatively. "Mr. William Monk?"

He was used to people's nervousness when first approaching him. It was not easy to engage an inquiry agent. Most matters about which one would wish such steps taken were of their very nature essentially private.

Monk rose to his feet and tried to compose his face into

1

an expression of friendliness without overfamiliarity. It was not easy for him; neither his features nor his personality lent itself to it.

"Yes ma'am. Please be seated." He indicated one of the two armchairs, a suggestion to the decor of his rooms made by Hester Latterly, his sometimes friend, sometimes antagonist, and frequent assistant, whether he wished it or not. However, this particular idea, he was obliged to admit, had been a good one.

Still gripping her shawl about her shoulders, the woman sat down on the very edge of the chair, her back ramrod straight, her fair face tense with anxiety. Her narrow, beautiful hazel eyes never left his.

"How may I help you?" He sat on the chair opposite her, leaning back and crossing his legs comfortably. He had been in the police force until a violent difference of opinion had precipitated his departure. Brilliant, acerbic, and at times ruthless, Monk was not used to setting people at their ease or courting their custom. It was an art he was learning with great difficulty, and only necessity had made him seek it at all.

She bit her lip and took a deep breath before plunging in.

"My name is Julia Penrose, or I should say more correctly, Mrs. Audley Penrose. I live with my husband and my younger sister just south of the Euston Road. . . ." She stopped, as if his knowledge of the area might matter and she had to assure herself of it.

"A very pleasant neighborhood." He nodded. It meant she probably had a house of moderate size, a garden of some sort, and kept at least two or three servants. No doubt it was a domestic theft, or a suitor for the sister about whom she entertained doubts.

She looked down at her hands, small and strong in their neat gloves. For several seconds she struggled for words.

His patience broke.

"What is it that concerns you, Mrs. Penrose? Unless you tell me, I cannot help."

"Yes, yes I know that," she said very quietly. "It is not

2

easy for me, Mr. Monk. I realize I am wasting your time, and I apologize. . . ."

"Not at all," he said grudgingly.

She looked up, her face pale but a flash of humor in her eyes. She made a tremendous effort. "My sister has been . . . molested, Mr. Monk. I wish to know who was responsible."

So it was not a petty matter after all.

"I'm sorry," he said gently, and he meant it. He did not need to ask why she had not called the police. The thought of making such a thing public would crush most people beyond bearing. Society's judgment of a woman who had been sexually assaulted, to whatever degree, was anything from prurient curiosity to the conviction that in some way she must have warranted such a fate. Even the woman herself, regardless of the circumstances, frequently felt that in some unknown way she was to blame, and that such things did not happen to the innocent. Perhaps it was people's way of coping with the horror it engendered, the fear that they might become similar victims. If it were in some way the woman's own fault, then it could be avoided by the just and the careful. The answer was simple.

"I wish you to find out who it was, Mr. Monk," she said again, looking at him earnestly.

"And if I do, Mrs. Penrose?" he asked. "Have you thought what you will do then? I assume from the fact that you have not called the police that you do not wish to prosecute?"

The fair skin of her face became even paler. "No, of course not," she said huskily. "You must be aware of what such a court case would be like. I think it might be even worse than the—the event, terrible as that must have been." She shook her head. "No—absolutely not! Have you any idea how people can be about . . ."

"Yes," he said quickly. "And also the chances of a conviction are not very good, unless there is considerable injury. Was your sister injured, Mrs. Penrose?"

Her eyes dropped and a faint flush crept up her cheeks.

3

"No, no, she was not—not in any way that can now be proved." Her voice sank even lower. "If you understand me? I prefer not to . . . discuss—it would be indelicate . . ."

"I see." And indeed he did. He was not sure whether he believed the young woman in question had been assaulted, or if she had told her sister that she had in order to explain a lapse in her own standards of morality. But already he felt a definite sympathy with the woman here in front of him. Whatever had happened, she now faced a budding tragedy.

She looked at him with hope and uncertainty. "Can you help us, Mr. Monk? 'Least—at least as long as my money lasts? I have saved a little from my dress allowance, and I can pay you up to twenty pounds in total." She did not wish to insult him, and embarrass herself, and she did not know how to avoid either.

He felt an uncharacteristic lurch of pity. It was not a feeling which came to him easily. He had seen so much suffering, almost all of it more violent and physical than Julia Penrose's, and he had long ago exhausted his emotions and built around himself a shell of anger which preserved his sanity. Anger drove him to action; it could be exorcised and leave him drained at the end of the day, and able to sleep.

"Yes, that will be quite sufficient," he said to her. "I should be able either to discover who it is or tell you that it is not possible. I assume you have asked your sister, and she has been unable to tell you?"

"Yes indeed," she responded. "And naturally she finds it difficult to recall the event—nature assists us in putting from our minds that which is too dreadful to bear."

"I know," he said with a harsh, biting humor she would never comprehend. It was barely a year ago, in the summer of 1856, just at the close of the war in the Crimea, that he had been involved in a coaching accident and woken in the narrow gray cot of a hospital, cold with terror that it might be the workhouse and knowing nothing of himself at all, not even his name. Certainly it was the crack to his head which had brought it on, but as fragments of memory had returned, snatches here and there, there was still a black

4

horror which held most of it from him, a dread of learning the unbearable. Piece by piece he had rediscovered something of himself. Still, most of it was unknown, guessed at, not remembered. Much of it had hurt him. The man who emerged was not easy to like and he still felt a dark fear about things he might yet discover: acts of ruthlessness, ambition, brilliance without mercy. Yes, he knew all about the need to forget what the mind or the heart could not cope with.

She was staring at him, her face creased with puzzlement and growing concern.

He recalled himself hastily. "Yes of course, Mrs. Penrose. It is quite natural that your sister should have blanked from her memory an event so distressing. Did you tell her you intended coming to see me?"

"Oh yes," she said quickly. "It would be quite pointless to attempt to do it behind her back, so to speak. She was not pleased, but she appreciates that it is by far the best way." She leaned a little farther forward. "To be frank, Mr. Monk, I believe she was so relieved I did not call the police that she accepted it without the slightest demur."

It was not entirely flattering, but catering to his self-esteem was something he had not been able to afford for some time.

"Then she will not refuse to see me?" he said aloud.

"Oh no, although I would ask you to be as considerate as possible." She colored faintly, raising her eyes to look at him very directly. There was a curiously firm set to her slender jaw. It was a very feminine face, very slight-boned, but by no means weak. "You see, Mr. Monk, that is the great difference between you and the police. Forgive my discourtesy in saying so, but the police are public servants and the law lays down what they must do about the investigation. You, on the other hand, are paid by me, and I can request you to stop at any time I feel it the best moral decision, or the least likely to cause profound hurt. I hope you are not angry that I should mark that distinction?"

Far from it. Inwardly he was smiling. It was the first

time he felt a spark of quite genuine respect for Julia Penrose.

"I take your point very nicely, ma'am," he answered, rising to his feet. "I have a duty both moral and legal to report a crime if I have proof of one, but in the case of rape—I apologize for such an ugly word, but I assume it is rape we are speaking of?"

"Yes," she said almost inaudibly, her discomfort only too apparent.

"For that crime it is necessary for the victim to make a complaint and to testify, so the matter will rest entirely with your sister. Whatever facts I learn will be at her disposal."

"Excellent." She stood up also and the hoops of her huge skirt settled into place, making her once more look fragile. "I assume you will begin immediately?"

"This afternoon if it will be convenient to see your sister then? You did not tell me her name."

"Marianne—Marianne Gillespie. Yes, this afternoon will be convenient."

"You said that you had saved from your dress allowance what seems to be a considerable sum. Did this happen some time ago?"

"Ten days," she replied quickly. "My allowance is paid quarterly. I had been circumspect, as it happens, and most of it was left from the last due date."

"Thank you, but you do not owe me an accounting, Mrs. Penrose. I merely needed to know how recent was the offense."

"Of course I do not. But I wish you to know that I am telling you the absolute truth, Mr. Monk. Otherwise I cannot expect you to help me. I trust you, and I require that you should trust me."

He smiled suddenly, a gesture which lit his face with charm because it was so rare, and so totally genuine. He found himself liking Julia Penrose more than he had anticipated from her rather prim and exceedingly predictable appearance—the huge hooped skirts so awkward to move in and so unfunctional, the neat bonnet which he loathed, the white gloves and demure manner. It had been a hasty judgment, a practice which he despised in others and even more in himself.

"Your address?" he said quickly.

"Number fourteen, Hastings Street," she replied.

"One more question. Since you are making these arrangements yourself, am I to assume that your husband is unaware of them?"

She bit her lip and the color in her cheeks heightened. "You are. I should be obliged if you would be as discreet as possible."

"How shall I account for my presence, if he should ask?"

"Oh." For a moment she was disconcerted. "Will it not be possible to call when he is out? He attends his business every weekday from nine in the morning until, at the earliest, half past four. He is an architect. Sometimes he is out considerably later."

"It will be, I expect, but I would prefer to have a story ready in case we are caught out. We must at least agree on our explanations."

She closed her eyes for a moment. "You make it sound so ... deceitful, Mr. Monk. I have no wish to lie to Mr. Penrose. It is simply that the matter is so distressing, it would be so much pleasanter for Marianne if he did not know. She has to continue living in his house, you see?" She stared up at him suddenly with fierce intensity. "She has already suffered the attack. Her only chance of recovering her emotions, her peace of mind, and any happiness at all, will lie in putting it all behind her. How can she do that if every time she sits down at the table she knows that the man opposite her is fully aware of her shame? It would be intolerable for her!"

"But you know, Mrs. Penrose," he pointed out, although even as he said it he knew that was entirely different.

A smile flickered across her mouth. "I am a woman, Mr. Monk. Need I explain to you that that brings us closer in a way you cannot know. Marianne will not mind me. With

7

Audley it would be quite different, for all his gentleness. He is a man, and nothing can alter that."

There was no possible comment to make on such a statement.

"What would you like to tell him to explain my presence?" he asked.

"I—I am not sure." She was momentarily confused, but she gathered her wits rapidly. She looked him up and down: his lean, smooth-boned face with its penetrating eyes and wide mouth, his elegant and expensively dressed figure. He still had the fine clothes he had bought when he was a senior inspector in the Metropolitan Police with no one to support but himself, before his last and most dreadful quarrel with Runcorn.

He waited with a dry amusement.

Evidently she approved what she saw. "You may say we have a mutual friend and you are calling to pay your respects to us," she replied decisively.

"And the friend?" He raised his eyebrows. "We should be agreed upon that."

"My cousin Albert Finnister. He is short and fat and lives in Halifax where he owns a woolen mill. My husband has never met him, nor is ever likely to. That you may not know Yorkshire is beside the point. You may have met him anywhere you choose, except London. Audley would wonder why he had not visited us."

"I have some knowledge of Yorkshire," Monk replied, hiding his smile. "Halifax will do. I shall see you this afternoon, Mrs. Penrose."

"Thank you. Good day, Mr. Monk." And with a slight inflection of her head she waited while he opened the door for her, then took her leave, walking straight-backed, head high, out into Fitzroy Street and north toward the square, and in a hundred yards or so, the Euston Road.

Monk closed the door and went back to his office room. He had lately moved here from his old lodgings around the corner in Grafton Street. He had resented Hester's interference in suggesting the move in her usual high-handed manner, but when she had explained her reasons, he was obliged to agree. In Grafton Street his rooms were up a flight of stairs and to the back. His landlady had been a motherly soul, but not used to the idea of his being in private practice and unwilling to show prospective clients up. Also they were obliged to pass the doors of other residents, and occasionally to meet them on the stairs or the hall or landing. This arrangement was much better. Here a maid answered the door without making her own inquiries as to people's business and simply showed them in to Monk's very agreeable ground-floor sitting room. Grudgingly at first, he conceded it was a marked improvement.

Now to prepare to investigate the rape of Miss Marianne Gillespie, a delicate and challenging matter, far more worthy of his mettle than petty theft or the reputation of an employee or suitor.

It was a beautiful day when he set out: a hot, high summer sun beating on the pavements, making the leafier squares pleasant refuges from the shimmering light hazy with the rising smoke of distant factory chimneys. Carriages clattered along the street past him, harnesses jingling, as people rode out to take the air or to pay early afternoon calls, drivers and footmen in livery, brasses gleaming. The smell of fresh horse droppings was pungent in the warmth and a twelve-year-old crossing sweeper mopped his brow under a floppy cap.

Monk walked to Hastings Street. It was little over a mile and the additional time would give him further opportunity to think. He welcomed the challenge of a more difficult case, one which would test his skills. Since the trial of Alexandra Carlyon he had had nothing but trivial matters, things that as a policeman he would have delegated to the most junior constable.

Of course the Carlyon case had been different. That had tested him to the utmost. He remembered it with a complexity of feelings, at once triumphant and painful. And with thought of it came memory of Hermione, and uncon-

9

sciously he lengthened his pace on the hot pavement, his body tightened and his mouth clenched shut in a hard line. He had been afraid when her face first came fleetingly into his mind; a shred of the past returned, uncertain, haunting him with echoes of love, tenderness, and terrible anxiety. He knew he had cared for her, but not when or how, if she had loved him, what had happened between them that he had nothing left, no letters, no pictures, no reference to her in his possessions.

But regardless of memory, his skill was always there, dedicated and ruthless. He had found her again. Fragment by fragment he had pieced it together until he stood on the doorstep and at last he knew her, the whole gentle almost childlike face, the brown eyes, the halo of hair. The entire memory flooded back.

He swallowed hard. Why was he deliberately hurting himself? The disillusion burned over him in anger as if it had been only moments ago, the searing knowledge that she preferred the comfortable existence of half love; emotions that did not challenge; commitment of the mind and body, but not of the heart; always a reservation to avoid the possibility of real pain.

Her gentleness was accommodation, not compassion. She had not the courage to do more than sip at life; she would never drain the cup.

He was walking so blindly he bumped into an elderly man in a frock coat and apologized perfunctorily. The man stared after him with irritation, his whiskers bristling. An open landau passed with a group of young women huddled together and giggling as one of them waved to some acquaintance. The ribbons on their bonnets danced in the breeze and their huge skirts made them seem to be sitting on mounds of flowered cushions.

Monk had already resolved to look no further into the emotions of his past. He knew more than he wanted to about Hermione; and he had detected or deduced enough about the man who had been his benefactor and mentor, and who would have introduced him into successful commerce had he not been cheated into ruin himself—a fate from which Monk had tried so hard to rescue him, and failed. It was then, in outrage at the injustice, that he had abandoned commerce and joined the police, to fight against such crime; although as far as he could remember, he had never caught that particular fraud. Please God at least he had tried. He could remember nothing, and he felt sick at the thought of trying, in case his discovery shed even further ugly light on the man he had been.

But he had been brilliant. Nothing cast shadow or doubt on that. Even since the accident he had solved the Grey case, the Moidore case, and then the Carlyon case. Not even his worst enemy—and so far that seemed to be Runcorn, although one never knew who else he might discover—but not even Runcorn had said he lacked courage, honesty, or the will to dedicate himself totally to the pursuit of truth, and labor till he dropped, without counting the cost. Although it seemed he did not count the cost to others either.

At least John Evan liked him, although of course he had known him only since the accident, but he had liked him whatever the circumstances. And he had chosen to continue something of a relationship even after Monk had left the force. It was one of the best things to have happened, and Monk hugged it to himself, a warm and acutely valuable thing, a friendship to be nurtured and guarded from his own hasty temper and biting tongue.

Hester Latterly was a different matter. She had been a nurse in the Crimea and was now home in an England that had no use for highly intelligent, and even more highly opinionated, young women—although she was not so young. She was probably at least thirty, too old to be considered favorably for marriage, and thus destined to either continue working to support herself or be permanently dependent upon the charity of some male relative. Hester would loathe that.

To begin with she had found a position in a hospital here in London, but in a very short time her outspoken counsel

11

to doctors, and finally her total insubordination in treating a patient herself, had earned her dismissal. The fact that she had almost certainly saved the patient's life only added to the offense. Nurses were for cleaning the ward, emptying slops, winding bandages, and generally doing as they were told. The practice of medicine was for doctors alone.

After that she had taken up private nursing. Goodness only knew where she was at this moment. Monk did not.

He was in Hastings Street. Number fourteen was only a few yards away, on the far side. He crossed over, climbed the steps, and rang the doorbell. It was a gracious house, neo-Georgian, and spoke of quiet respectability.

After a moment or two the door was opened by a maid in a blue stuff dress and white cap and apron.

"Yes sir?" she said inquiringly.

"Good afternoon." He held his hat in his hand courteously, but as if fully expecting to be admitted. "My name is William Monk." He produced a card which gave his name and address but not his occupation. "I am an acquaintance of Mr. Albert Finnister of Halifax, whom I believe to be a cousin of Mrs. Penrose and Miss Gillespie. Since I was in the area, I wondered if I might pay my respects?"

"Mr. Finnister, you said, sir?"

"That is correct, of Halifax in Yorkshire."

"If you'd like to wait in the morning room, Mr. Monk, I will see if Mrs. Penrose is at home."

The morning room where he waited was comfortably furnished but with a care which spoke of a well-managed economy. There was no unnecessary expense. Decoration was a home-stitched sampler modestly framed, a print of a romantic landscape, and a rather splendid mirror. The chair backs were protected by well-laundered antimacassars, and the armrests were worn where countless hands had rubbed them. Certainly there was something of a track across the carpet from door to fireplace. A nicely arranged vase of white daisies sat on the low central table, a pleasingly feminine touch. The bookcase had one brass doorknob which was not quite the same as the others. Altogether it was an agreeable, unexceptional room, designed for comfort rather than to impress.

The door opened and the maid informed him that Mrs. Penrose and Miss Gillespie would be delighted to receive him, if he would come to the withdrawing room.

He followed her obediently back across the hall again to another, larger room, but this time there was no opportunity to look about him. Julia Penrose was standing by the window in a rose-colored afternoon dress, and a young woman about eighteen or nineteen, whom he assumed to be Marianne, was sitting on the small sofa. She looked very pale in spite of her darker natural coloring, hair almost black and springing from her brow in a remarkable widow's peak. She also had a small mole high on her left cheekbone in what Monk thought the Regency dandies would have called the "gallant" position. Her eyes were very blue.

Julia came forward, smiling. "How do you do, Mr. Monk. How charming of you to call upon us," she said for the maid's benefit. "May we offer you some refreshment? Janet, please bring us some tea and cakes. You will have cakes, Mr. Monk?"

He accepted politely, but as soon as the maid was gone the charade fell away. Julia introduced him to Marianne and invited him to begin his task. She stood behind her sister's chair with her hand on the younger woman's shoulder as if she would give her of her own strength and resolve.

Monk had dealt with a case of assault upon a woman only once before. Rape was very seldom reported because of the shame and the scandal attached. He had given a great deal of thought how to begin, but still he was uncertain.

"Please tell me what you remember, Miss Gillespie," he said quietly. He was not sure whether to smile or not. She might take it as a lightness on his part, as if he had no sympathy with her. And yet if he did not, he knew his features were of a naturally grim cast.

She swallowed and cleared her throat, then cleared it again. Julia's hand tightened on her shoulder.

13

"I really don't remember very much, Mr. Monk," she apologized. "It was very—unpleasant. At first I tried to forget it. Maybe you cannot understand that, and I daresay I am to blame—but I did not realize . . ." She stopped.

"It is quite natural," he assured her with more sincerity than she could know. "We all try to forget what hurts us. It is sometimes the only way we can continue."

Her eyes widened in sudden surprise and a faint flush touched her cheeks.

"How sensitive of you." There was profound gratitude in her face, but no easing of the tension which gripped her.

"What can you tell me about it, Miss Gillespie?" he asked again.

Julia made as if to speak, then with an effort changed her mind. Monk realized she was some ten or twelve years older than her sister and felt a fierce sense of protection toward her.

Marianne looked down at her small square hands clenched in the lap of her enormous skirt.

"I don't know who it was," she said very quietly.

"We know that, dear," Julia said quickly, leaning forward a little. "That is what Mr. Monk is here to find out. Just tell him what you know—what you told me."

"He won't be able to find out," Marianne protested. "How could he, when I don't know myself? Anyway, you cannot undo it, even if you did know. What good will it do?" Her face was set in utter determination. "I'm not going to accuse anyone."

"Of course not!" Julia agreed. "That would be terrible for you. Quite unthinkable. But there are other ways. I shall see that he never comes near you again, or any other decent young woman. Please just answer Mr. Monk's questions, dear. It is an offense which cannot be allowed to happen. It would be quite wrong of us to continue as if it did not matter."

"Where were you when it happened, Miss Gillespie?" Monk interrupted. He did not want to be drawn into the argument as to what action could be taken if they discovered

14

the man. That was for them. They knew the consequences far better than he.

"In the summerhouse," Marianne replied.

Instinctively Monk glanced toward the windows, but he could see only sunlight through the cascading leaves of a weeping elm and the lush pink of a rose beyond.

"Here?" he asked. "In your own garden?"

"Yes. I go there quite often—to paint."

"Often? So anyone familiar with your day might have expected to find you there?"

She colored painfully. "I—suppose so. But I am sure that can having nothing to do with it."

He did not reply to that. "What time of day was it?" he asked instead.

"I am not certain. About half past three, I think. Or perhaps a little later. Maybe four." She shrugged very slightly. "Or even half past. I was not thinking of time."

"Before or after tea?"

"Oh—yes—I see. After tea. I suppose it must have been half past four then."

"Do you have a gardener?"

"It wasn't he!" she said, jerking forward in some alarm.

"Of course not," he soothed. "Or you would have known him. I was wondering if he had seen anyone. If he had been in the garden it might help to determine where the man came from, which direction, and perhaps how he left, even the precise time."

"Oh yes—I see."

"We do have a gardener," Julia said with keenness quickening in her face and some admiration for Monk lighting her eyes. "His name is Rodwell. He is here three days a week, in the afternoons. That was one of his days. Tomorrow he will be back again. You could ask him then."

"I shall do," Monk promised, turning back to Marianne. "Miss Gillespie, is there anything at all about the man you can recall? For example," he continued quickly, seeing her about to deny it, "how was he dressed?"

"I—I don't know what you mean." Her hands knotted

15

more tightly in her lap, and she stared at him with mounting nervousness.

"Was he dressed in a dark jacket such as a man of business might wear?" he explained. "Or a working smock, like a gardener? Or a white shirt, like a man of leisure?"

"Oh." She seemed relieved. "Yes. I see. I think I recall something—something pale." She nodded, becoming more assured. "Yes, a pale jacket, such as gentlemen sometimes wear in the summer."

"Was he bearded, or clean shaven?"

She hesitated only a moment. "Clean shaven."

"Can you remember anything else about his appearance? Was he dark or fair, large or small?"

"I—I don't know. I—" She took a sharp breath. "I suppose I must have had my eyes closed. It was . . ."

"Hush, dear," Julia said quickly, tightening her hand on Marianne's shoulder again. "Really, Mr. Monk, she cannot tell you anything more of him. It is a most terrible experience. I am only glad it has not turned her mind. Such things have been known to."

Monk retreated, uncertain just how far he ought to press. It was a terror and revulsion he could only imagine. Nothing could show to him her experience.

"Are you sure you wish to pursue it?" he asked as gently as he could, looking not at Julia but at Marianne.

However, as before, it was Julia who answered.

"We must." There was resolute decision in her voice. "Quite apart from justice, she must be protected from ever encountering this man again. You must persevere, Mr. Monk. What else is there that we can tell you that may be of use?"

"Perhaps you would show me the summerhouse?" he asked, rising to his feet.

"Of course," Julia agreed immediately. "You must see it, or how else can you judge for yourself?" She looked at Marianne. "Do you wish to come, dear, or would you rather not?" She turned back to Monk. "She has not been there since it happened."

Monk was about to say that he would be present to protect her from any danger, then realized just in time that being alone with a man she had newly met might in itself be enough to alarm her. He felt he was foundering. It was going to be even harder than he had anticipated.

But Marianne surprised him.

"No—that is quite all right, Julia," she said firmly. "I will take Mr. Monk and show him. Perhaps tea will come while we are out, and we shall be able to return to it." And without waiting for Julia's reply, she led the way out into the hall and to the side door into the garden.

After a glance at Julia, Monk followed her and found himself outside in a small but extremely pleasant paved yard under the shade of a laburnum tree and a birch of some sort. Ahead of them stretched a long, narrow lawn and he could see a wooden summerhouse about fifteen yards away.

He walked behind Marianne over the grass under the trees and into the sun. The summerhouse was a small building with glassed windows and a seat inside. There was no easel there now, but plenty of room where one might have stood.

Marianne turned around on the step.

"It was here," she said simply.

He regarded his surroundings with care, absorbing the details. There was at least a twenty-foot distance of grass in every direction, to the herbaceous border and the garden walls on three sides, to the arbor and the house on the fourth. She must have been concentrating very profoundly on her painting not to have noticed the man approach, and the gardener must have been at the front of the house or in the small kitchen herb garden at the side.

"Did you cry out?" he asked, turning to her.

Her face tightened. "I—I don't think so. I don't remember." She shuddered violently and stared at him in silence. "I—I might have. It is all . . ." She stared at him in silence again.

"Never mind," he dismissed it. There was no use in

17

making her so distressed that she could recall nothing clearly. "Where did you first see him?"

"I don't understand."

"Did you see him coming toward you across the grass?" he asked.

She looked at him in total confusion.

"Have you forgotten?" He made an effort to be gentle with her.

"Yes." She seized on it. "Yes—I'm sorry . . ."

He waved his hand, closing the matter. Then he left the summerhouse and walked over the grass toward the border and the old stone wall which marked the boundary between this and the next garden. It was about four feet high and covered in places by dark green moss. He could see no mark on it, no scuff or scratch where anyone had climbed over. Nor were there any broken plants in the border, although there were places where one might have trodden on the earth and avoided them. There was no point in looking for footprints now; the crime had been ten days ago, and it had rained several times since then, apart from whatever repairs the gardener might have made with a rake.

He heard the faint brush of her skirts over the grass and turned to find her standing just behind him.

"What are you doing?" she asked, her face puckered with anxiety.

"Looking to see if there are any traces of someone having climbed in over the wall," he replied.

"Oh." She drew in her breath as if about to continue speaking, then changed her mind.

He wondered what she had been about to say, and what thought had prevented her. It was an ugly feeling, and yet he could not help wondering if she had, after all, known her attacker—or even whether it had truly been an attack and not a seduction. He could well understand how a young woman who had lost her most precious commodity, her virtue in the eyes of others, and who thus was ruined for the marriage market, might well claim an attack rather than a yielding on her own part, whatever the temptation. Not that

18

being the victim of rape would be any more acceptable. Perhaps it was only to her own family that it might make any difference. They would do all they could to see that the rest of the world never knew.

He walked over to the wall at the end of the garden where it abutted the opposite property. Here the stones were crumbling in one or two places, and an agile man might have climbed over without leaving a noticeable trace. She was still with him and she read his thoughts, her eyes wide and dark, but she said nothing. Silently he looked at the third wall separating them from the garden to the west.

"He must have come over the end wall," she said very quietly, looking down at the grass. "No one could have come through the herb garden to the side because Rodwell must have been there. And the door from the yard on the other side is locked." She was referring to the paved area to the east side where the rubbish was kept and where the coal chute to the cellar and the servants' entrance to the scullery and kitchen were located.

"Did he hurt you, Miss Gillespie?" He asked it as respectfully as he could, but even so it sounded intrusive and disbelieving.

She avoided his eyes, a dark rush of blood staining her cheeks.

"It was most painful," she said very quietly. "Most painful indeed." There was undisguised surprise in her voice, as if the fact amazed her.

He swallowed. "I mean did he injure you, your arms or your upper body? Did he restrain you violently?"

"Oh—yes. I have bruises on my wrists and arms, but they are growing paler now." Carefully she pushed up her long sleeves to show him ugly yellow-gray bruising on the fair skin of her wrists and forearms. This time she looked up at him.

"I'm sorry." It was an expression of sympathy for her hurt, not an apology.

She flashed him a sudden smile; he saw a glimpse of the person she had been before this event had robbed her of her

19

confidence, pleasure, and peace of mind. Suddenly he felt a furious anger toward whoever had done this to her, whether it had been seduction to begin with, or always a violation.

"Thank you," she said, then straightened her shoulders. "Is there anything else you would care to see out here?"

"No, thank you."

"What will you do next?" she asked curiously.

"About this? Speak to your gardener, and then your neighbors' servants, to see if they saw anything unusual, anyone in the area not known to them."

"Oh. I see." She turned away again. The scent of flowers was heavy around them, and somewhere close he could hear bees.

"But first I shall take my leave of your sister," he said.

She took a step toward him.

"About Julia—Mr. Monk . . ."

"Yes?"

"You must forgive her being a little . . . overprotective of me." She smiled fleetingly. "You see, our mother died a few days after I was born, when Julia was eleven." She shook her head a little. "She might have hated me for it: it was my birth which caused Mama's death. Instead she looked after me right from that moment. She has always been there to give me all the tenderness and the patience when I was small, and later to play with me when I was a child. Then as I grew older she taught me and shared in all my experiences. No one could have been sweeter or more generous." She looked at him very candidly, an urgency in her face that he should do more than believe, that he should understand.

"Sometimes I fear she gave me the devotion she might have given to a child of her own, had she one." Now there was guilt in her. "I hope I have not been too demanding, taken from her too much time and emotion."

"You are quite able to care for yourself, and must have been for some time," he replied reasonably. "Surely she

20

would not still devote so much to you unless she wished to."

"I suppose not," she agreed, still looking at him earnestly. The slight breeze stirred the muslin of her skirt. "But I shall never be able to repay her for all she has done for me. You must know that, Mr. Monk, so you will understand a little better, and not judge her."

"I do not judge, Miss Gillespie," he lied. He was very prone to judge, and frequently harshly. However in this particular case he saw no fault in Julia Penrose's care for her sister, and perhaps that redeemed the untruth.

As they reached the side door to the house, they were met by a man in his mid-thirties. He was slender, of average height, with a face whose features and coloring were ordinary enough, but their expression gave him an air of crumpled vulnerability overlying a volatile temper and a huge capacity to be hurt.

Marianne moved a little closer to Monk and he could feel the warmth of her body as her skirts brushed around his ankles.

"Good afternoon, Audley," she said with a slight huskiness in her voice, as though speaking had come unexpectedly. "You are home early. Have you had an agreeable day?"

His eyes moved from her to Monk, and back again.

"Quite commonplace, thank you. Whom do I have the pleasure of addressing?"

"Oh—this is Mr. Monk," she explained easily. "He is a friend of cousin Albert's, from Halifax, you know."

"Good afternoon, sir." Audley Penrose's manner was polite, but without pleasure. "How is cousin Albert?"

"He was in good spirits the last time I saw him," Monk replied without a flicker. "But that was some little time ago. I was passing in this area, and since he spoke so kindly of you, I took the liberty of calling."

"No doubt my wife has offered you tea? I saw it set out in the withdrawing room."

"Thank you." Monk accepted because it would have

21

called for considerable explanation to leave without it now, and half an hour or so in their company might give him a better feel for the family and its relationships.

However, when he did leave some forty-five minutes later he had neither altered nor added to his original impression, nor his misgivings.

"What troubles you?" Callandra Daviot asked over supper in her cool green dining room. She sat back in her chair regarding Monk curiously. She was middle-aged, and not even her dearest friend would have called her beautiful. Her face was full of character; her nose was too long, her hair obviously beyond the ability of her maid to dress satisfactorily, let alone fashionably, but her eyes were wide, clear, and of remarkable intelligence. Her gown was a most pleasing shade of dark green, though of a cut neither one thing nor another, as though an unskilled dressmaker had tried to update it.

Monk regarded her with total affection. She was candid, courageous, inquisitive, and opinionated in the best possible way. Her sense of humor never failed her. She was everything he liked in a friend, and she was also generous enough to have engaged him as a business partner, sustaining him during those times when his cases were too few or too paltry to provide an adequate income. In return she required to know all he was able to tell her of each affair in which he involved himself. Which was what he was doing this evening in the dining room, over an excellent supper of cold pickled eel and fresh summer vegetables. He knew, because she had told him, that there was plum pie and cream to follow, and a fine Stilton cheese.

"It is totally unprovable," he answered her question. "There is nothing whatever except Marianne's word for it that the whole event ever took place at all, let alone that it took place as she described it."

"Do you doubt her?" she said curiously, but there was no offense in her voice.

He hesitated several moments, unsure, now that she

asked, whether he did or not. She did not interrupt his silence, nor draw the obvious conclusion, but went on eating her fish.

"Some of what she says is the truth," he said finally. "But I think she is also concealing something of importance."

"That she was willing?" She looked up at him, watching his face.

"No—no I don't think so."

"Then what?"

"I don't know."

"And what do they intend to do if you should discover who it is?" she asked with raised eyebrows. "After all, who could it be? Total strangers do not vault over suburban garden walls in the hope of finding some maiden alone in the summerhouse whom they can ravish, sufficiently quietly not to rouse the gardener or servants, and then leap back again and disappear."

"You make it sound absurd," he said dryly, taking a little more of the eel. It really was excellent.

"Life is often absurd," she replied, passing him the sauce. "But this is also unlikely, don't you agree?"

"Yes I do." He spooned sauce onto his plate liberally. "What is most unlikely is that it is really someone who was a complete stranger to her. If it was someone she knew, who came through the house, and therefore was aware that there was no one within earshot, and that his mere presence would not alarm her, as a stranger would, then it becomes much less unlikely."

"What concerns me far more," Callandra went on thoughtfully, "is what they intend to do when you tell them who it is—if you do."

It was something which had troubled him also.

Callandra grunted. "Sounds like a private revenge. I think perhaps you should consider very carefully what you tell them. And William . . ."

"Yes?"

"You had better be absolutely sure you are right!"

23

Monk sighed. It was getting uglier and more complicated with each new thought that came to him.

"What impression did you form of the sister and her husband?" Callandra pursued.

"Of them?" He was surprised. "Very sympathetic to her. I can't believe she has anything to fear from them, even if she did not resist as thoroughly as she might."

Callandra said nothing. They finished their course in companionable silence and the plum pie was brought in and served. It was so delicious that they both ate without speaking for several minutes, then finally Callandra set her spoon down.

"Have you seen Hester lately?"

"No."

She smiled with some inner amusement. He felt annoyed and then unaccountably foolish.

"I have not seen her," he went on. "The last time we parted it was with less than amiability. She is the most opinionated and abrasive woman I have ever met, and dogmatic to the degree that she does not listen to anyone else. And she is absurdly complacent about it, which makes it insufferable."

"Qualities you do not like?" she asked innocently.

"Good God no!" he exploded. "Does anyone?"

"You find firmly held opinions and spirited defense of them displeasing?"

"Yes!" he said vehemently, setting down his spoon momentarily. "It is unbecoming, irritating in manner, and makes all intelligent and open conversation impossible. Not that most men would be seeking an intelligent conversation with a woman of her age," he added.

"Especially when her views are mistaken," she said with her eyes bright.

"That adds to it, of course," he conceded, quite sure now that she was laughing.

"You know she said something very similar about you when she was here about three weeks ago. She is nursing an elderly lady with a broken leg, but at that point the

24

woman was almost recovered, and I don't think she has a further position offered her yet."

"Perhaps if she were to guard her tongue a little and make herself more obliging—and modest?" he suggested.

"I am sure you are right," Callandra agreed. "With your own experience of the value of such qualities, perhaps you might give her some excellent advice." She made the suggestion with a face almost wiped of humor.

He looked at her more closely. There was the slightest curl of a smile on her mouth and her eyes avoided his.

"After all," she continued, keeping a sober expression with an effort, "intelligent conversation with the open-minded is so agreeable, don't you think?"

"You are twisting my words," he said between his teeth.

"No I am not," she denied, looking up at him with quite open affection and amusement. "You mean that when Hester has an opinion and will not move from it, it is dogmatic and unbecoming and it annoys you incredibly. When you have one it is courageous and committed, and the only path for anyone with integrity. That is what you said, one way or another, and I am quite sure it is what you mean."

"You think I am wrong." He leaned forward on the table.

"Oh frequently. But I should never dare to say so. Would you care for more cream with your pie? I suppose you have not heard from Oliver Rathbone lately either?"

He helped himself to the cream.

"I looked into a minor case for him ten days ago." Rathbone was the highly successful barrister with whom Monk had worked on all his outstanding cases since the accident. He admired Rathbone's professional ability profoundly and found the man himself both attractive and irritating. There was a suaveness and a self-confidence in him which caught a nerve in Monk's nature. They were too alike in some aspects, and too unlike in others. "He seemed in excellent health," he finished with a tight smile, meeting Callandra's eyes. "And how are you? We have spoken of everything else. . . ."

She looked down at her plate for a moment, then up again at him.

"I am very well, thank you. Do I not look it?"

"Indeed, you look exceptionally well," he replied truthfully, although he had actually just noticed it for the first time. "You have found an interest?"

"How perceptive of you."

"I am a detective."

She looked at him very steadily and for that moment there was honest and equal friendship between them, without barrier of words.

"What is it?" he said quietly.

"I am on the Board of Governors in the Royal Free Hospital."

"I am delighted." He knew her late husband had been an army surgeon. It was a position which would suit her experience and her natural abilities and inclinations admirably. He was genuinely pleased for her. "How long?"

"Only a month, but already I feel I have been of some service." Her face was quickened with excitement and her eyes brilliant. "There is so much to be done." She leaned forward across the table. "I know a little about the new methods, Miss Nightingale's beliefs about air and cleanliness. It will take time, but we can accomplish what will seem like miracles if we work hard enough." Unconsciously she was beating her forefinger on the tablecloth. "There are so many progressive doctors, as well as the diehards. And the difference it makes to have anesthetic! You have no idea how things have changed in the last ten or twelve years."

She pushed the sugar scuttle away, her eyes intent upon his. "Do you know they can make a person completely senseless, oblivious of pain, and then recover him without harm!" Again her finger beat on the cloth. "That means all manner of surgery can be performed. There is no longer any need to tie a person down and hope to complete everything in a matter of two minutes or so. Now speed is not the primary consideration: one may take time—and care. I never imagined I would see such things—it is absolutely marvelous."

Her face darkened and she leaned back again. "Of course, the trouble is we still lose at least half the patients to infection afterwards. That is where we must improve things." Again she leaned forward. "But I am sure it can be done—there are brilliant and dedicated men here. I really feel I may make some difference." Suddenly the earnestness vanished and she smiled with total candor. "Finish your pie and have some more."

He laughed, happy for her enthusiasm, even though he knew so much of it would end in defeat. Still, any victory was precious. "Thank you," he accepted. "It is really exceedingly good."

2

THE FOLLOWING DAY about ten o'clock Monk walked along to Hastings Street again and called at number fourteen. This time Julia received him in a state of some concern.

"Good morning, Mr. Monk," she said, coming in and closing the door behind her. She was dressed in pale blue-gray and it became her delicate coloring, even though it was a very ordinary day dress with a high neck and the barest of trimmings. "You will be circumspect, won't you?" she said anxiously. "I don't know how you can possibly make inquiries without either telling people what you are seeking or arousing their suspicions. It would be disastrous if they were to learn the truth, or even to imagine it!" She stared up at him with puckered brows and a flush in her cheeks. "Even Audley, Mr. Penrose, was curious yesterday as to why you called. He is not especially fond of cousin Albert, and had not thought that I was either. Which is true, I am not; he was just the most suitable excuse that came to my mind."

"There is no need to be concerned, Mrs. Penrose," he said gravely. "I shall be very discreet."

"But how?" she pressed urgently, her voice sharpening. "What could you possibly say to explain away such questions? Servants talk, you know." She shook her head sharply. "Even the best of them. And what would my neighbors think? What imaginable reason does a respectable person have for employing a private inquiry agent?"

"Do you wish to cease the inquiry, ma'am?" he asked quite quietly. He would understand it very well if she did; indeed, he still did not know what use she would make of the information he sought, even if he found it for her, since no prosecution was planned.

"No," she said fiercely, gritting her teeth. "No I do not. It's just that I must think very clearly before I allow you to proceed. It would be reckless to go ahead and do more damage simply because I feel strongly about the matter."

"I had planned to say there had been a small unpleasantness of damage in the garden," Monk told her. "A few broken plants, and if you have them, glass frames. I will ask if the gardeners or servants have seen any boys playing who might have trespassed and done the harm. That will hardly be a cause for scandal or unseemly speculation."

Her face flickered with amazement, then relief. "Oh, what an excellent idea," she said eagerly. "I should never have thought of that. It sounds so simple and everyday a thing. Thank you, Mr. Monk, my mind is quite at ease."

He smiled in spite of himself. "I'm glad you are satisfied. But your own gardener will not be quite so easy."

"Why not?"

"Because he is perfectly aware that no one has broken your cold frames," he replied. "I had better make it someone else's, and hope they do not compare notes all along the road."

"Oh!" But she gave a little laugh, and the thought of it seemed to amuse her rather than trouble her. "Would you like to see Rodwell today? He is in the back garden now."

"Yes, thank you. This would seem a good opportunity." And without further discussion she led him to the side door into the arbor and left him to find the gardener, who was bent to his knees pulling weeds from the border.

"Good morning, Rodwell," Monk said pleasantly, stopping beside him.

"Mornin' sir," Rodwell answered without looking up.

"Mrs. Penrose gave me permission to speak to you about some breakages locally, in case you happened to have seen any strangers in the area," Monk continued.

"Oh?" Rodwell sat back on his haunches and regarded Monk curiously. "Breakages o' what, sir?"

"Cold frames, bedding plants, that sort of thing."

Rodwell pursed his lips. "No, I can't say as I've seen anyone strange 'round 'ere. Sounds like boys to me, that does—playing, like as not." He grunted. "Throwin' balls, cricket, and that sort o' thing. Mischief, more'n like, not downright wickedness."

"Probably," Monk agreed, nodding. "But it is not a pleasant thought that some stranger might be hanging around, doing malicious damage, even if it's only slight."

"Mrs. Penrose never said nothing about it." Rodwell screwed up his face and peered at Monk doubtfully.

"She wouldn't." Monk shook his head. "Nothing broken in your garden, I daresay."

"No—nothing at all—well . . . no but a few flowers, like, against the west wall. But that could 'a bin anything."

"You haven't seen anyone you don't know hanging around in the last two weeks or so? You are sure?"

"No one at all," Rodwell said with absolute certainty. "I'd 'a chased them orf smart if I 'ad. Don't 'old wi' strangers in gardens. Things get broke, just like you said."

"Oh well, thank you for your time, Rodwell."

"You're welcome, sir." And with that the gardener adjusted his cap to a slightly different angle and resumed his weeding.

Next Monk called at number sixteen, explained his purpose, and asked if he might speak to the lady of the house. The maid took the message and returned within ten minutes to admit him to a small but extremely pleasant writing room where a very elderly lady with many ropes of pearls around her neck and across her bosom was sitting at a rosewood bureau. She turned and looked at Monk with curiosity, and then as she regarded his face more closely, with considerable interest. Monk guessed she must be at least ninety years old.

"Well," she said with satisfaction. "You are an odd-looking young man to be inquiring about broken glass in the garden." She looked him up and down, from his discreet polished boots up his immaculate trouser legs to his elegant jacket, and lastly to his hard, lean face with its penetrating eyes and sardonic mouth. "You don't look to me as if you would know a spade or a hoe if you tripped over one," she went on. "And you certainly don't earn your living with your hands."

His own interest was piqued. She had an amiable face, deeply lined, full of humor and curiosity, and there was nothing critical in her remarks. The anomaly appeared to please her.

"You had better explain yourself." She turned away from the bureau completely as if he interested her far more than the letters she had been writing.

He smiled. "Yes ma'am," he conceded. "I am not really concerned with the glass. It can very easily be replaced. But Mrs. Penrose is a little alarmed at the thought of strangers wandering around. Miss Gillespie, her sister, is given to spending time in the summerhouse, and it is not pleasant to think that one might be being watched when one is unaware of it. Perhaps the concern is unnecessary, but it is there nonetheless."

"A Peeping Tom. How very distasteful," the old lady said, grasping the point instantly. "Yes, I can understand her pursuing the matter. A girl of spirit, Mrs. Penrose, but a very delicate constitution, I think. These fair-skinned girls sometimes are. It must be very hard for them all."

Monk was puzzled; it seemed an overstatement. "Hard for them all?" he repeated.

"No children," the old lady said, looking at him with her head a trifle on one side. "But you must be aware of that, young man?"

"Yes, yes of course I am. I had not thought of it in connection with her health."

"Oh dear—isn't that a man all over." She made a little tut-tut noise. "Of course it is to do with her health. She has been married some eight or nine years. What else would it be? Poor Mr. Penrose puts a very good face on it, but he cannot help but feel it all the same. Another cross for her to bear, poor creature. Afflictions of health are among the worst." She let out her breath in a little sigh. She regarded him closely with a slight squint of concentration. "Not that you would know, by the look of you. Well, I haven't seen any Peeping Toms, but then I cannot see beyond the garden window anyway. My sight is going. Happens when you get to my age. Not that you'd know that either. Don't suppose you are more than forty-five."

Monk winced, but forbore from saying anything. He preferred to think he did not look anything like forty-five, but this was not the time for vanity, and this outspoken old lady was certainly not the person with whom to try anything so transparent.

"Well, you had better ask the outdoor servants," she went on. "Mind you, that is only the gardener and sometimes the scullery maid, if she can escape the cook's eye. Made it sound like a whole retinue, didn't I? Ask them, by all means. Let me know if they tell you anything interesting. There's little enough of interest ever happens here nowadays."

He smiled. "The neighborhood is too quiet for you?"

She sighed. "I don't get about as much as I used to, and nobody brings me the gossip. Perhaps there isn't any." Her eyes widened. "We've all become so terribly respectable these days. It's the Queen. When I was a girl it was different." She shook her head sadly. "We had a king then, of course. Wonderful days. I remember when they brought the news of Trafalgar. It was the greatest naval victory in Europe, you know." She looked at Monk sharply to be sure he appreciated the import of what she was saying. "It was a matter of England's survival against the Emperor of the

French, and yet the fleet came in with mourning flags flying, and in silence—because Nelson had fallen." She gazed beyond Monk into the garden, her eyes misty with remembrance. "My father came into the room and my mother saw his face and we all stopped smiling. 'What is it?' she said immediately. 'Are we defeated?' My father had tears on his cheeks. It was the only time I ever saw him weep."

Her face was alight with the wonder of it still, all the myriad lines subtly altered by the innocence and the emotions of youth.

" 'Nelson is dead,' my father said very gravely. 'Have we lost the war?' my mother asked. 'Shall we be invaded by Napoleon?' 'No,' my father answered. 'We won. The French fleet is all sunk. No one will land on England's shores again.' " She stopped and stared up at Monk, watching to see if he caught the magnitude of it.

He met her eyes and she perceived that he had caught her vision.

"I danced all night before Waterloo," she went on enthusiastically, and Monk imagined the colors, the music, and the swirling skirts she could still see in her mind. "I was in Brussels with my husband. I danced with the Iron Duke himself." All the laughter vanished from her expression. "And then, of course, the next day there was the battle." Her voice was suddenly husky and she blinked several times. "And all that night we heard news and more news of the dead. The war was over, the Emperor beaten forever. It was the greatest victory in Europe, but dear God, how many young men died! I don't think I knew anyone who had not lost somebody, either dead or so injured as never to be the same again."

Monk had seen the carnage left by the Crimean War and he knew what she meant; even though that conflict had been so much smaller, the spirit and the pain were the same. In a sense it was worse, because there was no perceivable purpose to it. England was under no threat, as it had been from Napoleon.

She saw the emotion and the anger in his face. Suddenly

her own sorrow vanished. "And of course I knew Lord Byron," she went on with sudden animation. "What a man! There was a poet for you. So handsome." She gave a little laugh. "So beautifully romantic and dangerous. What wonderful scandal there was then. Such burning ideals, and men did something about them then." She gave a little gasp of fury, her ancient hands clenched into fists on her lap. "And what have we today? Tennyson."

She groaned and then looked at Monk with a sweet smile. "I suppose you want to see the gardener about your Peeping Tom? Well, you had better go and do so, with my blessing."

He smiled back at her with genuine regard. It would have been much pleasanter to remain and listen to her reminiscences, but he had undertaken a duty.

He rose to his feet. "Thank you, ma'am. Courtesy compels me, or I should not leave so readily."

"Ha! Very nicely said, young man." She nodded. "I think from your face there is more to you than chasing trivia, but that is your affair. Good day to you."

He bowed his head and took his leave of her. However, neither the gardener nor the scullery maid could tell him anything of use whatever. They had not seen any stranger in the area. There was no access to the garden of number fourteen except if someone chose to climb the wall, and the flower beds on either side had not been damaged or disturbed. A Peeping Tom, if indeed there had been such a person, must have come some other way.

The occupant of number twelve was of no assistance either. He was a fussy man with gray hair, which was sparse in front, and gold-rimmed eyeglasses. No, he had seen no one in the area who was not known to him and of excellent character. No, he had suffered no breakages in his cold frames. He was sorry, but he could be of no help, and since he was extremely busy, would Mr. Monk be so good as to excuse him.

The residents of the house whose garden abutted number fourteen at the end were considerably more lively. There were at least seven children whom Monk counted, three of them boys, so he abandoned the broken cold frames and returned to the Peeping Tom.

"Oh dear," Mrs. Hylton said with a frown. "What a foolish thing. Men with too little to occupy themselves, no doubt. Everyone ought to be busy." She poked a strand of hair back into its place and smoothed her skirts. "Keep themselves out of trouble. Miss Gillespie, you said? What a shame. Such a nice young lady. And her sister as well. Devoted, they are, which is so pleasant to see, don't you think?" She waved Monk toward the window where he could have a good view of their garden, the wall dividing it from the Penroses', but gave him no time to answer her rhetorical question. "And a very agreeable man, Mr. Penrose is too, I am sure."

"Do you have a gardener, Mrs. Hylton?"

"A gardener?" She was obviously surprised. "Dear me, no. I am afraid the garden is rather left to its own devices, apart from my husband cutting the grass every so often." She smiled happily. "Children, you know? I was afraid at first you were going to say someone had been too wild with the cricket ball and broken a window. You have no idea what a relief it was!"

"The action of a Peeping Tom does not frighten you, ma'am?"

"Oh dear no." She looked at him narrowly. "I doubt if there really was one, you know. Miss Gillespie is very young. Young girls are given to fancies at times, and to nerves." She smoothed her skirts again and rearranged the billowing fabric. "It comes of just sitting around waiting to meet a suitable young man, and hoping he will choose her above her fellows." She took a deep breath. "Of course, she is very pretty, and that will help, but entirely dependent upon her brother-in-law to support her until then. And as I understand it, there is no dowry to mention. I shouldn't be too concerned, if I were you, Mr. Monk. I expect it was a cat in the bushes, or some such thing."

"I see," Monk said thoughtfully, not that his mind was

on any kind of animal, or Marianne's possible imagination, but upon her financial dependence. "I daresay you are right," he added quickly. "Thank you, Mrs. Hylton. I think I shall take your advice and abandon the pursuit. I wish you good day, ma'am."

He had luncheon in a small, busy public house in the Euston Road, and then walked for some time in deep thought, hands in his pockets. The more he considered the evidence the more he disliked the conclusions it suggested. He had never thought it likely anyone came over the garden wall, now he considered it so improbable as to exclude it from his mind. Whoever had attacked Marianne had come through her own house, and therefore was known either to her or to her sister, almost certainly both.

Since they did not intend to prosecute, why had they called Monk? Why had they mentioned the matter at all?

The answer to that was obvious. Julia did not know of it. Marianne had been forced to explain the bruises in some way, and her state of distress; probably her clothes were torn or stained with grass or even blood. And for her own reasons she had not been willing to tell Julia who it was. Perhaps she had encouraged him to begin with, and then become frightened, and since she was ashamed, had claimed it was a stranger, the only answer that would be morally acceptable. No one would believe she would yield to a complete stranger or give him the slightest encouragement.

It was after three when he returned to Hastings Street and again sought admittance. He found Julia in the withdrawing room with Marianne and Audley, who had apparently come home early yet again.

"Mr. Monk?" he said with quite open surprise. "I had not realized cousin Albert had spoken of us so exceedingly well!"

"Audley!" Julia rose to her feet, her cheeks hot pink. "Please come in, Mr. Monk. I am sure my husband did not mean to make you feel less than welcome." Her eyes searched Monk's face with an anxiety she could not conceal, but she studiously avoided looking at Marianne. "It is a little early for tea, but may we offer you some cold lemonade? It is really a very hot day."

"Thank you." Monk accepted both because he was thirsty and because he wished to observe them all a little more closely, especially the two women. How deep was the trust between them, and how much was Julia really misled? Did she suspect her sister of an unwise dalliance? Was it all perhaps to protect her from Audley's moral outrage if he thought she were less than a victim? "That is very kind of you," he added, sitting in the chair she indicated.

She rang the bell and dispatched the maid to fetch the refreshments.

Monk felt he owed Julia some explanation for Audley, and racked his brain to think of an acceptable lie. To say he had left something behind would be too transparent. Audley would be suspicious immediately, so would Monk in his place. Dare he suggest an errand? Would Julia be quick enough?

But she preempted him.

"I am afraid I have not got it ready yet," she said, swallowing hard.

"What ready?" Audley asked, frowning at her.

She turned to him with a guileless smile. "Mr. Monk said he would be kind enough to take a small parcel back to cousin Albert for me, but I have been remiss and it is not yet ready."

"What are you sending to Albert?" Audley demanded, frowning. "I didn't know you were so fond of him. You did not give me that impression."

"I suppose I am not, really." She was elaborately casual, but Monk saw that her hands were clenched tight. "It is a relationship I feel I should keep. After all, he is family." She forced a smile. "I thought a small gift would be a good beginning. Besides, he has several family records I should be most obliged to share."

"You have not mentioned this before," he argued. "What records?"

37

"Of our grandparents," Marianne put in quickly, her voice sharp. "They are his also, and since he is older than we, he has memories which are far more vivid. I should like to know more. After all, I never knew my mother. Julia was kind enough to suggest cousin Albert might help."

Audley drew breath to say something further, then changed his mind. For a young woman utterly dependent upon him, Marianne had a forthright manner and appeared to have little awe of him. Or perhaps she was sufficiently devoted to Julia that she would have charged to her defense regardless, and only thought of her own peril afterwards.

"Very civil of you." Audley disregarded her and nodded to Monk. "Are you from Halifax also?"

"No, Northumberland," Monk replied. "But I shall pass through on my way north." He was getting deeper and deeper in the lie. He would have to post the parcel and hope cousin Albert replied with the necessary information. Presumably if he did not, they would use the excuse that he was obdurate.

"Indeed." Audley apparently had no further interest, and they were spared the necessity of small talk by the arrival of the maid to announce that Mrs. Hylton had called and wish to see Mrs. Penrose.

She was shown in and arrived looking flustered and full of curiosity. Both Monk and Audley rose to greet her, but before they could speak she rushed into words, turning from one to another of them.

"Oh, Mr. Monk! I am so glad you have not yet left. My dear Mrs. Penrose, how very pleasant to see you. Miss Gillespie. I am so sorry about your experience, but I am quite sure it will prove to have been no more than a stray cat or something of the sort. Mr. Penrose. How are you?"

"In good health, thank you, Mrs. Hylton," Audley replied coolly. He turned to his sister-in-law. "What experience is this? I have heard nothing!" He was very pale, with two spots of color in his cheeks. His hands were clenched by his sides and his knuckles showed white from the pressure.

"Oh dear!" Mrs. Hylton said hastily. "Perhaps I should

38

not have spoken of it. I'm so sorry. I hate indiscretion, and here I am committing it."

"What experience?" Audley demanded again, his voice catching. "Julia?"

"Oh . . ." Julia was lost, foundering. She dared not turn to Monk, or Audley would know she had confided in him, if he did not guess already.

"Only something in the bushes in the garden," Monk said quickly. "Miss Gillespie feared it might be some tramp or stray person who was peeping. But I am sure Mrs. Hylton is correct and it was simply a cat. It can be startling, but no more. I am certain there is no danger, Miss Gillespie."

"No." Marianne swallowed. "No, of course not. I fear I was foolish. I—I have been . . . hasty."

"If you sent Mr. Monk looking for a tramp you most certainly were," Audley agreed testily, his breath harsh in his throat. "You should have mentioned it to me! To have troubled a guest was quite unnecessary and unfortunate."

"Miss Gillespie did not ask me," Monk said defensively. "I was in the garden in her company at the time. It was the most natural thing in the world to offer to see if there were anyone trespassing."

Audley fell silent with the best grace he could muster, but it was less than comfortable.

"I was afraid one of my children might have thrown a ball too far and came to retrieve it," Mrs. Hylton said apologetically, looking from one to the other of them, curiosity alight in her face, and a taste for drama. "Most inconsiderate, I know, but children tend to be like that. I am sure you will find it so, when you have your own. . . ."

Audley's face was white, his eyes glittering, but his hard glance was not directed at Mrs. Hylton, nor at Julia, but out the window into the trees. Julia's cheeks were scarlet, but she too was mute.

It was Marianne who spoke, her voice quivering with pain and indignation.

"That may be so, Mrs. Hylton, but we do not all wish to

have the same patterns of life. And for some of us the choices are different. I am sure you have sufficient sensitivity to appreciate that. . . ."

Mrs. Hylton realized she had made an appalling blunder and blushed deeply, although from the confusion in her face, she still did not fully understand what it had been.

"Yes," she said hastily. "Of course. I see, yes. Naturally. Well, I am sure you have done the right thing, Mr. Monk. I—I just wished to—well—good day to you." And she turned around and retreated in disorder.

Monk had seen more than sufficient to confirm his fears. He would have to speak to Marianne alone, but he would not do it with Audley in the house. He would return tomorrow morning, when he could be almost certain he would find the women alone.

"I don't wish to intrude," he said aloud, looking first at Julia, then at Audley. "If it is acceptable, ma'am, I shall call again in the near future to pick up your gift for Mr. Finnister?"

"Oh. Thank you," Julia accepted quickly, relief flooding her face. "That would be most kind."

Audley said nothing, and with a few more words, Monk excused himself and left, walking out rapidly into the heat of Hastings Street and the noise and clatter of passing carriages and the trouble of his thoughts.

In the morning he stood in the summerhouse with Marianne. A dozen yards away there were birds singing in the lilac tree and a faint breeze blew a few fallen leaves across the grass. It was Rodwell's day off.

"I think I have made all the inquiries I can," Monk began.

"I cannot blame you if you can discover very little," Marianne answered with a tiny smile. She was leaning against the window, the pale sprigged muslin of her dress billowing around her. She looked very young, but oddly less vulnerable than Julia, even though Monk was aware of the fear in her.

"I discovered several things," he went on, watching her carefully. "For instance, no one came over the wall into the garden, from any direction."

"Oh?" She was very still, almost holding her breath, staring away from him across the grass.

"And you are sure it was not Rodwell?"

Now she was incredulous, swinging around to look at him with wide eyes. "Rodwell? You mean the gardener? Of course it was not him! Do you think I wouldn't recognize our own gardener? Oh—oh no! You can't think . . ." She stopped, her face scarlet.

"No I don't," he said quickly. "I simply had to be sure. No, I don't think it was Rodwell, Miss Gillespie. But I do think you know who it was."

Now her face was very pale except for the splashes of color high in her cheeks. She looked at him in hot, furious accusation.

"You think I was willing! Oh dear heaven, how could you! How could you?" She jerked away and her voice was filled with such horror his last vestiges of doubt vanished.

"No I don't," he answered, aware of how facile that sounded. "But I think you are afraid that people will believe it, so you are trying to protect yourself." He avoided using the word *lying*.

"You are wrong," she said simply, but she did not turn back to face him. She still stood with shoulders hunched and staring toward the shrubbery and the end wall of the garden beyond which came the intermittent shouts of the Hylton children playing.

"How did he get in?" he asked gently. "No stranger could come through the house."

"Then he must have come through the herb garden," she replied.

"Past Rodwell? He said he saw no one."

"He must have been somewhere else." Her voice was flat, brooking no argument. "Maybe he went 'round to the kitchen for a few minutes. Perhaps he went for a drink of

41

water, or a piece of cake or something, and didn't like to admit it."

"And this fellow seized his chance and came through into the back garden?" He did not try to keep the disbelief from his voice.

"Yes."

"What for? There's nothing here to steal. And what a risk! He couldn't know Rodwell would leave again. He could have been caught here for hours."

"I don't know!" Her voice rose desperately.

"Unless he knew you were here?"

Finally she swung around, her eyes brilliant. "I don't know!" she shouted. "I don't know what he thought! Why don't you just admit you can't find him and go away? I never thought you would. It's only Julia who even wants to, because she's so angry for me. I told you you would never find anyone. It's ridiculous. There's no way to know." Her voice caught in her throat huskily. "There cannot be. If you don't want to explain to her, then I will."

"And honor will be satisfied?" he said dryly.

"If you like." She was still furious.

"Do you love him?" he asked her softly.

The anger vanished from her face, leaving it totally shocked.

"What?"

"Do you love him?" he repeated.

"Who? What are you talking about? Love whom?"

"Audley."

She stared at him as if mesmerized, her eyes dark with pain and some other profound emotion he thought was horror.

"Did he force you?" he went on.

"No!" she gasped. "You are quite wrong! It wasn't Audley! That's a dreadful thing to say—how dare you? He is my sister's husband!" But there was no conviction in her voice and it shook even as she tried to uphold her outrage.

"It is exactly because he is your sister's husband that I cannot believe you were willing," he persisted, but he felt a profound pity for her distress, and his own emotion was thick in his voice.

Her eyes filled with tears. "It wasn't Audley," she said again, but this time it was a whisper, and there was no anger in it, and no conviction. It was a protest for Julia's sake, and even she did not expect him to believe it.

"Yes it was," he said simply.

"I shall deny it." Again it was a statement of fact.

He had no doubt she would, but she seemed not to be certain he was convinced. "Please, Mr. Monk! Say nothing," she implored. "He would deny it, and I should look as if I were a wicked woman as well as immoral. Audley has given me a home and looked after me ever since he married Julia. No one would believe me, and they would think me totally without gratitude or duty." Now there was real fear in her voice, far sharper than the physical fear or revulsion of the assault. If she were branded with such a charge she would find herself not only homeless in the immediate future, but without prospects of marriage in the distance. No respectable man would marry a woman who first took a lover, whether reluctantly or not, and then made such a terrible charge against her sister's husband, a man who had been so generous to her.

"What do you want me to say to your sister?" he asked her.

"Nothing! Say you cannot find out. Say he was a stranger who came in somehow and has long ago escaped." She put out her hand and clasped his arm impulsively. "Please, Mr. Monk!" It was a cry of real anguish now. "Think what it would do to Julia! That would be the worst of all. I couldn't bear it. I had rather Audley said I was an immoral woman and put me out to fend for myself."

She had no idea what fending for herself would mean: the sleeping in brothels or doss houses, the hunger, the abuse, the disease and fear. She had no craft with which to earn her living honestly in a sweatshop working eighteen hours a day, even if her health and her nerve would stand

43

it. But he easily believed she would accept it rather than allow Julia to know what had really happened.

"I shall not tell her it was Audley," he promised. "You need not fear."

The tears spilled over and ran down her cheeks. She gulped and sniffed.

"Thank you. Thank you, Mr. Monk." She fished for a handkerchief a few inches square and mostly lace. It was useless.

He passed her his and she took it silently and wiped her eyes, hesitated, then blew her nose as well. Then she was confused, uncertain whether to offer it back to him or not.

He smiled in spite of himself. "Keep it," he offered.

"Thank you."

"Now I had better go and give your sister my final report."

She nodded and sniffed again. "She will be disappointed, but don't let her prevail upon you. However put out she is by not knowing, knowing would be infinitely worse."

"You had better stay here."

"I shall." She gulped. "And—thank you, Mr. Monk."

He found Julia in the morning room writing letters. She looked up as soon as he came in, her face quick with anticipation. He loathed the need to lie, and it cut his pride to have to admit defeat at all, and when he had actually solved the case it was acutely bitter.

"I am sorry, Mrs. Penrose, but I feel that I have pursued this case as far as I can, and to follow it any further would be a waste of your resources—"

"That is my concern, Mr. Monk," she interrupted quickly, laying her pen aside. "And I do not consider it a waste."

"What I am trying to say is that I shall learn nothing further." He said it with difficulty. Never previously that he could recall had he flinched from telling someone a truth, regardless of its ugliness. Perhaps he should have. It was another side of his character it would probably be painful to look into.

"You cannot know that," she argued, her face already beginning to set in lines of stubbornness. "Or are you saying that you do not believe that Marianne was assaulted at all?"

"No, I was not saying that," he said sharply. "I believe without question that she was, but whoever did it was a stranger to her, and we have no way of finding him now, since none of your neighbors saw him or any evidence that might lead to his identity."

"Someone may have seen him," she insisted. "He did not materialize from nowhere. Maybe he was not a tramp of any sort, but a guest of someone in the neighborhood. Have you thought of that?" Now there was challenge in her voice and in her eyes.

"Who climbed over the wall in the chance of finding mischief?" he asked with as little sarcasm as was possible to the words.

"Don't be ridiculous," she said tartly. "He must have come in through the herb garden when Rodwell was not there. Maybe he mistook the house and thought it was that of someone he knew."

"And found Miss Gillespie in the summerhouse and assaulted her?"

"It would seem so. Yes," she agreed. "I daresay he indulged in some sort of conversation first, and she cannot remember it because the whole episode was so appalling she has cut it all from her mind. Such things happen."

He thought of his own snatches of memory and the cold sweat of horror, the fear, the rage, the smell of blood, confusion, and blindness again.

"I know that," he said bitterly.

"Then please continue to pursue it, Mr. Monk." She looked at him with challenge, too consumed in her own emotion to hear his. "Or if you are unable or unwilling to, then perhaps you can recommend me the name of another person of inquiry who will."

"I believe you have no chance of success, Mrs. Penrose," he said a little stiffly. "Not to tell you so would be less than honest."

"I commend your integrity," she said dryly. "Now you have told me, and I have heard what you say, and requested you to continue anyway."

He tried one more time. "You will learn nothing!"

She stood up from her desk and came toward him. "Mr. Monk, have you any idea how appalling a crime it is for a man to force himself upon a woman? Perhaps you imagine it is merely a matter of modesty and a little reluctance, and that really when a woman says no she does not truly mean it?"

He opened his mouth to argue, but she rushed on. "That is a piece of meretricious simplicity men use to justify to themselves an act of brutality that can never be excused. My sister is very young, and unmarried. It was a violation of the very worst nature. It has introduced her to—to bestiality—instead of to a—a . . ." She blushed but did not avoid his eyes. "A sacred relationship which she—oh—really." She lost patience with herself. "No one has a right to behave toward anyone else in such a way, and if your nature is too insensitive to appreciate that, then there is no way for me to tell you."

Monk chose his words carefully. "I agree with you that it is a base offense, Mrs. Penrose. My reluctance to continue has no relation to the seriousness of the crime, only to the impossibility of finding the offender now."

"I suppose I should have come to you sooner," she conceded. "Is that what you are saying? Marianne did not tell me the true nature of the event until several days after it had happened, and then it took me some little while to make up my mind what was best to do. After that it took me another three days to locate you and inquire something of your reputation—which is excellent. I am surprised that you have given in so quickly. That is not what people say of you."

The anger hardened inside him and only Marianne's anguish stopped him retaliating.

"I shall return tomorrow and we shall discuss it further,"

he said grimly. "I will not continue to take your money for something I believe cannot be done."

"I will be obliged if you will come in the morning," she replied. "As you have observed, my husband is not aware of the situation, and explanations are becoming increasingly difficult."

"Perhaps you should give me a letter to your cousin Mr. Finnister," he suggested. "In case anything is said, I shall post it, so there will be no unfortunate repercussions in the future."

"Thank you. That is most thoughtful of you. I will do so."

And still angry, and feeling disturbed and confused, he took his leave, walking briskly back toward Fitzroy Street and his rooms.

He could come to no satisfactory conclusion himself. He did not understand the events and the emotions profoundly enough to be confident in a decision. His anger toward Audley Penrose was monumental. He could have seen him punished with intense satisfaction; indeed, he longed to see it. And yet he could understand Marianne's need to protect not only herself but also Julia.

For once his own reputation as a detective was of secondary importance. Whatever the outcome of his entering the case, he could not even consider improving his professional standing at the expense of ruining either of the women.

Miserable, and in a very short temper, he went to see Callandra Daviot, and his ill humor was exacerbated immediately on finding Hester Latterly present. It was several weeks since he had last seen her, and their parting had been far from friendly. As so often happened, they had quarreled about something more of manner than of substance. In fact, he could not remember what it was now, only that she had been abrasive as usual and unwilling to listen or consider his view. Now she was sitting in Callandra's best chair, the one he most preferred, looking tired and far from the gently feminine creature Julia Penrose was. Hester's hair was thick and nearly straight and she had taken little trouble to dress it with curls or braids. Pulled as it was it showed the fine, strong bones of her face and the passionate features, the intelligence far too dominant to be attractive. Her gown was pale blue and the skirt, without hoops, a trifle crushed.

He ignored her and smiled at Callandra. "Good evening, Lady Callandra." He intended it to be warm, but his general unhappiness flavored it more than he wished.

"Good evening, William," Callandra replied, the tiniest smile touching the corners of her wide mouth.

Monk turned to Hester. "Good evening, Miss Latterly," he continued coolly, his disappointment undisguised.

"Good evening, Mr. Monk," Hester answered, turning around but not rising. "You look out of temper. Have you a disagreeable case?"

"Most criminal cases are disagreeable," he responded. "Like most illnesses."

"They both happen," Hester observed. "Very often to people we like and can help. That is immeasurably pleasing—at least it is to me. If it is not to you, then you should look for another form of employment."

Monk sat down. He was unexpectedly tired, which was ridiculous because he had done very little. "I have been dealing with tragedy all day, Hester. I am in no mind for trivial sophistry."

"It is not sophistry," she snapped. "You were being self-pitying about your work. I pointed out what is good about it."

"I am not self-pitying." His voice rose in spite of his resolution that it would not. "Good God! I pity everyone in the affair, except myself. I wish you would not make these slipshod judgments when you know nothing about the situation or the people."

She stared at him in fury for a moment, then her face lit up with appreciation and amusement. "You don't know what to do. You are confounded for the moment."

48

The only answer that came to his lips was in words he would not use in front of Callandra.

It was Callandra who replied, putting her hand on Hester's arm to restrain her.

"You should not feel badly about it, my dear," she said to Monk gently. "There was never much of a chance of learning who it was—if it was anyone. I mean, if it was really an assault."

Hester looked to Callandra, then to Monk, but she did not interrupt.

"It was an assault," Monk said more calmly. "And I know who it was, I just don't know what to do about it." He ignored Hester, but he was very aware of the change in her; the laughter was gone and suddenly her attention was total and serious.

"Because of what Mrs. Penrose will do with the knowledge?" Callandra asked.

"No—not really." He looked at her gravely, searching her curious, clever face. "Because of the ruin and the pain it will bring."

"To the offender?" Callandra asked. "To his family?"

Monk smiled. "No—and yes."

"Can you speak of it?" Hester asked him, all friction between them brushed aside as if it did not exist. "I assume you have to make a decision, and that is what troubles you?"

"Yes—by tomorrow."

"Can you tell us?"

He shrugged very slightly and sat back farther in his chair. She had the one he really wanted, but it hardly mattered now. His irritation was gone.

"Marianne lives with her married sister, Julia, and her sister's husband, Audley Penrose. Marianne says she was raped when she was in the summerhouse in the garden, but she did not know the man."

Neither Hester nor Callandra interrupted him, nor did their faces betray any disbelief.

49

"I questioned everyone in the neighborhood. No one saw any stranger."

Callandra sighed. "Audley Penrose?"

"Yes."

"Oh dear. Does she love him? Or think she does?"

"No. She is horrified—and apparently hurt," he said wearily. "She would rather be put out in the street as an immoral woman than have Julia know what happened."

Hester bit her lip. "Has she any conception what that would be like?"

"Probably not," he replied. "But that hardly matters. Julia won't allow that to happen—I don't think. But Marianne doesn't want me to tell anyone. She says she will deny it anyway, and I can understand that. Audley will deny it, naturally. He has to. I have no idea what Julia will believe, or what she will have to say she believes."

"Poor creature," Hester said with sudden passion. "What a fearful dilemma. What have you told her?"

"That I cannot find out who assaulted Marianne and I wish to be released from the case."

Hester looked across at him, her face lit with warmth of admiration and respect.

He was caught unaware by how sweet it was to him. Without warning the bitterness vanished from the decision. His own pride slipped away.

"And you are content with that?" Callandra broke the moment.

"Not content," he replied. "But I can think of nothing better. There is no honorable alternative."

"And Audley Penrose?" she pressed.

"I'd like to break his neck," he said savagely. "But that is a luxury I can't afford."

"I am not thinking of you, William," Callandra said soberly. She was the only person who called him by his given name, and while it pleased him with its familiarity, it also brought her close enough that pretense was impossible.

"What?" he said somewhat abruptly.

"I was not thinking of your satisfaction in revenge," she

50

elaborated. "Sweet as that would be. Or the demands of justice, as you see it. I was thinking of Marianne Gillespie. How can she continue to live in that house, with what has happened to her, and may well happen again if he believes he has got away with it?"

"That is her choice," Monk returned, but it was not a satisfying answer and he knew it. "She was extremely insistent on it," he went on, trying to justify himself. "She begged me to promise that I would not tell Julia, and I gave her my word."

"And what disturbs you now?" Callandra asked, her eyes wide.

Hester looked from one to the other of them, waiting, her concentration intense.

Monk hesitated.

"Is it purely vanity, because you do not like to appear to be defeated?" Callandra pursued. "Is that all it is, William, your own reputation?"

"No—no, I'm not sure what it is," he confessed, his anger temporarily abated.

"Have you considered what her life will be if he continues his behavior?" Callandra's voice was very quiet but the urgency in it filled the room. "She will feel terrified every time she is alone with him in case it happens again. She will be terrified in case Julia ever discovers them and is devastated with grief." She leaned farther forward in her chair. "Marianne will feel she has betrayed her sister, although it is none of her choosing, but will Julia know that? Will she not always have that gnawing fear that in her heart Marianne was willing, and that in some subtle way she encouraged him?"

"I don't believe that," he said fiercely. "She would rather be put out on the street than have Julia know it."

Callandra shook her head. "I am not speaking of now, William. I am speaking of what will happen if she says nothing and remains in the house. She may not have thought of it yet, but you must. You are the only one who knows all the facts and is in a position to act."

Monk sat silent, the thoughts and fears crowding his mind.

It was Hester who spoke.

"There is something worse than that," she said quietly. "What if she became with child?"

Monk and Callandra both turned slowly toward her and it was only too apparent in their faces that such an idea had not occurred to them, and now that it had they were appalled.

"Whatever you promised, it is not enough," Callandra said grimly. "You cannot simply walk away and leave her to her fate."

"But no one has the right to override her choice," Hester argued, not out of obstructiveness but because it had to be said. Her own conflicting emotions were plain in her face. For once Monk felt no animosity toward her, only the old sense of total friendship, the bond that unites people who understand each other and care with equal passion in a single cause.

"If I don't give her an answer I think Julia may well seek another agent who will," Monk added miserably. "I didn't tell Marianne that because I didn't see her again after I spoke to Julia."

"But what will happen if you tell Julia?" Hester asked anxiously. "Will she believe you? She will be placed in an impossible situation between her husband and her sister."

"And there is worse," Monk went on. "They are both financially dependent upon Audley."

"He can't throw his wife out." Hester sat upright, her face hot with anger. "And surely she would not be so— oh, of course. You mean she may choose to leave. Oh dear." She bit her lip. "And even if his crime could be proved, which it almost certainly could not, and he were convicted, then there is not money for anyone and they would both be in the street. What a ridiculous situation." Her fists clenched in her lap and her voice was husky with fury and frustration.

Suddenly she rose to her feet. "If only women could earn

a living as men can. If women could be doctors or architects and lawyers too." She paced to the window and turned. "Or even clerks and shopkeepers. Anything more than domestic servants, seamstresses, or whores! But what woman earns enough to live in anything better than one room in a lodging house if she's lucky, and in a tenement if she's not? And always hungry and always cold, and never sure next week will not be even worse."

"You are dreaming," Monk said, but not critically. He understood her feeling and the facts that inspired it. "And even if it happens one day, which is unlikely because it is against the natural social order, it won't help Julia Penrose or her sister. Anything I tell her—or don't—will cause terrible harm."

They all remained in silence for several minutes, each wrestling with the problem in his or her own way, Hester by the window, Callandra leaning back in her chair, Monk on the edge of his. Finally it was Callandra who spoke.

"I think you should tell Julia," she said very quietly, her voice low and unhappy. "It is not a good solution, but I believe it is better than not telling her. If you do, then at least the decision what to do is hers, not yours. And as you say, she may well press the matter until she learns something, whatever you do. And please God that is the right decision. We can only hope."

Monk looked at Hester.

"I agree," she answered. "No solution is satisfactory, and you will ruin her peace whatever you say, but I think perhaps that is ruined anyway. If he continues, and Marianne is either seriously hurt or with child, it will be worse. And then Julia would blame herself—and you."

"What about my promise to Marianne?" he asked.

Her eyes were filled with unhappiness.

"Do you suppose she knows what dangers there are ahead? She is young, unmarried. She may not even be aware of what they are. Many girls have no idea of childbirth, or even what brings it about; they only discover in the marriage bed."

53

"I don't know." It was not enough of an answer. "I gave her my word."

"Than you will have to tell her that you cannot keep it," Callandra replied. "Which will be very hard. But what is your alternative?"

"To keep it."

"Will that not be even harder—if not at first, then later?"

He knew that was true. He would not be able to turn his back on the affair and forget it. Every tragic possibility would haunt his imagination, and he would have to accept at least part of the responsibility for all of them.

"Yes," he admitted. "Yes—I shall have to go back and tell Marianne."

"I'm sorry." Hester touched his arm briefly, then withdrew.

They did not discuss it further. There was nothing more to say, and they could not help him. Instead they spoke of things that had nothing to do with the work of any of them, of the latest novels to be published and what they had heard said of them, of politics, of affairs in India and the fearful news of the mutiny, and the war in China. When they parted late into the summer night and Monk and Hester shared a hansom back to their respective lodgings, even that was done in companionable conversation.

Naturally they stopped at Hester's rooms first, the very sparsest of places because so frequently she was living in the house of her current patient. She was the only resident in her rooms at the moment because her patient was so nearly recovered she required attention only every other day, and did not see why she should house and feed a nurse from whom she now had so little service.

Monk alighted and opened the door for her, handing her down to the pavement. It came to his lips to say how pleasant it had been to see her, then he swallowed the words. There was no need of them. Small compliments, however true, belonged to a more trivial relationship, one that sailed on the surface of things.

"Good night," he said simply, walking across the stones with her to the front door.

"Good night, Monk," she answered with a smile. "I shall think of you tomorrow."

He smiled back, ruefully, knowing she meant it and feeling a kind of comfort in the thought that he would not be alone.

Behind him in the street the horse stamped and shifted position. There was nothing else to say. Hester let herself in with her key, and Monk returned to the hansom and climbed up as it moved off along the lamplit street.

He was at Hastings Street at quarter to ten in the morning. It was mild and raining very slightly. The flowers in the gardens were beaded with moisture and somewhere a bird was singing with startling clarity.

Monk would have given a great deal to have been able to turn and go back again to the Euston Road and not call at number fourteen. However, he did not hesitate on the step or wait before pulling the bell. He had already done all the thinking he could. There was no more debate left, no more arguments to put for either action.

The maid welcomed him in with some familiarity now, but she was slightly taken aback when he asked to see not Mrs. Penrose but Miss Gillespie. Presumably Julia had said she was expecting him.

He was alone in the morning room, pacing in restless anxiety, when Marianne came in. As soon as she saw him her face paled.

"What is it?" she asked quickly. "Has something happened?"

"Before I left here yesterday," he replied, "I spoke to your sister and told her that I would not be able to learn who assaulted you, and it would be pointless to continue seeking. She would not accept that. If I do not tell her then she will employ someone else who will."

"But how could anyone else know?" she said desperately. "I wouldn't tell them. No one saw, no one heard."

"They will deduce it from the evidence, as I did." This was every bit as hard as his worst fears. She looked so crushed. "Miss Gillespie—I am sorry, but I am going to have to take back the pledge I gave you and tell Mrs. Penrose the truth."

"You can't!" She was aghast. "You promised you would not do that!" But even as she spoke the innocent indignation was dying in her face and being replaced by understanding—and defeat.

He felt wretched. He had no alternative, and yet he was betraying her and he could not argue himself out of it.

"There are other things that have to be considered also. . . ."

"Of course there are." Her voice was harsh with anger and misery. "The worst of this is how Julia will feel about it. She will be destroyed. How can she ever feel the same about me, even if she truly believes it was the farthest thing from my wishes? I did nothing whatsoever to lead him to think I would ever be willing, and that is true, Mr. Monk! I swear it by all I hold dear——"

"I know that," he said, interrupting her. "That is not what I mean."

"Then what?" she demanded abruptly. "What else could be of importance beside that?"

"Why do you believe that it will never happen again?"

Her face was white. She swallowed with difficulty. She started to speak, and then stopped.

"Have you any protection against it happening again?" he insisted quietly.

"I—but . . ." She looked down. "Surely that was just one terrible lapse in—in an otherwise exemplary man? I am sure he loves Julia. . . ."

"What would you have said about the possibility of it ever happening a week before it did? Did you know or expect him to do such a thing?"

Now her eyes were blazing.

"Of course not. That is a dreadful thing to say. No! No,

56

I had no idea! Never!" She turned away abruptly, violently, as if he had offered her some physical attack.

"Then you cannot say that it will not happen again," he reasoned. "I'm sorry." He hovered on the edge of adding the possibility of becoming with child, and then remembered what Hester and Callandra had said. Marianne might not even be aware of how children were begotten, and he said nothing. Helplessness and inadequacy choked him.

"It must have cost you to tell me that." She looked back at him slowly, her face drained. "There are many men who would not have found the courage. Thank you at least for that."

"Now I must see Mrs. Penrose. I wish I could think of another way, but I cannot."

"She is in the withdrawing room. I shall wait in my bedroom. I expect Audley will ask me to leave and Julia will wish me to." And with quivering lips she turned and walked to the door too rapidly for him to reach it ahead of her. She fumbled with the knob, then flung it open and went out across the hall to the stairway, head high, her step clumsy.

He stood still for a moment, tempted to try one more time to think of another way. Then intelligence reasserted itself over emotion, and he went the now familiar way to knock on the withdrawing room door.

He was bidden to enter. Julia was standing at the central table before a vase of flowers, a long, bright stem of delphinium in her hand. Apparently she had not liked the position of it and had chosen to rearrange it herself. When she saw who it was she poked the flower in the back lopsidedly and without bothering to adjust it.

"Good morning, Mr. Monk." Her voice shook a little. She searched his face and saw something in its expression that frightened her. "What is it?"

He closed the door behind him. This was going to be acutely painful. There was no escape, no way even to mitigate it.

"I am afraid that what I told you yesterday was not the truth, Mrs. Penrose."

She stared at him without speaking. The shadow of surprise and anger across her eyes did not outweigh the fear.

This was like looking at something and deliberately killing it. Once he had told her it would be irretrievable. He had already made the decision, and yet he found himself hesitating even now.

"You had better explain yourself, Mr. Monk," she said at last, her voice catching. She swallowed to clear her throat. "Merely to say that is not sufficient. In what respect have you lied to me, and why?"

He answered the second question first. "Because the truth is so unpleasant that I wished to spare you from it, ma'am. And it was Miss Gillespie's wish also. Indeed, she denied it at first, until the weight of evidence made that no longer possible. Then she implored me not to tell you. She was prepared to accept any consequence of it herself rather than have you know. That was why it was necessary for me to speak to her this morning to tell her I could no longer keep my word to her."

Julia was so white he was afraid she would faint from lack of blood. Very slowly she backed away from the table with its bright flowers and reached behind her for the arm of the settee. She sank into it, still staring at him.

"You had better tell me what it is, Mr. Monk. I have to know. Do you know who raped my sister?"

"Yes, I am afraid I do." He took a deep breath. He tried one last thing, although he knew it would be futile. "I still think it would be better if you did not pursue the matter. You cannot prosecute. Perhaps if you were to find some other area for your sister to live, where she could not encounter him again? Do you have a relative, an aunt perhaps, with whom she could stay?"

Her eyebrows rose. "Are you suggesting that this man who did this thing should be allowed to go entirely unpunished, Mr. Monk? I am aware that the law will not punish him, and that a prosecution would in any case be as painful

58

for Marianne as it would ever be for him." She was sitting so tensely her body must ache with the rack of her muscles. "But I will not countenance his escaping scot-free! It seems you do not think it a crime after all. I confess I am disappointed. I had thought better of you."

Anger boiled up in him, and it cost him dearly to suppress it. "Fewer people would be hurt."

She stared at him.

"That is unfortunate, but it cannot be helped. Who was it? Please do not prevaricate any further. You will not change my mind."

"It was your husband, Mrs. Penrose."

She did not protest outrage or disbelief. She sat totally motionless, her face ashen. Then at last she licked her lips and tried to speak. Her throat convulsed and no sound came. Then she tried again.

"I assume you would not have said this—if—if you were not totally sure?"

"Of course not." He longed to comfort her, and there was no possible comfort. "Even then I would prefer not to have told you. Your sister begged me not to, but I felt I had to, in part because you were determined to pursue the matter, if not through me, then with another agent. And also because there is the danger of it happening again, and there is the possibility she may become with child—"

"Stop it!" This time the cry was torn from her in a frenzy of pain. "Stop it! You have told me. That is sufficient." With a terrible effort she mastered herself, although her hands were shaking uncontrollably.

"When I taxed her with it, she denied it at first, to protect you." He went on relentlessly. It had to be finished now. "Then when it was obviously true from her own testimony, and that of your neighbors, she admitted it, but implored me not to say so. I think the only reason she made any mention of the incident at all was to account for her extreme distress after it, and for the bruising. Otherwise I think she would have remained silent, for your sake."

"Poor Marianne." Her voice trembled violently. "She would endure that for me. What harm have I done her?"

He moved a step nearer to her, undecided whether to sit without invitation or remain standing, towering over her. He opted to sit.

"You cannot blame yourself," he said earnestly. "You of all people are the most innocent in this."

"No I am not, Mr. Monk." She did not look at him but at some distance far beyond the green shadow of leaves across the window. Her voice was now filled with self-loathing. "Audley is a man with natural expectations, and I have denied him all the years we have been married." She hunched into herself as if suddenly the room were intolerably cold, her fingers gripping her arms painfully, driving the blood out of the flesh.

He wanted to interrupt her and tell her the explanation was private and quite unnecessary, but he knew she needed to tell him, to rid herself of a burden she could no longer bear.

"I should not have, but I was so afraid." She was shivering very slightly, as if her muscles were locked. "You see, my mother had child after child between my birth and Marianne's. All of them miscarried or died. I watched her in such pain." Very slowly she began rocking herself back and forth as if in some way the movement eased her as the words poured out. "I remember her looking so white, and the blood on the sheets. Lots of it, great dark red stains as though her life were pouring out of her. They tried to hide them from me, and keep me in my own room. But I heard her crying with the pain of it, and I saw the maids hurrying about with bundles of linen, and trying to fold it so no one saw." The tears were running down her own face now and she made no pretense of concealing them. "And then when I was allowed in to see her, she would look so tired, with dark rings 'round her eyes, and her lips white. I knew she had been crying for the baby that was lost, and I couldn't bear it!"

Without thinking Monk put out his hands and held hers.

Unconsciously she clung to him, her fingers strong, gripping him like a lifeline.

"I knew she had dreaded it, every time she was with child. I felt the terror in her, even though I didn't know then what caused it. And when Marianne was born she was so pleased." She smiled as she remembered, and for a moment her eyes were tender and brilliant with gentleness. "She held her up and showed her to me, as if we had done it together. The midwife wanted to send me away, but Mama wouldn't let her. I think she knew then she was dying. She made me promise to look after Marianne as if I were in her place, to do for her what Mama could not."

Julia was weeping quite openly now. Monk ached for her, and for his own helplessness, and for all the terrified, lost, and grieving women.

"I stayed with her all that night," she went on, still rocking herself. "In the morning the bleeding started again, and they took me out, but I can remember the doctor being sent for. He went up the stairs with his face very grave and his black bag in his hand. There were more sheets carried out, and all the maids were frightened and the butler stood around looking sad. Mama died in the morning. I don't remember what time, but I knew it. It was as if suddenly I was alone in a way I never had been before. I have never been quite as warm or as safe since then."

There was nothing to say. He felt furious, helpless, stupidly close to weeping himself, and drenched with the same irredeemable sense of loneliness. He tightened his grasp a little closer around her hands. For several moments they remained in silence.

At last she looked up and straightened her back, fishing for a handkerchief. Monk gave her his, and she accepted it without speaking.

"I have never been able to think of getting with child myself. I could not bear it. It frightens me so much I should rather simply die with a gunshot than go through the agony that Mama did. I know it is wrong, probably wicked. All women are supposed to yield to their husbands and bear

61

children. It is our duty. But I am so terrified I cannot. This is a judgment on me. Now Marianne has been raped because of me."

"No! That's nonsense," he said furiously. "Whatever is between you and your husband, that is no excuse for what he did to Marianne. If he could not maintain continence, there are women whose trade it is to cater to appetites and he could perfectly easily have paid one of them." He wanted to shake her to force her to understand. "You must not blame yourself," he insisted. "It is wrong and foolish, and will be of no service to you or to Marianne. Do you hear me?" His voice was rougher than he had intended, but it was what he meant and it could not be withdrawn.

She looked up at him slowly, her eyes still swimming in tears.

"To blame yourself would be self-indulgent and debilitating," he said again. "You have to be strong. You have a fearful situation to deal with. Don't look back—look forward, only forward. If you cannot bring yourself to consummate your marriage, then your husband must look elsewhere, not to Marianne. Never to Marianne."

"I know," she whispered. "But I am still guilty. He has a right to expect it of me—and I have not given it him. I am deceitful, I cannot escape that."

"Yes—that is true." He would not evade it either. It would not serve either of them. "But your deceit does not excuse his offense. You must think what you are going to do next, not what you should have done before."

"What *can* I do?" Her eyes searched his desperately.

"This is a decision no one else can make for you," he answered. "But you must protect Marianne from it ever happening again. If she were to bear a child it would ruin her." He did not need to explain what he meant. They both knew no respectable man would marry a woman with an illegitimate child. Indeed, no man at all would regard her as anything but a whore, no matter how untrue that was.

"I will," she promised, and for the first time there was steel in her voice again. "There is no other answer for it.

I will have to swallow my fear." Again for a moment her eyes overflowed and there was a choking in her voice. Then with a superlative effort she mastered herself. "Thank you, Mr. Monk. You have discharged your duty honorably. I thank you for it. You may present your account, and I shall see that it is met. If you will be so kind as to show yourself out. I do not wish to appear before the servants looking in a state of distress."

"Of course." He stood up. "I am truly sorry. I wish there had been any other answer I could have given you." He did not wait for a reply which could only be meaningless. "Good-bye, Mrs. Penrose."

He went out into the hazy sun of Hastings Street feeling physically numb, and so crowded with emotion he was barely aware of the passersby, the clatter, the heat, or the people who stared at him as he strode on.

3

CALLANDRA DAVIOT had been deeply moved by the story that Monk had brought her regarding Julia Penrose and her sister, but she was helpless to do anything about it, and she was not a woman to spend time and emotion uselessly. There was too much else to do, and at the forefront of her mind was her work in the hospital of which she had spoken when Monk had called only a few short weeks before.

She was a member of the Board of Governors, which generally meant a fairly passive role of giving advice which doctors and treasurers would listen to more or less civilly, and then ignore, and of lecturing nurses on general morality and sobriety, a task she loathed and considered pointless.

There were so many better things to do, beginning with the reforms proposed by Florence Nightingale, which Hester had so fiercely advocated. Light and air in hospital wards were considered quite unnecessary here at home in England, if not downright harmful. The medical establishment was desperately conservative, jealous of its knowledge and privilege, loathing change. There was no place for women except as drudges, or on rare occasions administrators, such as hospital matron, or charitable workers such as herself and other ladies of society who played at the edges, watching other people's morality and using their connections to obtain donations of money.

She set out from home instructing her coachman to take her to the Gray's Inn Road with a sense of urgency which had only partly to do with her plans for reform. She would not have told Monk the truth of it—she did not even admit to herself how profoundly she looked forward to seeing Dr. Kristian Beck again, but whenever she thought of the hospital it was his face that came to her mind, his voice in her ears.

She brought her attention back sharply to the mundane matters in hand. Today she would see the matron, Mrs. Flaherty, a small tense woman who took offense extremely easily and forgave and forgot nothing. She managed her wards efficiently, terrorized the nurses into a remarkable degree of diligence and sobriety, and had a patience with the sick which seemed almost limitless. But she was rigid in her beliefs, her devotion to the surgeons and physicians who ruled the hospital, and her absolute refusal to listen to newfangled ideas and all those who advocated them. Even the name of Florence Nightingale held no magic for her.

Callandra alighted and instructed the coachman when to return for her, then climbed the steps and went in through the wide front doors to the stone-flagged foyer. A middle-aged woman trudged across with a pail of dirty water in one hand and a mop in the other. Her face was pale and her wispy hair screwed into a knot at the back of her head. She banged the pail with her knee and slopped the water over onto the floor without stopping. She ignored Callandra as if she were invisible.

A student surgeon appeared, scarlet arterial blood spatters on his collarless shirt and old trousers, mute evidence of his attendance in the operating theater. He nodded at Callandra and passed by.

There was a smell of coal dust, the heat of bodies in fevers and sickness, stale dressings, and of drains and undisposed sewage. She should go and see the matron about nurses' moral discipline. It was her turn to lecture them again. Then she should see the treasurer about funds and the disposition of certain monies to hand, the review of charity cases. She would do these things first, then she would be free to go and see Kristian Beck.

She found the matron in one of the wards filled with surgical patients, both those awaiting operations and those recovering. Several had developed fevers during the night or become worse, their infections already well advanced. One man was comatose and close to death. Although the recent discovery of anesthesia had made all sorts of procedures possible, many who survived operations died afterwards of infection. Those who survived were a minority. There was no way known to prevent septicemia or gangrene, and little that would treat even the symptoms, let alone provide a cure.

Mrs. Flaherty came out of the small room where the medicines and clean bandages were kept; her thin face was pale, her white hair screwed back so tightly it pulled the skin around her eyes. There were two spots of angry color on her cheeks.

"Good morning, your ladyship," she said brusquely. "There is nothing you can do here today, and I do not want to hear anything more about Miss Nightingale and fresh air. We've got poor souls dying of fevers, and outside air will kill the rest if we listen to you." She consulted the watch hanging from a pin on her thin shoulder, then she looked back at Callandra. "I'd be obliged, ma'am, if next time you talk to the nurses about morals and behavior, you would particularly mention honesty. We've had more thefts from patients. Just small things, of course, they haven't got much or they'd not be here. Although I don't know what good you think it will do, I'm sure."

She came out into the ward, a long room with a high ceiling, lined on both sides with narrow beds, each blanketed in gray and with someone either sitting or lying in it. Some were pale-faced, others feverish, some restless, tossing from side to side, some lying motionless, breathing shallowly, gasping for air. The room was hot and smelled stale and close.

A young woman in a soiled overall walked down the length of the floor between the beds carrying an uncovered pail of slops. The odor of it, strong and sour, assailed Callandra's nostrils as she passed.

"I'm sorry," Callandra replied, snatching her attention back to the matron's request. "Lecturing them isn't the answer. We need to get a different kind of woman into the trade, and then treat them accordingly."

Mrs. Flaherty's face creased with irritation. She had heard these arguments before and they were fanciful and completely impractical.

"All very nice, your ladyship," she said tartly. "But we have got to deal with what we have, and we have laziness, drunkenness, thieving, and complete irresponsibility. If you want to help, you'll do something about that, not talk about situations that will never be."

Callandra opened her mouth to argue, but her attention was distracted by a woman halfway down the ward starting to choke, and the patient next to her calling out for help.

A pale, obese woman appeared with an empty slop pail and lumbered over to the gasping patient, who began to vomit.

"That's the digitalis leaves," Mrs. Flaherty said matter-of-factly. "The poor creature is dropsical. Passed no urine for days, but this will help. She's been in here before and recovered." She turned away and looked back toward her table, where she had been writing notes on medications and responses. The heavy keys hanging in her belt jangled against each other. "Now if you will excuse me," she went on, her back to Callandra, "I've got a great deal to do, and I'm sure you have." Her voice on the last remark was tight with sarcasm.

"Yes," Callandra said equally tartly. "Yes I have. I am afraid you will have to ask someone else to lecture the nurses, Mrs. Flaherty; perhaps Lady Ross Gilbert would do that. She seems very capable."

"She is," Mrs. Flaherty said meaningfully, then sat down at her table and picked up her pen. It was dismissal.

Callandra left the ward, walking along a dim corridor past a woman with a bucket and scrubbing brush, and another woman seeming no more than a heap of laundry piled up against the wall, insensible with alcohol.

At the end of the corridor she encountered a group of three young student doctors talking together eagerly, heads close, hands gesticulating.

"It's this big," one red-haired youth said, holding up his clenched fist. "Sir Herbert is going to cut it out. Thank God I live when I do. Just think how hopeless that would have been twelve years ago before anesthetic. Now with ether or nitrous oxide, nothing is impossible."

"Greatest thing since Harvey and the circulation of blood," another agreed enthusiastically. "My grandfather was a naval surgeon in Nelson's fleet. Had to do everything with a bottle of rum and a leather gag, and two men to hold you down. My God, isn't modern medicine wonderful. Damn, I've got blood all over my trousers." He pulled his handkerchief out of his pocket, dabbed at himself without effect, except to stain the handkerchief scarlet.

"Don't know why you're wasting your time," the third young man said, regarding his efforts with a smile. "You're assisting, aren't you? You'll only get covered again. Shouldn't have worn a good suit. I never do. That'll teach you to be vain just because it's Sir Herbert."

They jostled each other in mock battle, passing Callandra with a brief word of acknowledgment, and went on across the foyer toward the operating theater.

A moment later Sir Herbert Stanhope himself came out of one of the large oak doorways. He saw Callandra and hesitated, as if searching his mind to recollect her name. He was a large man, not especially tall but portly and of imposing manner. His face was ordinary enough at a glance: narrow eyes, sharp nose, high brow, and receding sandy hair. It was only with closer attention one was acutely

68

aware of the power of his intellect and the emotional intensity of his concentration.

"Good morning, Lady Callandra," he said with sudden satisfaction.

"Good morning, Sir Herbert," she replied, smiling very slightly. "I'm glad I've managed to see you before you begin operating."

"I'm somewhat in a hurry," he said with a flicker of irritation. "My staff will be waiting for me in the theater, and I daresay my patient will be coming any moment."

"I have an observation which may be able to reduce infection to some extent," she continued, regardless of his haste.

"Indeed," he said skeptically, a tiny wrinkle of temper between his brows. "And what idea is that, pray?"

"I was in the ward a moment ago and observed, not for the first time, a nurse carrying a pail of slops the length of the room without a lid."

"Slops are inevitable, ma'am," he said impatiently. "People pass waste, and frequently it is disagreeable when they are ill. They also vomit. It is in the nature, both of disease and of cure."

Callandra kept her patience with difficulty. She was not a short-tempered woman, but being patronized she found exceedingly hard to bear.

"I am aware of that, Sir Herbert. But by the very nature that it is waste expelled by the body, the fumes are noxious and cannot be good to inhale again. Would it not be a simple thing to have the nurses use covers for the pails?"

There was a burst of raucous laughter somewhere around the corner of the corridor. Sir Herbert's mouth tightened with distaste.

"Have you ever tried to teach nurses to observe rules, ma'am?" He said it with a faint touch of humor, but there was no pleasure in it. "As was observed in the *Times* last year—I cannot quote precisely, but it was to the effect that nurses are lectured by committees, preached at by chaplains, scowled on by treasurers and stewards, scolded by matrons, bullied by dressers, grumbled at and abused by patients, insulted if old, treated with flippancy if middle-aged and agreeable-natured, seduced if young." He raised his thin eyebrows. "Is it any wonder they are such as they are? What manner of woman would one expect to take such employment?"

"I read the same piece," she agreed, moving to keep level with him as he began to walk toward the distant operating theater. "You omitted to mention that they are also sworn at by surgeons. It said that too." She ignored the momentary flicker of temper in his eyes. "That is perhaps the best of all the arguments for employing a better class of woman, and treating them as professionals rather than the roughest of servants."

"My dear Lady Callandra, it is all very well to talk as if there were hundreds of wellborn and intelligent young women of good moral character queuing up to perform the service, but since the glamour of war is past that is very far from being the case." He shook his head sharply. "Surely a moment's investigation would show you that? Idealistic daydreams are all very pleasant, but I have to deal in reality. I can only work with what there is, and the truth is that the women you see keep the fire stoked, the slops emptied, the bandages rolled, and most of them, when sober, are kind enough to the sick."

The hospital treasurer passed them, dressed in black and carrying a pile of ledgers. He nodded in their direction but did not stop to speak.

"By all means," Sir Herbert continued even more brusquely, "if you wish to provide covers for the pails, do what you can to see that they are used. In the meantime, I must report to the operating theater where my patient will come any minute. Good day to you ma'am." And without waiting for her to reply, he turned on his well-shod and polished heel and went across the foyer to the far corridor.

Callandra had scarcely drawn breath when she saw an ashen-faced woman, supported on both sides by solemn-eyed men, making her painful way toward the corridor

70

where Sir Herbert had gone. Seemingly she was the patient whom he had expected.

It was only after a tedious but dutiful hour with the black-coated treasurer discussing finances, donations, and gifts that Callandra encountered one of the other governors, the one of whom Mrs. Flaherty had spoken so approvingly, Lady Ross Gilbert. Callandra was on the landing at the top of the stairs when Berenice Ross Gilbert caught up with her. She was a tall woman who moved with a kind of elegance and ease which made even the most ordinary clothes seem as if they must be in the height of fashion. Today she wore a gown with a waist deeply pointed at the front and a soft green muslin skirt with three huge flounces, scattered randomly with embroidered flowers. It flattered her reddish hair and pale complexion, and her face with its heavy-lidded eyes and rather undershot jaw was extremely handsome in its own way.

"Good morning, Callandra," she said with a smile, swinging her skirts around the newel post and starting down the stairs beside her. "I hear you had a slight difference with Mrs. Flaherty earlier today." She pulled a face expressive of amused resignation. "I should forget Miss Nightingale if I were you. She is something of a romantic, and her ideas hardly apply to us."

"I didn't mention Miss Nightingale," Callandra replied, going down beside her. "I simply said I did not wish to lecture the nurses on honesty and sobriety."

Berenice laughed abruptly. "It would be a complete waste of your time, my dear. The only difference it would produce would be to make Mrs. Flaherty feel justified that she made an attempt."

"Has she not asked you to do it?" Callandra asked curiously.

"But of course. And I daresay I shall agree, and then say what I wish when the time comes."

"She will not forgive you," Callandra warned. "Mrs. Flaherty forgives nothing. By the way, what do you want to say?"

"I really don't know," Berenice replied airily. "Nothing as fiercely as you do."

They came to the bottom of the stairs.

"Really, my dear, you know you have no hope of getting people to keep windows open in this climate. They would freeze to death. Even in the Indies, you know, we kept the night air out. It isn't healthy, warm as it is."

"That is rather different," Callandra argued. "They have all manner of fevers out there."

"We have cholera, typhoid, and smallpox here," Berenice pointed out. "There was a serious outbreak of cholera near here only five years ago, which argues my point. One should keep the windows closed, in the sickroom especially."

They began to walk along the corridor.

"How long did you live in the Indies?" Callandra asked. "Where was it, Jamaica?"

"Oh, fifteen years," Berenice answered. "Yes, Jamaica most of the time. My family had plantations there. A very agreeable life." She shrugged her elegant shoulders. "But tedious when one longs for society and the excitement of London. It is the same people week after week. After a time one feels one has met everyone of any significance and heard everything they have to say."

They had reached a turn in the corridor and Berenice seemed to intend going into a ward to the left. Callandra wished to find Kristian Beck and thought it most likely that at this time of day he would be in his own rooms, where he studied, saw patients, and kept his books and papers, and that lay to the right.

"It must have been a wrench for you to leave, all the same," she said without real interest. "England would be very different, and you would miss your family."

Berenice smiled. "There was not so much to leave by the time I came away. Plantations are no longer the profitable places they used to be. I can remember going to the slave market in Kingston when I was a child, but of course slaving is illegal now and has been for years." She brushed her hand over her huge skirts, knocking off a piece of loose thread that cling to the cloth.

With that she laughed a little dryly and walked away along the corridor, leaving Callandra to go the other way toward Kristian Beck's rooms. Suddenly she was nervous, her hands hot, her tongue clumsy. This was ridiculous. She was a middle-aged widow, of no glamour at all, going to call upon a busy doctor, nothing more, nothing of any other meaning.

She knocked on the door abruptly.

"Come in." His voice was startlingly deep and touched by an almost imperceptible trace of accent she could not place. It was mid-European, but from which country she did not know, and had not asked him.

She turned the handle and pushed the door open.

He was standing at the table in front of the window, papers spread out in front of him, and he looked around to see who it was who had come in. He was not a tall man but there was a sense of power in him, both physical and emotional. His face was dominated by dark eyes that were of a beautiful shape and a mouth both sensual and humorous. His expression of preoccupation vanished when he saw her and was replaced immediately with one of pleasure.

"Lady Callandra. How good to see you again. I hope your visit does not mean that there is something wrong?"

"Nothing new." She closed the door behind her. Before she came she had formulated a good excuse for being here, but now the words escaped her. "I have been trying to prevail upon Sir Herbert to have the nurses cover the slop pails," she said rather too quickly. "But I don't think he sees much purpose to it. He was on his way to the operating theater, and I had the feeling his mind was on his patient."

"So you are going to persuade me instead?" His smile was sudden and wide. "I have never yet found above two or three nurses in the hospital who can remember an order for more than a day at a time, never mind carrying it out. The poor souls are harried from every quarter, hungry half

73

the time and drunk the other half." His smile vanished again. "They do their best according to their lights, for the most part."

His eyes lit with enthusiasm and he leaned against the table, engaging her attention. "You know, I have been reading the most interesting paper. This doctor, sailing from the Indies home to England, contracted a fever and treated himself by going out on deck at night, stripped of his clothes, and taking a cold shower with buckets of seawater. Can you believe that?" He was watching her, searching the expression in her eyes. "It relieved his symptoms marvelously and he slept well and was restored by morning. Then in the evening his fever returned and he treated it the same way, and was again restored. Each time the attack was slighter, and by the time the ship docked he was fully himself."

She was astounded, but his eagerness carried her along.

"Can you imagine Mrs. Flaherty if you tried drenching your patients with buckets of cold water?" She tried not to laugh but her voice was shaking, not so much with amusement as with nervousness. "I cannot even persuade her to open the windows in the sunlight let alone at night!"

"I know," he said quickly. "I know, but we are making new discoveries every year." He grasped the chair between them and turned it so it was convenient for her to sit, but she ignored it. "I've just been reading a paper by Carl Vierordt on counting human blood corpuscles." He moved closer to her in his keenness. "He has devised a way, can you imagine that?" He held up the paper as he said it, his eyes alight. "With this kind of precision, think what we might learn!" He offered her the paper as if he would share with her his pleasure.

She took it, smiling in spite of herself and meeting his gaze.

"Look," he commanded.

Obediently she looked down at the paper. It was in German. He saw her confusion, "Oh, I'm sorry." A faint pink flushed up his cheeks. "I find I speak with you so easily, I forget you do not read German. Shall I tell you what it says?" He so obviously wanted to that it was impossible to deny him, even had she thought of it.

"Please do," she encouraged. "It sounds a most desirable treatment."

He looked surprised. "Do you think so? I should hate to be drenched with buckets of cold water."

She smiled broadly. "Not from the patient's view perhaps. I was thinking of ours. Cold water is cheap and readily available almost everywhere, and requires no skill to administer, nor can the dosage be mistaken. A bucketful too much or too little will make no difference."

His face relaxed into sudden, delightful laughter. "Oh, of course. I fear you are far more practical than I. I find women often are." Then as quickly his expression became grim again, brows drawn down. "That is why I wish we could draw more intelligent and confident women into the treatment of the sick. We have one or two nurses here who are excellent, but there is little future for them unless beliefs change a great deal." He regarded her earnestly. "There is one in particular, a Miss Barrymore, who was with Miss Nightingale in the Crimea. She is remarkable in her perception, but I regret not everyone admires her as they might." He sighed, smiling at her with sudden total candor, an intimacy that sent a warmth racing through her. "I seem to have caught your zeal for reform."

He was saying it as if joking, but she knew he meant it with the utmost seriousness, and that he intended her to know it.

She was about to reply when there was a shout of anger in the passage outside, a woman's voice raised in furious temper. Instinctively both of them turned toward the door, listening.

Another angry shout followed a moment later, then a shriek as of pain and rage.

Kristian went to the door and opened it. Callandra followed and looked outside. There were no windows, and no gas lit during the day. A few yards along in the dim light two women were struggling together, the long hair of one of them hanging loose and untidy, and even as they watched, her opponent made another lunge to snatch at it and pull.

"Stop it!" Callandra shouted as she passed Kristian and advanced on the women. "What is it? What's the matter with you?"

They stopped for a moment, largely out of sheer surprise. One of them was in her late twenties, plain-faced, but not unappealing. The other was at least ten years older and already looking worn and aged by hard living and too many drunken nights.

"What is it?" Callandra demanded again. "What are you fighting about?"

"The laundry chute," the younger said sullenly. "She blocked it by putting the linen in it all in a bundle." She glared at the older woman. "Now nothing will go through and we'll all have to carry everything right down to the boilers ourselves. As if there weren't enough to do without going up and down them stairs every time there is a sheet to change."

For the first time, Callandra noticed the bundle of soiled sheets on the floor by the wall.

"I didn't," the older woman said defiantly. "I put one sheet down. How can you block it with one sheet?" Her voice rose in indignation. "You've got to be a real clever bitch to put down less than one at a time. What do you want? I should tear it in 'alf, then sew it back together when it's clean again?" She stared belligerently at her foe.

"Let us see," Kristian said behind Callandra. He excused himself between the nurses and looked down the open chute which took linen straight to the laundry and the huge copper boilers where it was washed. He peered down it for several seconds and they all waited in silence.

"I cannot see anything," he said finally, stepping back again. "There must be something blocking the way or I would be able to see the baskets at the bottom, or at least a light. But we will argue later as to who put it there. In the meantime, the thing is to remove it." He looked around for something to accomplish the task, and saw nothing.

"A broom?" Callandra suggested. "Or a window pole. Anything with a long handle."

The nurses stood still.

"Go on," Callandra commanded impatiently. "Go and find one. There must be a window pole in the ward." She pointed at the nearest ward entrance along the corridor. "Don't stand around, fetch it!"

Grudgingly the younger woman started, hesitated, and glared back at her companion, then continued on her way.

Callandra peered down the chute. She could see nothing either. Obviously the obstruction blocked it entirely, but how far down it was, she could not judge.

The nurse came back with a long-handled window pole and gave it to Kristian, who poked it down the chute. But even when he leaned as far as he could, he met with no resistance. The obstruction, whatever it was, was beyond his reach.

"We'll have to go down and see if we can dislodge it from below," he said after another unsuccessful try.

"Er—" The younger nurse cleared her throat.

They all turned and looked at her.

"Dr. Beck, sir."

"Yes?"

"Lally, she's one of the skivvies what does in the operating theater and like. She's only thirteen and she's made like a nine-penny rabbit. She could slide down there easy, and there's laundry baskets at the bottom, so she wouldn't hurt herself."

Kristian hesitated only a moment.

"Good idea. Fetch her, will you?" He turned to Callandra. "We should go down to the laundry room to make sure there's a soft landing for her."

"Yes sir, I'll go for her," the younger nurse said, and she went quickly, breaking into a run as she turned the corner.

Callandra, Kristian, and the other nurse went the opposite way, to the stairs and down to the basement and the dark, gas-lit passages to the laundry room where the huge coppers belched steam and the pipes clanked and rattled and poured out boiling water. Women with rolled-up sleeves heaved wet linen on the end of wooden poles, muscles straining, faces flushed, hair dripping. One or two looked around at the unusual intrusion of a man, then immediately returned to their labor.

Kristian went over to the base of the laundry chute and peered up, then backed out again and glanced at Callandra. He shook his head.

She pushed one of the large wicker baskets closer under the bottom of the chute and picked up a couple of bundles of dirty sheets to soften the fall.

"It shouldn't have got stuck," Kristian said, frowning. "Sheets are soft enough to slide, even if too many are poked down at once. Maybe someone has been putting rubbish in as well."

"We'll soon know," she replied, standing beside him and looking up expectantly.

They had not long to wait. There was a muffled call from above, faint and completely indistinguishable, then a moment's silence, a shriek, a curious shuffling noise, another shriek. A woman landed in the laundry basket, her skirts awry, arms and legs awkward. Straight after came the small, thin form of the skivvy, who shrieked again and scrambled to her feet, clambering like a monkey to escape the basket and falling onto the floor, wailing loudly.

Kristian bent forward to help the other woman up, then his face darkened and he moved his hand to hold Callandra back. But it was too late. She had already looked down and knew as soon as she saw her that the woman was dead. There was no mistaking the ashen quality of her skin, the bluish lips, and above all, the terrible bruises on her throat.

"It's Nurse Barrymore," Kristian said huskily, his voice catching in his throat. He did not add that she was dead; he saw in Callandra's eyes that she knew not only that, but also that it had been no illness or accident which had caused it. Instinctively he stretched out his hand as if to touch her, almost as if some compassion could still reach her.

"No," Callandra said softly. "Don't . . ."

He opened his mouth as though to remonstrate, then realized its uselessness. He stared down at the dead woman's body, his eyes filled with sadness. "Why would anyone want to do this to her?" he said helplessly. Without thinking, Callandra put her hand on his arm, gripping it gently.

"We can't know yet. But we must call the police. It seems to be murder."

One of the laundrywomen turned around, perhaps her attention caught by the skivvy, who was beginning to shriek again, and she saw the arm of the dead woman above the edge of the laundry basket. She came over and gaped at the corpse, then screamed.

"Murder!" She drew in her breath and screamed again, piercingly, her voice high and shrill even above the hiss of steam and clatter of pipes. "Murder! Help! Murder!"

All the other women stopped their work and crowded around, some wailing, some shrieking, one slithering to the floor in a faint. No one took any notice of the skivvy.

"Stop it!" Kristian ordered sharply. "Stop this minute and go back to your work!"

Some power in him, some tone or manner, caught their innate fear of authority, and one by one they fell silent, then retreated. But no one returned to the coppers or the piles of steaming laundry gradually cooling on the slabs and in the tubs.

Kristian turned to Callandra.

"You had better go and inform Sir Herbert, and have him call the police," he said quietly. "This is not something we can deal with ourselves. I'll stay here and make sure no one disturbs her. And you'd better take the skivvy, poor child, and have someone look after her."

"She'll tell everyone," Callandra warned. "No doubt with a great deal added. We'll have half the hospital thinking there's been a massacre. There'll be hysterics and the patients will suffer."

He hesitated a moment, weighing what she had said.

"Then you'd better take her to the matron and explain why. Then go and see Sir Herbert. I'll keep the laundry-women here."

She smiled and nodded very slightly. There was no need for further words. She turned away and went to where the skivvy was standing, pressed up against the capacious form of one of the silent laundrywomen. Her thin face was bloodless and her skinny arms were folded tightly around her body as if hugging herself to keep from shaking so violently she would fall over.

Callandra held out her hand toward her.

"Come," she said gently. "I'll take you upstairs where you can sit down and have a cup of tea before you go back to work." She did not mention Mrs. Flaherty; she knew most of the nurses and skivvies were terrified of her, and justly so.

The child stared at her, but there was nothing awe-inspiring in her mild face and untidy hair and rather comfortable figure in its stuff gown. She bore no resemblance whatever to the thin fierce person of Mrs. Flaherty.

"Come on," she said again, this time more briskly.

Obediently the child detached herself and followed a step behind as she was accustomed.

It did not take long to find Mrs. Flaherty. All the hospital knew where she was. Word ran like a warning whenever she passed. Bottles were put away, mops were pushed harder, heads bent in attention to labor.

"Yes, your ladyship, what is it now?" she said grimly, her eyes going to the skivvy with displeasure. "Not sick, is she?"

"No, Matron, only badly frightened," Callandra answered. "I'm afraid we have discovered a corpse in the laundry chute, and this poor child was the one who found her. I'm about to go to Sir Herbert and have him fetch the police."

"Whatever for?" Mrs. Flaherty snapped. "For goodness sake, there's nothing odd about a corpse in a hospital, although for the life of me, I can't think how it got to be in the laundry chute." Her face darkened with disapproval. "I hope it is not one of the young doctors with a puerile sense of what is amusing."

"No one could find this amusing, Mrs. Flaherty." Callandra was surprised to find her voice so calm. "It was Nurse Barrymore, and she has not died naturally. I am going to report the matter to Sir Herbert and I should be obliged if you would see to this child and make sure she does not unintentionally cause hysteria by speaking of it to others. It will be known soon enough, but for the meantime it would be better if we were prepared for it."

Mrs. Flaherty looked startled. "Not naturally? What do you mean?"

But Callandra was not going to discuss it further. She smiled bleakly and left without answering, Mrs. Flaherty staring after in confusion and anger.

Sir Herbert Stanhope was in the operating theater and apparently due to remain there for some considerable time. The matter would not wait, so she simply opened the door and went in. It was not a large room; a side table with instruments laid out took much of the space and there were already several people inside. Two student doctors assisted and learned, a third more senior watched the bottles of nitrous oxide and monitored the patient's breathing. A nurse stood by to pass instruments as required. The patient lay insensible upon the table, white-faced, her upper body naked and a bloody wound in the chest half closed. Sir Herbert Stanhope stood at her side, needle in his hand, blood staining his shirtsleeves and forearms.

Everyone stared at Callandra.

"What are you doing here, madam?" Sir Herbert demanded. "You have no business to interrupt an operation! Will you please leave immediately!"

She had expected a reception of this nature and she was not perturbed.

"There is a matter which cannot wait until you are concluded, Sir Herbert," she replied.

"Get some other doctor!" he snapped, turning away from her and resuming his stitching.

"Please keep your attention upon what I am doing, gentlemen," he went on, addressing the student doctors. He obviously assumed that Callandra would accept his dismissal and leave without further ado.

"There has been a murder in the hospital, Sir Herbert," Callandra said loudly and distinctly. "Do you wish me to inform the police, or would you prefer to do that yourself?"

He froze, his hands in the air with needle poised. Still he did not look at her. The nurse sucked in her breath sharply. One of the student doctors made a choking sound and grasped the edge of the table.

"Don't be absurd!" Sir Herbert snapped. "If a patient has died unexpectedly I will attend to it when I'm finished here." He turned slowly to look at Callandra. His face was pale and there were sharp lines of anger between his brows.

"One of the nurses has been strangled and stuffed down the laundry chute," Callandra said slowly and very clearly. "That can hardly be called a misjudgment. It is beyond question a crime, and if you cannot leave here to summon the police, I will do so on your behalf. The body will remain where it is. Dr. Beck is seeing that it is not disturbed."

There was a sharp hiss of breath between teeth. One of the student doctors let slip a blasphemy.

Sir Herbert lowered his hands, still holding the bloody needle and its long thread. He faced Callandra, his eyes bright, his face tight.

"One of the nurses?" he repeated very slowly. "Are you sure?"

"Of course I'm sure," Callandra answered. "It is Barrymore."

"Oh." He hesitated. "That is appalling. Yes, by all means, you'd better call the police. I shall finish here and be available to meet them by the time they arrive. You had better take a hansom yourself rather than send a messenger, and for goodness sake be as discreet as you can. We don't want a panic in the place. The sick will suffer." His expression darkened. "Who else knows of it already, apart from Dr. Beck?"

"Mrs. Flaherty, the laundrywomen, and one skivvy whom I asked Mrs. Flaherty to watch over, for that reason."

"Good." His expression relaxed a little. "Then you had better leave immediately. I should be ready when you return." He did not apologize for not having listened to her immediately, or for his rudeness, not that she had expected him to.

She took a hansom cab, as he had suggested, and ordered the driver to take her to Monk's old police station. It was probably the closest, and it was certainly the one of which she knew the address and where she was confident of finding a senior officer with a proper sense of discretion. She used her title to obtain immediate attention.

"Lady Callandra." Runcorn rose from his seat as soon as she was shown in. He came over to greet her, extending his hand, then changing his mind and bowing very slightly instead. He was a tall man with a narrow face bordering on handsome in a certain manner, but it was belied by lines of temper around his mouth and a lack of assurance which one would not have expected in an officer of his seniority. One had only to look at him to know that he and Monk could never be at ease with each other. Monk was assured, even arrogant, his convictions deeply seated and dominated by intellect, his ambition boundless. Runcorn held his convictions equally deeply, but lacked the personal confidence. His emotions were uncertain, his humor simple. His ambition was also keen but his vulnerability was plain in his face. He could be swayed and cut by what other people thought of him.

"Good morning, Mr. Runcorn," Callandra replied with a light smile. She accepted the seat he offered her. "I regret I have a crime to report and it may prove to be a sensitive matter. I wished to tell you of it in person rather than find a constable in the street. I'm afraid it is very serious."

"Indeed." Already he looked in some indefinable way satisfied, as though the fact she had confided in him were

83

an accolade. "I am sorry to hear it. Is it a matter of robbery?"

"No." She dismissed robbery as of no consequence. "It is murder."

His complacency disappeared but his attention quickened. "Who has been killed, ma'am? I will see that my very best officer is on the case straightaway. Where did this happen?"

"In the Royal Free Hospital on the Gray's Inn Road," she replied. "One of the nurses has been strangled and placed down the laundry chute. I have come straight from there. Sir Herbert Stanhope is the chief medical officer and a surgeon of some note."

"I've heard of him, of course. An excellent man." Runcorn nodded. "Indeed, an excellent man. He sent you to report this matter?"

"In a sense." It was foolish to resent the reference to Sir Herbert, as if he had taken charge and she were merely a messenger, and yet she knew that was what it would come to in the end. "I was one of those who found the body," she added.

"Most distressing for you," Runcorn said sympathetically. "May I send for something to restore you? Perhaps a cup of tea?"

"No thank you," she said rather more briskly than she had meant. She was shaken and her mouth felt dry. "No thank you. I should prefer to return to the hospital and allow your officer to begin his investigation of the matter," she added. "I have left Dr. Beck standing guard over the corpse to see that nothing is moved or altered. He has been there for some time by now."

"Of course. Most commendable of you, ma'am." Runcorn said it with what he doubtless intended to be approval, but to Callandra it sounded intolerably condescending. She nearly asked him if he had expected her to behave like a fool and leave the body for anyone to move or alter, but recalled herself only just in time. She was more distressed than she had thought. She found to her surprise that her hands were trembling. She thrust them into the concealing folds of her skirt so Runcorn would not see them. She stared at him expectantly.

He rose to his feet, excusing himself, and went to the door, opening it and calling in a constable. "Send Inspector Jeavis up here right away. I have a new case for him and Sergeant Evan."

The answer was indistinguishable, but it was barely a few moments before a dark saturnine man put his head around the door inquiringly, then followed immediately, his lean body dressed in very formal black trousers and a black frock coat. A white winged collar made him look like a city clerk or an undertaker. His manner was peculiarly both hesitant and assured. He looked at Runcorn and then at Callandra, as if to ask permission, though he did not wait for it but stood equally between them.

"Jeavis, this is Lady Callandra Daviot," Runcorn began, then he realized he had made a social error. He should have presented him to her, not the other way around. He blushed angrily but there was no way to retrieve it.

Without thought Callandra rescued him. It was the instinctive thing to do.

"Thank you for sending for Mr. Jeavis so rapidly, Mr. Runcorn. I'm sure it will prove to be the best arrangement possible. Good morning, Mr. Jeavis."

"Good morning, ma'am." He bowed very slightly, and she found him instantly irritating. He had a sallow face and thick black hair and very fine eyes, the darkest she had ever seen, but curiously light brows. It was unfair to prejudge the man, and she knew it even while she did it. "Perhaps you would be good enough to tell me what crime you have suffered?" he inquired.

"None at all," she replied hastily. "I am on the Board of Governors at the Royal Free Hospital in the Gray's Inn Road. We have just discovered the corpse of one of our young nurses in the laundry chute. She appears to have been strangled."

"Oh dear. How very unpleasant. When you say 'we,'

ma'am, whom precisely do you mean?" Jeavis asked. In spite of his obsequious manner his look was penetrating and highly intelligent. She had the sense of being very thoroughly weighed and that the judgment would have none of the social deference he suggested outwardly.

"Myself and Dr. Kristian Beck, who is one of the physicians at the hospital," she replied. "And in a sense the women in the laundry room, and a child who is employed as a skivvy."

"Indeed. What caused you to be examining the laundry chute, ma'am?" His head cocked curiously to one side. "Surely that is not part of the duties of a lady such as yourself?"

She explained to him how it had come about and he listened without taking his eyes from her face.

Runcorn fidgeted from one foot to the other, uncertain whether to interrupt or not, and at a loss for something to say to keep his place in the proceedings.

There was a knock on the door, and on Runcorn's command John Evan came in. His lean young face lit up when he saw Callandra, but in spite of past circumstances and commitments shared he had enough aplomb to affect merely recognition and no more.

"Good morning, Sergeant," she said formally.

"Good morning, ma'am," he replied, then looked inquiringly at Runcorn.

"A murder in the Royal Free Hospital," Runcorn said, seizing the chance to regain control. "You will go with Inspector Jeavis and investigate. Keep me informed of all your findings."

"Yes sir."

"Oh, Jeavis," Runcorn added as Jeavis opened the door for Callandra.

"Yes sir."

"Don't forget to report to Sir Herbert Stanhope at the hospital. Don't go blundering in as if it were a manhunt down the Whitechapel Road. Remember who he is!"

"Naturally sir," Jeavis said soothingly, but his face tightened with a quick flick of temper. He did not like to be reminded of social niceties.

Evan shot a rapid glance at Callandra, amusement glinting in his hazel eyes, and a wealth of memory and silent humor passed between them.

Back in the hospital it was entirely different. By the time they came in, in spite of Mrs. Flaherty's best efforts, the news was everywhere. The chaplain hurried up to them, coattails flapping, his round eyes startled. Then when he realized just who Jeavis was, he recovered again hastily, muttered something no one could distinguish, offered a hurried imprecation, and disappeared clutching his prayer book in both hands.

A young nurse stared inquisitively before going away about her duty. The treasurer shook his head with foreboding and directed them to Sir Herbert's rooms.

Sir Herbert met them at the door, opening it wide to show the gracious interior, carpeted in Prussian blue, gleaming with polished wood, and a bar of sunlight across the floor from the southern window.

"Good day, Inspector," he said gravely. "Please come in and I shall give you all the information I have in this affair. Thank you, Lady Callandra. You have discharged your duty excellently. Indeed, more than your duty, and we are all most obliged." As he ushered Jeavis and Evan inside, at the same time he stood so that he blocked the way for Callandra. There was nothing she could do but accept the dismissal and go back down to the laundry room to see if Kristian was still there.

The huge basement was full of steam again; copper pipes gurgled and clanked, the vast boiler hissed when the lid was lifted off and the laundrywomen poked in wooden poles to lever out the linen and carried it, arms straining, over to the sinks that lined the far wall. The sinks were mounted with giant mangles through which the linen was pressed to remove as much of the water as possible. Work had resumed, time and taskmasters waited for no one, and the corpse had lost their immediate interest. Most of the women had seen plenty of corpses before. Death came often enough.

Kristian was still standing near the laundry basket, his back to it, leaning a little on its rim to take his weight. As soon as he saw Callandra his head lifted and his eyes met her questioningly.

"The police are in with Sir Herbert," she said in answer to his unspoken question. "A man called Jeavis; I suppose he's quite good."

He looked at her more closely. "You sound doubtful."

She sighed. "I wish it were William Monk."

"The detective who went into private work?" There was a flash of humor across his face, so quick she barely caught it.

"He would have had . . ." She stopped, unsure what she meant. No one could say that Monk was sensitive. He was as ruthless as a juggernaut.

Kristian was waiting, trying to read her meaning.

She smiled at him. "Imagination, intelligence," she said, knowing that was still not quite what she meant. "The perception to see beyond the obvious," she went on. "And no one would have fobbed him off with a suitable answer if it was not the truth."

"You have a high regard for him," Kristian observed, his dry rueful smile returning. "Let us hope Mr. Jeavis is as gifted." He looked back at the basket. There was an unwashed sheet now folded over to cover the dead face. "Poor woman," he said very gently. "She was a good nurse, you know; in fact, I think she was the best here. What a ridiculous tragedy that she should come all through the campaigns in the Crimea, the danger and the disease, and the ocean voyages, to die at the hands of some criminal in a London hospital." He shook his head and there was a terrible sadness in his face. "Why would anyone want to kill such a woman?"

"Why indeed?" Jeavis had arrived without either of them being aware of him. "You knew her, Dr. Beck?"

Kristian looked startled. "Of course." His voice rose with irritation. "She was a nurse here. We all knew her."

"But you knew her personally?" Jeavis persisted, his dark eyes fixed almost accusingly on Kristian's face.

"If you mean did I know her outside her duties here in the hospital, no I did not," Kristian answered, his expression narrowing.

Jeavis grunted and moved over to the laundry basket. With delicate fingers he picked up the sheet and pulled it back. He looked at the dead woman. Callandra looked at her again carefully.

Prudence Barrymore had been in her early thirties, a very tall woman, slender. Perhaps in life she had been elegant; now with the awkwardness of death, there was no grace in her at all. She lay with arms and legs sprawled, one foot poking up, her skirts fallen back to reveal a long shapely leg. Her face was ashen now, but even with the blood coursing she must have been pale-skinned. Her hair was medium brown, her brows level and delicately marked, her mouth wide and sensitive. It was a passionate face, individual, full of humor and strength.

Callandra could remember her vividly, even though they had always met hastily, and about their separate duties. But Prudence Barrymore had been a reformer with a burning zeal, and few people in the hospital had been unaware of her. Not many were as interesting alive as she had been, and it seemed a vicious mockery that she should be lying here emptied of all that had made her vivid and special, nothing left but a vacated shell beyond feeling or awareness, and yet looking so terribly vulnerable.

"Cover her up," Callandra said instinctively.

"In a moment, ma'am." Jeavis held up his arm as if to prevent Callandra from doing it herself. "In a moment. Strangled, you said? Yes indeed. Looks like it. Poor creature." He stared at the deep-colored marks on her neck. It was horribly easy to imagine them as fingerprints of someone pressing harder and harder until there was no air left, no breath, no life.

"A nurse, was she?" Jeavis was looking at Kristian. "Work with you, did she, Doctor?"

"Sometimes," Kristian agreed. "She worked more often with Sir Herbert Stanhope, especially on his more difficult cases. She was an excellent nurse, and to the best of my belief, a fine woman. I never heard anyone speak ill of her."

Jeavis stood motionless, his dark eyes beneath their pale brows fixed on Kristian.

"Most interesting. What made you look in the laundry chute, Doctor?"

"It was blocked," Kristian replied. "Two of the nurses were having trouble trying to put soiled sheets down, and unable to get them to go all the way. Lady Callandra and I went to their assistance."

"I see. And how did you dislodge the body?"

"We sent one of the skivvies who works here, a child of about thirteen. She slid down the chute and her weight moved the body."

"Very efficient," Jeavis said dryly. "If a little hard on the child. Still, I suppose working in a hospital she's seen many dead bodies before." His sharp nose wrinkled very slightly.

"We did not know it was a dead body," Kristian said in distaste. "We assumed it was a bundle of sheets."

"Did you?" Jeavis walked over, pushed the basket out of the way, and peered up the chute for several moments. "Where is the top of this?" he said at last, withdrawing to look at Callandra.

"In the corridor on the ground floor," she replied, disliking him more by the moment. "In the west wing corridor, to be precise."

"A very odd place to put a body, don't you think?" Jeavis remarked. "Not easy to do without being observed." He turned to Kristian, then back to Callandra, his eyes very wide open.

"That is not entirely correct," Kristian answered. "The corridor has no windows, and during the daytime the gas is not lit, it saves expense."

"Still," Jeavis argued, "one would be bound to notice a

person standing or sitting around, and certainly one would see a person lifting a body and putting it down the chute. Wouldn't one?" There was a faint lift of inquiry in his tone, less than sarcasm but more than courtesy.

"Not necessarily," Callandra said defensively. "Bundles of sheets are sometimes left on the floor. The nurses occasionally sit in the corridors, if they are intoxicated. In the dim light a corpse could look like a pile of linen. And certainly if I saw someone putting laundry down the chute, I would assume it was merely a bundle of sheets. I image anyone else would also."

"Dear me." Jeavis looked from one to the other of them. "Are you saying that anyone could have stuffed the poor creature down the chute in full sight of respectable medical people, and no one would have thought anything amiss?"

Callandra was uncomfortable. She glanced at Kristian.

"More or less," she agreed at length. "One is not usually watching what other people are doing, one has one's own affairs." In her imagination she visualized a dim figure, shapeless in the half-light, lifting a bundle, heavier than it should have been, shrouded in sheets, and pressing it down the open chute. Her voice, when she continued, was husky and a little choked. "I myself passed what I assumed was a nurse in either intoxication or sleep this morning. But I do not know which it was. I didn't look at her face." She swallowed with a sudden sick realization. "It could have been Prudence Barrymore!"

"Really!" Jeavis's pale brows rose. "Do your nurses often lie about in the corridor, Lady Callandra? Do they not have beds to sleep in?"

"The ones who live in the dormitory do," she said tartly. "But many of them live out, and they have very little indeed. There is no place for them to sleep here, and precious little to eat. And yes, they frequently drink too much."

Jeavis looked temporarily disconcerted. He turned back to Kristian.

"I shall want to speak to you again, Doctor. Anything you can tell me about this unfortunate woman." He cleared

91

his throat. "To begin with, how long do you estimate she has been dead? Not, of course, that we won't have our own police surgeon tell us his opinion, but it will save time if you can give us yours now."

"About two hours, perhaps three," Kristian replied succinctly.

"But you haven't looked at her," Jeavis exclaimed.

"I looked at her before you came," Kristian answered.

"Did you! Did you indeed?" Jeavis's face sharpened. "I thought you said you had not disturbed the body! Was that not why you remained here, to see that no one tampered with the evidence?"

"I looked at her, Inspector. I did not move her."

"But you touched her."

"Yes, to see if she was cold."

"And she was?"

"Yes."

"How do you know she has not been dead all night?"

"Because rigor had not yet passed away."

"You moved her!"

"I did not."

"You must have," Jeavis said sharply. "Otherwise how could you know whether she was stiff or not?"

"She fell out of the chute, Inspector," Kristian explained patiently. "I saw her fall, and how she collapsed into the basket, the movement of her limbs. It's my estimate that she has been dead between two and four hours. But by all means ask your own surgeon."

Jeavis looked at him suspiciously. "You are not English, are you, sir? I detect a certain accent, shall we say? Very slight, but it is there. Where are you from?"

"Bohemia," Kristian replied with a faint flicker of amusement in his eyes.

Jeavis drew in his breath, Callandra thought, to ask where that was, then realized even the laundrywomen were watching him, and changed his mind.

"I see," he said thoughtfully. "Well now, perhaps you would be good enough to tell me, Doctor, where you were early this morning? For example, what time did you come here?" He looked at Kristian inquiringly. "Take a note of it please, Sergeant," he added with a nod at Evan, who had been watching silently some two or three yards away all through the exchange.

"I have been here all night," Kristian replied.

Jeavis's eyes widened. "Indeed. And why was that, sir?" He invested it with a great deal of meaning.

"I had a patient who was extremely ill," Kristian answered, watching Jeavis's face. "I stayed with him. I believed I could save him, but I was wrong. He died a little after four in the morning. It was hardly worth going home. I lay down on one of the hospital beds and slept till about half past six."

Jeavis frowned, glanced at Evan to make sure he was noting everything down, then back at Kristian. "I see," he said portentously. "So you were here when Nurse Barrymore met her death."

For the first time Callandra felt a sharp flick of anxiety. She looked at Kristian but saw nothing in his face beyond a mild curiosity, as if he did not entirely understand Jeavis's implication.

"Yes, it would seem so."

"And did you see this Nurse Barrymore?"

Kristian shook his head. "I don't think so, but I can't be sure. I certainly don't recall speaking to her."

"And yet she seems to be very sharp in your mind?" Jeavis said quickly. "You know precisely who she is, and you speak very well of her."

Kristian looked down, his eyes full of sadness.

"The poor creature is dead, Inspector. Of course she is sharp in my mind. And she was a fine nurse. There are not so many people dedicated to the care of others that one forgets them easily."

"Isn't everyone here dedicated to the care of the sick?" Jeavis asked with some surprise.

Kristian stared at him, then sighed deeply. "If there is nothing further, Inspector, I would like to go about my duties. I have been here in the laundry room nearly two hours. I have patients to see."

"By all means," Jeavis said, pursing his lips. "But don't go out of London, sir, if you please."

Kristian was startled, but he agreed without argument, and a few moments later he and Callandra left the steam and clank of the laundry room and climbed back up the stairs to the main hallway. Callandra's mind was teeming with things she wished to say to him, but they all sounded officious or overconcerned, and above all, she did not want him to know of the fear that was beginning to rise in her. Perhaps it was foolish. There was no reason Jeavis should suspect Kristian, but she had seen miscarriages of justice before. Innocent men had been hanged. It was so easy to suspect anyone who was different, whether it was in manner, appearance, race, or religion. If only Monk were conducting the investigation.

"You look tired, Lady Callandra," he said quietly, intruding into her thoughts.

"I beg your pardon?" She was startled, then realized what he had said. "Oh no, not tired so much as sad, afraid for what will come next."

"Afraid?"

"I have seen investigations before. People become frightened. One learns so much more about them than one ever wishes to know." She forced herself to smile. "But that is foolish. I daresay it will all be over quite quickly." They reached the top of the stairs and stopped. Two student doctors were arguing fiercely a dozen yards away. "Take no notice of what I said," she went on hastily. "If you have been up most of the night, I'm sure you must wish to rest for a while. It must be nearly time for luncheon by now."

"Of course. I am keeping you. I apologize." And with a quick smile, meeting her eyes for a moment, he excused himself and went rapidly along the corridor toward the nearest ward.

* * *

It was early evening before Callandra found Monk, and she observed no ceremony, but plunged straight in to her purpose for coming to his rooms.

"There has been a murder in the hospital," she said bluntly. "One of the nurses, an exceptional young woman, both honest and diligent. She was strangled, or so it appears, and stuffed into the laundry chute." She looked at him expectantly.

His hard gray eyes searched her face for several moments before he answered. "What bothers you?" he said at length. "There is something more."

"Runcorn sent an Inspector Jeavis to investigate," she replied. "Do you know him?"

"Slightly. He's very sharp. He'll probably do an adequate job. Why? Who did it? Do you know, or suspect?"

"No!" she said too quickly. "I have no idea at all. Why would anybody want to murder a nurse?"

"Any number of reasons." He pulled a face. "The most obvious that come to mind are a lover jilted, a jealous woman, and blackmail. But there are others. She may have witnessed a theft, or another murder that looked like natural death. Hospitals are full of deaths. And there are always love, hate, and jealousy. Was she handsome?"

"Yes, yes she was." Callandra stared at him. He had said so many ugly things in a bare handful of words, and yet any one of them could be true. At least one of them almost certainly was. One did not strangle a woman without some intense passion. Unless it was the act of a lunatic.

As if reading her thoughts, he spoke.

"I assume the hospital is for the physically sick? It is not a madhouse?"

"No, not at all. What a vile thought."

"A madhouse?"

"No, I meant that someone quite sane murdered her."

"Is that what troubles you?"

She considered lying to him, or at least evading the truth, then looked at his face and decided against it.

"Not entirely. I'm afraid Jeavis suspects Dr. Beck, pri-

95

marily because he is a foreigner and it is he and I who found the body."

He looked at her closely. "Do you suspect Dr. Beck?"

"No!" Then she blushed for the fierceness of her reply, but it was to late to retreat. He had seen her eagerness and then her immediate knowledge that she had betrayed herself. "No, I think it is extremely unlikely," she went on. "But I have no confidence in Jeavis. Will you please look into the matter? I will employ you myself, at your usual rate."

"Don't be ridiculous!" he said acidly. "You have contributed to my well-being ever since I took up this occupation. You are not paying me now because you wish a job done."

"But I have to." She looked at him and the words he had intended died on his lips. Callandra continued: "Will you please investigate the murder of Prudence Barrymore? She died this morning, probably between six o'clock and half past seven. Her body was found in the laundry chute at the hospital, and the cause of death seems to have been strangulation. There is not a great deal more I can tell you, except that she was an excellent nurse, one of Miss Nightingale's women who served in the Crimea. I judge her to be in her early thirties, and of course not married."

"All very pertinent information," he agreed. "But I have no way of involving myself in the matter. Jeavis certainly won't call upon me, and I think there is no chance whatsoever that he will share with me any information that he might have. Nor will anyone in the hospital answer my questions, should I have the temerity to ask." Then his face softened with regret. "I'm sorry. I would if I could."

But it was Kristian's features, not Monk's, which were in her mind.

"I appreciate it will be hard," she said without hesitation. "But it is a hospital. I shall be there. I can observe things and tell you. And perhaps it would be more effective if we could get Hester a position there? She would see much that I would not, and indeed that Inspector Jeavis would not."

"Callandra!" he interrupted. Calling her by her given

name without her title was a familiarity—indeed, an arrogance—which she did not mind. If she had, she would have corrected him rapidly enough. It was the pain in his voice which chilled her.

"Hester has a gift for observation," she carried on, disregarding him, Kristian's face still vivid in her mind. "And she is as good as you are at piecing together information. She has an excellent understanding of human nature, nor is she afraid to pursue a cause."

"In that case you will hardly need me." He said it waspishly, but it was redeemed at the last instant by a flash of humor in his eyes.

She was spoiling her own case by pressing too hard.

"Perhaps I overstated it a trifle," she conceded. "But she would certainly be an asset, and be able to observe those things you were not in a position to. Then she could report to you so you could make deductions and tell her what next to inquire into?"

"And if there is a murderer in this hospital of yours, have you considered what danger you might be putting her into? One nurse has already been killed," he pointed out.

She saw in his face that he was aware of his own victory.

"No, I had not thought of that," she confessed. "She would have to be most careful, and look without asking. Still, even so, she would be of invaluable assistance to you."

"You speak as though I were going to take the case."

"Am I mistaken?" This time it was her victory, and she also knew it.

Again the smile lit his face, showing an unaccustomed gentleness. "No, no you are not. I shall do what I can."

"Thank you." She felt a rush of relief which surprised her. "Did I mention it, John Evan is the sergeant assisting Jeavis?"

"No, you did not mention it, but I happened to know that he was working with Jeavis."

"I thought you might. I am glad you are still keeping your friendship with him. He is an excellent young man."

Monk smiled.

Callandra rose to her feet and he rose automatically also.

"Then you had better go and see Hester," she instructed. "There is no time to be lost. I would do it myself, but you can tell her what you wish her to do for you better than I. You may tell her I shall use my influence to see that she obtains a position. They will be looking for someone to take poor Prudence Barrymore's place."

"I shall ask her," he agreed, pulling a slight face. "I promise," he added.

"Thank you. I shall arrange it all tomorrow." And she went out of the door as he held it for her, and then through the front door into the warm evening street. Now that there was nothing more that she could do, she felt tired and extraordinarily sad. Her coach was waiting for her and she rode home in somber mood.

Hester received Monk with a surprise which she did not bother to conceal. She led him into the tiny front room and invited him to sit. She looked far less tired today; there was a vigor about her, a good color to her skin. Not for the first time he was aware of how intensely alive she was—not so much physically, but in the mind and in the will.

"This cannot be a social call," she said with a slight smile of amusement. "Something has happened." It was a statement, not a question.

He did not bother with prevarication.

"Callandra came to see me earlier this evening," he began. "This morning there was a nurse murdered in the hospital where she is on the Board of Governors. A nurse from the Crimea, not just a woman to fetch and carry." He stopped, seeing the shock in her face and quite suddenly realizing that in all probability it was someone she knew, maybe well, someone she might even have cared for. Neither he nor Callandra had thought of that.

"I'm sorry." He meant it. "It was Prudence Barrymore. Did you know her?"

"Yes." She took a deep, shaky breath, her face pale. "Not

98

well, but I liked her. She had great courage—and great heart. How did it happen?"

"I don't know. That is what Callandra wants us to find out."

"Us?" She looked startled. "What about the police? Surely they have called the police?"

"Yes of course they have," he said tartly. Suddenly all his old contempt for Runcorn boiled up again, and his own resentment that he was no longer on the force with his rank and power and the respect he had worked so long and hard to earn, even had it been laced with fear. "But she doesn't have any confidence that they will solve it."

Hester frowned and looked at him carefully.

"Is that all?"

"All? Isn't it enough?" His voice rose incredulously. "We have no power, no authority, and there are no obvious answers so far." He stabbed his finger viciously on the chair arm. "We have no right to ask questions, no access to the police information, medical reports, or anything else. What more do you want to provide a challenge?"

"An arrogant and disagreeable colleague," she said. "Just to make it really difficult!" She stood up and walked over to the window. "Really, there are times when I wonder how you succeeded for so long in the police." She looked at him. "Why is Callandra so concerned, and why does she doubt that the police will be able to solve it? Isn't it a little early to be so skeptical?"

He could feel his body tighten with anger, and yet there was also a strange kind of comfort in being with someone so quick to grasp the essential facts—and the nuances that might in the end matter even more. There were times when he loathed Hester, but she never bored him, nor had he ever found her trivial or artificial. Indeed, sometimes to quarrel with her gave him more satisfaction than to be agreeable with someone else.

"No," he said candidly. "I think she is afraid they may blame a Dr. Beck because he is a foreigner, and it may well be easier than questioning an eminent surgeon or dignitary.

With luck it may turn out to have been another nurse"—his voice was hard-edged with contempt—"or someone equally socially dispensable, but it may not. And there are no men in the hospital who are not eminent in some way, either as doctors, treasurers, chaplains, or even governors."

"What does she think I can offer?" Hester frowned, leaning a little against the windowsill. "I know less of the people of the hospital than she does. London is nothing like Scutari! And I was hardly in any hospital here long enough to learn much." She pulled a rueful face, but he knew the memory of her dismissal still hurt.

"She wishes you to take a position at the Royal Free." He saw her expression harden and hurried on. "Which she will obtain for you, possibly even as soon as tomorrow. They will require someone to take Nurse Barrymore's place. From that position of advantage, you might be able to observe much that would be of use, but you are not to indulge in questioning people."

"Why not?" Her eyebrows shot up. "I can hardly learn a great deal if I don't."

"Because you may well end up dead yourself, you fool," he snapped back. "For Heaven's sake, use your wits! One outspoken, self-opinionated young woman has already been murdered there. We don't need a second to prove the point."

"Thank you for your concern." She swung around and stared out of the window, her back to him. "I shall be discreet. I did not say so because I had assumed that you would take it for granted, but apparently you did not. I have no desire to be murdered, or even to be dismissed for inquisitiveness. I am perfectly capable of asking questions in such a way that no one realizes my interest is more than casual and quite natural."

"Are you," he said with heavy disbelief. "Well, I shall not permit you to go unless you give me your word that you will simply observe. Just watch and listen, no more. Do you understand me?"

"Of course I understand you. You are practically speaking in words of one syllable," she said scathingly. "I simply do not agree, that is all. And what makes you imagine you can give me orders, I have no idea. I shall do as I think fit. If it pleases you that is good. If it does not, as far as I am concerned that is just as good."

"Then don't come screaming to me for help if you're attacked," he said. "And if you are murdered I shall be very sorry, but not very surprised!"

"You will have the satisfaction, at my funeral, of being able to say that you told me so," she replied, staring at him with wide eyes.

"Very little satisfaction," he retorted, "if you are not there to hear me."

She swung away from the window and walked across the room.

"Oh do stop being so ill-tempered and pessimistic about it. It is I who have to go back and work in the hospital, and obey all the rules and endure their suffocating incompetence and their old-fashioned ideas. All you have to do is listen to what I report and work out who killed Prudence, and of course why."

"And prove it," he added.

"Oh yes." She flashed him a sudden brilliant smile. "That at least will be good, won't it?"

"It would, it would be very good indeed," he admitted frankly. It was another of those rare moments of perfect understanding between them, and he savored it with a unique satisfaction.

4

Monk began his investigation not in the hospital—where he knew they would still be highly suspicious and defensive, and he might even jeopardize Hester's opportunities—but by taking the train on the Great Western line to Hanwell, where Prudence Barrymore's family lived. It was a bright day with a gentle breeze, and it would have been a delightful walk from the station through the fields into the village and along Green Lane toward the point where the river Brent met the Grand Junction Canal, had he not been going to see people whose daughter had just been strangled to death.

The Barrymore house was the last on the right, with the water rushing around the very end of the garden. At first, in the sunlight, with the windowpanes reflecting the image of the climbing roses and the air full of birdsong and the sound of the river, it was easy to overlook the drawn blinds and the unnatural stillness of the house. It was only when he was actually at the door, seeing the black crepe on the knocker, that the presence of death was intrusive.

"Yes sir?" a red-eyed maid said somberly.

Monk had had several hours to think of what he would say, how to introduce himself so they would not find him prying and meddlesome in a tragedy that was none of his business. He had no official standing now, which still stung him. It would be foolish to resent Jeavis, but his dislike of Runcorn was seated deep in the past, and even though he still remembered only patches of it, their mutual antagonism was one thing of which he had no doubt. It was in everything Runcorn said, in his gestures, in the very bearing of his body, and Monk felt it in himself as instinctive as flinching when something passed too close to his face.

"Good morning," he said respectfully, offering her his card. "My name is William Monk. Lady Callandra Daviot, a governor of the Royal Free Hospital and a friend of Miss Barrymore's, asked me if I would call on Mr. and Mrs. Barrymore, to see if I could be of assistance. Would you ask them if they would be kind enough to spare me a little time? I realize the moment is inopportune, but there are matters which unfortunately will not wait."

"Oh—well." She looked doubtful. "I'll ask, sir, but I can't say as I think they will. We just had a bereavement in the family, as I suppose you know, from what you say."

"If you would?" Monk smiled slightly.

The maid looked a trifle confused, but she acceded to his request, leaving him in the hallway while she went to inform her mistress of his presence. Presumably the house did not boast a morning room or other unoccupied reception room where unexpected callers might wait.

He looked around curiously as he always did. One could learn much from the observation of people's homes, not merely their financial situations but their tastes, a guess at their educations, whether they had traveled or not, sometimes even their beliefs and prejudices and what they wished others to think of them. In the case of family homes of more than one generation, one could also learn something of parents, and thus of upbringing.

The Barrymores' hallway did not offer a great deal. The house was quite large, but of a cottage style, low-windowed, low-ceilinged, with oak beams across. It had apparently been designed for the comfort of a large family, rather than to entertain guests or to impress. The hall was wooden-floored, pleasant; two or three chintz-covered chairs sat against the walls, but there were no bookcases, no portraits or samplers from which to judge the taste of the occupants, and the single hat stand was not of particular character and boasted no walking stick, and only one rather well worn umbrella.

The maid returned, still looking very subdued.

"If you will come this way, sir, Mr. Barrymore will see you in the study."

Obediently he followed her across the hall and down a narrow passage toward the rear of the house, where a surprisingly pleasant room opened onto the back garden. Through French doors he saw a closely clipped lawn shaded at the end by willows leaning over the water. There were few flowers, but instead delicate shrubs with a wonderful variety of foliage.

Mr. Barrymore was a tall, lean man with a mobile face full of imagination. Monk could see that the man in front of him had lost not only a child, but some part of himself. Monk felt guilty for intruding. What did law, or even justice, matter in the face of this grief? No solution, no due process or punishment, would bring her back or alter what had happened. What on earth use was revenge?

"Good morning, sir," Barrymore said soberly. The marks of distress were plain in his face, and he did not apologize for them or make useless attempts at disguise. He looked at Monk uncertainly. "My maid said you had called with regard to our daughter's death. She did not mention the police, but do I assume that that is who you are? She mentioned a Lady Daviot, but that must have been a misunderstanding. We know no one of that name."

Monk wished he had some art or gift to soften what must be said, but he knew of none. Perhaps simple truth was the best. Prevarication would lengthen it to no purpose.

"No, Mr. Barrymore, I used to be in the police, but I left the force. Now I work privately." He loathed saying that. It sounded grubby, as if he chased sneak thieves and errant wives. "Lady Callandra Daviot"—that sounded better—"is a member of the Board of Governors of the hospital, and had a deep regard for Miss Barrymore. She is concerned in case the police do not learn all the facts of the case, or do not pursue it thoroughly, should it lead to troubling any authorities or persons of consequence. Therefore she asked me, as a personal favor to her, if I would pursue the matter myself."

A wan smile flickered over Barrymore's face and vanished again.

"Does it not concern you to disturb important people, Mr. Monk? I would have thought you more vulnerable to disfavor than the police. One assumes they have the force of government to back them."

"That rather depends on who the important people are," Monk pointed out.

Barrymore frowned. They were still standing in the middle of the charming room with the garden beyond. It did not seem an occasion to sit.

"Surely you cannot suspect anyone of that nature to be involved in Prudence's death." Barrymore said the last word as if he still found it difficult to grasp, and none of the first agonizing pain had yet dulled.

"I have no idea," Monk replied. "But it is very usual for a murder investigation to uncover a great many other events and relationships which people would prefer to have kept secret. Sometimes they will go to considerable lengths to see that they remain so, even if it means concealing the real crime."

"And you imagine you will be able to learn something that the police will not?" Barrymore asked. He was still courteous but his disbelief was undeniable.

"I don't know, but I shall try. I have in the past succeeded where they have failed."

"Have you?" It was not a challenge, not even a question, merely a noting of fact. "What can we tell you? I know nothing of the hospital at all." He stared out of the window at the sunlight on the leaves. "Indeed, I know very little of the practice of medicine. I am a collector of rare butterflies,

105

myself. Something of an authority on the subject." He smiled sadly, looking back at Monk. "It all seems rather pointless now, doesn't it?"

"No," Monk said quietly. "The study of what is beautiful can never be wasted, especially if you are seeking to understand and preserve it."

"Thank you," Barrymore said with a flash of gratitude. It was a minor thing, but at such times of numb tragedy the mind remembers the smallest kindness and clings to it amid the confusion and despair of events. Barrymore looked up at Monk and suddenly realized they were both standing and he had offered no hospitality of any sort. "Please sit down, Mr. Monk," he asked, sitting himself. "And tell me what I can do that will help. I really don't understand. . . ."

"You could tell me something about her."

Barrymore blinked. "How can that help? Surely it was some madman? What sane person would do that to . . ." He was obliged to struggle to retain command of himself.

"That may be so," Monk interposed, to save Barrymore embarrassment. "But it is also possible that it was someone she knew. Even madmen have to have some sort of reason, unless they are simply lunatics, and there is no reason so far to suppose that there was a lunatic loose in the hospital. It is a place for the treatment of illnesses of the body, not of the mind. But of course, the police will make extensive inquiries to see if there were any strangers observed at all. You may be quite sure of that."

Barrymore was still confused. He looked at Monk without comprehension.

"What do you want to know about Prudence? I cannot conceive of any reason at all why anyone who knew her would wish her harm."

"I heard she served in the Crimea?"

Unconsciously Barrymore straightened his shoulders. "Yes, indeed she did." There was pride in his voice. "She was one of the first to go out there. I remember the day she left home. She looked so terribly young." His eyes looked far beyond Monk into some place in his own inner vision.

106

"Only the young are so very confident. They have no idea what the world may bring them." He smiled with intense sadness. "They don't imagine that failure or death may come to them. It will always be someone else. That is immortality, isn't it? The belief."

Monk did not interrupt.

"She took one tin trunk," Barrymore went on. "Just a few plain blue gowns, clean linen, a second pair of boots, her Bible and journal, and her books on medicine. She wanted to be a doctor, you see. Impossible, I understand that, but it didn't stop her wanting it. She knew a great deal." For the first time he looked directly at Monk. "She was very clever, you know, very diligent. Studying came naturally to her. Nothing like her sister, Faith. She is quite different. They loved one another. After Faith was married and moved north, they wrote to each other at least once a week." His voice was thick with emotion. "She's going to be . . ."

"How were they different?" Monk asked, interrupting him for his own sake.

"How?" He was still gazing into the park, and the memories of happiness. "Oh, Faith was always laughing. She loved to dance. She cared about things, but she was such a flirt, then, so pretty. She found it easy to make people like her." He was smiling. "There were a dozen young men who were longing to court her. She chose Joseph Barker. He seemed so ordinary, a little shy. He even stuttered now and again when he was nervous." He shook his head a little as if it still surprised him. "He couldn't dance, and Faith loved to dance. But she had more sense than her mother or I. Joseph has made her very happy."

"And Prudence?" Monk prompted.

The light died out of his face.

"Prudence? She did not want to marry, she only cared about medicine and service. She wanted to heal people and to change things." He sighed. "And always to know more! Of course her mother wanted her to marry, but she turned away all suitors, and there were several. She was a lovely

107

girl. . . ." Again he stopped for a moment, his feelings too powerful to hide.

Monk waited. Barrymore needed time to recover control and master the outward show of his pain. Somewhere beyond the garden a dog barked, and from the other direction came the sound of children laughing.

"I'm sorry," Barrymore said after a few moments. "I loved her very much. One should not have favorite children, but Prudence was so easy for me to understand. We shared so many things—ideas—dreams . . ." He stopped, again his voice thick with tears.

"Thank you for sparing me your time, sir." Monk rose to his feet. The interview was unbearable, and he had learned all he could. "I will see what I can find from the hospital, and perhaps any other friends you think she may have spoken to lately and who may have some knowledge."

Barrymore recalled himself. "I have no idea how they could help, but if there is anything . . ."

"I would like to speak to Mrs. Barrymore, if she is well enough."

"Mrs. Barrymore?" He seemed surprised.

"She may know something of her daughter, some confidence perhaps, which might seem trivial but could lead us to something of importance."

"Oh—yes, I suppose so. I will ask her if she feels well enough." He shook his head very slightly. "I am amazed at her strength. She has borne this, I think, better than I." And with that observation, he excused himself and went to seek his wife.

He returned a few moments later and conducted Monk to another comfortable well-furnished room with flowered sofas and chairs, embroidered samplers on the walls, and many small ornaments of various types. A bookcase was filled with books, obviously chosen for their contents, not their appearance, and a basket of silks lay open next to a tapestry on a frame.

Mrs. Barrymore was far smaller than her husband, a neat little woman in a huge skirt, her fair hair graying only slightly, pulled back under a lace cap. Of course today she was wearing black, and her pretty, delicately boned face showed signs that she had wept very recently. But she was perfectly composed now and greeted Monk graciously. She did not rise, but extended to him a beautiful hand, partially covered by a fingerless lace mitten.

"How do you do, Mr. Monk? My husband tells me you are a friend of Lady Callandra Daviot, who was a patron of poor Prudence's. It is most kind of you to take an interest in our tragedy."

Monk silently admired Barrymore's diplomacy. He had not thought of such an elegant way of explaining it.

"Many people are moved by her loss, ma'am," he said aloud, brushing her fingertips with his lips. If Barrymore chose to present him as a gentleman, he would play the part; indeed, he would find acute satisfaction in it. Even though undoubtedly it was done for Mrs. Barrymore's benefit, to spare her the feeling that her life was being pried into by lesser people.

"It is truly terrible," she agreed, blinking several times. Silently she indicated where he might be seated, and he accepted. Mr. Barrymore remained standing beside his wife's chair, a curiously remote and yet protective attitude. "Although perhaps we should not be taken totally by surprise. That would be naive, would it not?" She looked at him with startlingly clear blue eyes.

Monk was confused. He hesitated, not wanting to preempt her by saying the wrong thing.

"Such a willful girl," Mrs. Barrymore went on, pinching in her mouth a little. "Charming and lovely to look at, but so set in her ways." She stared beyond Monk toward the window. "Do you have daughters, Mr. Monk?"

"No ma'am."

"Then my advice would be of little use to you, except of course that you may one day." She turned back to him, her lips touched by the ghost of a smile. "Believe me, a pretty girl can be an anxiety, a beauty even more so, even if she is aware of it, which does guard against certain dangers—

109

and increases others." Her mouth tightened. "But an intellectual girl is immeasurably worse. A modest girl, comely but not ravishing, and with enough wit to know how to please but no ambitions toward learning, that is the best of all possible worlds." She looked at him carefully to make sure he understood. "One can always teach a child to be obedient, to learn the domestic arts and to have good manners."

Mr. Barrymore coughed uncomfortably, shifting his weight to the other foot.

"Oh, I know what you are thinking, Robert," Mrs. Barrymore said as if he had spoken. "A girl cannot help having a fine mind. All I am saying is that she would have been so much happier if she had contented herself with using it in a suitable way, reading books, writing poetry if she so wished, and having conversations with friends." She was still perched on the edge of her chair, her skirts billowed around her. "And if she desired to encourage others, and had a gift for it," she continued earnestly, "then there is endless charitable work to be done. Goodness knows, I have spent hours and hours upon such things myself. I cannot count the numbers of committees upon which I have served." She counted them off on her small mittened fingers. "To feed the poor, to find suitable accommodation for girls who have fallen from virtue and cannot be placed in domestic service anymore, and all manner of other good causes." Her voice sharpened in exasperation. "But Prudence would have none of that. She would pursue medicine! She read all sorts of books with pictures in them, things no decent woman should know!" Her face twisted with distaste and embarrassment. "Of course I tried to reason with her, but she was obdurate."

Mr. Barrymore leaned forward, frowning. "My dear, there is no use in trying to make a person different from the way she is. It was not in Prudence's nature to abandon her learning." He said it gently, but there was a note of weariness in his voice as if he had said the same thing many times before and, as now, it had fallen on deaf ears.

Her neck stiffened and her pointed chin set in determination.

"People have to learn to recognize the world as it is." She looked not at him but at one of the paintings on the wall, an idyllic scene in a stable yard. "There are some things one may have, and some one may not." Her pretty mouth tightened. "I am afraid Prudence never learned the difference. That is a tragedy." She shook her head. "She could have been so happy, if only she had let go of her childish ideas and settled down to marry someone like poor Geoffrey Taunton. He was extremely reliable and he would have had her. Now, of course, it is all too late." Then without warning her eyes filled with tears. "Forgive me," she said with a ladylike sniff. "I cannot help but grieve."

"It would be inhuman not to," Monk said quickly. "She was a remarkable woman by all accounts, and one who brought comfort to many who were in the throes of intense suffering. You must be very proud of her."

Mr. Barrymore smiled, but was too filled with emotion to speak.

Mrs. Barrymore looked at Monk with faint surprise, as if his praise for Prudence puzzled her.

"You speak of Mr. Taunton in the past tense, Mrs. Barrymore," he continued. "Is he no longer alive?"

Now she looked thoroughly startled. "Oh yes. Yes indeed, Mr. Monk. Poor Geoffrey is very much alive. But it is too late for Prudence, poor girl. Now, no doubt, Geoffrey will marry that Nanette Cuthbertson. She has certainly been pursuing him for long enough." For a moment her face changed and an expression came on it not unlike spite. "But as long as Prudence was alive, Geoffrey would never look at her. He was 'round here only last weekend, asking after Prudence, how she was doing in London and when we expected her home again."

"He never understood her," Mr. Barrymore said sadly. "He always believed it was only a matter of waiting and she would come 'round to his way of thinking, that she'd forget nursing and come home and settle down."

111

"And so she would," Mrs. Barrymore said hastily. "Only she might have left it too late. There are only so many years when a young woman is attractive to a man who wishes to marry and have a family." Her voice rose in exasperation. "Prudence did not seem to appreciate that, though goodness knows how often I told her. Time will not wait for you, I said. One day you will realize that." Again her eyes filled with tears and she turned away.

Mr. Barrymore was embarrassed. He had already argued with his wife once on this issue in front of Monk, and there seemed nothing more to say.

"Where would I find Mr. Taunton?" Monk asked. "If he saw Miss Barrymore quite often, he may even know of someone who was causing her anxiety or distress."

Mrs. Barrymore looked back at him, jerked out of her grief momentarily by a question which she found extraordinary.

"Geoffrey? Geoffrey would not know anyone likely to—to commit murder, Mr. Monk! He is a most excellent young man, as respectable as one could wish. His father was a professor of mathematics." She invested the last word with great importance. "Mr. Barrymore knew him, before he died about four years ago. He left Geoffrey very well provided for." She nodded. "I am only surprised he has not married before now. Usually it is a financial restriction that prevents young men from marrying. Prudence did not know how fortunate she was that he was prepared to wait for her to change her mind."

Monk could offer no opinion on that.

"Where does he live, ma'am?" he asked.

"Geoffrey?" Her eyebrows rose. "Little Ealing. If you go down Boston Lane and turn right, then follow the road about a mile and a quarter or so, then on your left you will find the Ride. Geoffrey lives along there. After that, you will have to ask. I think that is simpler than my trying to describe the house, although it is most attractive; but then they all are along there. It is a most desirable area."

"Thank you, Mrs. Barrymore, that is very clear. And

how about Miss Cuthbertson, who apparently fancied herself Miss Barrymore's rival? Where might I find her?"

"Nanette Cuthbertson?" Again the look of dislike marred her expression. "Oh, she lives on Wyke Farm, right at the other side of the railway line, on the edge of Osterley Park." She smiled again, but with her lips only.

"Very agreeable really, especially for a girl who is fond of horses and that type of thing. I don't know how you will get there. It is a long way 'round, by Boston Lane. Unless you can hire a vehicle of some sort, you will have to walk over the fields." She waved her mittened hand in the air in a curiously graceful gesture. "If you begin westwards as you are level with Boston Farm, that should bring you to about the right place. Of course I always go by pony cart, but I think my judgment is correct."

"Thank you, Mrs. Barrymore." He rose to his feet, inclining his head courteously. "I apologize for intruding, and am most grateful for your help."

Barrymore looked at him quickly. "If you learn anything, would it be within the ethics of your profession to let us know?"

"I shall report to Lady Callandra, but I have no doubt she will tell you," Monk answered. He would have no compunction whatever in telling this quiet, grieving man anything that would help him, but he thought Barrymore would find it easier from Callandra, and it would be a way to avoid telling him anything that might be true but merely painful, and of no consequence in pursuing or convicting whoever murdered Prudence Barrymore. He thanked them again, and again expressed his condolences. Mr. Barrymore accompanied him to the door, and he took his leave.

It was a very pleasant day, and he enjoyed the half hour it took him to walk from Green Lane to Little Ealing and find the home of Geoffrey Taunton. And the time gave him the opportunity to formulate in his mind what he would say. He did not expect it to be easy. Geoffrey Taunton might even refuse to see him. People react differently to grief. With some, the anger comes first, long before the simple acceptance of pain. And of course it was perfectly possible that Geoffrey Taunton might have been the one who killed her. Perhaps he was not as willing to wait as he had been in the past, and his frustration had finally boiled over? Or maybe it was passion of a different sort which had run out of control, and then he regretted it and wished to marry this Nanette Cuthbertson instead. He must remember to ask Evan precisely what the medical examiner's report had said. For example, had Prudence Barrymore been with child? From her father's account of her, that seemed unlikely, but then fathers are frequently ignorant of that aspect of their daughters' lives, from preference or by design.

It really was a splendid day. The fields stretched out on either side of the lane, light wind rippling through the wheat, already turning gold. In another couple of months the reapers would be out, backs bent in the heat and the grain dust, the smell of hot straw everywhere, and the wagon somewhere behind them with cider and loaves of bread. In his imagination he could hear the rhythmic swishing of the scythe, feel the sweat on his bare skin, and the breeze, and then the shelter of the wagon, the thirst, and the cool sweet cider, still smelling of apples.

When had he ever done farm laboring? He searched his mind and nothing came. Was it here in the south, or at home in Northumberland, before he had come to London to learn commerce, make money, and becoming something of a gentleman?

He had no idea. It was gone, like so much else. And perhaps it was as well. It might belong to some personal memory, like the one of Hermione, which still cut so deep into his emotions. It was not losing her, that was nothing. It was his own humiliation, his misjudgment, the stupidity of having loved so much a woman who had not in her the capacity to love in return. And she had been honest enough to admit that she did not even wish to. Love was dangerous. It could hurt. She did not want hostages to fortune and she said so.

No, definitely any memories he chased from now on

would be professional ones. There at least he was safe. He was brilliant. Even his bitterest enemy, and so far that was Runcorn, had never denied his skill, his intelligence, or his intuition, and the dedication which harnessed them all and had made him the best detective in the force. He strode briskly. There was no sound but his own steps and the wind across the fields, faint and warm. In the early morning there could have been larks, but now it was too late.

And there was another reason, apart from the gratification of pride, why he should remember all he could. He needed to make his living by detection now, and without the memory of his past contacts with the criminal underworld, the minutiae of his craft, the names and faces of those who owed him debts or who feared him, those who had knowledge he would find useful, those who had secrets to hide. Without all this he was handicapped, starting again as a beginner. He needed to know more fully who his friends and his enemies were. Blindfolded by forgetting, he was at their mercy.

The warm sweet scent of honeysuckle was thick around him. Here and there long briers of wild rose trailed pink or white sprays of bloom.

He turned right into the Ride and after a hundred yards found an old carter leading his horse along the lane. He inquired after Geoffrey Taunton, and, after a few minutes' suspicious hesitation, was directed.

The house was gracious from the outside, and the plaster showed signs of having been fairly recently embellished with new pargetting in rich designs. The half timbering was immaculate. Presumably that was all done when Geoffrey Taunton came into his father's money.

Monk walked up the neat gravel drive, which was weedless and recently raked, and knocked at the front door. It was now early afternoon and he would be fortunate to find the master of the house at home; but if he were out, then he would endeavor to make an appointment for a later time.

The maid who answered the door was young and bright-eyed, full of curiosity when she saw a smartly dressed stranger on the step.

"Yes sir?" she said pleasantly, looking up at him.

"Good afternoon. I have no appointment, but I should like to see Mr. Taunton, if he is at home. If I am too early, perhaps you would tell me when would be a more convenient time?"

"Oh not at all, sir, this is an excellent time." Then she stopped and hesitated, realizing she had defied the social convention of pretending her employer was not in until she had ascertained whether the visitor was to be received or not. "Oh, I mean . . ."

Monk smiled in spite of himself. "I understand," he said dryly. "You had better go and ask if he will see me." He handed her his card, which showed his name and his residence, but not his occupation. "You may tell him it is in connection with one of the Board of Governors of the Royal Free Hospital in Gray's Inn, a Lady Callandra Daviot." That sounded impressive, not too personal, and it was true, in fact if not in essence.

"Yes sir," she said with a lift of interest in her voice. "And if you'll excuse me, I'll go and ask, sir." With a swish of skirts, she turned and was gone after having left Monk in the morning room in the sun.

Geoffrey Taunton himself came less than five minutes later. He was a pleasant-looking man in his early thirties, tall and well built, now dressed in the fashionless black of mourning. He was of medium coloring and good features, regular and well proportioned. His expression was mild, and at the moment marred by grief.

"Mr. Monk? Good afternoon. What may I do to be of service to you and the Board of Governors?" He held out his hand.

Monk took it with a twinge of guilt for his misrepresentation, but it was easily dismissed. There were greater priorities.

"Thank you for sparing me the time, sir, and excusing my calling without notice," he apologized. "But I heard of

116

you only through Mr. Barrymore when I called upon him this morning. As you may have assumed, it is in connection with the death of Miss Prudence Barrymore that I have been consulted."

"Consulted?" Taunton frowned. "Surely it is a police matter?" His expression was one of sharp disapproval. "If the Board of Governors are concerned about scandal, there is nothing whatever I can do to assist them. If they employ young women in such a calling, then there are all sorts of unfortunate circumstances which may arise, as I frequently tried to impress upon Miss Barrymore, but without success.

"Hospitals are not salubrious places," he continued with asperity. "Either physically or morally. It is bad enough to have to visit them if one should require surgery which cannot be performed in one's own home, but a woman who seeks employment there runs horrible risks. Most especially if the woman concerned is of gentle birth and has no need whatever to earn her living." His face darkened with pain at the uselessness of it, and he pushed his hands deep into his pockets. He looked stubborn, bewildered, and acutely vulnerable.

Evan would have been sorry for him; Runcorn would have agreed. Monk could only feel angry at his blindness. They were still standing in the morning room facing each other across the green carpet, neither willing to sit.

"I imagine she served out of compassion for the sick rather than for the financial reward," Monk said dryly. "From what I have heard said of her, she was a woman of remarkable gifts and great dedication. That she did not work from necessity can only be to her credit."

"It cost her her life," Taunton said bitterly, his wide eyes full of fury. "That is a tragedy and a crime. Nothing can bring her back, but I want to see whoever did this hanged."

"If we catch him, I daresay that will be your privilege, sir," Monk replied harshly. "Although watching a hanging is a vile affair, in my opinion. I have only seen two, but they were both experiences I would prefer to forget."

Taunton looked startled and his mouth went slack, then

117

he winced with displeasure. "I did not mean it literally, Mr. Monk. That is, as you say, a vile thought. I simply meant that I desire it to be done."

"Oh I see. Yes, that is different, and a quite common sentiment." His voice carried all his contempt for those who visit others to perform the unpleasant deeds so they do not suffer the distress of their reality and can sleep without nightmare and the horror of guilt, doubt, and pity. Then with an effort he recollected his purpose for having come. He forced himself to meet Taunton's eyes with something like courtesy. "And I assure you that anything that falls within my power to see that that is accomplished I shall do with all purpose and diligence at my command, you may be assured."

Taunton was mollified. He too forgot his sense of offense and returned his mind to Prudence and her death.

"Why have you come to see me, Mr. Monk? What can I do to assist you? I am aware of nothing whatever to account for what happened, except the very nature of hospitals and the people who inhabit them, the type of women employed there, of which you must be aware yourself."

Monk evaded the question slightly. "Can you think of any reason why another nurse should wish Miss Barrymore harm?" he asked.

Taunton looked thoughtful. "Many possibilities come to mind. Would you care to come through to my study, where we may discuss it in more comfortable surroundings?"

"Thank you," Monk accepted, following him back through the hallway and into a charming room much larger than he had expected, facing a rose garden with open fields beyond. A fine stand of elms rose two hundred yards away. "What a splendid view," he said involuntarily.

"Thank you," Taunton acknowledged with a tight smile. He waved at one of the large chairs, inviting Monk to sit, and then occupied another opposite it. "You asked about the nurses," he said, addressing the subject again. "Since you are consulted by the Board of Governors, I assume you are familiar with the kind of women who become nurses?

They have little or no education and the morals one would expect from such people." He regarded Monk gravely. "It would hardly be surprising if they resented a woman such as Miss Barrymore, who had what must have seemed to them to be wealth, and who worked not from necessity but because she wished to. Quite obviously she had education, gentle birth, and all the blessings of life they would have asked for themselves." He looked at Monk to make sure he understood the nuances of what he was saying.

"A quarrel?" Monk asked with surprise. "It would have taken a very vicious woman, and one of considerable physical strength, to have attacked Miss Barrymore and strangled her without drawing the attention of other people. The corridors are often empty for periods of time, but the wards are not far. A scream would have brought people running."

Taunton frowned. "I do not see the burden of your remark, Mr. Monk. Are you trying to say that Miss Barrymore was not killed in the hospital?" His expression hardened into contempt. "Is that what the Board of Governors wants, to disclaim responsibility and say the hospital is not involved?"

"Certainly not." Monk might have been amused had he not been so angry. He despised pomposity; coupled with foolishness, as it usually was, it was intolerable. "I am trying to point out that a quarrel between two women is unlikely to have ended by one of them being strangled," he said impatiently. "A quarrel would have been heard; indeed, it was two women quarreling which brought Dr. Beck and Lady Callandra to the scene and resulted in their finding Miss Barrymore."

"Oh." Taunton looked suddenly pale as the argument receded and they both remembered it was Prudence's death they were discussing, not some academic exercise. "Yes, I see. Then you are saying it must have been premeditated, done in a manner of cold blood, without warning." He looked away, his face filled with emotion. "Good God, how appalling! Poor Prudence." He swallowed with some difficulty. "Is it—is it possible she knew little of it, Mr. Monk?"

119

Monk had no idea. "Yes, I should think so," he lied. "It may have been very quick, especially if the attacker were strong."

Taunton blinked hastily.

"A man. Yes, that does seem far more likely." He seemed satisfied with the answer.

"Did Miss Barrymore mention any man to you who had been causing her anxiety and with whom she might have had an unsatisfactory acquaintance?" Monk asked.

Taunton frowned, looking at Monk uncertainly. "I am not quite sure what you mean by that."

"I do not know what other phrase to use. I mean either personal or professional, a doctor, chaplain, treasurer, governor, relation of a patient, or anyone with whom she had dealings in the course of her duties," Monk tried to explain.

Taunton's face cleared. "Oh yes, I see."

"Well, did she? Of whom did she speak?"

Taunton considered for a moment, his eyes on the elms in the distance, their great green bowers bright in the sun. "I am afraid we did not often discuss her work." His lips tightened, but it was not possible to say if it was in anger or pain. "I did not approve of it. But she did mention her high regard for the chief surgeon, Sir Herbert Stanhope, a man more of her own social class, of course. She had the greatest regard for his professional ability. But I gained no impression that her feelings were personal." He scowled at Monk. "I hope that is not what you are suggesting?"

"I am not suggesting anything," Monk said impatiently, his voice rising. "I am trying to learn something about her, and who may have wished her harm for whatever reason: jealousy, fear, ambition, revenge, greed, anything at all. Did she have any admirers that you know of? I believe she was a most attractive person."

"Yes she was, for all her stubbornness. She was quite lovely." For a moment he turned away from Monk and endeavored to mask his distress.

Monk thought of apologizing, then felt it would only embarrass Taunton further. He had never learned the right thing to say. Probably there was no right thing.

"No," Taunton said after several minutes. "She never spoke of anyone. Although it is possible she would not have told me, knowing how I felt. But she was transparently honest. I think if there had been anyone, her own candor would have compelled her to tell me." His face creased with total incomprehension. "She always spoke as if medicine were her sole love and she had no time for ordinary womanly pursuits and instincts. If anything, I should say she was increasingly devoted lately." He looked at Monk earnestly. "You did not know her before she went to the Crimea, Mr. Monk. She was different then, quite different. She had not the . . ." He stopped, struggling for a word to describe what he meant. "She was . . . softer, yes that is it, softer, far more truly womanly."

Monk did not argue, although the words were on the edge of his tongue. Were women really soft? The best women he knew, the ones that leaped to his mind, were anything but. Convention demanded their outer manners were yielding, but inside was a core of steel that would put many a man to shame, and a strength of will and endurance that knew no master. Hester Latterly had had courage to fight on for his vindication when he himself had given up. She had bullied, cajoled, and abused him into hope, and then into struggle, regardless of her own welfare.

And he would have sworn Callandra would do as much, if occasion demanded. And there were others. Perhaps Prudence Barrymore had been one like these, passionate, brave, and single-minded to her convictions. Difficult for a man like Geoffrey Taunton to accept, still less to understand. Perhaps difficult for anyone to associate with. Lord knew, Hester could be abrasive, willful, obstructive, and thoroughly sharp-tongued—and always opinionated.

In fact, Monk's irritation with Taunton lessened considerably as he thought about it. If he had been in love with Prudence Barrymore, he probably had had a great deal to endure.

"Yes, yes I see," he said aloud with a ghost of a smile. "It must have been most trying for you. When was the last time you saw Miss Barrymore?"

"I saw her the morning she died—was killed," Taunton replied, his face pale. "Probably very shortly before."

Monk was puzzled. "But she was killed very early in the morning, between six o'clock and half past seven."

Taunton blushed. "Yes, it was early; in fact, it was no more than seven o'clock at the most. I had spent the night in town and went in to the hospital to see her before catching the train home."

"It must have been something of great importance to you to take you there at that hour."

"It was." Taunton offered nothing further. His face was set, his expression closed.

"If you prefer not to tell me, you leave it to my imagination," Monk challenged with a hard smile. "I shall assume you quarreled over your disapproval of her occupation."

"You may assume what you wish," Taunton said equally tersely. "It was a private conversation which I should not have reported had nothing untoward happened. And now that poor Prudence is dead, I certainly shall not." He looked at Monk with defiance. "It was not to her credit, that is all you need to know. The poor creature was in a high temper when I left, most unbecoming, but she was in excellent health."

Monk let that go by without comment. Apparently Taunton had not yet even thought of himself as suspect. "And she at no time indicated to you that she was afraid of anyone?" Monk asked. "Or that anyone had been unpleasant or threatening toward her?"

"Of course not, or I should have informed you. You would not have needed to ask."

"I see. Thank you, you have been most cooperative. I am sure Lady Callandra will be grateful to you." Monk knew he should add his condolences, but the words stuck in his mouth. He had contained his temper, that was sufficient. He stood up. "Now I will not take any more of your time."

"It does not seem you have progressed very far." Taunton rose also, unconsciously smoothing his clothes and regarding Monk critically. "I cannot see how you can hope to catch whoever it was by such methods."

"I daresay I could not do your job either, sir," Monk said with a tight smile. "Perhaps that is just as well. Thank you again. Good day, Mr. Taunton."

It was a hot walk back along the Ride, over Boston Lane and through the fields to Wyke Farm, but Monk enjoyed it enormously. It was exquisite to feel the earth beneath his feet instead of pavement, to smell the wind across open land, heavy with honeysuckle, and hear nothing but the ripening ears of wheat rustling and the occasional distant bark of a dog. London and its troubles seemed another country, not just a few miles away on the railway line. For a moment he forgot Prudence Barrymore and allowed peace to settle in his mind and old memory to creep in: the wide hills of Northumberland and the clean wind off the sea, the gulls wheeling in the sky. It was all he had of childhood: impressions, a sound, a smell that brought back emotions, a glimpse of a face, gone before he could see it clearly.

His pleasure was snapped and he was returned to the present by a woman on horseback looming suddenly a few yards away. Of course she must have come over the fields, but he had been too preoccupied to notice her until she was almost on top of him. She rode with the total ease of someone to whom it is as natural as walking. She was all grace and femininity, her back straight, her head high, her hands light on the reins.

"Good afternoon, ma'am," he said with surprise. "I apologize for not having seen you earlier."

She smiled. Her mouth was wide, her face soft with dark eyes, perhaps a little deep set. Her brown hair was drawn back under her riding hat but the heavy curl softened it. She was pretty, almost beautiful.

"Are you lost?" she said with amusement, looking down at his smart clothes and dark boots. "There is nothing here along this track except Wyke Farm." She held her horse in tight control, standing only a yard in front of him, her hands strong, skilled, and tight.

"Then I am not lost," he answered, meeting her gaze. "I am looking for Miss Nanette Cuthbertson."

"You need go no farther. I am she." Her surprise was good-natured and welcoming. "What may I do for you, sir?"

"How do you do, Miss Cuthbertson. My name is William Monk. I am assisting Lady Callandra Daviot, who is a member of the Board of Governors of the Royal Free Hospital. She is eager to clear up the matter of Miss Barrymore's death. You were acquainted with her, I believe?"

The smile disappeared from her face, but there was no curiosity in her, simply a decent acknowledgment of tragedy. To have remained looking so cheerful would have been indelicate.

"Yes, of course I was. But I have no idea how I can help you." Gracefully she dismounted, without asking his help and before he could give it. She held the reins loosely, all but leaving the horse to follow her of itself. "I know nothing about it, except what Mr. Taunton has told me, which was simply that poor Prudence had met with a sudden and fearful death." She looked at him with soft innocent eyes.

"She was murdered," he replied, his words violent, his voice gentle.

"Oh." She paled visibly, but whether it was the news or his manner of delivering it, he could not tell. "How dreadful! I am sorry. I didn't realize . . ." She looked at him with puckered brows. "Mr. Taunton said that hospitals were not good places at all, but he did not say more than that. I had no idea they were so dangerous. Illness, of course I understand. One expects it. But not murder."

"The place of it may have been coincidental, Miss

Cuthbertson. People are murdered in houses also; we do not say that houses are therefore dangerous places."

An orange-and-black butterfly flew erratically between them and disappeared.

"I don't understand. . . ." And her expression made it quite obvious that she did not.

"Did you know Miss Barrymore well?"

She began to walk very slowly back toward the farm buildings. There was room on the hard track for him to walk beside her, the horse trailing behind, head low.

"I used to," she replied thoughtfully. "When we were much younger, growing up. Since she went to the Crimea I don't think any of us would say we knew her anymore. She changed, you see." She looked around at him to make sure he understood.

"I imagine it is an experience which would change anyone," he agreed. "How could one see the devastation and the suffering without being altered by it?"

"I suppose not," she agreed, glancing behind her to make sure the horse was still following obediently. "But it made her very different. She was always . . . if I say headstrong, please do not think I wish to speak ill of her, it is simply that she had such fierce desires and intentions." She paused for a moment, ordering her thoughts. "Her dreams were different from other people's. But after she came home from Scutari she was . . ." She frowned, searching for the word. "Harder—harder inside." Then she glanced up at Monk with a brilliant smile. "I'm sorry. Does that sound very unkind? I did not mean to be."

Monk looked at the warm brown eyes and the delicate cheeks and thought that was exactly what she meant to be, but the last thing she wished anyone to think of her. He felt part of himself respond to her and he hated his own gullibility. She reminded him of Hermione, and God knew how many other women in the past, whose total femininity had appealed to him and deluded him. Why had he been such a fool? He despised fools.

There was a large part of him which was skeptical, even

125

cynical. If Mrs. Barrymore were right, then this charming woman with her soft eyes and smiling mouth had wanted Geoffrey Taunton for herself for a long time, and must have bitterly resented his devotion to Prudence. How old had Prudence been? Callandra had said something about late twenties. Geoffrey Taunton was certainly that and more. Was Nanette Cuthbertson contemporary, or only a little younger? If so, then she was old for marriage, time was running out for her. She would soon be considered an old maid, if not already, and definitely old for bearing her first child. Might she feel more than jealousy, a sense of desperation, panic as the years passed and still Geoffrey Taunton waited for Prudence and she refused him for her career?

"Did you not," he said noncommittally. "I daresay it is true, and I am asking for truth, hard or not. A polite lie will serve no good now; in fact, it will obscure facts we need to know." His voice had been cold, but she saw justification in it. She kept the horse close behind her with a heavy pressure on the reins.

"Thank you, Mr. Monk, you set my mind at rest. It is unpleasant to speak ill of people, even slightly."

"I find many people enjoy it," he said with a slow smile. "In fact, it is one of their greatest pleasures, particularly if they can feel superior at the time."

She was taken aback. It was not the sort of thing one acknowledged. "Er—do you think so?"

He had nearly spoiled his own case. "Some people," he said, knocking the head off a long stalk of wheat that had grown across the path. "But I regret I have to ask you to tell me something more of Prudence Barrymore, even if it is distasteful to you, because I do not know who else to ask, who will be frank. Eulogies are no help to me."

This time she kept her eyes straight ahead. They were almost to the farm gate and he opened it for her, waited while the horse followed her through, then went through himself and closed it carefully. An elderly man in a faded smock and trousers tied around the ankles with string smiled shyly, then took the animal. Nanette thanked him

126

and led Monk across the yard toward the kitchen garden, and he opened the door of the farmhouse. It was not into the kitchen as he had expected, but a side entrance to a wide hallway.

"May I offer you some refreshment, Mr. Monk?" Nanette said with a smile. She was of more than average height and slender, a tiny waist and slight bosom. She moved with skill to maneuver the skirts of her riding habit so they seemed part of her and not an encumbrance, as they were to some women.

"Thank you," he accepted. He did not know if he could learn anything useful from her, but he might not have another opportunity. He should use this one.

She laid her hat and crop on the hall table, then rang for a maid, requested tea, and conducted him to a pretty sitting room full of flowered chintz. They made trivial conversation till the tea was brought and they were alone again and could remain uninterrupted.

"You wish to know about poor Prudence," she said immediately, passing him his cup.

"If you please." He accepted it.

She met his eyes. "Please understand that I am speaking so frankly only because I am aware that kindness is of no use in finding out who killed her, poor soul."

"I have asked you to be frank, Miss Cuthbertson," he encouraged her.

She settled back in her chair and began to speak, her gaze unflinching.

"I have known Prudence since we were both girls. She always had a curiosity much greater than most people's, and a dedication to learn all she could. Her mother, who is a dear creature, most sensible, tried to dissuade her, but to no avail. Have you met her sister, Faith?"

"No."

"A very nice person," she said with approval. "She married and went to live in York. But Prudence was always her father's favorite, and I regret the necessity to say so, but I think he indulged her when it might have been in her greater interest to have exercised a little more discipline." She shrugged, looking at Monk with a smile. "Anyway, the result was that when we here in England began to learn a little of how serious the war in the Crimea had become, Prudence decided to go out there and nurse our soldiers, and nothing on earth would deter her."

Monk forbore from interruption with difficulty. He wanted to tell this equally determined, rather complacent, pretty woman who was discreetly flirting with him something of the horror of the battlefield and the hospital as he had learned it from Hester. He forced himself to keep silent, merely looking at her to continue.

She did not need prompting.

"Of course we all assumed that when she came home she would have had enough of it," she said quickly. "She had served her country and we were all proud of her. But not at all. She then insisted on continuing with nursing and took up a post in the hospital in London." She was watching Monk's face closely, all the time biting her lip as if uncertain what to say, although he knew from the strength in her voice that that was anything but the case. "She became very—very forceful," she continued. "Very outspoken in her opinions and extremely critical of the medical authorities. I am afraid she had ambitions that were totally impossible and quite unsuitable anyway, and she was bitter about it." She searched Monk's eyes, trying to judge his thoughts. "I can only assume that some of her experiences in the Crimea were so fearful that they affected her mind and destroyed her judgment to some extent. It is really very tragic." As she said it her face was very sober.

"Very," Monk agreed tersely. "It is also tragic that someone should have killed her. Did she ever say anything to you about anyone who might have threatened her or wished her ill?" It was an ingenuous question, but there was always the remote chance she might give a surprising answer.

Nanette shrugged very slightly, a delicate, very feminine gesture of her shoulders.

"Well, she was very forthright, and she could be highly

critical," she said reluctantly. "I fear it is not impossible that she offended someone sufficiently that he became violent, which is a fearful thought. But some men do have ungovernable tempers. Perhaps her insult was very serious, threatening his professional reputation. She did not spare people, you know."

"Did she mention anyone by name, Miss Cuthbertson?"

"Oh not to me. But then their names would mean nothing to me even if I heard them."

"I see. What about admirers? Were there any men, do you know, who might have felt rejected by her, or jealous?"

The blush on her cheek was very slight, and she smiled as if the question were of no consequence to her.

"She did not confide that sort of thing to me, but I gathered the impression that she had no time for such emotions." She smiled at the absurdity of such a nature. "Perhaps you had better ask someone who knew her from day to day."

"I shall. Thank you for your candor, Miss Cuthbertson. If everyone else is as frank with me, I shall be very fortunate."

She leaned forward in her chair a little. "Will you find out who killed her, Mr. Monk?"

"Yes." He was quite unequivocal, not because he had any conviction, still less any knowledge, but he would not admit the possibility of defeat.

"I am so glad. It is most comforting to know that in spite of tragedy, there are people who will see that at least justice is done." Again she smiled at him, and he wondered why on earth Geoffrey Taunton had not wooed this woman, who seemed so excellently suited to his life and his personality, but had chosen instead to waste his time and his emotion on Prudence Barrymore. She could never have made either him or herself happy in such an alliance, which to him would have been fraught with tension and uncertainty, and to her would have been at once barren and suffocating.

But then he had imagined himself so in love with Hermione Ward, who would have hurt and disappointed

129

him at every turn and left him in the bitterest loneliness. Perhaps in the end he would even have hated her.

He finished his tea and excused himself. Thanking her again, he took his leave.

The return journey to London was hot and the train crowded. He was suddenly very tired and closed his eyes, leaning back against the seat. The rattle and sway of the carriage was curiously soothing.

He woke up with a start to find a small boy staring at him with intense curiosity. A fair-haired woman pulled at the child's jacket and ordered him to mind his manners and not to be so rude to the gentleman. Then she smiled shyly at Monk and apologized.

"There is no harm in it, ma'am," he replied quietly, but his mind was suddenly jolted by a vivid fragment of memory. It was a sensation he had felt many times since his accident, and more and more frequently in the last few months, but it never ceased to bring with it a frisson of fear. So much of what he learned of himself showed him only actions, not reasons, and he did not always like the man he discovered.

This memory was sharp and bright, and yet distant. He was not the man of today, but very much of yesterday. The picture in his mind was full of sunlight, and for all its clarity there was a sense of distance. He was younger, far younger, new at his job with all the eagerness and the need to learn that comes with being a novice. His immediate senior was Samuel Runcorn, that was perfectly clear. He knew it as one knows things in dreams; there is no visible evidence, and yet the certainty is unquestionable. He could picture Runcorn as sharply as the young woman on the seat opposite him in the clanking train as it rushed past the houses toward the city. Runcorn, with his narrow face and deep-set eyes. He had been handsome then: bony nose, good brow, broad mouth. Even now it was only his expression, the mixture of temper and apology in his eyes, which marred him.

130

What had happened in the intervening years? How much of it had been Monk's doing? That was a thought which returned to him again and again. And yet that was foolish. Monk was not to blame. Whatever Runcorn was, it was his own doing, his own choice.

Why had that memory returned? Just a snatch, a journey in a train with Runcorn. Runcorn had been an inspector, and Monk a constable working on a case under his direction.

They were coming into the outskirts of Bayswater, not far to go to the Euston Road and home. It would be good to get out of this noisy, jiggling, confined space and walk in the fresh air. Not that Fitzroy Street would be like Boston Lane with the wind over the wheat fields.

He was aware of a sharp inner sense of frustration, of questions and answers that led nowhere, of knowing that someone was lying, but not who. They had been days on the case and learned nothing that made sense, no string of evidence that began to form a story.

Except that this was the first day. Prudence Barrymore had died only yesterday. The emotion came from the past, whatever he and Runcorn had been doing however many years ago—was it ten, fifteen? Runcorn had been different. He had had more confidence, less arrogance, less need to exert his authority, less need to show he was right. Something had happened to him in the years between which had destroyed an element of belief in himself, injuring some inner part so that now it was maimed.

Did Monk know what it was? At least had he known before the accident? Was Runcorn's hatred of him born of that: his vulnerability, and Monk's use of it?

The train was going through Paddington now. Not long till he was home. He ached to be able to stand up.

He closed his eyes again. The heat in the carriage and the rhythmic swinging to and fro, the incessant clatter as the wheels passed over the joins in the rails, were hypnotic.

There had been another constable on the case as well, a slight young man with dark hair that stood up from the brow. The memory of him was vivid and acutely uncomfortable, but Monk had no idea why. He racked his brain but nothing came. Had he died? Why was there this unhappiness in his mind when he pictured him?

Runcorn was different; for him he felt anger and a swift harsh contempt. It was not that he was stupid. He was not: his questions were perceptive enough, well phrased, well judged, and he obviously weighed the answers. He was not gullible. So why did Monk find himself unconsciously curling his lip?

What had the case been? He could not remember that either! But it had mattered, of that he had no doubt at all. It was serious. The superintendent had been asking them every day for progress. The press had been demanding someone be caught and hanged. But for what?

Had they succeeded?

He sat up with a jolt. They were at Euston Road and it was time he got off or he would be carried past his stop. Hastily, apologizing for treading on people's feet, he scrambled out of his seat and made his way out onto the platform.

He must stop dwelling in the past and think what next to do in the murder of Prudence Barrymore. There was nothing to report to Callandra yet, but she might have something to tell him, although it was a trifle early. Better to leave it a day or two, then he might have something to say himself.

He strode along the platform, threading his way among the people, bumping into a porter and nearly tripping over a bale of papers.

What had Prudence Barrymore been like as a nurse? Better to begin at the beginning. He had met her parents, her suitor, albeit unsuccessful, and her rival. In time he would ask her superiors, but they were, or might be, suspects. The best judge of the next stage in her career would be someone who had known her in the Crimea, apart from Hester. He dodged around two men and a woman struggling with a hat box.

What about Florence Nightingale herself? She would know something about all her nurses, surely? But would she see Monk? She was now fêted and admired all over the city, second in public affection only to the Queen.

It was worth trying.

Tomorrow he would do that. She was immeasurably more famous, more important, but she could not be more opinionated or more acid-tongued than Hester.

Unconsciously he quickened his step. It was a good decision. He smiled at an elderly lady who glared back at him.

Florence Nightingale was smaller than he had expected, slight of build and with brown hair and regular features, at a glance quite unremarkable. It was only the intensity of her eyes under the level brows which held him, and the way she seemed to look right into his mind, not with interest, simply a demand that he meet her honesty with equal candor. He imagined no one dared to waste her time.

She had received him in some sort of office, sparsely furnished and strictly functional. He had gained admittance only with difficulty, and after explaining his precise purpose. It was apparent she was deeply engaged in some cause and had set it aside only for the duration of the interview.

"Good afternoon, Mr. Monk," she said in a strong clear voice. "I believe you have come in connection with the death of one of my nurses. I am extremely sorry to hear of it. What is it you wish of me?"

He would not have dared prevaricate, even if it had been his intention.

"She was murdered, ma'am, while serving in the Royal Free Hospital. Her name was Prudence Barrymore." He saw the shadow of pain pass over Florence Nightingale's calm features, and liked her the better for it. "I am inquiring into her murder," he went on. "Not with the police but at the wish of one of her friends."

"I am deeply sorry. Please be seated, Mr. Monk." She indicated a hard-backed chair and sat in one opposite, holding her hands in her lap and staring at him.

He obeyed. "Can you tell me something of her nature and her abilities, ma'am?" he asked. "I have already heard that she was dedicated to medicine to the exclusion of all else, that she had refused a man who had admired her for many years, and that she held her opinions with great conviction."

A flicker of amusement touched Florence Nightingale's mouth. "And expressed them," she agreed. "Yes, she was a fine woman, with a passion to learn. Nothing deterred her from seeking the truth and acknowledging it."

"And telling it to others?" he asked.

"Of course. If you know the truth, it takes a gentler and perhaps a wiser woman than Prudence Barrymore not to speak it aloud. She did not understand the arts of diplomacy. I fear that perhaps I do not either. The sick cannot wait for flattery and coercion to do their work."

He did not flatter her with agreement. She was not a woman who would have valued the obvious.

"Might Miss Barrymore have made enemies profound enough to have killed her?" he asked. "I mean, was her zeal to reform or her medical knowledge sufficient for that?"

For several moments Florence Nightingale sat silent, but Monk knew perfectly well that she had understood him and that she was considering the question before answering.

"I find it unlikely, Mr. Monk," she said at last. "Prudence was more interested in medicine itself than in ideas of reforming such as I have. I desire above all things to see the simple changes that would save so many lives and cost little, such as proper ventilation of hospital wards." She looked at him with brilliant eyes, burning with the intensity of her feeling. Already the timbre of her voice had altered and there was a new quality of urgency in it. "Have you any idea, Mr. Monk, how stuffy most wards are, how stale the air and full of noxious vapors and fumes? Clean air will do as much to heal people as half the medicines they are

134

given." She leaned forward a fraction. "Of course our hospitals here are nothing like the hospitals in Scutari, but still they are places where as many people die of infections caught there as of the original complaints that brought them! There is so much to do, so much suffering and death which could be avoided." She spoke quietly, and yet Monk, listening to her, felt a quiver of excitement inside himself. There was a passion in her eyes which lit them from within. No longer could Monk possibly say she was ordinary. She possessed a fierceness, a solitary fire, and yet a vulnerability which made her unique. He caught a glimpse of what it was that had inspired an army to love her and the nation to revere her, and yet leave her with such a core of inner loneliness.

"I have a friend"—he used the word without thinking—"who nursed with you in the Crimea, a Miss Hester Latterly . . ."

Her face softened with instant pleasure. "You know Hester? How is she? She had to return home early because of the death of both of her parents. Have you seen her recently? Is she well?"

"I saw her two days ago," he answered readily. "She is in excellent health. She will be most pleased to know you asked after her." He felt slightly proprietorial. "She is largely nursing privately at present. I am afraid her outspokenness cost her her first hospital post." He found himself smiling, although at the time he had been both angry and critical. "She knew more of fever medicine than the doctor, and acted upon it. He never forgave her."

Florence smiled, a peaceful inward amusement, and he thought a certain pride. "I am not surprised," she admitted. "Hester never suffered fools easily, especially military ones, and there are a great many of those. She used to get so angry at the waste and told them how stupid they were and what they should have done." She shook her head. "I think had she been a man, Hester might have made a good soldier. She had all the zeal to fight and a good instinct for strategy, at least of a physical sort."

135

"A physical sort?" He did not understand. He had not noticed Hester being particularly good at planning ahead—in fact, rather the opposite.

She saw his confusion and the doubt in him.

"Oh, I don't mean of a type that would be any use to her," she explained. "Not as a woman, anyway. She could never bide her time and manipulate people. She had no patience for that. But she could understand a battlefield. And she had the courage."

He smiled in spite of himself. That was the Hester he knew.

But Florence was not looking at him. She was lost in memory, her mind in the so recent past.

"I am so sorry about Prudence," she said, more to herself than to Monk, and her face was suddenly unbearably sad and lonely. "She had such a passion to heal. I can remember her going out more than once with field surgeons. She was not especially strong, and she was terrified of crawling things, insects and the like, but she would sleep out in order to be there when the surgeons most needed her. She would be sick with the horror of some of the wounds, but only afterwards. She never gave way at the time. How she would work. Nothing was too much. One of the surgeons told me she knew as much about amputating a limb as he did himself, and she was not afraid to do it, if she had to, if there was no one else there."

Monk did not interrupt. The quiet sunlit room in London disappeared and the slender woman in her drab dress was the only thing he saw, her intense and passionate voice all he heard.

"It was Rebecca who told me," she went on. "Rebecca Box. She was a huge woman, a soldier's wife, nearly six feet tall she was, and as strong as an ox." The smile of memory touched her lips. "She used to go out into the battlefield, ahead of the guns even, and pick up the wounded men far beyond where anyone else would go, right up to the enemy. Then she would put them across her back and carry them home."

136

She turned to Monk, searching his face. "You have no idea what women can do until you have seen someone like Rebecca. She told me how Prudence first took off a man's arm. It had been hacked to the bone by a saber. It was bleeding terribly, and there was no chance of saving it and no time to find a surgeon. Prudence was as white as the man himself, but her hand was steady and her nerve held. She took it off just as a surgeon would have. The man lived. Prudence was like that. I am so sorry she is gone." Still her gaze was fixed on Monk's as if she would assure herself he shared her feeling. "I shall write to her family and convey my sympathies."

Monk tried to imagine Prudence in the flare of an oil lamp, kneeling over the desperately bleeding man, her strong steady fingers holding the saw, her face set in concentration as she used the skill she had so often watched and had thus learned. He wished he had known her. It was painful that where there had been this brave and willful woman now there was a void, a darkness. A passionate voice was silenced and the loss was raw and unexplained.

It would not remain so. He would find out who had killed her, and why. He would have a kind of revenge.

"Thank you very much for sparing me your time, Miss Nightingale," he said a little more stiffly than he had meant. "You have told me something of her which no one else could."

"It is a very small thing," she said, dismissing its inadequacy. "I wish I had the remotest idea who could have wished her dead, but I have not. When there is so much tragedy and pain in the world that we cannot help, it seems incomprehensible that we should bring even more upon ourselves. Sometimes I despair of mankind. Does that sound blasphemous, Mr. Monk?"

"No ma'am, it sounds honest."

She smiled bleakly. "Shall you see Hester Latterly again?"

"Yes." In spite of himself his interest was so sharp he spoke before he thought. "Did you know her well?"

"Indeed." The smile returned to her mouth. "We spent many hours working together. It is strange how much one knows of a person laboring in a common cause, even if one said nothing of one's own life before coming to the Crimea, nothing of one's family or youth, nothing of one's loves or dreams, still one learns of another's nature. And perhaps that is the real core of passion, don't you think?"

He nodded, not wishing to intrude with words.

"I agree," she went on thoughtfully. "I know nothing of her past, but I learned to trust her integrity as we worked night after night to help the soldiers and their women, to get food for them, blankets, and to make the authorities allow us space so the beds were not crammed side by side." She gave an odd, choked little laugh. "She used to get so angry. I always knew if I had a battle to fight that Hester would be by my side. She never retreated, never pretended or flattered. And I knew her courage." She hunched her shoulders in a gesture of distaste. "She loathed the rats, and they were all over the place. They climbed the walls and fell off like rotten plums dropping off a tree. I shall never forget the sound of their bodies hitting the floor. And I watched her pity, not useless, not maudlin, just a long slow ache inside as she knew the pain of others and did everything within her human power to ease it. One has a special feeling for someone with whom one has shared such times, Mr. Monk. Yes, please remember me to her."

"I will," he promised.

He rose to his feet again, suddenly acutely conscious of the passage of time. He knew she was fitting him in between one meeting and another of hospital governors, architects, medical schools, or organizations of similar nature. Since her return from the Crimea she had never ceased to work for the reforms in design and administration in which she believed so fervently.

"Whom will you seek next?" She preempted his farewell. She had no need to explain to what matter she was referring and she was not a woman for unnecessary words.

"The police," he answered. "I still have friends there

who may tell me what the medical examiner says, and perhaps what the official testimony is of other witnesses. Then I shall appeal to her colleagues at the hospital. If I can persuade them to speak honestly of her and of one another, I may learn a great deal."

"I see. May God be with you, Mr. Monk. It is more than justice you must seek. If women like Prudence Barrymore can be murdered when they are about their work, then we are all a great deal the poorer, not only now, but in the future as well."

"I do not give up, ma'am," he said grimly, and he meant it, not only to match his determination with hers, but because he had a consuming personal desire to find the one who had destroyed such a life. "He will rue the day, I promise you. Good afternoon, ma'am."

"Good afternoon, Mr. Monk."

5

John Evan was not happy with the case of Prudence Barrymore. He hated the thought of a young woman with such passion and vitality having been killed, and in this particular instance all the other circumstances also confused and troubled him. He did not like the hospital. The very smell of it caught in his throat even without his awareness of the pain and the fear that must reside here. He saw the bloodstained clothes of the surgeons as they hurried about the corridors, and the piles of soiled dressings and bandages, and every now and again he both saw and smelled the buckets of waste that were carried away by the nurses.

But deeper than all these was a matter disturbing him more because it was personal, something about which he not only could, but was morally bound to, do something. It was the way in which the investigation was being conducted. He had been angry and bitter when Monk had been maneuvered into resigning by events in the Moidore case and Runcorn's stand on the issue. But he had grown accustomed to working with Jeavis now, and while he did not either like or admire him, as he did Monk, he knew that he was a competent and honorable man.

But in this case Jeavis was out of his depth, or at least

Evan thought so. The medical evidence was fairly clear. Prudence Barrymore had been attacked from the front and strangled to death manually; no ligature had been used. The marks of such a thing would have been plain enough, and indeed the bruises on her throat corresponded to the fingers of a powerful person of average enough size; it could have been any of dozens of people who had access to the hospital. And it was easy enough to enter from the street. There were so many doctors, nurses, and assistants of one sort or another coming and going, an extra person would be unnoticed. For that matter, even someone drenched in blood would cause no alarm.

At first Jeavis had thought of other nurses. It had crossed Evan's mind that he had done so because it was easier for him than approaching the doctors and surgeons, who were of a superior education and social background, and Jeavis was nervous of them. However, when a large number of the individual nurses could account for their whereabouts, in each others' company or in the company of a patient from the time Prudence Barrymore was last seen alive until the skivvy found her in the laundry chute, he was obliged to cast his net wider. He looked to the treasurer, a pompous man with a high winged collar that seemed to be too tight for him. He constantly eased his neck and stretched his chin forward as if to be free of it. However, he had not been on the premises early enough, and could prove himself to have been still at his home, or in a hansom on his way up the Gray's Inn Road, at the appropriate time.

Jeavis's face had tightened. "Well, Mr. Evan, we shall have to look to the patients at the time. And if we do not find our murderer among them, then to the doctors." His expression relaxed a little. "Or of course there is always the possibility that some outsider may have come in, perhaps someone she knew. We shall have to look more closely into her character. . . ."

"She wasn't a domestic servant," Evan said tartly.

"Indeed not," Jeavis agreed. "The reputation of nurses being what it is, I daresay most ladies that have servants wouldn't employ them." His face registered a very faint suggestion of a smile.

"The women who went out to nurse with Miss Nightingale were ladies!" Evan was outraged, not only for Prudence Barrymore but also for Hester and (he was surprised to find) for Florence Nightingale too. Part of his mind was worldly, experienced, and only mildly tolerant of such foibles as hero worship, but there was a surprisingly large part of him that felt an uprush of pride and fierce defense when he thought of "the lady with the lamp" and all she had meant to agonized and dying men far from home in a nightmare place. He was angry with Jeavis for his indirect slight. A flash of amusement lit him also and he knew what Monk would say, he could hear his beautiful, sarcastic voice in his head: "A true child of the vicarage, Evan. Believe any pretty story told you, and make your own angels to walk the streets. You should have taken the cloth like your father!"

"Daydreaming?" Jeavis said, cutting into his thoughts. "Why the smile, may I ask? Do you know something that I don't?"

"No sir!" Evan pulled himself together. "What about the Board of Governors? We might find some of them were here, and knew her, one way or another."

Jeavis's face sharpened. "What do you mean, 'one way or another'? Men like the governors of hospitals don't have affairs with nurses, man!" His mouth registered his distaste for the very idea and his disapproval of Evan for having put words to it.

Evan had been going to explain himself, that he had meant either socially or professionally, but now he felt obstructive and chose to make it literal.

"By all accounts she was a handsome woman, and full of intelligence and spirit," he argued. "And men of any sort will always be attracted to women like that."

"Rubbish!" Jeavis treasured an image of certain classes of gentleman, just as did Runcorn. Their relationship had become a mutually agreeable one, and both were finding it increasingly to their advantage. It was one of the few things in Jeavis which truly irritated Evan more than he could brush aside.

"If Mr. Gladstone could give assistance to prostitutes off the street," Evan said decisively, looking Jeavis straight in the eye, "I'm quite sure a hospital governor could cherish a fancy for a fine woman like Prudence Barrymore."

Jeavis was too much of a policeman to let his social pretensions deny his professionalism.

"Possibly," he said grudgingly, pushing out his lip and scowling. "Possibly. Now get about your job, and don't stand around wasting time." He poked his finger at the air. "Want to know if anyone saw strangers here that morning. Speak to everyone, mind, don't miss a soul. And then find out where all the doctors and surgeons were—exactly. I'll see about the governors."

"Yes sir. And the chaplain?"

A mixture of emotions crossed Jeavis's face: outrage at the idea a chaplain could be guilty of such an act, anger that Evan should have said it, sadness that in fact it was not impossible, and a flash of amusement and suspicion that Evan, a son of the clergy himself, was aware of all the irony of it.

"You might as well," he said at last. "But you be sure of your facts. No 'he said' and 'she said.' I want eyewitnesses, you understand me?" He fixed Evan fiercely with his pale-lashed eyes.

"Yes sir," Evan agreed. "I'll get precise evidence, sir. Good enough for a jury."

But three days later when Evan and Jeavis stood in front of Runcorn's desk in his office, the precise evidence amounted to very little indeed.

"So what have you?" Runcorn leaned back in his chair, his long face somber and critical. "Come on, Jeavis! A nurse gets strangled in a hospital. It's not as if anyone could walk in unnoticed. The girl must have friends, enemies, people she'd quarreled with." He tapped his finger on the desk. "Who are they? Where were they when she was killed? Who saw her last before she was found? What about this Dr. Beck? A foreigner, you said? What's he like?"

Jeavis stood up to attention, hands at his side.

"Quiet sort o' chap," he answered, his features carefully composed into lines of respect. "Smug, bit of a foreign accent, but speaks English well enough, in fact too well, if you know what I mean, sir? Seems good at his job, but Sir Herbert Stanhope, the chief surgeon, doesn't seem to like him a lot." He blinked. "At least that's what I sense, although of course he didn't exactly say so."

"Never mind Sir Herbert." Runcorn dismissed it with a brush of his hand. "What about the dead woman? Did she get on with this Dr. Beck?" Again his finger tapped the table. "Could there be an affair there? Was she nice-looking? What were her morals? Loose? I hear nurses are pretty easy."

Evan opened his mouth to object and Jeavis kicked him sharply below the level of the desktop where Runcorn would not see him.

Evan gasped.

Runcorn turned to him, his eyes narrowing.

"Yes? Come on, man. Don't just stand there!"

"No sir. No one spoke ill of Miss Barrymore's morals, sir. On the contrary, they said she seemed uninterested in such things."

"Not normal, eh?" Runcorn pulled his long face into an expression of distaste. "Can't say that surprises me a great deal. What normal woman would want to go off to a foreign battlefield and take up such an occupation?"

It flashed into Evan's mind that if she had shown interest in men, Runcorn would have said she was loose principled and immoral. Monk would have pointed that out, and asked what Runcorn would have considered right. He stared at Jeavis beside him, then across at Runcorn's thoughtful face, his brows drawn down above his long narrow nose.

"What should we take for normal, sir?" Evan let the

144

words out before his better judgment prevailed, almost as if it were someone else speaking.

Runcorn's head jerked up. "What?"

Evan stood firm, his jaw tightening. "I was thinking, sir, that if she didn't show any interest in men, she was not normal, and if she did she was of loose morals. What, to your mind, would be right—sir?"

"What is right, Evan," Runcorn said between his teeth, the blood rising up his cheeks, "is for a young woman to conduct herself like a lady: seemly, modest, and gentle, not to chase after a man, but to let him know in a subtle and genteel way that she admires him and might not find his attentions unwelcome. That is what is normal, Mr. Evan, and what is right. You are a vicar's son. How is it that I should have to tell you that?"

"Perhaps if anybody's attentions had been welcome, she'd have let him know it," Evan suggested, ignoring the last question and keeping his eyes wide open, his expression innocent.

Runcorn was thrown off balance. He had never known exactly what to make of Evan. He looked so mild and inoffensive with his long nose and hazel eyes, but seemed always to be on the brink of amusement, and Runcorn was never comfortable with it, because he did not know what was funny.

"Do you know something, Sergeant, that you haven't told us?" he said tartly.

"No sir!" Evan replied, standing even more upright.

Jeavis shifted his weight to the other foot. "She did have a visitor that morning, sir, a Mr. Taunton."

"Did she?" Runcorn's eyebrows rose and he jerked forward in his chair. "Well, man! What do we know about this Mr. Taunton? Why didn't you tell me about this in the first place, Jeavis?"

"Because he is a very respectable gentleman," Jeavis defended himself, keeping his temper with difficulty. "And he came and went again inside ten minutes or so, an' at least one of the other nurses thinks she saw Barrymore alive after Mr. Taunton left."

"Oh." Runcorn's face fell. "Well, make sure of it. He might have come back again. Hospitals are big places. You can get in and out of them easy enough. Just walk in off the street, seems to me," he said, contradicting his earlier statement. Then his expression sharpened. "Haven't you got anything, Jeavis? What've you been doing with your time? There's two of you. You must have learned something!"

Jeavis was aggrieved. "We have learned something, sir," he said coldly. "Barrymore was a very bossy, ambitious sort of a person, always giving orders to other people, but very good at her job. Even them that liked her least gave her that. Seems she used to work a lot with Dr. Beck—that's the foreign doctor—then she switched to working mostly with Sir Herbert Stanhope. He's the head of the place and a very fine doctor. Has a spotless reputation both as a surgeon and as a man."

Runcorn's face twitched. "Of course he has. I've heard of him. What about this Beck fellow? She worked with him, you say?"

"Yes sir," Jeavis replied, his smooth features taking on a satisfied look. "He is a different matter altogether. Mrs. Flaherty—she's the matron, a superior sort of person, I judged—she overheard Beck and Barrymore quarreling only a few days ago."

"Did she indeed?" Runcorn looked better pleased. "Can't you be more exact, Jeavis? What do you mean a 'few days'?"

"She wasn't sure, or I'd 'ave said," Jeavis responded sourly. "Two or three. Seems days and nights all melt into one another in a hospital."

"So what did they quarrel about?"

Evan was growing more and more uncomfortable, but he could think of no reasonable protest to make, nothing they would listen to.

"Not certain," Jeavis replied. "But she said it was definitely a powerful difference." He hurried on, seeing

Runcorn's impatience growing. "Beck said 'It won't get you anywhere,' or something to that effect. And she said that if there was no other course open to her she'd have to go to the authorities. And he said 'Please don't do that! I am quite sure it will gain you nothing, in fact it will harm you if anything.'" He ignored the smile on Evan's face at the "he said" and "she said," but his neck grew pinker. "And she said again as she was determined, and nothing would put her off, and he begged her again, and then got angry and said she was a foolish and destructive woman, that she risked ruining a fine medical career through her waywardness, but she just shouted something at him and stormed out, slamming the door." Jeavis finished his account and looked squarely at Runcorn, waiting to see the effect his revelation had had upon him. He totally ignored Evan, who was keeping sober-faced with an effort.

He should have been well pleased. Runcorn sat bolt upright, his face glowing.

"Now there you have something, Jeavis," he said enthusiastically. "Get on with it, man! Go and see this Beck. Pin him down. I expect an arrest within days, with all the evidence we need for a conviction. Just don't spoil it by acting precipitately."

A flicker of uncertainty crossed Jeavis's black eyes. "No sir. It would be precipitate, sir." Evan felt a twinge of sympathy for Jeavis. He was almost certain he did not know the meaning of the word. "We have no idea what the quarrel was about—" Jeavis went on.

"Blackmail," Runcorn said sharply. "It's obvious, man. She knew something about him which could ruin his career, and if he didn't cough up, she was going to tell the authorities. Nasty piece of work, all right." He snorted. "Can't say I grieve much when a blackmailer gets killed. All the same, can't let it happen and get away with it, not here in London! You go and find out what the blackmail was about." His finger jabbed the desk once more. "Look to the man's history, his patients, his qualifications, anything you can. See if he owes money, plays fast and loose with women."

His long nose wrinkled. "Or boys—or whatever. I want to know more about the man than he knows himself, do you understand?"

"Yes sir," Evan said grimly.

"Yes sir," Jeavis agreed.

"Well, get on with it then." Runcorn leaned back in his chair, smiling. "Get to work!"

"Now then, Dr. Beck." Jeavis rocked back and forth on the balls of his feet, his hands thrust deep in his pockets. "A few questions, if you please."

Beck looked at him curiously. He had exceptionally fine eyes, well shaped and very dark. It was a face at once sensuous and refined, but there was something different in the shape of the bones, something indefinably foreign.

"Yes, Inspector?" he said politely.

Jeavis was full of confidence, perhaps remembering Runcorn's satisfaction.

"You worked with the deceased Nurse Barrymore, didn't you, Doctor." It was more of a statement than an inquiry. He knew the answer and his knowledge sat on him like armor.

"I imagine she worked with all the doctors in the hospital," Beck replied. "Although lately, I believe she assisted Sir Herbert most often. She was extremely capable, far more so than the average nurse." A flicker of amusement touched with anger curled his mouth.

"Are you saying that the deceased was different from other nurses, sir?" Jeavis asked quickly.

"Of course I am." Beck was surprised at Jeavis's stupidity. "She was one of Miss Nightingale's nurses from the Crimea! Most of the others are simply female employees who clean up here rather than in some domestic establishment. Frequently because to work in a domestic establishment of any quality you have to have references as to character, morals, sobriety, and honesty, which many of these women could not obtain. Miss Barrymore was a lady

148

who chose nursing in order to serve. She probably had no need to earn her living at all."

Jeavis was thrown off balance.

"Be that as it may," he said dubiously. "I have a witness who overheard you quarreling with Barrymore a couple of days before she was murdered. What do you say to that, Doctor?"

Beck looked startled and his face tightened minutely.

"I say that your witness is mistaken, Inspector," he replied levelly. "I had no quarrel with Miss Barrymore. I had a great respect for her, both personally and professionally."

"Well you wouldn't say different now, sir, would you, seeing as how she's been murdered!"

"Then why did you ask me, Inspector?" Again the flash of humor crossed Beck's face, then vanished, leaving him graver than before. "Your witness is either malicious, frightened for himself, or else overheard part of a conversation and misunderstood. I have no idea which."

Jeavis pinched his lip doubtfully. "Well that could be the case, but it was a very reputable person, and I still want a better explanation than that, sir, because from what was overheard, it looks very like Miss Barrymore was black-mailing you and threatening to go to the hospital authorities and tell them something, and you begged with her not to. Would you care to explain that, sir?"

Beck looked paler.

"I can't explain it," he confessed. "It's complete nonsense."

Jeavis grunted. "I don't think so, sir. I don't think so at all. But we'll leave that for now." He looked at Beck sharply. "Just don't take it into your head to go for a trip back to France, or wherever it is you come from. Or I'll have to come after you!"

"I have no desire whatever to go to France, Inspector," Beck said dryly. "I shall be here, I assure you. Now if there is nothing further, I must return to my patients." And without waiting to see if Jeavis agreed, he walked past the two policemen and out of the room.

"Suspicious," Jeavis said darkly. "Mark my words, Evan, that's our man."

"Maybe." Evan did not agree, not because he knew anything, or suspected anyone else, but out of contrariness. "And maybe not."

Callandra became increasingly aware of Jeavis's presence in the hospital, and then, with a sick fear, of his suspicion of Kristian Beck. She did not believe for an instant that he was guilty, but she had seen enough miscarriage of justice to know that innocence was not always sufficient to save one even from the gallows, let alone from the damage of suspicion, the ruin to reputation, the fear and the loss of friends and fortune.

As she walked down the wide corridor of the hospital she felt a peculiar breathlessness and something not unlike a dizziness as she turned the corner, and almost bumped into Berenice Ross Gilbert.

"Oh! Good afternoon," she said with a gasp, regaining her balance somewhat ungracefully.

"Good afternoon, Callandra," Berenice said with her elegant eyebrows raised. "You look a trifle flustered, my dear. Is there something wrong?"

"Of course something is wrong," Callandra replied testily. "Nurse Barrymore has been murdered. Isn't that as wrong as anything can be?"

"It is fearful, naturally," Berenice answered, adjusting the drape of her fichu. "But to judge from your expression, I thought there must be something new. I'm relieved there is not." She was dressed in a rich shade of brown with gold lace. "The whole place is at sixes and sevens. Mrs. Flaherty cannot get sense out of any of the nurses. Stupid women seem to think there is a lunatic about and they are all in danger." Her rather long-nosed face with its ironic amusement was full of contempt as she stared at Callandra. "Which is ridiculous. It's obviously a personal crime— some rejected lover, as like as not."

150

"Rejected suitor, perhaps," Callandra corrected. "Not lover. Prudence was not of that nature."

"Oh really, my dear." Berenice laughed outright, her face full of scornful amusement. "She may have been gauche, but of course she was of that nature. Do you suppose she spent all that time out in the Crimea with all those soldiers out of a religious vocation to help the sick?"

"No. I think she went out of a sense of frustration at home," Callandra snapped back. "Adventure to travel and see other places and people, do something useful, and above all to learn about medicine, which had been her passion since she was a girl."

Berenice tossed her head in laughter, a rich gurgling sound. "You are naive, my dear! But by all means think what you will." She moved a little closer to Callandra, as if to impart a confidence, and Callandra caught a breath of rich musky perfume. "Have you seen that fearful little policeman? What an oily creature, like a beetle. Have you noticed he has hardly any eyebrows, and those black eyes like stones." She shuddered. "I swear they look just like the prune stones I used to count to know my future. You know, tinker, tailor, and so on. I am quite sure he thinks Dr. Beck did it."

Callandra tried to speak and had to swallow an obstruction in her throat.

"Dr. Beck?" She should not have been surprised. It was only her fear spoken aloud. "Why? Why on earth should Dr. Beck have—have—killed her?"

Berenice shrugged. "Who knows? Perhaps he pursued her and she rejected him, and he was furious and lost his temper and strangled her?"

"Pursued her?" Callandra stared, turmoil in her mind and a hot, sick feeling of horror rippling through her body.

"For Heaven's sake, Callandra, stop repeating everything I say as if you were half-witted!" Berenice said tartly. "Why not? He is a man in the prime of life, and married to a woman who at best is quite indifferent to him, and at worst, if I were unkind, refuses to fulfill her conjugal duties. . . ."

Callandra cringed inside. It was inexpressibly offensive to hear Berenice speaking in such terms of Kristian and his most personal life. It hurt more than she could have foreseen.

Berenice continued, apparently with total unawareness of the horror she was causing.

"And Prudence Barrymore was quite a handsome woman, in her own fashion, one has to grant that. Not really a demure face, or traditionally pretty, but I imagine some men may have found it interesting, and poor Dr. Beck may have been in a desperate state. Working side by side can prove peculiarly powerful." She shrugged her elegant shoulders. "Still, it is hardly anything we can affect, and I have too much to do to spend more time on it. I have to find the chaplain, then I am invited to take tea with Lady Washbourne. Do you know her?"

"No," Callandra replied abruptly. "But I know someone probably more interesting, whom I must see. Good day to you." And with that she walked off smartly before Berenice could be the one to depart first.

She had had Monk in mind when she spoke, but actually the next person she saw was Kristian Beck himself. He came out of one of the wards into the corridor just as she was passing. He looked preoccupied and anxious, but he smiled when he recognized her and the candor of it sent a warmth through her, which only sharpened her fear. She was forced to admit she cared for him more profoundly than anyone else she could recall. She had loved her husband, but it was a friendship, a companionship of long familiarity and a number of shared ideals over the years, not the sharp, strange vulnerability she felt over Kristian Beck, and not the swift elation and the painful excitement, the inner sweetness, in spite of the pain.

He was smiling and she had no idea what he had said. She blushed at her stupidity.

"I beg your pardon?" she stammered.

He was surprised. "I said 'Good morning,' " he repeated. "Are you well?" He looked at her more closely. "Has that wretched policeman been bothering you?"

"No." She smiled in sudden relief. It was ridiculous. She could have dealt with Jeavis without a hesitation in her stride. Good heavens, she was a match for Monk, let alone one of Runcorn's junior minions appointed in his stead. "No," she said again. "Not at all. But I am concerned about his efficiency. I fear he may not be as capable of the skill as this unhappy case requires."

Kristian gave a twisted smile. "He is certainly diligent enough. He has already questioned me three times, and to judge from his expression, believed nothing I said." He gave a sad little laugh. "I think he suspects me."

She caught the edge of fear in his voice, and pretended she had not, then changed her mind and met his eyes. She longed to be able to touch him, but she did not know how much he felt, or knew. And this was hardly the time.

"He will be eager to prove himself by solving the case as quickly and satisfactorily as possible," she said with an effort at composure. "And he has a superior with social ambitions and a keen sense of what is politically judicious." She saw his face tighten as he appreciated exactly what she meant, and the consequent danger to himself as a foreigner and a man with no social connections in England. "But I have a friend, a private inquiry agent," she went on hastily, aching to reassure him. "I have engaged him to look into the case. He is quite brilliant. He will find the truth."

"You say that with great confidence," he observed quietly, halfway between amusement and a desperate need to believe her.

"I have known him for some time and seen him solve cases the police could not." She searched his face, the anxiety in his eyes, the smile on his lips belying it. "He is a hard man, ruthless, and sometimes arrogant," she went on intently. "But he has imagination and brilliance, and he has absolute integrity. If anyone can find the truth, it will be Monk." She thought of the past cases through which she had known him and felt a surge of hope. She made herself smile and saw an answering flicker in Kristian's eyes.

"If he has your confidence to that degree, then I must rest my trust in him also," he replied.

She wanted to say something further, but nothing came to her mind that was not forced. Rather than appear foolish, she excused herself and walked away to look for Mrs. Flaherty, to discuss some charitable business.

Hester found returning to hospital duty after private nursing a severe strain on her temper. She had grown accustomed to being her own mistress since her dismissal roughly a year ago. The restrictions of English medical practice were almost beyond bearing after the urgency and freedom of the Crimea, where there had frequently been so few army surgeons that nurses such as herself had had to take matters into their own hands, and there had been little complaint. Back at home again it seemed that every pettifogging little rule was invoked, more to safeguard dignity than to ease pain or preserve life, and that reputation was more precious than discovery.

She had known Prudence Barrymore and she felt a sharply personal sense of both anger and loss at her death. She was determined to give Monk any assistance she could in learning who had killed her. Therefore she would govern her temper, however difficult that might prove; refrain from expressing her opinions, no matter how severely tempted; and not at any time exercise her own medical judgment.

So far she had succeeded, but Mrs. Flaherty tried her sorely. The woman was set in her ways. She refused to listen to anyone's instructions about opening windows, even on the warmest, mildest days. Twice she had told the nurses to put a cloth over buckets of slops as they were carrying them out, but when they had forgotten on all subsequent occasions she had said nothing further. Hester, as a disciple of Florence Nightingale, was passionately keen on fresh air to cleanse the atmosphere and carry away harmful effluvia and unpleasant odor. Mrs. Flaherty was terrified of chills and preferred to rely on fumigation. It was with the greatest of difficulty that Hester kept her own counsel.

Instinctively she liked Kristian Beck. There seemed to be both compassion and imagination in his face. His modesty and dry humor appealed to her and she felt he was greatly skilled at his profession. Sir Herbert Stanhope she liked less, but was obliged to concede he was a brilliant surgeon. He performed operations lesser men might not have dared, and he was not so careful of his reputation as to fear novelty or innovation. She admired him and felt she should have liked him better than she did. She thought she detected in him a dislike of nurses who had been in the Crimea. Perhaps she was reaping a legacy of Prudence Barrymore's abrasiveness and ambition.

The first death to occur after her arrival was that of a thin little woman, whom she judged to be about fifty and who had a growth in the breast. In spite of all that Sir Herbert could do, she died on the operating table.

It was late in the evening. They had been working all day and they had tried everything they knew to save her. It had all been futile. She had slipped away even as they struggled. Sir Herbert stood with his bloodstained hands in the air. Behind him were the bare walls of the theater, to the left the table with instruments and swabs and bandages, to the right the cylinders of anesthetic gases. A nurse stood by with a mop, brushing the hair out of her eyes with one hand.

There was no one in the gallery, only two students assisting.

Sir Herbert looked up, his face pale, skin drawn tight across his cheekbones.

"She's gone," he said flatly. "Poor creature. No strength left."

"Had she been ill long?" one of the two student doctors asked.

"Long?" Sir Herbert said with an abrupt jerky laugh. "Depends how you think of it. She's had fourteen children,

155

and God knows how many miscarriages. Her body was exhausted."

"She must have stopped bearing some time ago," the younger one said with a squint down at her scrawny body. It was already looking bloodless, as if death had been hours since. "She must be at least fifty."

"Thirty-seven," Sir Herbert replied with a rasp to his voice as though he were angry and held this young man to blame, his ignorance causing the situation, not resulting from it.

The young man drew breath as if to speak, then looked more closely at Sir Herbert's tired face and changed his mind.

"All right, Miss Latterly," Sir Herbert said to Hester. "Inform the mortuary and have her taken there. I'll tell the husband."

Without thinking Hester spoke. "I'll tell him, if you wish, sir?"

He looked at her more closely, surprise wiping away the weariness for a moment.

"That's very good of you, but it is my job. I am used to it. God knows how many women I've seen die either in childbirth or after bearing one after another until they were exhausted, and prey to the first fever that came along."

"Why do they do it?" the young doctor asked, his confusion getting the better of his tact. "Surely they can see what it will do to them? Eight or ten children should be enough for anyone."

"Because they don't know any differently, of course!" Sir Herbert snapped at him. "Half of them have no idea how conception takes place, or why, let alone how to prevent it." He reached for a cloth and wiped his hands. "Most women come to marriage without the faintest idea what it will involve, and a good many never learn the connection between conjugal relations and innumerable pregnancies." He held out the soiled cloth. Hester took it and replaced it with a clean one. "They are taught it is their duty, and the will of God," he continued. "They believe in a God who has nei-

156

ther mercy nor common sense." His face was growing darker as he spoke and his narrow eyes were hard with anger.

"Do you tell them?" the young doctor asked.

"Tell them what?" he said between his teeth. "Tell them to deny their husbands one of the few pleasures the poor devils have? And then what? Watch them leave and take someone else?"

"No of course not," the young man said irritably. "Tell them some way of . . ." He stopped, realizing the futility of what he said. He was speaking about women of whom the great majority could neither read nor count. The church sanctioned no means of birth control whatever. It was God's will that all women should bear as many children as nature would permit, and the pain, fear, and loss of life were all part of Eve's punishment, and should be borne with fortitude, and in silence.

"Don't stand there, woman!" Sir Herbert said, turning on Hester sharply. "Have the poor creature's remains taken to the mortuary."

Two days later, Hester was in Sir Herbert's office, having brought some papers for him from Mrs. Flaherty.

There was a knock at the door, and Sir Herbert gave permission for the person to enter. Hester was at the back of the room in a small alcove, and her first thought was that he had forgotten she was still present. Then as the two young women came in, she realized that perhaps he wished her to remain.

The first was approximately thirty, fair-haired, her face very pale, with high cheekbones and curiously narrow and very beautiful hazel eyes. The second was much younger, perhaps no more than eighteen. Although there was a slight resemblance of feature, her coloring was dark, her eyebrows very clearly marked over deep blue eyes, and her hair grew from her brow in a perfect widow's peak. She also had a beauty spot high on her cheekbone. It was most attractive. However now she looked tired and very pale.

157

"Good afternoon, Sir Herbert." The elder spoke with a catch of nervousness in her voice, but with her chin high and her eyes direct.

He rose very slightly from his seat, only a gesture. "Good afternoon, ma'am."

"Mrs. Penrose," she said in answer to the unspoken question. "Julia Penrose. This is my sister, Miss Marianne Gillespie." She indicated the younger woman a little behind her.

"Miss Gillespie." Sir Herbert acknowledged her with a nod of his head. "How can I help you, Mrs. Penrose? Or is your sister the patient?"

She looked a little startled, as if she had not expected him to be so perceptive. Neither of them could see Hester in the alcove, motionless, her hand in the air half raised to put a book away, peering through the space where it should have sat on the shelf. The names ran like an electric charge in her mind.

Julia was talking, answering Sir Herbert.

"Yes. Yes, it is my sister who requires your help."

Sir Herbert looked at Marianne inquiringly, but also with an appraising eye, regarding her color, her build, the anxiety with which she wound her fingers together in front of her, the bright frightened look in her eyes.

"Please sit down, ladies," he invited, indicating the chairs on the other side of the desk. "I assume you wish to remain during the consultation, Mrs. Penrose?"

Julia lifted her chin a little in anticipation of an attempt to dismiss her. "I do. I can verify everything my sister says."

Sir Herbert's eyebrows rose. "Am I likely to doubt her, ma'am?"

Julia bit her lip. "I do not know, but it is an eventuality I wish to guard against. The situation is distressing enough as it is. I refuse to have any more anguish added to it." She shifted in her seat as if to rearrange her skirts. There was nothing comfortable in her bearing. Then suddenly she plunged on. "My sister is with child. . . ."

Sir Herbert's face tightened. Apparently he had noted that she had been introduced as an unmarried woman.

"I am sorry," he said briefly, his disapproval unmistakable.

Marianne flushed hotly and Julia's eyes glittered with fury.

"She was raped." She used the word deliberately, with all its violence and crudeness, refusing any euphemism. "She is with child as a result of it." She stopped, her breath choking in her throat.

"Indeed," Sir Herbert said with neither skepticism nor pity in his face. He gave no indication whether he believed her or not.

Julia took his lack of horror or sympathy as disbelief.

"If you need proof of it, Sir Herbert," she said icily, "I shall call upon the private inquiry agent who conducted the investigation, and he will confirm what I say."

"You did not report the matter to the police?" Again Sir Herbert's fine pale eyebrows rose. "It is a very serious crime, Mrs. Penrose. One of the most heinous."

Julia's face was ashen. "I am aware of that. It is also one in which the victim may be as seriously punished as the offender, both by public opinion and by having to relive the experience for the courts and for the judiciary, to be stared at and speculated over by everyone with the price of a newspaper in his pocket!" She drew in her breath; her hands, in front of her, were shaking. "Would you subject your wife or daughter to such an ordeal, sir? And do not tell me they would not find themselves in such a position. My sister was in her own garden, painting in the summerhouse, quite alone, when she was molested by someone she had every cause to trust."

"The more so is it a crime, my dear lady," Sir Herbert replied gravely. "To abuse trust is more despicable than simply to enact a violence upon a stranger."

Julia was white. Standing in the alcove, Hester was afraid she was going to faint. She moved to intervene, to offer a glass of water, or even some physical support, and

159

suddenly Sir Herbert glanced at her and motioned her to remain where she was.

"I am aware of the enormity of it, Sir Herbert," she said so quietly that he leaned forward, screwing up his eyes, in his concentration. "It is my husband who committed the offense. You must surely appreciate why I do not wish to bring the police into the matter. And my sister is sensible of my feelings, for which I am profoundly grateful. She is also aware that it would do no good. He would naturally deny it. But even if it could be proved, which it cannot, we are both dependent upon him. We should all be ruined, to no purpose."

"You have my sympathies, ma'am," he said with more gentleness. "It is a truly tragic situation. But I fail to see how I can be of any assistance to you. To be with child is not an illness. Your regular physician will give you all the aid that you require, and a midwife will attend you during your confinement."

Marianne spoke for the first time, her voice low and clear. "I do not wish to bear the child, Sir Herbert. It is conceived as a result of an event which I shall spend the rest of my life trying to forget. And its birth would ruin us all."

"I well understand your situation, Miss Gillespie." He sat back in his chair, looking at her gravely. "But I am afraid that it is not a matter in which you have a choice. Once a child is conceived, there is no other course except to await its birth." The ghost of a smile touched his neat mouth. "I sympathize with you profoundly, but all I can suggest is that you counsel with your parson and gain what comfort you may from him."

Marianne blinked, her face painfully hot, her eyes downcast.

"Of course there is an alternative," Julia said hastily. "There is abortion."

"My dear lady, your sister appears to be a healthy young woman. There is no question of her life being in jeopardy, and indeed no reason to suppose she will not deliver a fine

160

child in due course." He folded his fine sensitive hands. "I could not possibly perform an abortion. It would be a criminal act, as perhaps you are not aware?"

"The rape was a criminal act!" Julia protested desperately, leaning far forward, her hands, white-knuckled, on the edge of his desk.

"You have already explained very clearly why you have brought no charge regarding that," Sir Herbert said patiently. "But it has no bearing upon my situation with regard to performing an abortion." He shook his head. "I am sorry, but it is not something I can do. You are asking me to commit a crime. I can recommend an excellent and discreet physician, and will be happy to do so. He is in Bath, so you may stay away from London and your acquaintances for the next few months. He will also find a place for the child, should you wish to have it adopted, which no doubt you will. Unless . . .?" He turned to Julia. "Could you make room for it in your family, Mrs. Penrose? Or would the cause of its conception be a permanent distress to you?"

Julia swallowed hard and opened her mouth, but before she could reply, Marianne cut across her.

"I do not wish to bear the child," she said, her voice rising sharply in something like panic. "I don't care how discreet the physician is, or how easily he could place it afterwards. Can't you understand? The whole event was a nightmare! I want to forget it, not live with it as a constant reminder every day!"

"I wish I could offer you a way of escape," Sir Herbert said again, his expression pained. "But I cannot. How long ago did this happen?"

"Three weeks and five days," Marianne answered immediately.

"Three weeks?" Sir Herbert said incredulously, his eyebrows high. "But my dear girl, you cannot possibly know that you are with child! There will be no quickening for another three or four months at the very earliest. I should go home and cease to worry."

161

"I am with child!" Marianne said with hard, very suppressed fury. "The midwife said so, and she is never wrong. She can tell merely by looking at a woman's face, without any of the other signs." Her own expression set in anger and pain, and she stared at him defiantly.

He sighed. "Possibly. But it does not alter the case. The law is very plain. There used to be a distinction between aborting a fetus before it had quickened and after, but that has now been done away with. It is all the same." He sounded weary, as if he had said all this before. "And of course it used to be a hanging offense. Now it is merely a matter of ruin and imprisonment. But whatever the punishment, Miss Gillespie, it is a crime I am not prepared to commit, however tragic the circumstances. I am truly sorry."

Julia remained sitting. "We should naturally expect to pay—handsomely."

A small muscle flickered in Sir Herbert's cheeks.

"I had not assumed you were asking it as a gift. But the matter of payment is irrelevant. I have tried to explain to you why I cannot do it." He looked from one to the other of them. "Please believe me, my decision is absolute. I am not unsympathetic, indeed I am not. I grieve for you. But I cannot help."

Marianne rose to her feet and put her hand on Julia's shoulder.

"Come. We shall achieve nothing further here. We shall have to seek help elsewhere." She turned to Sir Herbert. "Thank you for your time. Good day."

Julia climbed to her feet very slowly, still half lingering, as if there were some hope.

"Elsewhere?" Sir Herbert said with a frown. "I assure you, Miss Gillespie, no reputable surgeon will perform such an operation for you." He drew in his breath sharply, and suddenly his face took on a curiously pinched look, quite different from the slight complacence before. This had a sharp note of reality. "And I beg you, please do not go to the back-street practitioners," he urged. "They will assuredly do it for you, and very possibly ruin you for life; at worst bungle it so badly you become infected and either bleed to death or die in agony of septicemia."

Both women froze, staring at him, eyes wide.

He leaned forward, his hands white-knuckled on the desk.

"Believe me, Miss Gillespie, I am not trying to distress you unnecessarily. I know what I am speaking about. My own daughter was the victim of such a man! She too was molested, as you were. She was only sixteen. . . ." His voice caught for a moment, and he had to force himself to continue. Only his inner anger overcame his grief. "We never found who the man was. She told us nothing about it. She was too frightened, too shocked and ashamed. She went to a private abortionist who was so clumsy he cut her inside. Now she will never bear a child."

His eyes were narrowed slits in a face almost bloodless. "She will never even be able to have a normal union with a man. She will be single all her life, and in pain—in constant pain. For God's sake don't go to a back-street abortionist!" His voice dropped again, curiously husky. "Have your child, Miss Gillespie. Whatever you think now, it is the better part than what you face if you go to someone else for the help I cannot give you."

"I . . ." Marianne gulped. "I wasn't thinking of anything so—I mean—I hadn't . . ."

"We hadn't thought of going to such a person," Julia said in a tight brittle voice. "Neither of us would know how to find one, or whom to approach. I had only thought of a reputable surgeon. I—I hadn't realized it was against the law, not when the woman was a victim—of rape."

"I am afraid the law makes no distinction. The child's life is the same."

"I am not concerned with the child's life," Julia said in little more than a whisper. "I am thinking of Marianne."

"She is a healthy young woman. She will probably be perfectly all right. And in time she will recover from the fear and the grief. There is nothing I can do. I am sorry."

163

"So you have said. I apologize for having taken up your time. Good day, Sir Herbert."

"Good day, Mrs. Penrose—Miss Gillespie." As soon as they were gone, Sir Herbert closed the door and returned to his desk. He sat motionless for several seconds, then apparently dismissed the matter and reached for a pile of notes.

Hester came out of the alcove, hesitated, then crossed the floor.

Sir Herbert's head jerked up, his eyes momentarily wide with surprise.

"Oh—Miss Latterly." Then he recollected himself. "Yes—the body's away. Thank you. That's all for the moment. Thank you."

It was dismissal.

"Yes, Sir Herbert."

Hester found the encounter deeply distressing. She could not clear it from her mind, and at the first opportunity she recounted the entire interview to Callandra. It was late evening, and they were sitting outside in Callandra's garden. The scent of roses was heavy in the air and the low sunlight slanting on the poplar leaves was deep golden, almost an apricot shade. There was no motion except the sunset wind in the leaves. The wall muffled the passing of hooves and made inaudible the hiss of carriage wheels.

"It was like the worst kind of dream," Hester said, staring at the poplars and the golden blue sky beyond. "I was aware what was going to happen before it did. And of course I knew every word she said was true, and yet I was helpless to do anything at all about it." She turned to Callandra. "I suppose Sir Herbert is right, and it is a crime to abort, even when the child is a result of rape. It is not anything I have ever had to know. I have nursed entirely soldiers or people suffering from injury or fevers. I have no experience of midwifery at all. I have not even cared for a child, much less a mother and infant. It seems so wrong."

She slapped her hand on the arm of the wicker garden chair. "I am seeing women suffer in a way I never knew before. I suppose I hadn't thought about it. But do you know how many women have come into that hospital in even the few days I've been there, who are worn out and ill as a result of bearing child after child?" She leaned a little farther to face Callandra. "And how many are there we don't see? How many just live lives in silent despair and terror of the next pregnancy?" She banged the chair arm again. "There's such ignorance. Such blind tragic ignorance."

"I am not sure what good knowledge would do," Callandra replied, looking not at Hester but at the rose bed and a late butterfly drifting from one bloom to another. "Forms of prevention have been around since Roman days, but they are not available to most people." She pulled a face. "And they are very often weird contraptions that the ordinary man would not use. A woman has no right in civil or religious law to deny her husband, and even if she had, common sense and the need to survive on something like equable terms would make it impractical."

"At least knowledge would take away some of the shock," Hester argued hotly. "We had one young woman in hospital who was so mortified when she discovered what marriage required of her she went into hysterics, and then tried to kill herself." Her voice rose with outrage. "No one had given her the slightest idea, and she simply could not endure it. She had been brought up with the strictest teachings of purity and it overwhelmed her. She was married by her parents to a man thirty years older than herself and with little patience or gentleness. She came into the hospital with broken arms and legs and ribs where she had jumped out of a window in an attempt to kill herself." She took a deep breath and made a vain attempt to lower her tone.

"Now, unless Dr. Beck can persuade the police and the Church that it was an accident, they will charge her with attempted suicide and either imprison her or hang her." She banged her fist down on the chair arm yet again. "And that monumental fool, Jeavis, is trying to say Dr. Beck killed Prudence Barrymore." She did not notice Callandra stiffen

165

in her seat or her face grow paler. "That is because that would be the easy answer, and save him from having to question the other surgeons and the chaplain and the members of the Board of Governors."

Callandra started to speak, and then stopped again.

"Is there nothing we can do to help Marianne Gillespie?" Hester persisted, her fists clenched, leaning forward in the chair. She glanced at the roses. "Is there nobody to which one could appeal? Do you know Sir Herbert said his own daughter had been assaulted and had become with child as a result?" She swung around to Callandra again. "And she went to a private abortionist in some back street who maimed her so badly she can now never marry, let alone bear children. And she is in constant pain. For Heaven's sake, there must be something we can do!"

"If I knew of anything I should not be sitting her listening to you," Callandra replied with a sad smile. "I should have told you what it was, and we should be on our way to do it. Please be careful, or you are going to put your arm right through my best garden chair."

"Oh! I'm sorry. It's just that I get so furious!"

Callandra smiled, and said nothing.

The following two days were hot and sultry. Tempers became short. Jeavis seemed to be everywhere in the hospital, getting in the way, asking questions which most people found irritating and pointless. The treasurer swore at him. A gentleman on the Board of Governors made a complaint to his member of Parliament. Mrs. Flaherty lectured him on abstinence, decorum, and probity, which was more than even he could take. After that he left her strictly alone.

But gradually the hospital was getting back to its normal routine and even in the laundry room they spoke less of the murder and more of their usual concerns: husbands, money, the latest music hall jokes, and general gossip.

Monk was concentrating his attention on learning the past and present circumstances of all the doctors, especially the students, and of the treasurer, chaplain, and various governors.

It was late in the evening and still oppressively warm when Callandra went to look for Kristian Beck. She had no real reason to speak to him; she had to manufacture one. What she wished was to see how he was bearing up under Jeavis's interrogations and less-than-subtle implication that Beck had had some shameful secret which he had begged Prudence Barrymore not to reveal to the authorities.

She had still no firm idea what she was going to say as she walked along the corridor toward his room, her heart pounding, nervousness making her mouth dry. In the heat after the long afternoon sun on the windows and roof, the air smelled stale. She could almost distinguish the cloying smell of blood from bandages and the acridness of waste. Two flies buzzed and banged blindly against the glass of a window.

She could ask him if Monk had spoken to him, and yet again assure him of Monk's brilliance and his past successes. It was not a good reason, but she could not bear the inaction any longer. She had to see him and do what she could to allay the fear he must feel. Over and over she had imagined his thoughts as Jeavis made his insinuations, as he saw Jeavis's black eyes watching him. It was impossible to argue or defend oneself against prejudice, the irrational suspicion of anything or anyone who was different.

She was at his door. She knocked. There was a sound, a voice, but she could not distinguish the words. She turned the handle and pushed the door wide.

The scene that met her burned itself into her brain. The large table which served as his desk was in the center of the room and lying on it was a woman, part of her body covered with a white sheet, but her abdomen and upper thighs clearly exposed. There were swabs bright with blood, and a bloodstained towel. There was a bucket on the floor, but with a cloth over it so she could not see what it contained. She had seen enough operations before to recognize the

167

tanks and flasks that held ether and the other materials used to anesthetize a patient.

Kristian had his back to her. She would recognize him anywhere, the line of his shoulder, the way his hair grew on his neck, the curve of his high cheekbone.

And she knew the woman also. Her hair was black with a deep widow's peak. Her brows were dark and unusually clearly marked, and there was a small neat mole on her cheek level with the corner of her eye. Marianne Gillespie! There was only one conclusion: Sir Herbert had denied her—but Kristian had not. He was performing the illegal abortion.

For seconds Callandra stood frozen, her tongue stiff, her mouth dry. She did not even see the figure of the nurse beyond.

Kristian was concentrating so intently upon what he was doing, his hands moving quickly, delicately, his eyes checking again and again to see the color of Marianne's face, to make sure she was breathing evenly. He had not heard Callandra's voice, nor the door opening.

At last she moved. She backed out and pulled the door after her, closing it without sound. Her heart was beating so violently her body shook, and she could not catch her breath. For a moment she was afraid she was going to choke.

A nurse passed by, staggering a little from fatigue, and Callandra felt just as dizzy, just as incapable of balance. Hester's words came back into her mind like hammer blows. Sir Herbert's daughter had gone to a secret abortionist and he had maimed her, operated so clumsily she would never be a normal woman again, and never be free from pain.

Had Kristian done that too? Was he the one she had gone to? As Marianne had? Funny, gentle, wise Kristian, with whom she had shared so many moments of understanding, to whom she did not need to explain the pain or the laughter of thoughts—Kristian, whose face she could see every time she closed her eyes, whom she longed to touch, though she knew she must never yield to the temptation. It would break the delicate unspoken barrier between a love that was acceptable and one that was not. To bring shame to him would be unbearable.

Shame! Could the man she knew possibly be the same man who would do what she had seen? And perhaps worse—far worse? The thought was sickening, but she could not cast it out of her mind. The picture was there in front of her every time she closed her eyes.

And then a thought came which was immeasurably more hideous. Had Prudence Barrymore known? Was that what he had begged her not to tell the authorities? Not simply the Board of Governors of the hospital, but the police? And had he killed her to keep her silent?

She leaned against the wall, overwhelmed with misery. Her brain refused to work. There was no one she could turn to. She dared not even tell Monk. It was a burden she would have to carry silently, and alone. Without realizing the full enormity of it, she chose to bear his guilt with him.

6

HESTER FOUND hospital routine increasingly difficult. She obeyed Mrs. Flaherty because her survival depended upon it, but she found herself grinding her teeth to keep from answering back, and more than once she had to change a sentence midway through in order to make it innocuous. Only the thought of Prudence Barrymore made it possible. She had not known her well. The battlefield was too large, too filled with confusion, pain, and a violent, sickening urgency for people to know each other unless they had had occasion to work together. And chance had dictated that she had worked with Prudence only once, but that once was engraven on her memory indelibly. It was after the battle of Inkermann, in November of '54. It was less than three weeks after the disaster of Balaclava and the massacre resulting from the Light Brigade's suicidal charge against the Russian guns. It was bitterly cold, and relentless rain meant that men stood or marched in mud up to their knees. The tents were worn with holes and they slept wet and filthy. Their clothes were growing ragged and there was nothing with which to mend them. They were underfed because supplies were in desperate straits, and they were exhausted with constant labor and anxiety.

The siege of Sebastopol was achieving nothing. The Russians were dug in deeper and deeper, and the winter was fast approaching. Men and horses died of cold, hunger, injuries, and above all disease.

Then had come the battle of Inkermann. It had been going badly for the British troops to begin with, and when they finally sent for the French reinforcements, three battalions of Zouaves and Algerians coming in at a run, bugles blowing, drums beating and their general shouting encouragement in Arabic, it had become a rout. Of the forty thousand Russians, over a quarter were killed, wounded, or taken prisoner. The British lost six hundred killed, the French a mere hundred and thirty. In each case three times as many were wounded. The whole battle was fought in shifting, swirling mists, and as often as not men stumbled on the enemy by chance, or were lost, and injured their own men in the confusion.

Hester could recall it vividly. Standing in the warm sunny London hospital ward, she did not even need to close her eyes to see it in her mind, or feel the cold, and hear the noise, the cries and groans, the voices thick with pain. Three days after the battle the burial parties were still working. She could see in her dreams their bent forms, huddled against the howling wind, shovels in their hands, heads down, shoulders hunched, trudging through the mud; or stopped to lift another corpse, often frozen in the violent positions of hand-to-hand fighting, faces disfigured with terror, and gored by terrible bayonet wounds. At least four thousand Russians were heaped in communal graves.

And the wounded were continually being discovered in the scrub and brushwood, screaming.

Hour after hour the surgeons had labored in the medical tents, striving to save lives, only to have men die on the long rough cart journeys to the ships, and then by sea to Scutari, where, if they survived that, they would die in the hospital of fevers or gangrene.

She could recall the smell and the exhaustion, the dim light of lanterns swaying, their yellow glare on the surgeon's face as he worked, knife or saw in his hand, striving above all to be quick. Speed was everything. There was seldom time for such niceties as chloroform, even though it was available. And many preferred the "stimulant" of a well-used knife rather than the silent slipping away into death of anesthetics.

She could remember the numberless white faces of men, haggard, shocked with injury, the knowledge of mutilation, the scarlet, and the warm smell of blood, the neat pile of amputated limbs just outside the tent flap in the mud.

She could see Prudence Barrymore's face, eyes intent, mouth drawn tight with emotion, smears of blood on her cheek and across her brow where she had pushed her hair out of her eyes. They had worked in silent unison, too weary to speak a word when a glance would serve. There was no need to express an emotion which was so completely shared. Their world was one of private horror, pity, need, and a kind of terrible victory. If one could survive this, then Hell itself could offer little worse.

It was not something you could call friendship; it was at once less and more. The sharing of such experiences created a bond and set them apart from all others. It was not something that could be told to another person. There were no words with a meaning both could understand which would impart the physical horror or the heights and depths of emotion.

It brought an extraordinary kind of loneliness that Prudence was gone, and a driving anger that it should be in this way.

On night duty—which Mrs. Flaherty gave her whenever she could; she disliked Crimean nurses and all the arrogance and the change they represented—Hester would walk around the wards by lamplight, and past memories crowded in on her. More than once she heard a dull thud and turned around with a shudder, expecting to see a rat stunned as it dropped off the wall, but there was nothing except a bundle of sheets and bandages and a slop pail.

Gradually she distinguished the other nurses and spoke to them when she had a natural opportunity. Very often she simply listened. They were frightened. Prudence's name was mentioned often, to begin with, with fear. Why had she been murdered? Was there a madman loose in the hospital, and might any one of them be next? Inevitably there were stories of sinister shadows in empty corridors, sounds of muffled screams and then silence, and almost every male member of staff was the subject of speculation.

They were in the laundry room. The huge coppers were silent, no clanking of steam in the pipes, no hissing and bubbling. It was the end of the day. There was little left to do but fold and collect sheets.

"What was she like?" Hester asked with casual innocence.

"Bossy," an elderly nurse replied, pulling a face. She was fat and tired, and her red-veined nose bore mute witness to her solace in the gin bottle. "Always telling other people what to do. Thought having been in the Crimea meant she knew everything. Even told the doctors sometimes." She grinned toothlessly. "Made 'em mad, it did."

There was laughter all around. Apparently, however unpopular Prudence might have been at times, the doctors were more so, and when she clashed with them, the women were amused and were on her side.

"Really?" Hester made her interest obvious. "Didn't she get told off for it? She was lucky not to be dismissed."

"Not her!" Another nurse laughed abruptly, pushing her hands into her pockets. "She was a bossy piece, all right, but she knew how to run a ward and care for the sick. Knew it better than Mrs. Flaherty, although if you say I said that, I'll push your eyes out." She put down the last sheet with a thump.

"Who is going to tell that vinegar bitch, you stupid cow?" the first woman said acidly. "But I don't think she was that good. Thought she was, mind."

"Yes she was!" Now the second woman was getting angry. Her face was flushed. "She saved a lot of lives in this God-awful place. Even made it smell better."

"Smell better!" There was a guffaw of laughter from a

173

big red-haired woman. "Where d'ya think yer are, some gennelman's 'ouse? Garn, ya fool! She thought she were a lady, not one o' the likes of us. A sight too good to work with scrubwomen and domestics. Got ideas about being a doctor, she 'ad. Right fool, she was, poor cow. Should have heard what his lordship had to say about that."

" 'Oo? Sir 'Erbert?"

" 'Course Sir 'Erbert. 'Oo else? Not old German George. 'E's a foreigner and full o' funny ideas anyway. Wouldn't be surprised if it were 'im wot killed 'er. That's what them rozzers are sayin' anyway."

"Are they?" Hester looked interested. "Why? I mean, couldn't it just as easily have been anyone else?"

They all looked at her.

"Wot yer mean?" the red-haired one said with a frown.

Hester hitched herself onto the edge of the laundry basket. This was the sort of opportunity she had been angling for. "Well, who was here when she was killed?"

They looked at her, then at each other.

"Wot yer mean? Doctors, and the like?"

" 'Course she means doctors and the like," the fat woman said derisively. "She don't think one of us did her in. If I were going to kill anyone, it'd be me ol' man, not some jumped-up nurse wi' ideas above 'erself. Wot do I care about 'er? I wouldn't 'av seen 'er dead, poor cow, but I wouldn't shed no tears either."

"What about the treasurer and the chaplain?" Hester tried to sound casual. "Did they like her?"

The fat woman shrugged. "Who knows? Why should they care one way or the other?"

"Well she weren't bad-looking," the old one replied with an air of generosity. "And if they can chase Mary 'Iggins, they could certainly chase 'er."

"Who chases Mary Higgins?" Hester inquired, not sure who Mary Higgins was, but assuming she was a nurse.

"The treasurer," the young one said with a shrug. "Fancies 'er, 'e does."

"So does the chaplain," the fat woman said with a snort.

174

"Dirty old sod. Keeps putting 'is arm 'round 'er an' calling 'er 'dear.' Mind, I wouldn't say as 'e didn't fancy Pru' Barrymore neither, come ter think on it. Maybe 'e went too far, and she threatened to report 'im? 'E could 'a done it."

"Would he have been here at that time in the morning?" Hester asked dubiously.

They looked at each other.

"Yeah," the fat one said with certainty. "'E'd bin 'ere all night 'cos of someone important dying. 'E were 'ere all right. Maybe 'e did it, and not German George? An' 'is patient snuffed it, an all," she added. "Wot were a surprise. Thought 'e were goin' ter make it—poor sod."

There were several such conversations in between the sweeping and fetching, rolling bandages, emptying pails and changing beds. Hester learned a great deal about where everybody was at about seven o'clock on the morning that Prudence Barrymore had died, but it still left a great many possibilities as to who could have killed her. She heard much gossip about motives, most of it scurrilous and highly speculative, but when she saw John Evan she reported it to him in the brief moment they had alone in one of the small side rooms where medicines were kept. Mrs. Flaherty had just left, after instructing Hester to roll an enormous pile of bandages, and Sir Herbert was not due for at least another half hour, after he had finished luncheon.

Evan half sat on the table, watching her fingers smoothing and rolling the cloth.

"Have you told Monk yet?" he asked with a smile.

"I haven't seen him since Sunday," she replied.

"What is he doing?" he asked, his voice light but his hazel eyes watching her with brightness.

"I don't know," she answered, piling another heap of bandages on the table beside him. "He said he was going to learn more about various governors on the board, in case one of them had some relationship with Prudence, or her family, that we don't know about. Or even some connection with her in the Crimea, in any way."

Evan grunted, his eyes roaming over the cabinet with its

jars of dried herbs, colored crystals, and bottles of wine and surgical spirits. "That's something we haven't even thought of." He pulled a face. "But then Jeavis wouldn't. He tends to think in terms of the obvious and usually he's right. Runcorn would never countenance disturbing the gentry, unless there is no other choice. Does Monk think it's personal, in that way?"

She laughed. "He's not told me. It could be anybody. It seems the chaplain was here all that night—and Dr. Beck . . ."

Evan's head jerked up. "The chaplain. I didn't know that. He didn't say so when we spoke to him. Although to be honest I'm not sure Jeavis asked him. He was more concerned with his opinion of Prudence, and anybody's feelings about her that the chaplain might know of."

"And did he know of any?" she asked.

He smiled, his eyes bright with amusement. He knew she would tell Monk whatever he said.

"Nothing promising," he began. "Mrs. Flaherty didn't like her, but that's not surprising. The other nurses largely tolerated her, but they had little in common. One or two of the younger ones admired her—a little hero worship there, I think. One of the student doctors seems to have felt rather the same, but she gave him little encouragement." His expression took on a shadow of wry sympathy, as if he could imagine it clearly. "Another one of the students, tall fellow with fair hair that falls over his brow, he didn't like her. Thought she had ambitions above a woman's place." His eyes met Hester's. "Arrogant fellow, he seemed to me," he added. "But then he doesn't care for policemen either. We get in the way of the real work, which of course is his work."

"You didn't like him," she stated the obvious, reaching for another heap of bandages. "But was he in the hospital that morning?"

He pulled a face. "Unfortunately not. Nor was the one who admired her."

"Who was, that you know?"

"About half the nurses, the treasurer, Dr. Beck, Sir Herbert, two student doctors named Howard and Cantrell, Mrs. Flaherty, one of the Board of Governors called Sir Donald MacLean, another called Lady Ross Gilbert. And the front doors were open so anyone could have come in unobserved. Not very helpful, is it?"

"Not very," she agreed. "But then I suppose opportunity was never going to be our best chance for evidence."

He laughed. "How very efficient you sound. Monk's right-hand man—I mean, woman."

She was about to explode in argument that she was most certainly not Monk's hand of any sort when Mrs. Flaherty's thin upright figure appeared in the doorway, her face pink with anger, her eyes brilliant.

"And what are you doing, Nurse Latterly, standing about talking to this young man? You are very new here, and regardless of your friendship with certain well-placed persons, I would remind you we set a very high moral standard, and if you fall below it, you will be dismissed!"

For an instant Hester was furious. Then she saw the absurdity of her morality's being questioned in regard to John Evan.

"I am from the police, Matron Flaherty," Evan said coldly, standing upright. "I was questioning Miss Latterly. She had no alternative but to answer me, as have all the staff in the hospital, if they wish to assist the law rather than be charged with obstructing it."

Color flared up Mrs. Flaherty's cheeks. "Fiddlesticks, young man!" she said. "Nurse Latterly was not even here when poor Nurse Barrymore met her death. If you have not even learned that, then you are hopelessly incompetent. I don't know what we pay you for!"

"Of course I am aware of that," Evan said angrily. "It is precisely because she could not be guilty that her observation is so useful."

"Observation of what?" Mrs. Flaherty's white eyebrows rose very high. "As I have just pointed out, young man, she was not here. What could she have seen?"

177

Evan affected extreme patience. "Mrs. Flaherty, seven days ago someone strangled one of your nurses and stuffed the body down the laundry chute. Such an act is not an isolated piece of lunacy. Whoever did it had a powerful motive, something which springs from the past. Similarly, the memory of that crime, and the fear of being caught, will carry forward into the future. There is much to observe now for those with the ability to see it."

Mrs. Flaherty grunted, looked at Hester: her strong face, her slender almost lean figure, very square-shouldered, very upright; then at Evan standing beside the table piled with bandages, his soft wing of brown hair waving off the brow, his long nosed, sensitive, humorous face; and snorted her disbelief. Then she swung on her heel and marched off.

Evan did not know whether to be angry or to laugh; the mixed emotions were plain in his expression.

"I'm sorry," he apologized. "I did not mean to compromise your reputation. It never occurred to me."

"Nor to me," Hester admitted with a faint heat in her cheeks. It was all so ridiculous. "Perhaps if we meet again, it had better be outside the hospital?"

"And outside Jeavis's knowledge too," he said quickly. "He would not appreciate me giving aid and comfort to the enemy."

"The enemy. Am I the enemy?"

"By extension, yes." He put his hands in his pockets. "Runcorn still hates Monk and never ceases to tell Jeavis how much more satisfactory he is, but the men still speak of Monk, and Jeavis is no fool. He knows why Runcorn prefers him, and he's determined to prove himself and lay Monk's ghost." He smiled. "Not that he ever will. Runcorn can't forget all the years Monk trod on his heels, the times he was right when Runcorn was wrong, the little things, the unspoken contempt, the better-cut suits, the voice a little rounder." He was watching Hester's eyes. "Just the fact that he tried so often to humiliate Monk, and could never quite succeed. He won in the end, but it didn't taste like victory.

He keeps wanting to bring him back so he can win again, and this time savor it properly."

"Oh dear." Hester rolled the last of the bandages and tied the end. She was sorry for Jeavis, and in a faint equivocal way for Runcorn, but mostly she had a sharp prickle of satisfaction on Monk's account. She was not quite smiling, but very nearly. "Poor Inspector Jeavis."

Evan looked startled for a moment, then comprehension lit his face, and an inner gentleness. "I had better go and see the chaplain." He inclined his head. "Thank you!"

That afternoon Hester was sent for to assist Sir Herbert in an operation. She was told by a large nurse with powerful shoulders, a coarse-featured face, and remarkable eyes. Hester had seen her several times, always with a feeling of unease, and it was only this time that she realized why her eyes were so arresting. One was blue and the other quite clear cold green. How could she have failed to notice it before? Perhaps the sheer physical strength of the woman had so filled her mind as to leave no room for other impressions.

"Sir 'Erbert wants yer," the woman said grimly. Her name was Dora Parsons; that much Hester remembered.

Hester put down the pail she was carrying. "Where?"

"In 'is office, o' course. I s'pose your goin' to take her place then? Or yer think y'are!"

"Whose place?"

The woman's huge, ugly face was sharp with contempt. "Don't act gormless wi' me, miss 'igh 'n' mighty. Jus' 'cos yer've bin ter the Crimea an' everybody's fallen over theirselves about yer, don't think yer can get away wi' anything at all, 'cos yer can't! Givin' yerself airs like yer too good fer the rest of us." She spat viciously to demonstrate her scorn.

"I assume you mean Nurse Barrymore?" Hester said icily, although the woman's physical power was intimidating. She would guard very carefully against finding herself alone with her in the laundry room, out of earshot. But bullies chase those in whom they sense fear.

"O' course I mean Nurse Barrymore." Dora mimicked Hester's voice. "Are there any other fancy Crimean nurses around 'ere?"

"Well, you are in a better position than I to know that," Hester retorted. "I assume from your words that you disliked her?"

"Me and 'alf a score others," Dora agreed. "So don't you go tryin' ter say I was the one what done 'er in, or I'll 'ave yer." She leered. "I could break your skinny little neck in two shakes, I could."

"It would seem unnecessary to tell the police." Hester controlled her voice with an effort. Deliberately she thought of Prudence in the surgeon's tent on the battlefield, and then lying dead in the laundry room, to make herself angry. It was better than being afraid of this wretched woman. "Your behavior makes it so obvious that the stupidest constable could see it for himself. Do you often break people's necks if they annoy you?"

Dora opened her mouth to reply, then realized that what she had been going to say led her straight into a trap.

"Well are you goin' ter Sir 'Erbert, or shall I tell him as yer declines to, seein' as yer too busy?"

"I'm going." Hester moved away, around the huge figure of Dora Parsons and swiftly out of the room and along the corridor, boot heels clattering on the floor. She reached Sir Herbert's door and knocked sharply, as if Dora were still behind her.

"Come!" Sir Herbert's voice was peremptory.

She turned the handle and went in.

He was sitting behind his desk, papers spread in front of him. He looked up.

"Oh—Miss—er . . . Latterly. You're the Crimean nurse, aren't you?"

"Yes, Sir Herbert." She stood straight, her hands clasped behind her in an attitude of respect.

"Good," he said with satisfaction, folding some papers and putting them away. "I have a delicate operation to perform on a person of some importance. I wish you to be on

180

hand to assist me and to care for the patient afterwards. I cannot be everywhere all the time. I have been reading some new theories on the subject. Most interesting." He smiled. "Not, of course, that I would expect them to be of concern to you."

He had stopped, as if he half thought she might answer him. It was of considerable interest to her, but mindful of her need to remain employed in the hospital (and that might depend upon Sir Herbert's view of her), she answered as she thought he would wish it.

"I hardly think it lies within my skill, sir," she said demurely. "Although, of course, I am sure it is most important, and may well be something I shall have to learn when the time is fit."

The satisfaction in his small intelligent eyes was sharp.

"Of course, Miss Latterly. In due time, I shall tell you all you need to know to care for my patient. A very fitting attitude."

She bit her tongue to refrain from answering back. But she did not thank him for what was undoubtedly intended as a compliment. She did not think she could keep her voice from betraying her sarcasm.

He seemed to be waiting for her to speak.

"Would you like me to see the patient before he comes to the operating room, sir?" she asked him.

"No, that will not be necessary. Mrs. Flaherty is preparing him. Do you sleep in the nurses' dormitory?"

"Yes." It was a sore subject. She hated the communal living, the rows of beds in the long room, like a workhouse ward, without privacy, no silence in which to sleep or to think or to read. Always there were the sounds of other women, the interruptions, the restless movements, the talking, sometimes the laughter, the coming and going. She washed under the tap in one of the two large sinks, ate what little there was as opportunity offered between the long twelve-hour shifts.

It was not that she was unused to hard conditions. Heaven knew the Crimea had been immeasurably worse.

She had been colder, hungrier, wearier, and often in acute personal danger. But there it had seemed unavoidable; it was war. And there had been a comradeship and a facing of common enemies. Here it was arbitrary, and she resented it. Only the thought of Prudence Barrymore made her endure it.

"Good." Sir Herbert smiled at her. It lit his face and made him look quite different. Even though it was only a gesture of politeness, she could see a softer, more human man behind the professional. "We do have a few nurses who maintain their own homes, but it is not a satisfactory arrangement, most particularly it they are to care for a patient who needs their undivided attention. Please make yourself available at two o'clock precisely. Good day to you, Miss Latterly."

"Thank you, Sir Herbert." And immediately she withdrew.

The operation was actually very interesting. For over two hours she totally forgot her own dislike of hospital discipline and the laxness she saw in nursing, living in the dormitory, and the threatening presence of Dora Parsons; she even forgot Prudence Barrymore and her own reason for being here. The surgery was for the removal of stones from a very portly gentleman in his late fifties. She barely saw his face, but the pale abdomen, swollen with indulgence, and then the layers of fat as Sir Herbert cut through them to expose the organs, was fascinating to her. The fact that the patient could be anesthetized meant that speed was irrelevant. That release from urgency, the agonizing consciousness of the patient's almost unbearable pain, brought her close to euphoria.

She watched Sir Herbert's slender hands, with their tapered fingers, with an admiration which was akin to awe. They were delicate and powerful and he moved rapidly but without haste. Never once did he appear to lose his intense concentration, nor did his patience diminish. His skill had a kind of beauty which drove everything else from her mind. She was oblivious of the tense faces of the students watching; one black-haired young man standing almost next to her kept sucking in his breath, and normally the sound of it would have irritated her beyond bearing. Today she hardly heard it.

When at last Sir Herbert was finished he stood back, his face radiant with the knowledge that he had performed brilliantly, that his art had cut away pain, and that with careful nursing and good luck the wound would heal and the man be restored.

"There now, gentlemen," he said with a smile. "A decade ago we could not have performed such a protracted operation. We live in an age of miracles. Science moves forward in giant steps and we are in the van. New horizons beckon, new techniques, new discoveries. Right, Nurse Latterly. I can do no more for him. It is up to you to dress the wound, keep his fever down, and at the same time make sure he is exposed to no chill. I shall come to see him tomorrow."

"Yes, Sir Herbert." For once her admiration was sufficiently sincere that she spoke with genuine humility.

The patient recovered consciousness slowly, and in considerable distress. He was not only in great pain, but he suffered nausea and vomiting, and he was deeply concerned lest he should tear the stitches in his abdomen. It occupied all her time and attention to do what she could to ease him and to check and recheck that he was not bleeding. There was little she could do to determine whether he bled internally except keep testing him for fever, clamminess of skin, or faintness of pulse.

Several times Mrs. Flaherty looked in to the small room where she was, and it was on the third of these visits that Hester learned her patient's name.

"How is Mr. Prendergast?" Mrs. Flaherty said with a frown, her eye going to the pail on the floor and the cloth cover over it. She could not resist passing comment. "I assume that is empty, Miss Latterly?"

"No. I am afraid he has vomited," Hester replied.

Mrs. Flaherty's white eyebrows rose. "I thought you Crimean nurses were the ones who were so determined not to have slops left anywhere near the patients? Not one to practice as you preach, eh?"

Hester drew in her breath to wither Mrs. Flaherty with what she considered to be obvious, then remembered her object in being here.

"I thought it was the lesser evil," she replied, not daring to meet Mrs. Flaherty's icy blue eyes in case her anger showed. "I am afraid he is in some distress, and without my presence he might have torn his stitches if he were sick again. Added to which, I have only one pail, and better that than soiling the sheets."

Mrs. Flaherty gave a wintry smile. "A little common sense, I see. Far more practical use than all the education in the world. Perhaps we'll make a good nurse of you yet, which is more than I can say for some of your kind." And before Hester could retaliate, she hurried on. "Is he feverish? What is his pulse? Have you checked his wound? Is he bleeding?"

Hester answered all those questions, and was about to ask if she could be relieved so she might eat something herself, since she had not had so much as a drink since Sir Herbert had first sent for her, but Mrs. Flaherty expressed her moderate satisfaction and whisked out, keys swinging, footsteps clicking down the corridor.

Perhaps she was doing her an injustice, but Hester thought Mrs. Flaherty knew perfectly well how long she had been there without more than momentary relief, for the calls of nature, and took some satisfaction in it.

Another junior nurse who had admired Prudence came in at about ten o'clock in the evening, when it was growing dark, a hot mug of tea in her hand and a thick mutton sandwich. She closed the door behind her swiftly and held them out.

"You must be gasping for something," she said, her eyes bright.

"I'm ravenous," Hester agreed gratefully. "Thank you very much."

184

"How is he?" the nurse asked. She was about twenty, brown-haired with an eager, gentle face.

"In a lot of pain," Hester answered, her mouth full. "But his pulse is still good, so I'm hoping he isn't losing any blood."

"Poor soul. But Sir Herbert's a marvelous surgeon, isn't he?"

"Yes." Hester meant it. "Yes, he's brilliant." She took a long drink at the tea, even though it was too hot.

"Were you in the Crimea too?" the nurse resumed, her face lit with enthusiasm. "Did you know poor Nurse Barrymore? Did you know Miss Nightingale?" Her voice dropped a fraction in awe at the great name.

"Yes," Hester said with very slight amusement. "I knew them both. And Mary Seacole."

The girl was mystified. "Who's Mary Seacole?"

"One of the finest women I ever met," Hester replied, knowing her answer was borne of perversity as well as truth. Profound as was her admiration for Florence Nightingale, and for all the women who had served in the Crimea, she had heard so much praise for most of them but nothing for the black Jamaican woman who had served with equal selflessness and diligence, running a boardinghouse which was a refuge for the sick, injured, and terrified, administering her own fever cures, learned in the yellow fever areas of her native West Indies.

The girl's face quickened with curiosity. "Oh? I never heard mention of her. Why not? Why don't people know?"

"Probably because she is Jamaican," Hester replied, sipping at the tea. "We are very parochial whom we honor." She thought of the still rigidly absurd social hierarchy even among the ladies who picnicked on the heights overlooking the battle, or rode their fine horses on parade the mornings before—and after, and the tea parties amid the carnage. Then with a jolt she recalled herself to the present. "Yes, I knew Prudence. She was a brave and unselfish woman—then."

"Then!" The girl was horrified. "What do you mean?

She was marvelous. She knew so much. Far more than some of the doctors, I used to think—Oh!" She clapped her hand to her mouth. "Don't tell anyone I said that! Of course she was only a nurse . . ."

"But she was very knowledgeable?" A new and ugly thought entered Hester's mind, spoiling her pleasure in the sandwich, hurrying as she was.

"Oh, yes!" the girl said vehemently. "I suppose it came with all her experience. Not that she talked about it very much. I used to wish she would say more. . . . It was wonderful to listen to her." She smiled a little shyly. "I suppose you could tell the same sort of thing, seeing as you were there too?"

"I could," Hester agreed. "But sometimes it is hard to find words to convey something that is so dreadfully different. How can you describe the smell, and the taste of it, or being so tired—or feeling such horror and anger and pity? I wish I could make you see it through my eyes for a moment, but I can't. And sometimes when you can't do a thing properly, it is better not to belittle it by doing it badly."

"I understand." Suddenly there was a new brightness in her eyes and a tiny smile as something unexplainable at last made sense.

Hester took a deep breath, finished the tea, then asked the questions that crowded her mind. "Do you think Prudence knew enough that she might have been aware if someone else had made a mistake—a serious one?"

"Oh . . ." The girl looked thoughtful, turning the possibility over in her mind. Then with a thrill of horror she realized what Hester meant. Her hand came up sharply, her eyes wide and dark. "Oh no! Oh dear Heaven! You mean did she see someone make a real mistake, a dreadful one, and he murdered her to keep her quiet? But who would do such a wicked thing?"

"Someone who was frightened his reputation would be ruined," Hester answered. "If the mistake was fatal . . ."

"Oh—I see." The girl continued to stare at her aghast.

186

"Whom did she work with recently?" Hester pursued. She was aware that she was treading into a dangerous area, dangerous for herself if this innocent, almost naive-seeming girl were to repeat the conversation, but her curiosity overpowered her sense of self-preservation. The danger was only possible, and some time in the future. The knowledge was now. "Who had been caring for someone who died unexpectedly?"

The girl's eyes were fixed on Hester's face. "She worked very close with Sir Herbert until just before she died. And she worked with Dr. Beck too." Her voice dropped unhappily. "And Dr. Beck's patient died that night—and that was unexpected. We all thought he'd live. And Prudence and him had a quarrel. . . . Everyone knows that, but I reckon as if he had done anything like that, she'd have told. She was as straight as they come. She wouldn't've hidden it to save anyone. Not her."

"So if it were that, then it happened probably the day before she was killed, or even that night?"

"Yes."

"But Dr. Beck's patient died that night," Hester pointed out.

"Yes," the girl conceded, the light brightening in her eyes again and her voice lifting.

"So whom did she work with that night?" Hester asked. "Who was even here that night?"

The girl hesitated for several moments, thinking so she remembered exactly. The patient in the bed turned restlessly, throwing the sheet off himself. Hester rearranged it more comfortably. There was little else she could do.

"Well, Sir Herbert was here the day before," the girl went on. "Naturally, but not through the night." She looked at the ceiling, her vision inward. "He hardly ever stays all night. He's married of course. Ever such a nice lady, his wife, so they say. And seven children. Of course he's a real gentleman, not like Dr. Beck—he's foreign, and that's different isn't it? Not that he isn't very nice too, and always so polite. I never heard a wrong word from him. He quite

187

often stops all night, if he's got a really bad patient. That isn't unusual."

"And other doctors?"

"Dr. Chalmers wasn't here. He usually only comes in the afternoon. He works somewhere else in the mornings. Dr. Didcot was away in Glasgow. And if you mean the students, they hardly ever come in before about nine o'clock." She pulled a face. "If you ask them, they'll say they were studying, or something of the sort, but I have my own ideas about that." She let her breath out in a highly expressive little snort.

"And nurses? I suppose nurses could make mistakes too," Hester pursued it to the end. "What about Mrs. Flaherty?"

"Mrs. Flaherty?" The girl's eyebrows shot up with a mixture of alarm and amusement. "Oh my goodness! I never thought of her. Well—she and Prudence fairly disliked each other." She gave a convulsive little shiver. "I suppose either would have been pleased enough to catch the other out. But Mrs. Flaherty is awful little. Prudence was tall, about two or three inches taller than you, I'd say, and six inches taller than Mrs. Flaherty."

Hester was vaguely disappointed. "Was she here?"

"Yes . . . she was." Her face lit up with a kind of glee and then she was instantly ashamed of it. "I remember clearly because I was with her."

"Where?"

"In the nurses' dormitory. She was telling them off to a standstill." She looked at Hester to gauge how far she dare go with her honesty. She met Hester's eyes, and threw caution to the winds. "Over an hour she was, inspecting everything in sight. I know she had a quarrel with Prudence, because I saw Prudence walk away, and Mrs. Flaherty went to take it out on the nurses in the dormitory. I think she must have got the worst of the argument."

"You saw Prudence that morning?" Hester tried to take the urgency out of her voice in case she precipitated the girl unwittingly into imagining rather than remembering.

188

"Oh yes," she said with certainty.

"Do you know what time?"

"About half past six."

"You must have been one of the last people to see her alive." She saw the girl pale and a mixture of fear and sadness cross her young face. "Have the police asked you about it?"

"Well—not really. They asked me if I saw Dr. Beck and Sir Herbert."

"Did you?"

"I saw Dr. Beck going along the corridor toward the wards. They asked me what he was doing and how he looked. He was just walking, and he looked terrible tired, like 'e'd been up all night—which I suppose he had. He didn't look furious or frightened like he'd just murdered someone, just sad."

"Who else did you see?"

"Lots of people," she said quickly. "There's lots of people around, even at that hour. The chaplain, and Mr. Plumstead—he's the treasurer. Don't know what he was doing here then." She shrugged. "And a gentleman I don't know, but dressed smart, like, with brownish hair. He didn't seem to know his way 'round. He walked into the linen room, then a second later came right out, looking awkward, like he knew he'd made a fool of himself. I reckon he wasn't a doctor. We don't get visiting doctors at that time. And he looked sort of angry, as if he'd been crossed in something. Not furious, just irritated."

She looked at Hester, her face troubled. "Do you think he could be the one? He didn't look like a madman to me, in fact he looked rather nice. Like somebody's brother, if you know what I mean? He probably came to visit a patient, and wasn't allowed in. It happens sometimes, especially if people call at the wrong time."

"That may be what he was," Hester agreed. "Was that before or after you saw Prudence?"

"Before. But he could have waited around, couldn't he?"

"Yes—if he even knew her."

189

"Don't seem very likely, does it," the girl said unhappily. "I reckon it was more likely one of us here. She quarreled something fierce with Mrs. Flaherty. Only last week Mrs. Flaherty swore either Prudence would have to go or she would. I reckoned it was temper, but maybe she meant it." She looked at Hester half hopefully.

"But you said you saw Prudence after the quarrel, then Mrs. Flaherty went to the dormitory, where she stayed for at least an hour," Hester pointed out.

"Oh—yes, so I did. I suppose it can't have been her." She pulled a small face. "Not that I really thought it was, for all that she hated Prudence. Not that she was the only one."

The patient stirred again, and they both stopped and looked at him, but after a muffled groan he sank back into sleep.

"Who else?" Hester prompted.

"Really hated? Well, I suppose Dora Parsons. But she curses at a lot of people, and she's certainly strong enough to have broken her back, never mind strangled her. Have you seen her arms?"

"Yes," Hester admitted with a shiver. But as much as she feared Dora Parsons herself, it was fear of being hurt, not killed. She found it hard to believe sheer ignorant dislike of a woman she believed to have ambitions that were arrogant and misplaced, and to imagine herself superior, was motive for a sane person to commit murder. And for all her coarseness, Dora Parsons was an adequate nurse, rough but not deliberately cruel, tireless and patient enough with the sick. The more Hester thought about it, the less did she think Dora would murder Prudence out of nothing more than hatred.

"Yes, I am sure she has the strength," she went on. "But no reason."

"No, I suppose." She sounded reluctant, but she smiled as she said it. "And I'd better go before Mrs. Flaherty comes back and catches me. Shall I empty the slop pail for you? I'll be quick."

"Yes please. And thank you for the sandwich and the tea."

The girl smiled with sudden brilliance, then blushed, took the pail, and disappeared.

It was a long night, and Hester got little sleep. Her patient dozed fitfully, always aware of his pain, but when daylight came a little before four in the morning his pulse was still strong and he had only the barest flush of fever. Hester was weary but well satisfied, and when Sir Herbert called in at half past seven she told him the news with a sense of achievement.

"Excellent, Miss Latterly." He spoke succinctly, beyond Prendergast's hearing, although he was barely half awake. "Quite excellent. But there is a long way to go yet." He looked at him dubiously, pushing out his lip. "He may develop fever any time in the next seven or eight days, which could yet prove fatal. I wish you to remain with him each night. Mrs. Flaherty can see to his needs during the day." He ignored her temporarily while he examined the patient, and she stepped back and waited. His concentration was total, his brows furrowed, eyes intent while his fingers moved dextrously, gently. He asked one or two questions, more for reassurance of his attention than from a need for information, and he was unconcerned when Prendergast gave few coherent replies, his eyes sunken with shock of the wound and the bleeding.

"Very good," Sir Herbert said at last, stepping back. "You are progressing very well, sir. I expect to see you in full health in a matter of weeks."

"Do you? Do you think so?" Prendergast smiled weakly. "I feel very ill now."

"Of course you do. But that will pass, I assure you. Now I must attend to my other patients. The nurses will care for you. Good day, sir." And with no more than a passing nod to Hester he left, striding along the corridor, shoulders squared, head high.

As soon as she was relieved, Hester also left. She was

barely halfway along the corridor in the direction of the nurses' dormitory when she encountered the imposing figure of Berenice Ross Gilbert. Although in any social circumstance she would have considered herself Lady Ross Gilbert's equal, even if perhaps that opinion had not been shared, in her gray stuff nursing dress, and with her occupation known, she was at every kind of disadvantage, and she was uncomfortably aware of it.

Berenice was dressed splendidly, as usual, her gown a mixture of rusts and golds with a touch of fuchsia pink, and cut to the minute of fashion. She smiled with casual charm, looking straight through Hester, and continued on her way. However, she had only gone a few steps when Sir Herbert came out of one of the doorways.

"Ah!" he said quickly, his face lighting up. "I was just hoping to . . ."

"Good morning, Sir Herbert," Berenice cut across him, her voice brittle and a trifle loud. "Another very pleasant day. How is Mr. Prendergast? I hear you performed a brilliant operation. It is an excellent thing for the reputation of the hospital, and of course for English medicine in general. How did he pass the night? Well?"

Sir Herbert looked a little taken aback. He was facing Berenice with his profile to Hester, whom he had not noticed standing in the shadows a dozen yards away. She was a nurse, so to some extent invisible, like a good domestic servant.

Sir Herbert's eyebrows rose in obvious surprise.

"Yes, he is doing very well so far," he replied. "But it is too early yet for that to mean a great deal. I didn't know you were acquainted with Mr. Prendergast."

"Ah no, my interest is not personal."

"I was going to say that I—" he began again.

"And of course," she cut across him again, "I am concerned with the hospital's reputation and your enhancement of it, Sir Herbert." She smiled fixedly. "Of course this whole wretched business of poor Nurse—whatever her name was."

"Barrymore? Really, Berenice . . ."

"Yes, of course, Barrymore. And we have another Crimean nurse, so I hear—Miss—er . . ." She half turned toward Hester and indicated her.

"Ah—yes." Sir Herbert looked startled and slightly out of composure. "Yes—it seems like a fortunate acquisition—so far. A very competent young woman. Thank you for your kind words, Lady Ross Gilbert." Unconsciously he pulled down the front of his jacket, straightening it a little. "Most generous of you. Now if you would excuse me, I have other patients I must attend. Charming to see you."

Berenice smiled bleakly. "Naturally. Good morning, Sir Herbert."

Hester moved at last toward the dormitory and the opportunity for an hour or two's rest. She was tired enough to sleep even through the constant comings and goings, the chatter, the movement of others, even though she longed for privacy. The peace of her own small lodging room seemed a haven it never had previously, when she had compared it with her father's home with its spaciousness, warmth, and familiar elegance.

She did not sleep long and woke with a start, her mind frantically trying to recall some impression she had gained. It was important, it meant something, and she could not grasp it.

An elderly nurse with a bald patch on one side of her head was standing a few feet away, staring at her.

"That there rozzer wants yer," she said flatly. "The one wi' the eyes like a ferret. You'd better look sharp. 'E ain't one to cross." And having delivered her message she took herself off without glancing backwards to see whether Hester obeyed or not.

Blinking, her eyes sore, her head heavy, Hester climbed out of the cot (she did not think of it as hers), pulled on her dress, and straightened her hair. Then she set off to find Jeavis; from the woman's description it could only be Jeavis who wanted her, not Evan.

She saw him standing outside Sir Herbert Stanhope's

room, looking along the corridor toward her. Presumably he knew where the dormitory was, and thus expected her the way she came.

"Morning, miss," he said when she was within a few feet of him. He looked her up and down with curiosity. "You'd be Miss Latterly?"

"Yes, Inspector. What may I do for you?" She said it more coolly than she had intended, but something in his manner irritated her.

"Oh yes. You were not here when Miss Barrymore met her death," he began unnecessarily. "But I understand you served in the Crimea? Perhaps you were acquainted with her there?"

"Yes, slightly." She was about to add that she knew nothing of relevance, or she would have told him without his asking, then she realized that it was just possible she might learn something from him if she prolonged the conversation. "We served side by side on at least one occasion." She looked into his dark, almost browless eyes, and unwittingly thought of the bald nurse's mention of a ferret. It was cruel, but not entirely inappropriate—a dark brown, highly intelligent ferret. Perhaps it was not such a good idea to try misleading him after all.

"Difficult to tell what a woman looked like," he said thoughtfully, "when you haven't seen her alive. They tell me she was quite handsome. Would you agree with that, Miss Latterly?"

"Yes." She was surprised. It seemed so irrelevant. "Yes, she had a very—very individual face, most appealing. But she was rather tall."

Jeavis unconsciously squared his shoulders. "Indeed. I assume she must have had admirers?"

Hester avoided his eyes deliberately. "Oh yes. Are you thinking such a person killed her?"

"Never mind what we're thinking," he replied smugly. "You just answer my questions the best you can."

Hester seethed with annoyance, and hid it with difficulty. Pompous little man!

194

"I never knew her to encourage anyone," she said between stiff lips. "She didn't flirt. I don't think she knew how to."

"Hmm . . ." He bit his lip. "Be that as it may, did she ever mention a Mr. Geoffrey Taunton to you? Think carefully now. I need an exact, honest answer."

Hester controlled herself with an intense effort. She wanted to slap him. But this conversation would be worth it if she learned something, however small. She gazed back at him with wide eyes.

"What does he look like, Inspector?"

"It doesn't matter what he looks like, miss," he said irritably. "What I want to know is, did she mention him?"

"She had a photograph," Hester lied without compunction. At least it was a lie in essence. Prudence had had a photograph, certainly, but it was one of her father, and Hester knew that.

Jeavis's interest was quickened. "Did she, now. What was he like, the man in this photograph?"

This was no use. "Well—er . . ." She screwed up her face as if in a concentrated effort to find the right words.

"Come on, miss. You must have some idea!" Jeavis said urgently. "Was he coarse or refined? Handsome or homely? Was he clean-shaven, a mustache, whiskers, a beard? What was he like?"

"Oh he was fine-looking," she prevaricated, hoping he would forget his caution. "Sort of—well—it's hard to say. . . ."

"Oh yes."

She was afraid if she did not give him a satisfactory answer soon he would lose interest. "She had it with her all the time."

Jeavis abandoned patience. "Was he tall, straight hair, regular features, smallish sort of mouth, light eyes, very level?"

"Yes! Yes, that's who he was, exactly," she said, affecting relief. "Is that him?"

"Never you mind. So she carried that with her, did she?

195

Sounds like she knew him pretty close. I suppose she got letters?"

"Oh yes, whenever the post came from England. But I didn't think Mr. Taunton lived in London."

"He didn't," he agreed. "But there are trains, and it's easy enough to come and go. Trip to Ealing only takes an hour or less. Easy enough to get in and out of the hospital. I'll have to have a good deal closer talk with Mr. Taunton." He shook his head darkly. "Nice-looking gentleman like that might have other ladies to set their caps at. Funny he chose to go on with her, even when she worked in a place like this and seemed set to continue with it."

"Love is funny, Inspector," Hester said tartly. "And while a great many people marry for other reasons, there are a few who insist on marrying for love. Perhaps Mr. Taunton was one of them?"

"You've got a very sharp tongue in your head, Miss Latterly," Jeavis said with a perceptive look at her. "Was Miss Barrymore like that too? Independent, and a bit waspish, was she?"

Hester was staring. It was not a pleasing description.

"Those would not have been my choice of words, Inspector, but essentially my meaning, yes. But I don't see how she could have been killed by a jealous woman. The sort of person who would have been in love with Mr. Taunton surely would not have had the strength to strangle her. Prudence was tall, and not weak by any means. Wouldn't there have been a fight? And such a person would be marked as well, scratched or bruised at least?"

"Oh no," Jeavis denied quickly. "There wasn't a struggle. It must have been very quick. Just powerful hands on her throat." He made a quick, harsh gesture, like closing a double fist, and his lips tightened with revulsion. "And it was all over. She might have scratched a hand or so, or even once at the neck or face. But there was no blood in any of her fingernails, nor anything else, no other scratches or bruises on her. There was no fight. Whoever it was, she was not expecting it."

"Of course you are right, Inspector." Hester concealed her triumph beneath humility and downcast eyes. Did Monk know there was no fight? It would be something to tell him that he might not have learned for himself. She refused to think of the human meaning of it.

"If it was a woman," Jeavis went on, brows drawn down. "It was a strong woman, one with powerful hands, like a good horse rider perhaps. It certainly wasn't any fancy lady who never held anything bigger than a cake fork in her fingers. Mind, surprise counts for a lot. Brave, was she, Miss Barrymore?"

Suddenly it was real again, Prudence's death.

"Yes—yes she was brave," Hester said with a catch in her voice. She forced memories out of her mind: Prudence's face in the lamplight, the surgeon's saw in her hand. Prudence sitting up in bed in Scutari, studying medical papers by candlelight.

"Hmm," Jeavis said thoughtfully, unaware of her emotion. "Wonder why she never screamed. You'd think she would, wouldn't you? Would you scream, Miss Latterly?"

Hester blinked away sudden tears.

"I don't know," she said honestly. "I should feel so inadequate."

Jeavis's eyes widened.

"Bit foolish, that, isn't it, miss? After all, if someone attacks you, you would be inadequate to defend yourself, wouldn't you? Miss Barrymore was, right enough. Doesn't seem there's so much noise going on here that a good scream wouldn't be heard."

"Then whoever attacked her was very quick," Hester said sharply, angry with him for his words and for the dismissive tone of them. Her emotions were too raw, too close to the surface. "Which suggests someone strong," she added unnecessarily.

"Quite so," he agreed. "Thank you for your cooperation, miss. She had an admirer when she was in the Crimea. That was really all I wished to know from you. You may continue in your duties."

"I wasn't at my duties," she said angrily. "I was asleep. I had been up with a patient all night."

"Oh, is that so." A flicker of oblique humor lit his eyes for an instant. "I'm so glad I wasn't taking you away from anything important."

Furious as she was, she liked him rather better for that than if he had become obsequious again.

When she saw Monk the following day in Mecklenburg Square, with all its hideous memories of murder, guilt, and the unknown, there was a tense, oppressive heat, and she was glad of the shade of the trees. They were walking side by side, quite casually, he carrying a stick as if it were a stroll after luncheon, she in a plain blue muslin dress, its wide skirts trailing on the grass at the edge of the path. She had already told him of her encounter with Jeavis.

"I knew Geoffrey Taunton was there," he said when she had finished. "He admitted that himself. I suppose he knew he was seen—by nurses, if no one else."

"Oh." She felt unreasonably crushed.

"But it is most interesting that there were no marks on her except the bruises on her throat," he went on. "I did not know that. Jeavis will give me nothing at all, which I suppose is natural. I wouldn't, in his place. But apparently he didn't tell Evan that either." Unconsciously he quickened his pace, even though they were merely walking in circles around the edge of the square. "That means whoever did it was powerful. A weak person could not kill her without a struggle. And probably also someone she knew, and wasn't expecting it from. Most interesting. It raises one most important question."

She refused to ask. Then quite suddenly she perceived it, and spoke even as the thought formed in her mind. "Was it premeditated? Did he, or she, go with the intention of killing her—or did it arise from something that Prudence said, without realizing what it meant, and thus precipitated a sudden attack with no warning?"

He looked at her with surprise and sudden bright, grudging appreciation.

"Precisely." He swiped at a loose stone on the path with his stick, and missed. He swore, and caught it the second time, sending it twenty yards through the air.

"Geoffrey Taunton?" she asked.

"Less likely." He caught another stone, more successfully this time. "She was no threat to him that we know of. And I cannot imagine what such a threat could be. No, I think if he killed her, it would be in hot blood, as a result of a quarrel and his temper finally snapping. They quarreled that morning but she was still alive at the end of it. He might have gone back later, but it seems unlikely." He looked at her curiously. "What do you make of Kristian Beck?"

They passed a nursemaid with a small child in a sailor's suit. Somewhere in the distance there was the sound of an organ-grinder and the music was familiar.

"I have seen very little of him," she answered. "But I like what I have seen."

"I don't care whether you like him or not," he said acidly. "I want to know if you think he could have killed Prudence."

"You think there was something unnatural about his patient's death that night? I doubt it. Lots of people die unexpectedly. You think they're recovering, and suddenly they don't. Anyway, how would Prudence know anything was wrong? If he had made a mistake in front of her, she would have told him and corrected it. He wasn't operated on that night."

"Nothing to do with that night." He took her elbow to guide her across the path out of the way of a man walking briskly about some business.

If it had been a protective gesture she would have welcomed it, but it was officious, impatient instead, as if she were unable to take care of herself. She pulled away sharply.

"She knew something which he begged her not to take to

the authorities, and she refused him," he went on regardless.

"That doesn't sound like Prudence as I knew her," she said instantly. "It must have been something very serious. She loathed authorities and had the utmost contempt for them. Anyone has who's been with the army! Are you sure you have that correctly?"

"The quarrel was overheard," he replied. "She said she would go to the authorities, and Beck pleaded with her not to. She was adamant."

"But you don't know what about?" she pressed.

"No of course I don't." He glared at her. "If I knew, I'd tackle Beck over it. Probably be able to tell Jeavis and have him arrested, which would hardly please Callandra. I think her main purpose in employing me is to prove it was not Beck. She holds him in great regard."

She was spoiling for a quarrel, but this was not the time; there was too much else more important than new emotions.

"Are you afraid it is he?" she said quietly.

He did not look at her. "I don't know. The field does not seem very wide. Did she quarrel with any of the nurses? I don't imagine she was popular, if her ideas of reform are anything like yours. I expect she infuriated several of the doctors. You certainly did, in your short stay in office."

Her good resolution died instantly.

"If you infuriate a doctor, he dismisses you!" she replied sharply. "It doesn't make sense to kill someone when there is such an easy way, without any risk to yourself, to get rid of her and at the same time make her suffer!"

He grunted. "You have a concise and logical mind. Which is useful—but unattractive. I wonder if she was the same? What about the nurses? Would they have disliked her equally?"

She felt hurt, which was ridiculous. She already knew he liked women to be feminine, vulnerable, and mysterious. She remembered how he had been charmed by Imogen, her sister-in-law. Although as she knew very well, under

Imogen's gentle manner there was no foolish or yielding woman, just one who knew how to comport herself with grace and allure. That was an art she was devoid of, and at this moment its absence was stupidly painful.

"Well?" he demanded. "You've seen them at work, you must have an idea."

"Some of them worshiped her," she said swiftly, her chin held high, her step more determined. "Others, fairly naturally, were jealous. You cannot succeed without running into risk of jealousy. You should know that!"

"Jealous enough to call it hatred?" He was being logical, unaware of any feelings.

"Possibly," she said, equally reasonably. "There is a very strong large woman called Dora Parsons who certainly loathed her. Whether it was enough to have killed her, I have no idea. Seems extreme—unless there was some specific issue."

"Had Prudence the power to have this woman dismissed if she were incompetent, or drunk—or if she stole?" He looked at her hopefully.

"I imagine so." She picked up her skirts delicately as they passed a patch of long grass by the path. "Prudence worked closely with Sir Herbert. He spoke very highly of her to me. I imagine he would take her word for such a thing." She let her skirts fall again. "Certainly Dora Parsons is the sort of woman who could be very easily replaced. There are thousands like her in London."

"And very few indeed like Prudence Barrymore," he finished the thought. "And presumably several more like Dora Parsons even within the Royal Free Hospital. So that thought is hardly conclusive."

They walked in silence for a while, absorbed in their own thoughts. They passed a man with a dog, and two small boys, one with a hoop, the other with a spinning top on a string, looking for a level place in the path to pull it. A young woman looked Monk up and down admiringly; her escort sulked. At length it was Hester who spoke.

"Have you learned anything?"

"What?"

"Have you learned anything?" she repeated. "You must have been doing something over the last week. What is the result?"

Suddenly he grinned broadly, as if the interrogation amused him.

"I suppose you have as much right to know as I," he conceded. "I have been looking into Mr. Geoffrey Taunton and Miss Nanette Cuthbertson. She is a more determined young woman than I first supposed. And she seems to have had the most powerful motive of all for wishing to be rid of Prudence. Prudence stood between her and love, respectability, and the family status she wishes for more than anything else. Time is growing short for her—very short." They had momentarily stopped under the trees and he put his hands in his pockets. "She is twenty-eight, even though she is still remarkably pretty. I imagine panic may be rising inside her—enough to do violence. If only I could work out how she achieved it," he said thoughtfully. "She is not as tall as Prudence by some two inches, and of slight build. And even with her head in the academic clouds, Prudence cannot surely have been so insensitive as to have been unaware of Nanette's emotions."

Hester wanted to snap back that twenty-eight was hardly ancient—and of course she was still pretty. And might well remain so for another twenty years—or more. But she felt a ridiculous tightening in her throat, and found the words remained unspoken. It hardly mattered if twenty-eight were old or not—if it seemed old to him. You cannot argue someone out of such a view.

"Hester?" He frowned at her.

Hester stared straight ahead and began walking again.

"She might have been," she replied briskly. "Perhaps she valued people for their worth—their humor, or courage, integrity, their intelligence, compassion, good companionship, imagination, honor, any of a dozen things that don't suddenly cease the day you turn thirty."

"For Heaven's sake, don't be so idiotic," he said in

amazement, striding along beside her. "We're not talking about worth. We're talking about Nanette Cuthbertson being in love and wanting to marry Geoffrey Taunton and have a family. That's got nothing to do with intelligence or courage or humor. What's the matter with you? Stop walking so fast or you'll fall over something! She wants children—not a halo. She's a perfectly ordinary woman. I would have thought Prudence would have had sufficient wit to see that. But talking to you—perhaps she wouldn't. You don't seem to have."

Hester opened her mouth to argue, but there was no logical answer, and she found herself at a loss for words.

He strode on in silence, still swiping occasionally at the odd stone on the path.

"Is that all you've done?" she said finally.

"What?"

"Discover that Nanette had a good motive, but no means, so far as you can find out."

"No of course it isn't." He hit another stone. "I've looked into Prudence's past, her nursing skills, her war record, anything I can think of. It's all very interesting, very admirable, but none of it suggests a specific motive for murdering her—or anyone who might have wished to. I am somewhat hampered by not having any authority."

"Well whose fault is that?" she said sharply, then immediately wished she had not, but was damned if she was going to apologize.

They walked for a further hundred yards in silence until they were back at Doughty Street, where she excused herself, pointing out that she'd had very little sleep and would be required to sit up all night with Mr. Prendergast again. They parted coolly, she back to the hospital, he she knew not where.

7

EVERYTHING THAT MONK had learned about Prudence Barrymore showed a passionate, intelligent, single-minded woman bent on caring for the sick to the exclusion of all else. While exciting his admiration, she had almost certainly not been an easy woman to know, either as a friend or as a member of one's family. No one had mentioned whether or not she had the least sense of humor. Humor was at times Hester's saving grace. No, that was not entirely true: he would never forget her courage, her will to fight for him, even when it seemed the battle was pointless and he not worth anyone's effort. But she could still be insufferable to spend time with.

He was walking along the street under a leaden, gray sky. Any moment there would be a summer downpour. It would drench the pedestrians, bounce off the busy thoroughfare, washing horse droppings into the gutter and sending the water swirling in huge puddles across the street. Even the wind smelled heavy and wet.

He was in the Gray's Inn Road going toward the hospital with the intention of seeing Evan again to ask him more about Prudence Barrymore's character, if he were willing to share any information. And in conscience, he might not be. Monk disliked having to ask him. In Jeavis's place he would not have told anyone else, and would verbally have flayed a junior who did.

And yet he did not think Jeavis's ability equal to this case, which was an opinion for which he had no grounds. He knew his own successes since the accident, and some of them were precarious enough and owed much to the help of others, especially Hester. As to cases before the accident, he had only written records on which to rely. They all pointed to his brilliance, anger at injustice, impatience with hesitation or timidity, and gave little credit to anyone else. But since they were largely in his own handwriting, how accurate were they?

What was the memory that had teased at the edge of his mind during the train journey back from Little Ealing? He and Runcorn had been on a case together a long time ago, when Monk was new to the force. He had struggled to recapture something more, any clue as to what the case had been, but nothing came, only a sense of anger, a deep, white-hot rage that was like a shield against—against what?

It was beginning to rain, huge warm drops falling faster and faster. Somewhere far away, audible even above the clatter of wheels, came the rumble of thunder. A man hurried past him, fumbling to open up his black umbrella. A newsboy stuffed his papers hastily into a canvas satchel without ceasing his cries. Monk turned up his coat collar and hunched forward.

That was it. The press! His rage had protected him from any vulnerability to the clamor for an arrest, and the pressure from superiors. He had not cared what anyone else thought or felt, all that mattered to him was his own overpowering emotion over the crime itself, the fury of it consumed him. But what was the crime? Nothing in his memory gave any clue to follow. Search as he could, it was a blank.

It was intensely frustrating. And that feeling was familiar. He had been frustrated then. The helplessness underlying the anger all the time. There had been one blind alley after another. He knew the upsurge of hope, the anticipation, and then the disappointment, the hollowness of failure. His fury had been at least partially directed at Runcorn because he was too timid, too careful of the sensibilities of witnesses. Monk had wished to press them regardless, not for cruelty's sake but because they were guarding their own petty little secrets when a far greater tragedy loomed over them with its brooding evil.

But what evil? All he could recall was a sense of darkness and a weight oppressing him, and always the rage.

The rain was heavy now, soaking through his trousers, making his ankles cold, and running down the back of his neck. He shivered violently, and quickened his pace. The water was rising in the gutter and swirling down the drains.

He needed to know. He needed to understand himself, the man he had been in those years, whether his anger was justified or merely the violence in his own nature finding an excuse—emotionally and intellectually dishonest. That was something he despised utterly.

And there was no excuse for self-indulgence at the expense of his task for Callandra. He had no idea who had murdered Prudence Barrymore, or why. There were too many possibilities. It could have been anything from a long hatred, frustration, or rejection such as that which must be felt by Geoffrey Taunton, or a mixture of the panic and jealousy which must have affected Nanette Cuthbertson as time passed by and still Geoffrey waited for Prudence and she kept him at bay, neither accepting him nor letting him go.

Or it could have been another lover, a doctor or hospital governor, a quarrel or an explosion of jealousy; or the blackmail that, according to Evan, Jeavis suspected of Kristian Beck.

Or if Prudence Barrymore were as opinionated, officious, and authoritarian as had been suggested, then it might as easily have been merely some nurse driven beyond the bounds of self-control by the constant abrasion to her temper and esteem. Perhaps one gibe, one criticism, had been the final straw, and someone had at last lashed out?

He was almost at the hospital entrance.

He ran the final few yards and climbed the steps two at a time to be in the shelter at last, then stood in the entrance hall dripping pools of water onto the floor. He turned down his collar and smoothed his lapels and pushed his fingers through his hair in unconscious vanity. He wanted to see Evan alone, but he could not wait for an opportunity to present itself. He would have to look for him and hope he found him without Jeavis. He set out, still trailing water.

As it happened he was unfortunate. He had planned using the excuse that he was seeking Callandra, if anyone asked him his business. But he almost bumped into Jeavis and Evan as he was going along the corridor and they were standing near the laundry chute.

Jeavis looked up in surprise, at first suspecting a governor from Monk's dress, then recognizing his face, and his own expression darkening in suspicion.

"Hello—what are you doing here, Monk?" He smiled bleakly. "Not sick, are you?" He looked at Monk's rain-darkened coat and wet footprints, but added nothing.

Monk hesitated, considering a lie, but the thought of excusing himself to Jeavis, even obliquely, was intolerable.

"I have been retained by Lady Callandra Daviot, as I daresay you know," he answered. "Is that the chute down to the laundry room?"

Evan looked acutely uncomfortable. Monk was tearing his loyalties and he knew it. Jeavis's face was hard. Monk had driven him onto the defensive. Perhaps that was clumsy. On the other hand, it might only have precipitated the inevitable.

"Of course it is," he said coldly. He raised his pale brows. "Is this the first time you've seen it? A bit slow for you, Monk."

"Don't see what I can learn from it," Monk replied edgily. "If there were much, you would have made an arrest already."

"If I'd found any evidence anywhere, I'd have made an arrest," Jeavis said with an odd flash of humor. "But I don't suppose that'll stop you padding around behind me, all the same!"

"Or the occasional place before you," Monk added.

Jeavis shot him a glance. "That's as may be. But you're welcome to peer down that chute all you wish. You'll see nothing but a laundry basket at the bottom. And at the top, there's a long corridor with few lights and half a dozen doors, but none along this stretch except Dr. Beck's office, and the treasurer's office over there. Make what you like out of that."

Monk looked around, gazing up and down the length of the corridor. The only definite thing he concluded was that if Prudence had been strangled here beside the chute, then she could not have cried out without being heard had there been anyone in Beck's office or the treasurer's. The other doors seemed to be far enough away to be out of earshot. Similarly, if she had been killed in one of the other rooms, then she must have been carried some distance along the open corridor, which might have posed a risk. Hospital corridors were never entirely deserted, as those in a house or an office might be. However, he was not going to say so to Jeavis.

"Interesting, isn't it?" Jeavis said dryly, and Monk knew his thoughts were precisely the same. "Looks unpleasantly like the good Dr. Beck, don't you think?"

"Or the treasurer," Monk agreed. "Or someone who acted on the spur of the moment, right here, and so swiftly and with such surprise she had no time to cry out."

Jeavis pulled a face and smiled.

"Seems to me like a woman who would have fought," he said with a little shake of his head. "Tall, too. Not weakly, by all accounts. Mind, some of the other nurses are built like cart horses." He looked at Monk with bland, challenging amusement. "Seems she had a tongue as sharp as one o' the surgeon's knives and didn't spare them if she thought they slacked in their duty. A very different sort of woman, Nurse Barrymore." Then he added under his breath, "Thank God."

"But good enough at her job to be justified in her comments," Monk said thoughtfully. "Or they'd have got rid of her, don't you think?" He avoided looking at Evan.

"Oh yes," Jeavis agreed without hesitation. "She seems to have been that, all right. Don't think anyone would have put up with her otherwise. At least, not those that disliked her. And to be fair, that wasn't everyone. Seems she was something of a heroine to some. And Sir Herbert speaks well enough of her."

A nurse with a pile of clean sheets approached and they moved aside for her.

"What about Beck?" Monk asked when she had gone.

"Oh, him too. But then, if he killed her, he's hardly going to tell us that he couldn't abide her, is he?"

"What do other people say?"

"Well now, Mr. Monk, I wouldn't want to rob you of your livelihood by doing your work for you, now would I?" Jeavis said, looking Monk straight in the eyes. "If I did that, how could you go to Lady Callandra and expect to be paid?" And with a smile he glanced meaningfully at Evan and walked away down the corridor.

Evan looked at Monk and shrugged, then followed dutifully. Jeavis had already stopped a dozen yards away and was waiting for him.

Monk had little else to do here. He had no authority to question anyone, and he resisted the temptation to find Hester. Any unnecessary association with him might lessen her ability to question people without arousing suspicion and destroy her usefulness.

He had the geography of the place firmly in his mind. There was nothing more to learn standing here.

He was on his way out again, irritated and short-tempered, when he saw Callandra crossing the foyer. She looked tired and her hair was even more unruly than usual. The characteristic humor had left her face and there was an air of anxiety about her quite out of her customary spirit.

She was almost up to Monk before she looked at him

clearly enough to recognize him, then her expression changed, but he could see the deliberate effort it cost her.

Was it simply the death of a nurse, one as outstanding as Prudence Barrymore, which grieved her so deeply? Was it the haste with which it had followed on the heels of the tragedy of Julia Penrose and her sister? Again he had that appallingly helpless feeling of caring for someone, admiring her and being truly grateful, and totally unable to help her pain. It was like the past all over again, his mentor who had helped him on his first arrival in London, and the tragedy that had struck him down and begun Monk's career in the police. And now, as then, he could do nothing. It was another emotion from the past crowding the present and tearing at him with all its old power.

"Hello William." Callandra greeted him politely enough, but there was no pleasure in her voice, no lift at all. "Are you looking for me?" There was a flicker of anxiety as she said it, as if she feared his answer.

He longed to be able to comfort her, but he knew without words that whatever distressed her so deeply was private and she would speak of it without prompting if ever she wished him to know. The kindest thing he could do now would be to pretend he had not noticed.

"Actually I was hoping to see Evan alone," he said ruefully. "But I ran into Jeavis straightaway. I'm on my way out now. I wish I knew more about Prudence Barrymore. Many people have told me their views of her, and yet I feel I am still missing something essential. Hester remembers her, you know. . . ."

Callandra's face tightened, but she said nothing.

A student doctor strode past, looking harassed.

"And I went to see Miss Nightingale. She spoke of Prudence very highly. And of Hester too."

Callandra smiled a trifle wanly.

"Did you learn anything new?"

"Nothing that throws any light on why she might have been killed. It seems she was an excellent nurse, even brilliant. Her father did not exaggerate her abilities, or her ded-

210

ication to medicine. But I wonder—" He stopped abruptly. Perhaps his thought was unfair and would hurt Callandra unnecessarily.

"You wonder what?" She could not leave it. Her face darkened, and the tiredness and the concern were there.

He had no idea what she feared, so he could not choose to avoid it.

"I wonder if her knowledge was as great as she thought it was. She might have misunderstood something, misjudged—"

Callandra's eyes cleared. "It is a possibility," she said slowly. "Although I cannot yet see how it could lead to murder. But pursue it, William. It seems to be all we have at present. Please keep me informed if you learn anything."

They nodded briefly to the chaplain as he passed, muttering to himself.

"Of course," Monk agreed. And after bidding her goodbye he went out through the foyer into the wet streets. It had stopped raining, and the footpath and the roadway were glistening in the brightness of the sun. The air was filled with myriad smells, most of them warm, heavy, and not very pleasant: horse droppings, overflowing drains unable to take the downpour. Rubbish swirled along the gutters in the torrent. Horses clattered by, flanks steaming, vehicle wheels sending up showers of water.

Where could he find out Prudence's real ability? No one in the hospital would give him an unbiased opinion, nor would her family, and certainly not Geoffrey Taunton. He had already learned all he could expect to from Florence Nightingale. There was no recognized body that passed judgment on the abilities of nurses, no school or college of training.

He might find an army surgeon who had known her, for whatever his opinion would be worth on the subject. They must have been hurried, always tired, overwhelmed by the sheer numbers of the sick and injured. How much would they remember of any individual nurse and her medical knowledge? Had there even been time for anything beyond the most hasty treatment, little more than amputation, cauterization of the stump, stitching, splinting, and prayer?

He was walking along the fast-drying pavement, ignoring the passersby and going generally southward without any destination in mind.

Had she thought to improve her knowledge since leaving the Crimea? How would she have gone about it? No medical school accepted women. The idea was unthinkable. What private study was there? What might she learn without a teacher?

Some hazy memory of his own youth intruded into his mind. When he had first come down to London from Northumberland, desperate to better himself, absorb every piece of knowledge he could, and arm himself against a busy, impatient, and suspicious world, he had gone to the reading room of the British Museum.

Hastily he turned on his heel and walked back the twenty yards to Guildford Street and increased his pace past the Foundling Hospital toward Russell Square, then Montague Street and the British Museum. Once inside he went straight to the reading room. Here she would find all manner of books and papers if she were really as thirsty for learning as her father had said.

He approached the attendant with a sense of excitement that was wildly out of proportion to the importance of his quest.

"Excuse me, sir, may I interrupt you for a little of your time?"

"Good afternoon, sir. Of course you may," the man replied with a civil smile. He was small and very dark. "How may I be of service to you? If there is something you wish to find . . ." His eye roamed in unconcealed awe around the vast expanse of books both visible and invisible. All the world's knowledge was here, and the miracle of it still amazed him. Monk could see it in his eyes.

"I am inquiring on behalf of the friends and family of a young lady whom I believe used to study here," Monk began, more or less truthfully.

"Oh dear." The man's face darkened. "Oh dear. You speak, sir, as if she were deceased."

"I am afraid she is. But as so often happens, those who mourn her wish to know anything they can of her. It is all there is left."

"Of course. Yes, of course." The man nodded several times. "Yes, I do understand. But people do not always leave their names, you know, particularly if it is newspapers and periodicals that they come to read. Or the sort of thing young ladies usually seek—I'm afraid."

"This young lady was tall, of a determined and intelligent manner, and would in all likelihood be plainly dressed, perhaps in blue or gray, and with few, if any, hoops in her skirts."

"Ah." The man's face lightened. "I think I may know the young lady you mean. Would she by any chance have been interested in medical books and papers? A most remarkable person, most serious-minded. Always very pleasant, she was, except to those who interrupted her unnecessarily and made light of her intention." He nodded quickly. "I do recall her being very brisk indeed with a young gentleman who was rather persistent in his attentions, shall we say?"

"That would be she." Monk felt a sudden elation. "She studied medical texts, you say?"

"Oh indeed yes; most diligent, she was. A very serious person." He looked up at Monk. "A trifle daunting, if you know what I mean, that a young lady should be so intent. I assumed, perhaps incorrectly, that someone in her family suffered a disease and she thought to learn as much of it as possible." His face fell. "Now it seems I was wrong and it was she herself. I am most deeply sorry. For all her solemnity, I rather took to her." He said it with a slight air of apology, as if it needed some explaining. "There was something in her that . . . oh well. I am very sorry to know it. How may I help you, sir? I have no recollection of what she read now, I am afraid. But perhaps I can look. It was very general . . ."

"No—no, that is not necessary, thank you," Monk declined. He had what he wished. "You have been most generous. Thank you, sir, for your time and your courtesy. Good day to you."

"Good day, Mr. er—good day, sir."

And Monk left with more knowledge than when he went in but no wiser, and with a feeling of success which had no basis at all in fact.

Hester also observed Callandra, but with a woman's eye and a far greater and more subtle sensitivity as to the cause of her distress. Only something deeply personal could trouble her so much. She could not be afraid for herself, surely? Jeavis would not suspect her of having murdered Prudence; she had no possible reason. And Monk had made no secret that it was Callandra who had hired him to investigate further.

Could it be that she knew, or thought she knew, who the murderer was, and feared for her own safety? It seemed unlikely. If she knew something, surely she would have told Monk immediately and taken steps to guard herself.

Hester was still turning over unsatisfactory possibilities in her mind when she was sent for to assist Kristian Beck. Mr. Prendergast was recovering well and no longer required her presence through the night. She was tired from too little sleep, the uncertainty of not being able to rest until she woke naturally.

Kristian Beck said nothing, but she knew from the occasional expression in his eyes that he was aware how weary she was, and he merely smiled at her occasional hesitations. He did not even criticize her when she dropped an instrument and had to reach down and pick it up, wipe it clean and then pass it to him.

When they were finished she was embarrassed at her ineptitude and eager to leave, but she could not forsake the opportunity to observe him further. He also was tired, and he was far too intelligent to be unaware of Jeavis's suspicions of him. It is at such times that people betray them-

214

selves: feelings are too raw to hide and there is no strength for the extra guard upon thought.

"I do not hold a great deal of hope for him," Kristian said to her quietly, regarding the patient. "But we have done all we can."

"Do you wish me to sit up with him?" she asked out of duty. She was dreading his reply.

But she need not have been worried. He smiled—a brief, illuminating, and gentle gesture. "No. No, Mrs. Flaherty will assign someone. You should sleep."

"But—"

"You must learn to let go, Miss Latterly." He shook his head very slightly. "If you do not, you will exhaust yourself—and then whom can you help? Surely the Crimea taught you that the first rule of caring for others is that you must maintain your own strength, and that if you come to the limit of your own resources your judgment will be affected." His eyes did not leave her face. "And the sick deserve the best you can give. Neither skill nor compassion are enough; you must also have wisdom."

"Of course you are right," she agreed. "Perhaps I was losing my sense of proportion."

A flash of humor crossed his face. "It is not hard to do. Come." And he led the way out of the theater, holding the door open for her. They were in the corridor, walking side by side in silence, when they almost bumped into Callandra as she came out of one of the wards.

She stopped abruptly, the color rushing up her cheeks. There was no apparent reason she should have been flustered, and yet it seemed she was. Hester drew breath to say something, then realized that Callandra was looking only at Kristian; she was scarcely aware of Hester to his left and half a step behind.

"Oh—good morning—Doctor," Callandra said hastily, trying to regain her composure.

He looked a little puzzled. "Good morning, Lady Callandra." His voice was soft and he spoke the words very distinctly, as if he liked her name on his tongue. He frowned. "Is all well?"

"Oh yes," she replied. Then she realized how ridiculous that was, in the circumstances. She smiled, but the effort it cost her was plain to Hester. "As good as we may hope, with police all over the place, I suppose. They do not seem to have achieved anything."

"I doubt they would tell us if they had," Kristian said ruefully. Then he gave a thin answering smile, full of doubt and self-mockery. "I'm sure they suspect me! Inspector Jeavis keeps on asking me about having quarreled with poor Nurse Barrymore. I've finally remembered it was over a mistake she felt one of the student doctors had made, which I overruled. It makes one wonder just what was overheard, and by whom." He shook his head a little. "I never before worried greatly what people thought of me, but now I confess it is in my mind more and more of the time."

Callandra did not look directly at him, and the color was high in her cheeks. "You cannot govern your life by what you fear others may think of you. If—if what you are doing is what you believe to be right—they will have to think as they please." She took a deep breath and then said nothing.

Both Hester and Kristian waited for her to continue, but she did not. Left as it was it sounded bare, and a little trite, not like Callandra at all.

"Does . . ." She looked at Kristian directly. "Does Jeavis disturb you?" This time her eyes searched his face.

"I dislike being suspected," he answered frankly. "But I know the man is only doing his duty. I wish I had some idea what actually happened to poor Nurse Barrymore, but hard as I think, nothing comes to me."

"There are innumerable reasons why someone might have killed her," Callandra said with sudden ferocity. "A rejected lover, a jealous woman, an envious nurse, a mad or disaffected patient, all sorts of people." She finished a little breathlessly, and without looking at Hester.

"I expect Jeavis will have thought of those things too."

Kristian pulled a slight face. His eyes never left Callandra's. "I hope he is pursuing them with equal diligence. Do you wish to speak to me about something? Or did we merely bump into you?"

"Just . . . chance," Callandra replied. "I am—on my way to see the chaplain."

Kristian bowed very slightly and excused himself, leaving Hester and Callandra alone in the corridor. Apparently without realizing it, Callandra watched him until he turned the corner into a ward and disappeared, then she looked back at Hester.

"How are you, my dear?" she asked with a sudden gentleness in her voice. "You look very tired." She herself looked exhausted. Her skin was pale and her hair wilder than ever, as if she had run her fingers through it distractedly.

Hester entirely dismissed her own feelings. There was obviously some deep trouble in Callandra and her whole concern was how to help. She was uncertain as to whether she should even acknowledge that she was aware of it, much less ask what it was. Something in Callandra's manner made her feel it was private, and in all possibility that was part of its burden.

She made herself assume a casual expression.

"I'm tired at the moment," she acknowledged. There was no point in a lie; it would be unbearably patronizing. "But the work is most rewarding. Sir Herbert really is a brilliant surgeon. He has not only skill but courage."

"Yes indeed," Callandra agreed with a flash of enthusiasm. "I hear he is high in line for appointment as medical adviser to someone in the Royal household—I forget whom."

"No wonder he is looking pleased with himself," Hester said immediately. "But I daresay it is well deserved. Still, it is a great honor."

"Indeed." Callandra's face darkened again. "Hester, have you seen William lately? Do you know how he is doing—if he has learned anything . . . pertinent?" There was an edge

217

to her voice and she looked at Hester with a nervousness she failed to conceal.

"I haven't seen him for a day or two," Hester replied, wishing she knew what better to say. What troubled Callandra so much? Usually she was a woman of deep sensitivity, of empathy and a great will to fight, but for all that, there was an inner calm in her, a certainty that no outside forces could alter. Suddenly that peace at the core of her was gone. Whatever it was she feared had struck at the root of her being.

And it concerned Kristian Beck. Hester was almost sure of that. Had she heard the rumors of his quarrel with Prudence and feared he was guilty? Even so, why would that cause her anything but the same grief it would bring everyone else? Why should it disturb her in this quite fundamental way?

The answer was obvious. There was only one possibility in Hester's mind, one reason such a thing would have disturbed her. Her mind flew back to a bitter night during the siege of Sebastopol. The snow had been deep, muffling the hills in white, deadening sound, laying a biting cold upon everything. The wind had got up so it bit through the thin blankets the men huddled in, shuddering with cold. Everyone was hungry. Even now she could not bear to think of the horses.

She had thought herself in love with one of the surgeons—although what was the difference between being in love and thinking yourself so? Surely an emotion is the same whether it lasts or not—like pain. If you believe you hurt, you feel it just the same.

It was that night that she had realized he had been so terrified on the battlefield that he had left wounded men to die. She could still remember the agony of that discovery now, years after she had ceased to feel anything for him except compassion.

Callandra was in love with Kristian Beck. Of course. Now that she realized it, she wondered how she had ever failed to see it. And she was terrified that he was guilty.

Was that merely because of Jeavis's suspicions over the half-heard quarrel? Or had she learned something further herself?

She looked at Callandra's pale, tired face and knew that she would tell her nothing, not that Hester would have asked. In her place, Hester would have told no one. She would have gone on believing there must be some reason, some explanation that cast a different light. She remembered the murder of Joscelin Grey, and all the doubt and pain that had cost, and knew that to be true.

"I had better find him and tell him my progress, though," she said aloud, jerking Callandra's attention back. "Little as it is."

"Yes—yes of course," Callandra agreed. "Then I shall not detain you longer. But do get some sleep, my dear. Everyone has to rest some time, or they cannot have the strength to be useful."

Hester smiled briefly, as if in agreement, and excused herself.

Before she found Monk again she wanted to have another look at the corridor near the laundry chute at seven in the morning, roughly the time at which Prudence had been killed. She took steps to see that she was awake at half past six, and by seven she was alone beside the chute. It was broad daylight, and it had been for nearly three hours, but the stretch of the passage was dim because there were no windows, and at this time of the year the gas was not lit.

She stood against the wall and waited. In thirty-five minutes one dresser passed her carrying a bundle of bandages, looking neither to right nor left. He appeared tired, and Hester thought that quite possibly he did not even see her. If he had, she doubted very much he could have said afterwards who she was.

One nurse passed, going in the opposite direction. She swore at Hester in a general impersonal anger without looking at her. She was probably tired, hungry, and saw nothing ahead of her but endless days and nights the same. Hester had no heart to swear back.

After another quarter hour, having seen no one, she was about to leave. She had learned all she wished to. Maybe Monk already knew it, but if he did, it was by other evidence. She knew it for herself. Anyone would have had time to kill Prudence and put her in the laundry chute without fear of being observed, or even if they were, of being recognized by a witness who would testify against them.

She turned and walked toward the stairs down—and almost bumped into the huge form of Dora Parsons, standing with her arms folded.

"Oh!" Hester stopped abruptly, a sudden chill of fear running through her.

Dora grasped hold of her like an immovable clamp. Struggle would have been pointless.

"And what were you doing standing there in the shadows by the laundry chute, miss?" Dora said very quietly, her voice no more than a husky whisper.

Hester's mind went numb. It was instinctive to deny the truth, but Dora's bright odd eyes were watching her intently, and there was nothing gullible in her—in fact, she looked hideously knowing.

"I—" Hester began, chill turning to hot panic. There was no one else within hearing. The deep stairwell was only two feet away. A quick lift by those huge shoulders and she would be over it, to fall twenty or thirty feet down onto the stone floor of the laundry room. Was that how it had been for Prudence? A few moments of throat-closing terror and then death? Was the whole answer as simple as this—a huge, ugly, stolid nurse with a personal hatred of women who were a threat to her livelihood with their new ideas and standards?

"Yeah?" Dora demanded. "What? Cat got your tongue? Not so smart now, are we?" She shook Hester roughly, like a rat. "What were you doing there? What were you waiting for, eh?"

There was no believable lie. She might as well die, if she

were going to, telling the truth. It did occur to her to scream, but that might well panic Dora into killing her instantly.

"I was . . ." Her mouth was so dry she had to gulp and swallow before she could form the words. "I was . . ." she began again, "trying to see how deserted the—the corridor was at this time of day. Who usually passed." She swallowed again. Dora's huge hands were gripping her arms so tightly she was going to have purple bruises there tomorrow—if there was a tomorrow.

Dora moved her face a fraction closer till Hester could see the open pores of her skin and the separate short black eyelashes.

"O' course you were," Dora hissed softly. "Just 'cos I ain't bin to school don't mean I'm stupid! 'Oo did yer see? An' why do you care? You weren't even 'ere when that bitch were done. What's it to you? That's wot I wanna know." She looked her up and down. "You just a nosy cow, 'r yer got some reason?"

Hester had a strong belief that merely being nosy would not excuse her in Dora's eyes. And a reason would be more believable.

"A—a reason," she gasped.

"Yeah? So what is it then?"

They were only a foot from the banister now, and the drop down the stairwell. A quick turn of those great shoulders and Hester would be over.

What would she believe? And what would she not hate her for? At this point truth was irrelevant.

"I—I want to make sure they don't blame Dr. Beck just because he's foreign," she gasped.

"Why?" Dora's eyes narrowed. "Wot's it ter you if they do?" she demanded. "You only just got here. Why do you care if they 'ang 'im?"

"I knew him before." Hester was warming to the lie now. It sounded good.

"Did yer, now? And where was that then? 'E didn't work in your 'ospital in the war! 'E were 'ere."

"I know that," Hester answered. "The war only lasted two years."

"Got a thing for 'im, 'ave yer?" Dora's grip relaxed a little. "Won't do yer no good. 'E's married. Cold bitch with a face like a dead 'addock and a body to match. Still, that's your trouble, not mine. I daresay as yer wouldn't be the first fine lady to take 'er pleasures wrong side of the blanket." She squinted at Hester narrowly, a new expression in her face, not entirely unkind. "Mind, you be careful as yer don't get yerself inter no trouble." Her grasp loosened even more. "Wot you learn, then?"

Hester took a deep breath.

"That hardly anyone comes along there, and those who do aren't looking right or left, and probably wouldn't recognize anyone in the shadows even if they noticed them. There's plenty of time to kill someone and stuff them into the chute."

Dora grinned suddenly and startlingly, showing several blackened teeth.

"That's right. So you watch yourself, miss! Or you could end up the same." And without warning she let go, pushing Hester away with a little shove, and turned on her heel to march away.

Hester's knees were so weak they nearly buckled underneath her and she sank to the floor, feeling it hard and cold below her, her back to the wall. She must look ridiculous. Then, on second thought, everyone passing would only think she was drunk—not collapsed with relief. She sat there for several more moments before climbing up, holding the railing and swallowing hard before setting out again along the passage.

Monk exploded with anger when he heard about it in his lodgings. His face was white and his eyes narrow and lips drawn back.

"You stupid creature," he said in a hard low voice. "You fatuous, dangerous, sheep-brained idiot! Callandra said you were tired, but she didn't say you'd taken leave of what little sense you have." He glared at her. "There's no point in asking you what you thought you were doing! Quite obviously you didn't think! Now I've got to go and look after you as if you were a child—a little child, not even a sensible one."

She had been profoundly frightened, but now she was sufficiently safe, she could give rein to anger also.

"Nothing happened to me," she said icily. "You asked me to go there—"

"Callandra asked you," he interrupted with a curl of his lip.

"If you like," she said equally quickly, and with a tight hard smile to match his. "Callandra asked me in order to assist you in getting the information that you could not have found yourself."

"That she thought I could not have found," he corrected again.

She raised her eyebrows very high. "Oh—was she mistaken? I cannot understand how. I have not seen you around the corridors or in the wards and operating rooms. Or was that dresser who fell over the slop pail yesterday you in heavy disguise?"

A flash of amusement crossed his eyes but he refused to give way to it.

"I do not risk my life in idiotic ways to get information!" he said coldly.

"Of course not," she agreed, aching to hit him, to feel the release of physical action and reaction, to contact him more immediately than with words, however stinging the sarcasm. But self-preservation restrained her hand. "You always play very safe, no risk at all," she went on. "No danger to yourself. To hell with the results. How unfortunate if the wrong man is hanged—at least we are all safe. I have noticed that is your philosophy."

In a cooler temper he would not have responded to that, but his anger was still boiling.

"I take risks when it is necessary. Not when it is merely stupid. And I think what I'm doing first!"

This time she did laugh, loudly, uproariously, and in a most undignified and unladylike fashion. It felt wonderful. All the tensions and fears fled out of her, the fury and the loneliness, and she laughed even harder. She could not have stopped even if she had tried and she did not try.

"Stupid woman," he said between his teeth, his face coloring. "God preserve me from the half-witted!" He turned away because he was about to laugh as well, and she knew it as surely as if he had.

Eventually, with tears streaming down her face, she regained control of herself and fished for a handkerchief to blow her nose.

"If you have composed yourself?" he said, still trying to maintain a frigid expression. "Then perhaps you will tell me if you have learned anything useful, either in this operation or in any other?"

"Of course," she said cheerfully. "That is what I came for." She had already decided, without even having to consider it, that she would not tell him about Callandra's feelings for Kristian Beck. It was a totally private matter. To mention it would be a kind of betrayal. "The corridor is almost deserted at that time of day, and the few who do pass along it are either rushed or too tired to remark anything, or both. They didn't notice me, and I don't think they would have noticed anyone else either."

"Not even a man?" he pressed, his attention fully back on the case again. "In trousers and jacket, rather than a dresser's clothes?"

"It's very dim. I don't think they would have," she said thoughtfully. "One would simply have to have turned one's back and pretended to be putting something down the chute. At that time in the morning people have been on duty all night and are too exhausted to mind anyone else's business. Their own is more than enough. They are thinking of lying down somewhere and going to sleep. That's about all that matters."

He looked at her more closely.

"You look tired," he said after a moment's consideration. "In fact, you look awful."

"You don't," she rejoined instantly. "You look very well. But then I daresay I have been working a great deal harder than you have."

He took her totally by surprise by agreeing with her.

"I know." He smiled suddenly. "Let us hope the sick are suitably grateful. I expect Callandra will be, and you can buy a new dress. You certainly need one. What else did you discover if anything?"

The remark about the dress stung. She was always aware of how very smart he was. She would never have let him know—he was more than vain enough—but she admired it. She also knew quite well that she was seldom fashionable herself, and never really feminine. It was an art which eluded her, and she had stopped trying. She would love to be as beautiful as Imogen, as graceful and romantic.

He was staring at her, waiting for a reply.

"Sir Herbert is very likely to be offered a position as medical adviser to a member of the Royal household," she said hastily. "I don't know who."

"Doesn't seem to be relevant." He shrugged, dismissing it. "But I suppose it may be. What else?"

"Sir John Robertson, one of the governors, has financial troubles," she recounted in a businesslike tone. "The chaplain drinks; not wildly, but more than is good for his judgment at times, and his balance. And the treasurer has wandering eyes, and hands, where the better-looking nurses are concerned. But he favors fair hair and generous bosoms."

Monk glanced at her but forbore from comment.

"Not likely to have bothered Prudence, then," he observed.

She felt as if his remark had been personal and included her.

"I think she could have dealt with him very adequately if he had," she answered fiercely. "I certainly could."

225

He grinned broadly, on the edge of laughter, but he said nothing aloud.

"And did you discover anything?" she inquired with raised eyebrows. "Or have you simply been waiting to see what I would learn?"

"Of course I discovered things. Are you requiring me to report to you?" He sounded surprised.

"Certainly I am."

"Very well. Both Geoffrey Taunton and Nanette Cuthbertson had excellent opportunity," he recounted, standing a little more upright, like a soldier reporting, but he was still smiling. "He was in the hospital that morning to see Prudence, and by his own admission he quarreled with her."

"She was seen alive after the quarrel," she interrupted.

"I know that. But there is no proof he left the hospital. He did not catch the next train. In fact, he did not return home until midday and cannot prove where he was. Do you think I would bother to mention it if he could?"

She shrugged. "Go on."

"And Miss Cuthbertson was also up in town that morning. She had been here since the previous night, when she attended a ball at Mrs. Waldemar's house, which is in Regent Square, only two streets away from the hospital." He was looking at her as he spoke. "And curiously, after having danced all night, she rose very early and was absent for breakfast. According to her, she went for a walk in the fresh air. She says it was not to the hospital, but there is no proof of where it was. No one saw her."

"And she had an excellent motive in jealousy," Hester agreed. "But would she be strong enough?"

"Oh yes," he said without hesitation. "She is a fine horsewoman. I watched her the other day reining in an animal any man would have trouble mastering. She has the strength, especially if she took someone by surprise."

"And I suppose she could have passed herself off as a nurse if she had a plain enough dress," she said thoughtfully. "But there is nothing to prove that she did."

226

"I know that." His voice rose sharply. "If there were I would have taken it to Jeavis."

"Anything else?"

"Nothing indicative."

"Then I suppose we had better return to work and try harder." She rose to her feet. "I think I shall see if I can learn more about some of the governors—and Sir Herbert and Dr. Beck."

He moved to stand between her and the door, his face suddenly completely serious, his eyes intent on hers.

"Be careful, Hester! Someone murdered Prudence Barrymore—not in a fight and not by accident. He will just as easily kill you if you let him think he has cause."

"Of course I will be careful," she said with a quick rush of warmth. "I am not asking questions, I am simply observing."

"Possibly," he conceded doubtfully.

"What are you going to do?"

"Investigate the student doctors."

"Tell me if there is anything I can do to be of help. I may learn something of them." He was standing close to her, listening, watching her face. "They seem very ordinary to me so far, overworked, eager to learn, arrogant toward the female staff, full of stupid jokes to offset the distress they feel when people die and their own inadequacy, always poor and often hungry and tired. They make bad jokes about Sir Herbert, but they admire him immensely."

"Do you?" Suddenly he seemed more interested.

"Yes," she answered with surprise. "Yes. I think I do, now."

"Be careful, Hester!" he said again, urgency mounting in his voice.

"You already said that, and I promised I would. Good night."

"Good night . . ."

The following day she had several hours off duty, and used them to visit two people for whom she had formed a

227

considerable friendship. One was Major Hercules Tiplady, although the "Hercules" was a secret between them which she had promised not to reveal. She had been nursing him privately during his recovery from a badly broken leg while she was involved in the Carlyon case, and she had grown unusually fond of him. She did not often feel more than a regard and a responsibility toward her patients, but for the major she had developed a genuine friendship.

She had known Edith Sobell before the case. It was their friendship which had drawn her into it, and through that hectic time they had become very close. When Edith had left home it had been Hester who had made it possible by introducing her to the major, and from that had sprung his offer to employ her, a widow with no professional skills, as his secretary and assistant to help him write his memoirs of his experiences in India.

Hester arrived in the early afternoon, without having given notice of her intention because there had been no time. However, she was welcomed in with delight and an immediate abandonment of all work.

"Hester! How wonderful to see you. How are you? You look so tired, my dear. Do come in and tell us how you are, and let us fetch tea for you. You are stopping, aren't you?" Edith's curious face, at once plain and beautiful, was shining with enthusiasm.

"Of course she is staying," the major said quickly. He was fully restored to health now and walked with only the barest limp. Hester had never seen him active before, and it was quite startling to have him upright and attending to her, rather than her assisting him. All the marks of pain and frustration were gone from his face and he still looked as scrubbed pink and clean and his hair stood up like a white crest.

She acquiesced with pleasure. It was a warm, very sweet feeling to be among friends again, and with no duties to perform and nothing expected of her beyond tea and conversation.

"Who are you with now? Where are you nursing?" Edith

asked eagerly, folding herself into a large armchair in a characteristic gawky mixture of grace and inelegance. It delighted Hester to see it: it meant she was utterly at home here. There was no perching on the edge of the chair, back straight, skirts arranged, hands folded as a lady should. Hester found herself relaxing also, and smiling for no particular reason.

"At the Royal Free Hospital on the Gray's Inn Road," she replied.

"A hospital?" Major Tiplady was amazed. "Not privately? Why? I thought you found it too . . ." He hesitated, unsure how to say what he meant diplomatically.

"Restricting to your temper," Edith finished for him.

"It is," Hester agreed, still smiling. "I am only there temporarily. It was very civil of you not to remind me that I am also fortunate to find a hospital which will take me after my last experience. Lady Callandra Daviot is on the Board of Governors. She obtained the position for me because their best nurse, another from the Crimea, was murdered."

"Oh how terrible!" Edith's face fell. "How did it happen?"

"We don't know," Hester replied with a return to gravity. "Lady Callandra has called Monk into the case, as well as the police, of course. And that is why I am there."

"Ah!" The major's eyes lit with enthusiasm. "So you are engaged upon detection again." Then he also became very grave. "Do be careful, my dear. Such an undertaking may become dangerous if your intent is realized."

"You have no need for concern," Hester assured him. "I am simply a nurse working like any other." She smiled broadly. "Such dislike as I have collected is because I served in the Crimea and am bossy and opinionated."

"And what was the dead nurse like?" Edith inquired.

"Bossy and opinionated." Hester gave a wry smile. "But truly, if that were a motive for murder there would be few of us left."

"Have you any idea why she was killed?" the major

asked, leaning over the back of the chair in which Edith was sitting.

"No—no we haven't. There are several possibilities. Monk is looking into some of them. I should like to find out more about a German doctor who is working there. I admit I like him and am more eager to prove his innocence than his guilt. I wonder if . . ." Then she stopped. What she had been going to say sounded impertinent now.

"We could help you," the major finished for her. "We should be delighted. Tell us his name, and what you know about him, and we shall search for the rest. You may depend upon us. Mayn't she, Edith?"

"Most certainly," Edith said keenly. "I have become really quite good at discovering things—in a literary sort of way, of course." She smiled ruefully, her individual face with its curved nose and humorous mouth showing her perception of the difference between research and detection as she thought Hester practiced it. "But I imagine much will be known of him by hospitals where he has worked before. I shall pursue it straightaway. There are medical authorities who have lists of all sorts." She rearranged herself a little more comfortably. "But tell us what else you have been doing. How are you? You do look rather tired."

"I shall order tea," the major said with decision. "You must be thirsty. It's terribly hot today, and no doubt you walked at least some of the way. Would you like some cucumber sandwiches? And perhaps tomato? I remember you were always fond of tomato."

"I should love some." Hester accepted with pleasure, for the refreshment itself, but even more for the friendship and the simple warmth of the occasion. She looked up at the major and smiled. "How thoughtful of you to remember."

He blushed very faintly and went off about his errand, beaming with satisfaction.

"Tell me," Edith said again, "everything that is fun and interesting and that you care about since we last met."

Hester wriggled a little farther down in her chair and began.

At about the same time that Hester was enjoying her tea and cucumber sandwiches with Edith and the major, Callandra was picking up a very elegant wafer-thin finger of bread and butter at the garden party of Lady Stanhope. She was not fond of garden parties, still less of the sort of people who usually attended them, but she had come because she wanted to meet the daughter that Hester had told her Sir Herbert had spoken of, the one maimed for life by the bungled abortion. Even thinking of it chilled her so deeply she felt a little sick.

All around her were the sounds of tinkling cups and glasses, murmured conversation, laughter, the swish and rustle of skirts. Footmen moved discreetly among the guests with fresh bottles of chilled champagne or tall glasses of iced lemonade. Maids in crisp lace aprons and starched caps offered trays of sandwiches and tiny pastries or cakes. A titled lady made a joke, and everyone around her laughed. Heads turned.

It had not been easy to obtain an invitation. She was not acquainted with Lady Stanhope, who was a quiet woman better pleased to remain at home with her seven children than involve herself in public affairs, and entered society only as much as was required of her to maintain her husband's standing, and not to find herself remarked upon. This garden party was a way of discharging a great many of her obligations in one event, and she was not totally conversant with her guest list. Consequently she had not seemed surprised to meet Callandra. Perhaps she supposed her to be someone whose hospitality she had accepted without remembering, and whom she had invited in order to cancel a debt.

Callandra had actually come in the company of a mutual friend, upon whom she felt quite free to call for a favor without any detail of explanation.

She'd had to dress far more formally than she enjoyed. Her maid, a most comfortable and agreeable creature who had worked for her for years, had always found hair difficult and possessed little natural art with it. On the other hand, she was extremely good-tempered, had excellent health, a pleasing sense of humor, and was supremely loyal. Since Callandra seldom cared in the slightest what her hair looked like, these virtues far outweighed her failings.

However, today it would have been appreciated had she had skill with the comb and pin. Instead, Callandra looked as if she had ridden to the event at a gallop, and every time she put her hand up to tidy away a stray strand, she made it worse and (if such a thing were possible) drew more attention to it.

She was dressed in a medium shade of blue, trimmed with white. It was not especially fashionable, but it was most becoming, and that, at her age, mattered far more.

She was not really sure what she hoped to achieve. Even in the most fluent and companionable conversation with Victoria Stanhope, should she contrive such a thing, she could hardly ask her who had operated on her so tragically, nor what money he had taken from her for the act—one could hardly call it a service.

She was standing at the edge of the lawn, next to the herbaceous border, which was now filled with soaring delphiniums, blazing peonies, rather overblown poppies, and some blue veronica and catmint which smelled delicious. She felt miserable, out of place, and extremely foolish. It was quite pointless to have come, and she was on the edge of looking for some socially acceptable excuse to leave when she was engaged in conversation by an elderly gentleman who was determined to explain to her his theories on the propagation of pinks, and assure that she understood precisely how to instruct her gardener in the matter of cuttings.

Three times she tried to persuade him that her gardener was quite skilled in the art, but his enthusiasm overrode all she could do, and it was a quarter of an hour later when she finally extricated herself and found herself face to face with young Arthur Stanhope, Sir Herbert's eldest son. He was a slender young man with a pale complexion and smooth brown hair. He was about nineteen and very obviously doing his duty at his mother's party. It would have been heartless to dismiss him. The only decent thing was to answer all his polite questions and try to keep her mind on the totally meaningless conversation.

She was saying yes and no at what she hoped were appropriate junctures when she became aware of a girl of about seventeen hovering a few yards away. She was very thin and seemed to stand almost lopsidedly, as if she might walk with a limp. Her dress was a pretty blush pink, and very well cut, but all the dressmaker's skill could not hide the drawn look on her face nor the smudges of tiredness under her eyes. Callandra had seen too many invalids not to recognize the signs of pain when she saw them so clearly, or the attitude of one who finds standing tiring.

"Excuse me," she said, interrupting Arthur without a thought.

"Eh?" He looked startled. "Yes?"

"I think the young lady is waiting for you." She indicated the girl in pink.

He turned around to follow her gaze. A mixture of emotions filled his face—discomfort, defensiveness, irritation, and tenderness.

"Oh—yes, Victoria, do come and meet Lady Callandra Daviot."

Victoria hesitated; now that attention was drawn to her, she was self-conscious.

Callandra knew what life lay ahead for a girl who could not ever hope to marry. She would be permanently dependent upon her father for financial support, and upon her mother for companionship and affection. She would never have a home of her own, unless she were an only child of wealthy parents, which Victoria was not. Arthur would naturally inherit the estate, apart from a suitable dowry for his marriageable sisters. His brothers would make their own way, having been given appropriate education and a handsome start.

For Victoria, by far the most consistently painful thing would be the pity, the well-meaning and desperately cruel remarks, the unthinking questions, the young men who paid her court—until they knew.

With an ache inside her that was almost intolerable, Callandra smiled at the girl.

"How do you do, Miss Stanhope," she said with all the charm she could muster, which was far more than she realized.

"How do you do, Lady Callandra," Victoria said with a hesitant smile in answer.

"What a delightful garden you have," Callandra went on. Not only was she considerably the elder, and therefore it was incumbent upon her to lead the conversation, it was quite apparent that Victoria found it hard to accomplish what duty required, and did not enjoy it. Social awkwardness was a pinprick compared with the mortal wound that had already been dealt her, but at that moment Callandra would have spared her even the thought of pain, much less its reality. "I see you have several fine pinks as well. I love the perfume of them, don't you?" She saw Victoria's answering smile. "A gentleman with an eyeglass was just explaining to me how they are propagated to cross one strain with another."

"Oh yes—Colonel Strother," Victoria said quickly, taking a step closer. "I'm afraid he does tend to elaborate on the subject rather."

"Just a little," Callandra conceded. "Still, it is a pleasant enough thing to discuss, and I daresay he meant it kindly."

"I had rather listen to Colonel Strother on pinks than Mrs. Warburton on immorality in garrison towns." Victoria smiled a little. "Or Mrs. Peabody on her health, or Mrs. Kilbride on the state of the cotton industry in the plantations of America, or Major Drissell on the Indian mutiny." Her enthusiasm grew with a sense of ease with Callandra. "We get the massacre at Amritsar every time he calls. I have even had it served up with fish at dinner, and again with the sorbet."

"Some people have very little sense of proportion," Callandra agreed with answering candor. "On their favorite subject, they tend to bolt like a horse with a bit between its teeth."

Victoria laughed; it seemed the analogy amused her.

"Excuse me." A nice-looking young man of perhaps twenty-one or twenty-two came up apologetically, a small lace handkerchief in his hand. He looked at Victoria, almost ignoring Callandra and apparently not having seen Arthur at all. He held up the scrap of lawn and lace. "I think you may have dropped this, ma'am. Excuse my familiarity in returning it." He smiled. "But it gives me the opportunity of presenting myself. My name is Robert Oliver."

Victoria's cheeks paled, then flushed deep red. A dozen emotions chased themselves across her face: pleasure, a wild hope, and then the bitterness of memory and realization.

"Thank you," she said in a small tight voice. "But I regret, it is not mine. It must belong to some other—some other lady."

He stared at her, searching her eyes to see whether it was really the dismissal it sounded.

Callandra longed to intervene, but she knew she would only be prolonging the pain. Robert Oliver had been drawn to something in Victoria's face, an intelligence, an imagination, a vulnerability. Perhaps he even glimpsed what she would have been. He could not know the wound to the body which meant she could never give him what he would so naturally seek.

Without willing it, Callandra found herself speaking.

"How considerate of you, Mr. Oliver. I am sure Miss Stanhope is obliged, but so will be the handkerchief's true owner, I have no doubt." She was also quite convinced that Robert Oliver had no intention of seeking anyone further. He had found the scrap of fabric and used it as an excuse, a gracious and simple one. It had no further purpose.

He looked at her fully for the first time, trying to judge who she was and how much her view mattered. He caught something of the grief in her, and knew it was real, although of course he could not know the cause of it. His thin, earnest young face was full of confusion.

Callandra felt a scalding hot anger well up in her. She hated the abortionist who had done this. It was a vile thing to make money out of other people's fear and distress. For an honest operation to go wrong was a common enough tragedy. This was not honest. God knew if the practitioner was even a doctor, let alone a surgeon.

Please—please God it had not been Kristian. The thought was so dreadful it was like a blow to the stomach, driving the breath out of her.

Did she want to know, if it had been? Would she not rather cling to what she had, the gentleness, the laughter, even the pain of not being able to touch, of knowing she never could have more than this? But could she live with not knowing? Would not the sick, crawling fear inside her mar everything, guilty or not?

Robert Oliver was still staring at her.

She forced herself to smile at him, although she felt it was a hideous travesty of pleasure.

"Miss Stanhope and I were just about to take a little refreshment, and she was to show me some flowers her gardener has propagated. I am sure you will excuse us?" Gently she took Victoria by the arm, and after only a moment's hesitation, Victoria came with her, her face pale, her lip trembling. They walked in silence, close to each other. Victoria never asked why Callandra had done such a thing, or what she knew.

A memorial service was held for Prudence Barrymore in the village church at Hanwell, and Monk attended. He went as part of his duty to Callandra, but also because he felt a growing respect for the dead woman, and a profound sense of loss that someone so alive and so valuable should have gone. To attend a formal recognition of that loss was some way of, if not filling the void, at least bridging it.

It was a quiet service but the church was crowded with people. It seemed many had come from London to show their respect and offer their condolences to the family. Monk saw at least a score who must have been soldiers, some of them only too obviously amputees, leaning on crutches or with empty sleeves hanging by their sides. Many others had faces which should have looked young but showed signs of premature strain and indelible memory, whom he took also to be soldiers.

Mrs. Barrymore was dressed entirely in black, but her fair face glowed with a kind of energy as she supervised affairs, greeted people, accepted condolences from strangers with a kind of amiable confusion. It obviously amazed her that so many people should have held a deep and personal regard for the daughter she had always found such a trial, and ultimately a disappointment.

Her husband looked much closer to the edge of emotion he could not contain, but there was an immense dignity about him. He stood almost silently, merely nodding his head as people filed past him and spoke of their sorrow, their admiration, their debt to his daughter's courage and dedication. He was so proud of her that his head was high and his back ramrod straight, as if for this day at least he too were a soldier. But his grief was more than would allow his voice to come unchoked, and he did not embarrass himself by trying more than a few words as courtesy made it completely unavoidable.

There were flowers in tribute, wreaths and garlands of summer blossoms. Monk had brought one himself—full-blown summer roses—and laid it among the rest. He saw one of wildflowers, small and discreet among the others, and he thought of the flowers of the battlefield. He looked at the card. It said simply, "To my comrade, with love, Hester."

For a moment he felt a ridiculous surge of emotion that forced him to raise his head away from the bouquets and sniff hard, blinking his eyes. He walked away, but not before he had noticed another wreath, of plain white daisies, and the card, "Rest in the Lord, Florence Nightingale."

Monk stood apart from the crowd, not wishing to be spoken to by anyone. He was not doing his duty. He was here to observe and not to mourn, and yet the emotion welled up inside him and would not be denied. It was not curiosity he felt, and just at that moment not anger; it was grief. The slow sad music of the organ, the ancient stone of the church arching over the small figures of the people, all in black, heads bared, spoke of unrelieved loss.

He saw Callandra, quiet and discreet, here for herself, not for the Board of Governors. Probably one of the solemn dignitaries at the far side of the aisle was serving that function. There had been a wreath from Sir Herbert and one from the hospital in general, white lilies soberly arranged and some suitable inscription.

After the service chance brought him inevitably to Mr. Barrymore, and it would have been ostentatiously rude to have avoided him. He could not bear to say anything trite. He met Barrymore's eyes and smiled very slightly.

"Thank you for coming, Mr. Monk," Barrymore said with sincerity. "That was generous of you, since you never knew Prudence."

"I know a great deal about her," Monk replied. "And everything I have learned makes me feel the loss more deeply. I came because I wished to."

Barrymore's smile widened, but his eyes suddenly filled with tears and he was obliged to remain silent for a moment until he mastered himself.

Monk felt no embarrassment. The man's grief was genuine, and nothing which should shame or trouble the onlooker. Monk held out his hand. Barrymore took it firmly and clasped it in a hard warm grip, then let go.

It was only then that Monk noticed the young woman standing half behind him and a little to his left. She was of average height with a finely chiseled, intelligent face, which in different circumstances would have been filled with humor and made charming by vivacity. Even as somber as this, the lines of her normal character were plain. The resemblance to Mrs. Barrymore was marked. She must be Faith Barker, Prudence's sister. Since Barrymore had said she lived in Yorkshire and was presumably down only for the service, he would have no other opportunity to speak with her. However unsuitable or insensitive it seemed, he must force the issue now.

"Mrs. Barker?" he inquired.

Her expression sharpened with interest immediately. She regarded him up and down in an unusually candid manner.

"Are you Mr. Monk?" she inquired with a courtesy which robbed it of the bluntness it would otherwise have had. Her face was remarkably pleasing, now that she had temporarily cast aside the complete solemnity of mourning. He could see in her the girl who danced and flirted that her mother had described.

"Yes," he acknowledged, wondering what had been said of him to her.

Her look was confidential, and she placed a black-gloved hand on his arm.

"May we speak alone for a few moments? I realize I am taking up your time, but I should appreciate it more than you can know."

"Of course," he said quickly. "If you don't mind coming back toward the house?"

"Thank you so much." She took his arm and they went together through the mourners out of the shadow of the church and into the sunlight, picking their way between the gravestones into a quiet corner in the long grass close to the wall.

She stopped and faced him.

"Papa said you were inquiring into Prudence's death, independently from the police. Is that correct?"

"Yes."

"But you will take to the police anything you find which may be of importance, and force them to act upon it?"

"Do you know something Mrs. Barker?"

"Yes—yes I do. Prudence wrote to me every two or three days, regardless of how busy she was. They were not merely letters, they were more in the nature of diaries, and notes upon the cases she worked on that she felt to be interesting or medically instructive." She was watching his face keenly. "I have them all here—at least all those from the last three months. I think that will be sufficient."

"Sufficient for what, ma'am?" He could feel excitement bubbling up inside him, but he dared not be precipitate, in case it should prove to be an ill-founded suspicion, a matter of guesses rather than fact, a sister's natural desire for revenge—or as she would see it, justice.

"To hang him," she said unequivocally. Suddenly the charm fled from her eyes and left them bleak, angry, and full of grief.

He held out his hand. "I cannot say until I have read them. But if they are, I give you my word I shall not rest until it is done."

"That is what I thought." A smile flashed across her mouth and vanished. "You have a ruthless face, Mr. Monk. I should not care to have you pursuing me." She fished in an unusually large black reticule and brought out a bundle of envelopes. "Here." She offered them to him. "I hoped you would come to the service. Please take these and do what you must. Perhaps one day I may have them back— after they have served their purpose in evidence?"

"If it lies within my power," he promised.

"Good. Now I must return to my father and be what comfort I can to him. Remember, you have given me your word! Good day, Mr. Monk." And without adding anything further, she walked away, very upright, head held stiff and straight, until she mingled with a group of soldiers, some one-armed or one-legged, who parted awkwardly to allow her through.

He did not open the letters to read until he reached his home and could do so in comfort and without haste.

The first had been written some three months earlier, as Faith Barker had said. The handwriting was small, untidy, and obviously written at speed, but there was nothing cramped or mean about it, and it was easily legible.

Dear Faith,

Another long and most interesting case today. A woman came in with a tumor of the breast. The poor creature had been in pain for some considerable time, but too frightened to consult anyone in the matter. Sir Herbert examined her, and told her it must be removed as soon as possible, and he would do it himself. He reassured her until she was almost without anxiety, and she was duly admitted to the hospital.

Then followed a detailed and highly technical description of the operation itself, and Sir Herbert's brilliance in its performance.

Afterwards I had a hasty meal with Sir Herbert (we had been working long without a break or refreshment of any sort). He explained to me many ideas of his on further procedure which could cut down the shock to the patient in such operations. I think his ideas are quite excellent, and would love to see him obtain the position where he has the opportunity to exercise them. He is one of the great ornaments to both the study and the practice of medicine. I sometimes think his hands are the most beautiful part of any human being I have ever seen. Some speak of hands in prayer as exquisite. I think hands in healing can never be superseded by anything.

I went to bed so tired! And yet so very happy!

Your loving sister.

Monk set it aside. It was personal, perhaps mildly suggestive—certainly far from accusing, let alone damning.

He read the next one, and the next. They were essentially similar, a great deal of medical comment and detail, and again the reference to Sir Herbert and his skill.

It was ridiculous to feel so disappointed. What had he expected?

He read three more, his attention increasingly waning.

Then quite suddenly he found his heart beating and his fingers stiff as he held the paper.

I spoke for over an hour with Sir Herbert last night. We did not finish until nearly midnight, and both of us were too overwrought by events to retire immediately. I have never admired a man's skills more, and I told him so. He was very gentle and warm toward me. Faith, I really believe true happiness is possible for me, in a way I only dreamed as a girl. I am on the brink of all I have wanted for so long. And Herbert is the one who can bring it about for me.

I went to bed so happy—and excited. I hope—I dream—I even pray! And it all lies with Herbert. God be with him.

Prudence.

Frantically Monk leafed through more letters, and found other passages in the same vein, full of hope and excitement, full of reference to happiness in the future, dreams coming true, in among the medical details and case histories.

He has it in his power to make me the happiest woman in the world. I know it sounds absurd, impossible, and I do understand what you tell me, all the cautions and warnings, and that you have only my happiness in mind. But if it all comes true . . . And he could make it happen, Faith—he could! It is not impossible after all. I have searched and thought, but I know of no law which cannot be fought or circumvented. Pray for me, my dear sister. Pray for me!

And then the tone changed, quite suddenly, only a week before her death.

Sir Herbert has betrayed me totally! At first I could hardly believe it. I went to him, full of hope—and, fool that I was, of confidence. He laughed at me and told me it was totally impossible and always would be.

I realized, like a hard slap in the face, that he had been using me, and what I could give him. He never intended to keep his word.

But I have a way of keeping him to it. I will not permit him the choice. I hate force—I abhor it. But what else is left me? I will not give up—I will not! I have the weapons, and I will use them!

Was that what had happened? She had gone to him with her threat and he had retaliated with his own weapon—murder?

Faith Barker was right. The letters were enough to bring Sir Herbert Stanhope to trial—and very possibly enough to hang him.

In the morning he would take them to Runcorn.

It was barely eight o'clock when Monk put the letters into his pocket and rode in a hansom to the police station. He alighted, paid the driver, and went up the steps savoring every moment, the bright air already warm. The sounds of shouting, the clatter of hooves, and the rattle of cart wheels over the stones, even the smells of vegetables, fish, rubbish, and old horse manure were inoffensive to him today.

"Good morning," he said cheerfully to the desk sergeant, and saw the man's look of surprise, and then alarm.

"Mornin' sir," he said warily, his eyes narrowing. "What can we do for you, Mr. Monk?"

Monk smiled, showing his teeth. "I should like to see Mr. Runcorn, if you please? I have important evidence in connection with the murder of Prudence Barrymore."

"Yes sir. And what would that be?"

"That would be confidential, Sergeant, and concerns a very important person. Will you tell Mr. Runcorn, please?"

The sergeant thought about it for a moment, regarding Monk's face. A flood of memories came back to him, transparent in his expression, and all the old fears of a quick and savage tongue. He decided he was still more afraid of Monk than he was of Runcorn.

"Yes, Mr. Monk. I'll go and ask him." Then he remembered that Monk no longer had any status. He smiled tentatively. "But I can't say as he'll see you."

"Tell him it's enough for an arrest," Monk added with acute satisfaction. "I'll take it elsewhere if he'd rather?"

"No—no sir. I'll ask him." And carefully, so as not to show any deferential haste, still less anything that could be taken for obedience, he left the desk and walked across the floor to the stairs.

He was gone for several minutes, and returned with an almost expressionless face.

"Yes sir, if you like to go up, Mr. Runcorn will see you now."

"Thank you," Monk said with elaborate graciousness. Then he went up the stairs and knocked on Runcorn's door. Now there were a host of memories crowding him too, countless times he had stood here with all manner of news, or none at all.

He wondered what Runcorn was thinking, if there was a flicker of nervousness in him, recollection of their past clashes, victories and defeats. Or was he now so sure of himself, with Monk out of office, that he could win any confrontation?

"Come." Runcorn's voice was strong and full of anticipation.

Monk opened the door and strode in, smiling.

Runcorn leaned a little back in his chair and gazed at Monk with bland confidence.

"Good morning," Monk said casually, hands in his pockets, his fingers closing over Prudence's letters.

For several seconds they stared at each other. Slowly Runcorn's smile faded a little. His eyes narrowed.

"Well?" he said testily. "Don't stand there grinning. Have you got something to give the police, or not?"

Monk felt all the old confidence rushing back to him, the knowledge of his superiority over Runcorn, his quicker mind, his harder tongue, and above all the power of his will. He could not recall specific victories, but he knew the flavor of them as surely as if it were a heat in the room, indefinable, but immediate.

"Yes, I have something," he replied. He pulled the letters out and held them where Runcorn could see them.

Runcorn waited, refusing to ask what they were. He stared at Monk, but the certainty was ebbing away. Old recollections were overpowering.

"Letters from Prudence Barrymore to her sister," Monk explained. "I think when you have read them you will have sufficient evidence to arrest Sir Herbert Stanhope." He said it because he knew it would rattle Runcorn, who was terrified of offending socially or politically important people, and even more of making a mistake from which he could not retreat, or blame anyone else. Already a flush of anger was creeping up his cheeks and a tightness around his mouth.

"Letters from Nurse Barrymore to her sister?" Runcorn repeated, struggling to gain time to order his thoughts. "Hardly proof of much, Monk. Word of a dead woman—unsubstantiated. Don't think we would be arresting anyone on that. Never get a conviction." He smiled, but it was a sickly gesture, and his eyes reflected nothing of it.

Memory came flashing back of that earlier time when they were so much younger, of Runcorn being equally timid then, afraid of offending a powerful man, even when it seemed obvious he was hiding information. Monk could feel the power of his contempt then as acutely as if they were both still young, raw to their profession and their own abilities. He knew his face registered it just as clearly now as it had then. And he saw Runcorn's recognition of it, and the hatred fire in his eyes.

"I'll take the letters and make my own decision as to what they're worth." Runcorn's voice was harsh and his lips curled, but his breathing was harder and his hand, thrust out to grasp the papers, was rigid. "You've done the right thing bringing them to the police." He added the last word with satisfaction and now his eyes met Monk's.

But time had telescoped, at least for Monk, and he thought in some sense for Runcorn too; the past was always there between them, with all its wounds and angers, resentments, failures, and petty revenges.

"I hope I have." Monk raised his eyebrows. "I'm beginning to think perhaps I should have taken them to someone with the courage to use them openly and let the court decide what they prove."

Runcorn blinked, his eyes hot, full of confusion. That defensive look was just the same as it had been when he and Monk had quarreled over the case years ago. Only Runcorn had been younger, his face unlined. Now the innocence had gone, he knew Monk and had tasted defeat, and final victory had not wiped it out.

What had that case been about? Had they solved it in the end?

"Not your place," Runcorn was saying. "You'd be withholding evidence, and that's a crime. Don't think I wouldn't prosecute you, because I would." Then a deep pleasure came into his eyes. "But I know you, Monk. You'll give them to me because you wouldn't miss the chance of showing up someone important. You can't abide success, people who have made it to the top, because you haven't yourself. Envious, that's what you are. Oh, you'll give me those letters. You know it, and I know it."

"Of course you know it," Monk said. "That's what terrifies you. You'll have to use them. You'll have to be the one to go and question Sir Herbert, and when he can't answer, you are going to have to press him, drive him into a corner, and in the end arrest him. And the thought of it scares you bloodless. It'll ruin your social aspirations. You'll always be remembered as the man who ruined the best surgeon in London!"

Runcorn was white to the lips, sweat beads on his skin. But he did not back down.

"I'll—" He swallowed. "I'll be remembered as the man

246

who solved the Prudence Barrymore murder," he said huskily. "And that's more than you will, Monk! You'll be forgotten!"

That stung, because it was probably true.

"You won't forget me, Runcorn," Monk said viciously. "Because you'll always know I brought you the letters. You didn't find them yourself. And you'll remember that every time someone tells you how clever you are, what a brilliant detective—you'll know it is really me they are talking about. Only you haven't the courage or the honor to say so. You'll just sit there and smile, and thank them. But you'll know."

"Maybe!" Runcorn rose in his seat, his face red. "But you damn well won't, because it will be in the clubs, and halls and dining rooms where you'll not be invited."

"Neither will you—you fool," Monk said with stinging scorn. "You are not a gentleman, and you never will be. You don't stand like one, you don't dress like one, you don't speak like one—and above all you haven't the nerve, because you know you aren't one. You are a policeman with ambitions above yourself. Especially for the policeman who is going to arrest Sir Herbert Stanhope—and that's how you'll be remembered!"

Runcorn's shoulders hunched as if he intended hitting Monk. For seconds they stared at each other, both poised to lash out.

Then gradually Runcorn relaxed. He sat back in his chair again and looked up at Monk, a very slight sneer curling his lips.

"You'll be remembered too, Monk, not among the great and famous, not among gentlemen—but here in the police station. You'll be remembered with fear—by the ordinary P.C.s you bullied and made miserable, by the men whose reputations you destroyed because they weren't as ruthless as you or as quick as you thought they should be. You ever read your Bible, Monk? 'How are the mighty fallen?' Remember that?" His smile widened. "Oh, they'll talk about you in the public houses and on the street corners, they'll

247

say how good it is now you're gone. They'll tell the new recruits who complain that they don't know they're born. They should see what a real hard man is—a real bully." The smile was all the way to his eyes. "Give me the letters, Monk, and go and get on with your prying and following and whatever it is you do now."

"What I do now is what I have always done," Monk said between his teeth, his voice choking. "Tidy up the cases you can't manage and clean up behind you!" He thrust the letters out and slammed them on the desk. "I'm not the only one who knows about them, so don't think you can hide them and blame some other poor sod who is as innocent as that poor bloody footman you hanged." And with that he turned on his heel and walked out, leaving Runcorn white-faced, his hands shaking.

8

SIR HERBERT STANHOPE was arrested and charged, and Oliver Rathbone was retained to conduct his defense. He was one of the most brilliant lawyers in London and, since Monk's first case after his accident, well acquainted with both Monk and Hester Latterly. To say it was a friendship would be both to understate it and to overstate it. With Monk it was a difficult relationship. Their mutual respect was high; indeed, it amounted to admiration. They also felt a complete trust not only in the competence but each in the professional integrity of the other.

However, on a personal level matters were different. Monk found Rathbone more than a little arrogant and complacent, and he had mannerisms which irritated Monk at times almost beyond bearing. Rathbone, on the other hand, found Monk also arrogant, abrasive, willful, and inappropriately ruthless.

With Hester it was quite different. Rathbone had a regard for her which had grown deeper and more intimate with time. He did not consider her totally suitable as a lifetime companion. She was too opinionated, had very little idea of what it was suitable for a lady to interest herself in—to wit, criminal cases. And yet, curiously, he enjoyed her company more than that of any other woman, and he found himself caring surprisingly deeply what she thought and felt for him. His mind turned to her more often than he could satisfactorily explain to himself. It was disconcerting, but not entirely unpleasant.

And what she thought and felt for him were emotions she had no intention of allowing him to know. At times he disturbed her profoundly—for example, when he had kissed her so suddenly and gently over a year ago. And there had been a sweetness in their time spent at Primrose Hill with his father, Henry Rathbone, whom Hester liked enormously. She would always remember the closeness she had felt walking in the garden in the evening, and the scents of summer in the wind, cut grass and honeysuckle, the leaves of the apple orchard beyond the hedge, dark against the stars.

And yet at the back of her mind there was always Monk. Monk's face intruded into her thoughts; his voice, and its words, spoke in the silence.

Rathbone was not in the least surprised to receive the call from Sir Herbert Stanhope's solicitors. Such a man would naturally seek the best defense available, and there were many who would aver without question that that was Oliver Rathbone.

He read all the papers and considered the matter with care. The case against Sir Herbert was strong, but far from conclusive. He had had the opportunity, along with at least a score of other people. He had had the means, as did anyone with sufficient strength in his or her hands—and with a group of women like the average nurses, that included almost everyone. The only evidence of motive was the letters written by Prudence Barrymore to her sister—but they were a powerful indictment, uncontested.

Reasonable doubt would be sufficient to gain an acquittal in law and avoid the hangman's noose. But to save Sir Herbert's reputation and honor there must be no doubt at all. That meant he must provide another suspect for the public to blame. They were the ultimate jury.

But first he must seek an acquittal before the court. He

read the letters again. They required an explanation, a different interpretation that was both innocent and believable. For that he would have to see Sir Herbert himself.

It was another hot day, sultry with an overcast sky. He disliked visiting the prison at any time, but in the close, oppressive heat it was more unpleasant than usual. The odors were of clogged drains, closed rooms containing exhausted bodies, fear ebbing slowly to despair. He could smell the stone as the doors closed behind him with a hard, heavy clang and the warder led him to the room where he would be permitted to interview Sir Herbert Stanhope.

It was bare gray stone with only a simple wooden table in the center and a chair on either side. One high window, barred and with an iron grille, let in the light high above the eye level of even the tallest man. The warder looked at Rathbone.

"Call when you want out, sir." And without adding anything further he turned and left Rathbone alone with Sir Herbert. In spite of the fact that they were both prominent men, they had not met before, and they regarded each other with interest. For Sir Herbert it might well prove to be a matter of his life or death. Oliver Rathbone's skill was the only shield between him and the noose. Sir Herbert's eyes narrowed and he concentrated intensely, weighing the face he saw with its broad forehead, curious very dark eyes for a man otherwise fair, long sensitive nose and beautiful mouth.

Rathbone also regarded Sir Herbert carefully. He was bound to defend this man, a famous public figure, at least in the medical world. The center of the case upon which would rest a good many reputations—his own included, if he did not conduct himself well. It was a terrible responsibility to have a man's life in one's hands—not as it was for Sir Herbert, where it lay on the dexterity of the fingers, but simply upon one's judgment of other human beings, the knowledge of the law, and the quickness of your wits and your tongue.

Was he innocent? Or guilty?

"Good afternoon, Mr. Rathbone," Sir Herbert said at last, inclining his head but not offering his hand. He was dressed in his own clothes. He had not yet stood trial, and therefore was legally innocent. He must still be treated with respect, even by jailers.

"How do you do, Sir Herbert," Rathbone replied, walking to the farther chair. "Please sit down. Time is precious, so I will not waste it with pleasantries we may both take for granted."

Sir Herbert smiled bleakly and obeyed. "This is hardly a social occasion," he agreed. "I assume you have acquainted yourself with the facts of the case as the prosecution is presenting it?"

"Naturally." He sat on the hard chair, leaning a little across the table. "They have a good case, but not impeccable. It will not be difficult to raise a reasonable doubt. But I wish to do more than that or your reputation will not be preserved."

"Of course." A look of dry, harsh amusement crossed Sir Herbert's broad face. Rathbone was impressed that he was disposed to fight rather than to sink into self-pity, as a lesser man might have. He was certainly not handsome, nor was he a man to whom charm came easily, but he quite obviously had a high intelligence and the willpower and strength of nerve which had taken him to the forefront of a most demanding profession. He was used to having other men's lives in his hands, to making instant decisions which weighed life and death, and he flinched from neither. Rathbone was obliged to respect him, an emotion he did not always feel toward his clients.

"Your solicitor has already informed me that you have absolutely denied killing Prudence Barrymore," he continued. "May I assume that you would give me the same assurance? Remember, I am bound to offer you the best defense I can, regardless of the circumstances, but to lie to me would be most foolish because it will impair my ability. I need to be in possession of all the facts or I cannot defend you against the prosecutor's interpretation of them." He watched closely as Sir Herbert looked at him steadily, but he saw no flicker in his face, no nervous movement, and he heard no wavering in his voice.

"I did not kill Nurse Barrymore," he answered. "Nor do I know who did, although I may guess why, but I have no knowledge. Ask me whatever you wish."

"I shall pursue those points myself." Rathbone leaned a little back in his chair, not comfortably, since it was wooden and straight. He regarded Sir Herbert steadily. "Means and opportunity are immaterial. A large number of people possessed both. I assume you have thought hard to see if there is anyone who could account for your time that morning and there is no one? No, I assumed not, or you would have told the police and we should not now be here."

The ghost of a smile lit Sir Herbert's eyes, but he made no comment.

"That leaves motive," Rathbone went on. "The letters Miss Barrymore wrote to her sister, and which are now in the hands of the prosecution, suggest most forcibly that you had a romantic liaison with her, and that when she realized that it could come to nothing she became troublesome to you, threatened you in some way, and to avoid a scandal you killed her. I accept that you did not kill her. But were you having an affair with her?"

Sir Herbert's thin lips tightened in a grimace.

"Most certainly not. The idea would be amusing, it is so far from the truth, were it not mortally dangerous. No, Mr. Rathbone. I had never even thought of Miss Barrymore in that light." He looked shiftily surprised. "Nor any woman other than my wife. Which may sound unlikely, most men's morals being as they are." He shrugged, a deprecating and amused gesture. "But I have put all my energy into my professional life, and all my passion."

His eyes were very intent upon Rathbone's face. He had a gift of concentration, as if the person to whom he was speaking at that moment were of the utmost importance to him, and his attention was absolute. Rathbone was acutely conscious of the power of his personality. But for all that, he believed the passion in him was of the mind, not of the body. It was not a self-indulgent face. He could see no weakness in it, no ungoverned appetite. "I have a devoted wife, Mr. Rathbone," Sir Herbert continued. "And seven children. My home life is amply sufficient. The human body holds much fascination for me, its anatomy and physiology, its diseases and their healing. I do not lust after nurses." The amusement was there again, briefly. "And quite frankly, if you had known Nurse Barrymore you would not have assumed I might. She was handsome enough, but unyielding, ambitious, and very unwomanly."

Rathbone pursed his lips a trifle. He must press the issue, whatever his own inner convictions. "In what way unwomanly, Sir Herbert? I have been led to suppose she had admirers; indeed, one who was so devoted to her he pursued her for years, in spite of her continued rejection of him."

Sir Herbert's light, thin eyebrows rose. "Indeed? You surprise me. But to answer your question: she was perverse, displeasingly outspoken and opinionated on certain subjects, and uninterested in home or family. She took little trouble to make herself appealing." He leaned forward. "Please understand me, none of this is criticism." He shook his head. "I have no desire to have hospital nurses flirting with me, or with anyone else. They are there to care for the sick, to obey orders, and to keep a reasonable standard of morality and sobriety. Prudence Barrymore did far better than that. She was abstemious in her appetites, totally sober, punctual, diligent in her work, and at times gifted. I think I can say she was the best nurse I had ever known, and I have known hundreds."

"A thoroughly decent, if somewhat forbidding, young woman," Rathbone summed up.

"Quite," Sir Herbert agreed, sitting back in his chair again. "Not the sort with whom one flirts, given one were so inclined, and I am not." He smiled ruefully. "But believe me, Mr. Rathbone, if I were, I should not choose such a public place in which to do so, still less would I indulge myself in my place of work, which to me is the most important in my life. I would never jeopardize it for such a relatively trivial satisfaction."

Rathbone did not doubt him. He had spent his professional life, and carved a brilliant reputation, by judging when a man was lying and when he was not. There were a score of tiny signs to watch for, and he had seen none of them.

"Then what is the explanation of her letters?" he asked levelly and quite quietly. There was no change in his tone; it was simply an inquiry to which he fully expected an acceptable answer.

Sir Herbert's face took on an expression of rueful apology.

"It is embarrassing, Mr. Rathbone. I dislike having to say this—it is highly unbecoming a gentleman to speak so." He took a deep breath and let it out in a sigh. "I—I have heard of occasions in the past when young women have become . . . shall I say enamored of . . . certain . . . prominent men." He looked at Rathbone curiously. "I daresay you have had the experience yourself? A young woman you have helped, or whose family you have helped. Her natural admiration and gratitude becomes . . . romantic in nature? You may have been quite unaware of it until suddenly some chance word or look brings to your mind the reality that she is nurturing a fantasy with you at its heart."

Rathbone knew the experience only too well. He could remember a very pleasant feeling of being admired suddenly turning into an acutely embarrassing confrontation with a breathless and ardently romantic young woman who had mistaken his vanity for shyness and a concealed ardor. He blushed hot at the recollection even now.

Sir Herbert smiled.

"I see you have. Most distressing. And one can find that, out of sheer blindness, one's mind occupied with one's work, one has not discouraged it plainly enough when it was still budding, and one's silence has been misunderstood." His eyes were still on Rathbone's face. "I fear that

255

is what happened with Nurse Barrymore. I swear I had no idea whatsoever. She was not the type of woman with whom one associates such emotions." He sighed. "God only knows what I may have said or done that she has taken to mean something quite different. Women seem to be able to interpret words—and silence—to mean all sorts of things that never crossed one's mind."

"If you can think of anything specific, it would help."

Sir Herbert's face wrinkled up in an effort to oblige.

"Really it is very difficult," he said reluctantly. "One does not weigh what one says in the course of duty. Naturally I spoke to her countless times. She was an excellent nurse. I told her a great deal more than I would a lesser woman." He shook his head sharply. "Ours was a busy professional relationship, Mr. Rathbone. I did not speak to her as one would a social acquaintance. It never occurred to me to watch her face to assure myself she had perceived my remarks in a correct light. I may often have had my back to her, or even spoken to her as I was walking away or doing something else. My regard for her was in no way personal."

Rathbone did not interrupt him, but sat waiting, watching his face.

Sir Herbert shrugged. "Young women are prone to fancies, especially when they reach a certain age and are not married." A fleeting smile of regret and sympathy touched his mouth and vanished. "It is not natural for a woman to devote herself to a career in such a way, and no doubt it places a strain upon the natural emotions, most particularly when that career is an unusual and demanding one like nursing." His gaze was earnest on Rathbone's face. "Her experiences in the war must have left her particularly vulnerable to emotional injury, and daydreaming is not an abnormal way of coping with circumstances that might otherwise be unendurable."

Rathbone knew that what he said was perfectly true, and yet he found himself feeling that it was vaguely patronizing, and without knowing why, he resented it. He could not imagine anyone less likely to indulge in unreality or romanctic daydreams than Hester Latterly, who in many of the ways Sir Herbert referred to, was in exactly the same circumstances as Prudence. Perhaps he would have found her easier if she had. And yet he would have admired her less, and perhaps liked her less too. With an effort he refrained from saying what sprang to his mind. He returned to his original request.

"But you can think of no particular occasion on which she may have misinterpreted a specific remark? It would be most helpful if we could rebut it in more than general terms."

"I realize that, but I am afraid I can think of nothing I have ever said or done to make any woman think my interest was more than professional." Sir Herbert looked at him with anxiety and, Rathbone judged, a totally innocent confusion.

Rathbone rose to his feet.

"That is sufficient for this visit, Sir Herbert. Keep your spirits up. We have some time yet in which to learn more of Miss Barrymore and her other possible enemies and rivals. But please continue to cast your mind back over all the times you worked together recently and see if anything comes to you which may be of use. When we get to court, we must have more than a general denial." He smiled. "But try not to worry overmuch. I have excellent people who can assist me, and we will no doubt discover a great deal more before then."

Sir Herbert rose also. He was pale and the marks of anxiety were plain in his face now that he had stopped concentrating on specific questions. The gravity of his situation overwhelmed him, and for all the force of logic and Rathbone's assurances, if the verdict was against him, he faced the rope, and the reality of that crowded out everything else.

He made as if to speak, and then found no words.

Rathbone had stood in cells like this more times than he could count, with all manner of both men and women, each facing the fear in their own way. Some were openly terrified, others masked their feelings with pride or anger. Sir Herbert was outwardly calm, but Rathbone knew the sick anxiety he must feel inside, and was helpless to do anything to help. Whatever he said, as soon as he was gone and the great door closed behind him, Sir Herbert would be alone for the long dragging hours, to swing from hope to despair, courage to terror. He must wait, and leave the battle to someone else.

"I will put my best people onto it," Rathbone said aloud, gripping Sir Herbert's hand in his own. "In the meantime, try to think over any conversation with Miss Barrymore that you can. It will be helpful to us to refute the interpretation they have put upon your regard for her."

"Yes." Sir Herbert composed his face into an expression of calm intelligence. "Of course. Good day, Mr. Rathbone. I shall look forward to your next visit. . . ."

"In two or three days' time," Rathbone said in answer to the unasked question, then he turned to the door and called for the jailer.

Rathbone had every intention of doing all he could to find another suspect in the case. If Sir Herbert were innocent, then someone else was guilty. There was no one in London better able to unearth the truth than Monk. Accordingly he sent a letter to Monk's lodgings in Fitzroy Street, stating his intention to call upon him that evening on a matter of business. It never occurred to him that Monk might be otherwise engaged.

And indeed Monk was not. Whatever his personal inclinations, he needed every individual job, and he needed Rathbone's goodwill in general. Many of his most rewarding cases, both professionally and financially, came through Rathbone.

He welcomed him in and invited him to be seated in the comfortable chair, himself sitting in the one opposite and regarding him curiously. There had been nothing in his letter as to the nature of the present case.

Rathbone pursed his lips.

"I have an extremely difficult defense to conduct," he began carefully, watching Monk's face. "I am assuming my client is innocent. The circumstantial evidence is poor, but the evidence of motive is strong, and no other immediate suspect leaps to mind."

"Any others possible?" Monk interrupted.

"Oh indeed, several."

"With motive?"

Rathbone settled a little more comfortably in his seat.

"Certainly, although there was no proof that it is powerful enough to have precipitated the act. One may deduce it rather than observe evidence of it."

"A nice distinction." Monk smiled. "I presume your client's motive is rather more evident?"

"I'm afraid so. But he is by no means the only suspect, merely by some way the best."

Monk looked thoughtful. "He denies the act. Does he deny the motive?"

"He does. He claims that the perception of it is a misunderstanding, not intentional, merely somewhat . . . emotionally distorted." He saw Monk's gray eyes narrow. Rathbone smiled. "I perceive your thoughts. You are correct. It is Sir Herbert Stanhope. I am quite aware that it was you who found the letters from Prudence Barrymore to her sister."

Monk's eyebrows rose.

"And yet you ask me to help you disprove their content?"

"Not disprove their content," Rathbone argued. "Simply show that Miss Barrymore's infatuation with Sir Herbert did not mean that he killed her. There are very credible other possibilities, one of which may prove to be the truth."

"And you are content with the possibility?" Monk asked. "Or do you wish me to provide proof of the alternative as well?"

"Possibility first," Rathbone said dryly. "Then when you have that, of course an alternative would be excellent. It is hardly satisfactory simply to establish doubt. It is not certain a jury will acquit on it, and it assuredly will not save

259

the man's reputation. Without the conviction of someone else, he will effectively be ruined."

"Do you believe him innocent?" Monk looked at Rathbone with acute interest. "Or is that something you cannot tell me?"

"Yes I do," Rathbone answered candidly. "I have no grounds for it, but I do. Are you convinced of his guilt?"

"No," Monk replied with little hesitation. "I rather think not, in spite of the letters." His face darkened as he spoke. "It seems she was infatuated with him, and he may have been flattered and foolish enough to encourage her. But on reflection—I have given it a great deal of thought—murder seems a somewhat hysterical reaction to a young woman's emotions, no doubt embarrassing but not dangerous to him. Even if she was intensely in love with him," he said the words as though they were distasteful to him, "there was nothing she could do that would do more than cause him a certain awkwardness." He seemed to retreat inside himself and Rathbone was aware that the thoughts hurt him. "I would have thought a man of his eminence, working very often with women," he continued, "must have faced similar situations before. I do not share your certainty of his innocence, but I am sure there is more to the story than we have discovered so far. I accept your offer. I shall be most interested to see what else I can learn."

"Why were you involved in it in the first place?" Rathbone asked curiously.

"Lady Callandra wished the matter looked into. She is on the Board of Governors of the hospital and had a high regard for Prudence Barrymore."

"And this answer satisfies her?" Rathbone did not conceal his surprise. "I would have thought as a governor of the hospital she would have been most eager to vindicate Sir Herbert! He is unquestionably their brightest luminary; almost anyone could be better spared than he."

A flicker of doubt darkened Monk's eyes.

"Yes," he said slowly. "She does seem to be well satisfied. She has thanked me, paid me, and released me from the case."

Rathbone said nothing, his mind filled with conjecture, conclusionless, one thought melting into another, but worrying.

"Hester does not believe it is the answer," Monk continued after a moment or two.

Rathbone's attention was jerked back by the sound of her name. "Hester? What has she to do with it?"

Monk smiled with a downturn of the corners of his mouth. He regarded Rathbone with amusement, and Rathbone had the most uncomfortable sensation that his uneasy and very personal feelings for Hester were transparent in his face. Surely she would have had confided in Monk? That would be too—no, of course she would not. He dismissed the thought. It was disturbing and offensive.

"She knew Prudence in the Crimea," Monk replied. The easy use of Nurse Barrymore's given name startled Rathbone. He had thought of her as the victim; his concern had been entirely with Sir Herbert. Now suddenly her reality came to him with a painful shock. Hester had known her, perhaps cared for her. With chilling clarity he saw again how like Hester she must have been. Suddenly he was cold inside.

Monk perceived the shock in him. Surprisingly there was none of the ironic humor Rathbone expected, instead only a pain devoid of adulteration or disguise.

"Did you know her?" he asked before his brain censored the words. Of course Monk had not known her. How could he?

"No," Monk replied quietly, his voice full of hurt. "But I have learned a great deal about her." His gray eyes hardened, cold and implacable. "And I intend to see the right man with the noose around his neck for this." Then suddenly the ruthless, bitter smile was there on his lips. "I don't only mean in order to avoid a miscarriage of justice. Of course I don't want that—but neither do I intend to see

Stanhope acquitted and no one in his place. I won't allow them to let this one go unresolved."

Rathbone looked at him closely, studying the passion so plain in his face.

"What did you learn of her which moves you this profoundly?"

"Courage," Monk answered. "Intelligence, dedication to learning, a will to fight for what she believed and what she wanted. She cared about people, and there was no equivocation or hypocrisy in her."

Rathbone had a sudden vision of a woman not unlike Monk himself, in some ways strange and complex, in others burningly simple. He was not surprised that Monk cared so much that she was dead, even that he felt an identity with her loss.

"She sounds like a woman who could have loved very deeply," Rathbone said gently. "Not one who would have accepted rejection without a struggle."

Monk pursed his lips, doubt in his eyes, reluctant and touched with anger.

"Nor one to resort to pleading or blackmail," he said, but his voice held more hurt than conviction.

Rathbone rose to his feet.

"If there is another story we have not touched yet, find it. Do whatever you can that will expose other motives. Someone killed her."

Monk's face set hard. "I will," he promised, not to Rathbone but to himself. His smile was sour. "I assume Sir Herbert is paying for this?"

"He is," Rathbone replied. "If only we could unearth a strong motive in someone else! There is a reason why someone killed her, Monk." He stopped. "Where is Hester working now?"

Monk smiled, the amusement going all the way to his eyes. "In the Royal Free Hospital."

"What?" Rathbone was incredulous. "In a hospital? But I thought she . . ." He stopped. It was none of Monk's business that Hester had been dismissed before, although of course he knew it. The thoughts, the amusement, the anger, and the instinct to defend, in spite of himself, were all there in his eyes as Rathbone stared at him.

There were times when Rathbone felt uniquely close to Monk, and both liked and disliked him intensely with two warring parts of his nature.

"I see," he said aloud. "Well, I suppose it could prove useful. Please keep me informed."

"Of course," Monk agreed soberly. "Good day."

Rathbone never doubted that he would also go to see Hester. He argued with himself, debating the reasons for and against such a move, but he did it with his brain, even while his feet were carrying him toward the hospital. It would be difficult to find her; she would be busy working. Quite possibly she knew nothing helpful about the murder anyway. But she had known Prudence Barrymore. Perhaps she also knew Sir Herbert. He could not afford to ignore her opinion. He could hardly afford to ignore anything!

He disliked the hospital. The very smell of the place offended his senses, and his consciousness of the pain and the distress colored all his thoughts. The place was in less than its normal state of busy, rather haphazard order since Sir Herbert's arrest. People were confused, intensely partisan over the issue of his innocence or guilt.

He asked to see Hester, explaining who he was and his purpose, and he was shown into a small, tidy room and requested to wait. He was there, growing increasingly impatient and short-tempered, for some twenty minutes before the door opened and Hester came in.

It was over three months since he had last seen her, and although he had thought his memory vivid, he was still taken aback by her presence. She looked tired, a little pale, and there was a splash of blood on her very plain gray dress. He found the sudden feeling of familiarity both pleasant and disturbing.

"Good afternoon, Oliver," she said rather formally. "I am told you are defending Sir Herbert and wish to speak to me on the matter. I doubt I can help. I was not here at the time of the murder, but of course I shall do all I can." Her eyes met his directly with none of the decorum he was used to in women.

In that instant he was powerfully aware that she had known and liked Prudence Barrymore, and that her emotions would crowd her actions in the matter. It both pleased and displeased him. It would be a nuisance professionally. He needed clarity of observation. Personally, he found indifference to death a greater tragedy than the death itself, and sometimes a more offensive sin than many of the other lies, evasions, and betrayals that so often accompanied a trial.

"Monk tells me you knew Prudence Barrymore," he said bluntly.

Her face tightened. "Yes."

"Are you aware of the content of the letters she wrote to her sister?"

"Yes. Monk told me." Her expression was guarded, unhappy. He wondered whether it was at the intrusion into privacy or at the subject matter of the letters themselves.

"Did it surprise you?" he asked.

She was still standing in front of him. There were no chairs in the room. Apparently it was used simply to store materials of one sort and another, and had been offered him because it afforded privacy.

"Yes," she said unequivocally. "I accept that is what she wrote, because I have to. But it sounds most unlike the woman I knew."

He did not wish to offend her, but he must not fall short of the truth either.

"And did you know her other than in the Crimea?"

It was a perceptive question, and she saw the meaning behind it immediately.

"No, I didn't know her here in England," she replied. "And I left the Crimea before she did because of my parents' death, nor have I seen her since then. But all the same, this is nothing like the woman I worked with." She frowned, trying to order her thoughts and find words for them. "She was—more sufficient in herself. . . ." It was half a question, to see if he understood. "She never allowed her happiness to rest in other people," she tried again. "She was a leader, not a follower. Am I explaining myself?" She regarded him anxiously, conscious of inadequacy.

"No," he said simply, with a faint smile. "Are you saying she was incapable of falling in love?"

She hesitated for so long he thought she was not going to answer. He wished he had not broached the subject, but it was too late to retreat.

"Hester?"

"I don't know," she said at last. "Of loving, certainly, but falling in love . . . I am not sure. *Falling* implies some loss of balance. It is a good word to use. I am not at all sure Prudence was capable of falling. And Sir Herbert doesn't seem . . ." She stopped.

"Doesn't seem?" he prompted.

She pulled a very slight face. "The sort of man to inspire an overwhelming passion." She made it almost a question, watching his face.

"Then what can she have meant in her letters?" he asked.

She shook her head fractionally. "I cannot see any other explanation. I just find it so hard to believe. I suppose she must have changed more than I would have thought possible." Her expression hardened. "There must have been something between them that we have not even guessed at, some tenderness, something shared which was uniquely precious to her, so dear she could not give it up, even at the cost of demeaning herself to use threats."

She shook her head again with a brisk impatient little movement, as if to brush away some troublesome insect. "She was always so direct, so candid. What on earth would she want with the affection of a man she had forced into giving it? It makes no sense!"

"Infatuation seldom does make sense, my dear," he said quietly. "When you care so fiercely and all-consumingly for someone you simply cannot believe that in time they will not learn to feel the same for you. If only you have the

265

chance to be with them, you can make things change." He stopped abruptly. It was all true, and relevant to the case, but it was far more than he had intended to say. And yet he heard his own voice carrying on. "Have you never cared for anyone in that way?" He was asking not only for Prudence Barrymore, but because he wanted to know if Hester had ever felt that wild surge of emotion that eclipses everything else and distracts all other needs and wishes. As soon as the words were out, he wished he had not asked. If she said no, he would feel her cold, something less than a woman, and fear she was not capable of such feelings. But if she said yes, he would be ridiculously jealous of the man who had inspired it in her. He waited for her answer, feeling utterly foolish.

If she were aware of the turmoil in him she betrayed none of it in her face.

"If I had, I should not wish to discuss it," she said primly, then gave a sudden smile. "I am not being of any assistance, am I? I'm sorry. You have to defend Sir Herbert, and this is no use at all. I suppose what you had better do is see if you can find out what pressure she intended to use. And if you can find none, it may tend to vindicate him." She screwed up her face. "That is not very good, is it?"

"Almost no good at all," he agreed, making himself smile back.

"What can I do that would be useful?" she asked frankly.

"Find me evidence to suggest that it was someone else."

He saw a flicker of doubt in her face, or perhaps it was anxiety, or unhappiness. But she did not explain it.

"What is it?" he pressed. "Do you know something?"

"No," she said too quickly. Then she met his eyes. "No, I know of no evidence whatever to implicate anyone else. I believe the police have looked fairly thoroughly at all the other people it might be. I know Monk thought quite seriously about Geoffrey Taunton and about Nanette Cuthbertson. I suppose you might pursue them?"

"I shall certainly do so, naturally. What of the other

nurses here? Have you formed any impression as to their feelings for Nurse Barrymore?"

"I'm not sure if my impressions are of much value, but it seems to me they both admired and resented her, but they would not have harmed her." She looked at him with a curious expression, half wry, half sad. "They are very angry with Sir Herbert. They think he did it, and there is no pity for him." She leaned a little against one of the benches. "You will be very ill-advised to call any of them as witnesses if you can help it."

"Why? Do they believe she was in love with him and he misled her?"

"I don't know what they think." She shook her head. "They simply accept that he is guilty. It is not a carefully reasoned matter, just the difference between the status of a doctor and that of a nurse. He had power, she had not. It is all the old resentments of the weak against the strong, the poor against the wealthy, the ignorant against the educated and the clever. But you will have to be very subtle indeed to gain anything good from them on the witness stand."

"I take your warning," he said grimly. The outlook was not good. She had told him nothing, but given him hope. "What is your own opinion of Sir Herbert? You have been working with him, haven't you?"

"Yes." She frowned. "It surprises me, but I find it hard to believe he used her as her letters suggest. I hope I am not being vain, but I have never caught in his eye even the slightest personal interest in me." She looked at Rathbone carefully to judge his response. "And I have worked closely with him," she continued. "Often late into the night, and on difficult cases when there was much room for emotion over shared success or failure. I have found him dedicated to his work, and totally correct in all particulars of his behavior."

"Would you be prepared to swear to that?"

"Of course. But I cannot see that is useful. I daresay any other nurse who has worked with him will do the same."

"I cannot call them without being sure they will say as you do," he pointed out. "I wonder, could you—"

"I have already," she interrupted. "I have spoken with a few others who worked with him now and then, most particularly the youngest and best-looking. None of them has ever found him anything but most correct."

He felt a slight lift of spirits. If nothing else, it established a pattern.

"Now that is helpful," he acknowledged. "Did Nurse Barrymore confide in anyone, do you know? Surely she had some particular friend."

"None of whom I am aware." She shook her head and made a little face. "But I shall look further. She didn't in the Crimea. She was totally absorbed in her work; there was no time and no emotion left for much more than the sort of silent understanding that requires no effort. England and all its ties were left behind. I suppose there must have been a great deal of her I didn't know—didn't even think about."

"I need to know," he said simply. "It would make all the difference if we knew what was going on in her mind."

"Of course." She looked at him gravely for a moment, then straightened her shoulders. "I shall inform you of anything that I think could possibly be of use. Do you require it written down, or will a verbal report be sufficient?"

With difficulty he kept himself from smiling. "Oh, a verbal report will be far better," he said soberly. "Then if I wish to pursue any issue further I can do it at the time. Thank you very much for your assistance. I am sure justice will be the better served."

"I thought it was Sir Herbert you were trying to serve," she said dryly, but not without amusement. Then she politely took her farewell and excused herself back to her duties.

He stood in the small room for a moment or two after she had gone. He felt a sense of elation slowly filling him. He had forgotten how exhilarating she was, how immediate and intelligent, how without pretense. To be with her was at once pleasingly familiar, oddly comfortable, and yet also disturbing. It was something he could not easily dismiss from his thoughts or choose when he would think about it and when he would not.

Monk had very mixed feelings about undertaking to work for Oliver Rathbone in Sir Herbert Stanhope's defense. When he had read the letters he had believed they were proof of a relationship quite different from anything Sir Herbert had admitted. It was both shameful, on a personal and professional level, and—if she were indiscreet, as she had so obviously threatened to be—a motive for murder . . . a very simple one which would easily be believed by any jury.

But on the other hand Rathbone's account of it having been all in Prudence's feverish overemotional imagination was something which with any other woman would have been only too easily believable. And was Monk guilty of having credited Prudence with a moral strength, a single-minded dedication to duty, that was superhuman, overlooking her very ordinary, mortal weaknesses? Had he once again created in his imagination a woman totally different from, and inferior to, the real one?

It was a painful thought. And yet wounding as it was, he could not escape it. He had read into Hermione qualities she did not have, and perhaps into Imogen Latterly too. How many other women had he so idealized—and hopelessly misread?

It seemed where they were involved he had neither judgment nor even the ability to learn from his mistakes.

At least professionally he was skilled—more than skilled, he was brilliant. His cases were record of that; they were a list of victory after victory. Even though he could remember few details, he knew the flavor, knew from other men's regard for him that he seldom lost. And no one spoke lightly of him or willingly crossed his will. Men who served with him gave of their best. They might dread it, obey with trepidation, but when success came they were elated and proud to be part of it. It was an accolade to have served with

269

Monk, a mark of success in one's career, a stepping-stone to greater things.

But with another, all too familiar, jar of discomfort, he was reminded of Runcorn's words by the memory of having humiliated the young constable who was working with him on that case so long ago which hovered on the edge of his memory with such vividness. He could picture the man's face as he lashed him with words of scorn for his timidity, his softheartedness with witnesses who were concealing truth, evading what was painful for them, regardless of the cost to others. He felt a sharp stab of guilt for the way he had treated the man, who was not dilatory, nor was he a coward, simply more sensitive to others' feelings and approaching the problem with a different way of solving it. Perhaps his way was less efficient than Monk's, but not necessarily of less moral worth. Monk could see that now with the wisdom of hindsight, the clearer knowledge of himself. But at the time he had felt nothing but contempt and he had made no effort to conceal it.

He could not remember what had happened to the man, if he had remained on the force, discouraged and unhappy, or if he had left. Please God, Monk had not ruined him.

But rack his brain as he might, he found no clue to memory at all, no shred of the man's life that stayed with him. And that probably meant that he had not cared one way or the other what happened to him—which was an added ugly thought.

Work. He must pursue Rathbone's problem and strive just as hard to prove Stanhope innocent as he had done to prove him guilty. Perhaps a great deal more was needed, even for his own satisfaction. The letters were proof of probability, certainly not proof conclusive. But the only proof conclusive would be that it was impossible for him to have done it, and since he had both means and opportunity, and certainly motive, they could not look for that. The alternative was to prove that someone else was guilty. That was the only way to acquit him without question. Mere doubt might help him elude the hangman's rope, but not redeem his honor or his reputation.

Was he innocent?

Far worse than letting a guilty man go free was the sickening thought of the slow, deliberate condemnation and death of an innocent one. That was a taste with which he was already familiar, and he would give everything he knew, all he possessed, every moment of his nights and days, rather than ever again contribute to that happening. That once still haunted his worst dreams, the white hopeless face staring at him in the middle of the night. The fact that he had struggled to prevent it was comfortless in its chill attempt at self-justification.

There may not be any evidential proof that anyone else was guilty; no footprints, pieces of torn cloth, witnesses who had seen or overheard, no lies in which to catch anyone.

If not Sir Herbert, who?

He did not know where to begin. There were two options: prove someone else guilty, which might not be possible; or cast such strong doubt on Sir Herbert's guilt that a jury could not accept it. He had already done all that he could think of in the former. Until some new idea occurred to him, he would pursue the latter. He would seek out Sir Herbert's colleagues and learn his reputation among them. They might prove impressive character witnesses, if nothing more.

There followed several days of routine, excessively polite interviews in which he struggled to provoke some comments deeper than fulsome professional praise, carefully expressed disbelief that Sir Herbert could have done such a thing, and rather nervous agreement to testify on his behalf—if it were strictly necessary. The hospital governors were transparently nervous of becoming involved in something which they feared might prove to be very ugly before it was finished. It was painfully apparent in their faces that they did not know whether he was guilty or not, or where they should nail their colors to avoid sinking with a lost cause.

From Mrs. Flaherty he got tight-lipped silence and a total refusal to offer any opinion at all or to testify in court should she be asked. She was frightened, and like many who feel themselves defenseless, she froze. Monk was surprised to find he understood her with more patience than he had expected of himself. Even as he stood in the bleak hospital corridor and saw her pinched face with its pale skin and bright spots of color on the cheekbones, he realized her vulnerability and her confusion.

Berenice Ross Gilbert was entirely different. She received him in the room where the Board of Governors normally met, a wide gracious chamber with a long mahogany table set around with chairs, sporting prints on the walls and brocade curtains at the windows. She was dressed in deepest teal green trimmed with turquoise. It was expensive, and remarkably flattering to her auburn coloring. Its huge skirts swept around her, but she moved them elegantly without effort.

She regarded Monk with amusement, looking over his features, his strong nose, high cheekbones, and level unflinching eyes. He saw the spark of interest light in her face and the smile curve her lips. It was a look he had seen many times before, and he understood its meaning with satisfaction.

"Poor Sir Herbert." She raised her arched brows. "A perfectly fearful thing. I wish I knew what to say to help, but what can I do?" She shrugged graceful shoulders. "I have no idea what the man's personal weaknesses may have been. I always found him courteous, highly professional, and correct at all times. But then"—she smiled at Monk, meeting his eyes—"if he were seeking an illicit romance, he would not have chosen me with whom to have it." The smile widened. He knew she was telling both the truth and a lie. She expected him to decipher its double meanings. She was no trivial pastime to be picked up and put down; but on the other hand, she was a sophisticated and elegant

272

woman, almost beautiful in her own way, perhaps better than beautiful—full of character. She had thought Prudence prim, naive, and immeasurably inferior to herself in all aspects of charm and allure.

Monk had no specific memories, and yet he knew he had stood in this position many times before, facing a wealthy, well-read woman who had found him exciting and was happy to forget his office and his purpose.

He smiled back at her very slightly, enough to be civil, not enough to betray any interest himself.

"I am sure it was part of your duties as a governor of the hospital, Lady Ross Gilbert, to be aware of the morals and failings of members of the staff. And I imagine you are an acute judge of human nature, particularly in that area." He saw her eyes glisten with amusement. "What is Sir Herbert's reputation? Please be honest—euphemisms will serve neither his interest nor the hospital's."

"I seldom deal in euphemisms, Mr. Monk," she said, still with the curl of a smile on her lips. She stood very elegantly, leaning a little against one of the chairs. "I wish I could tell you something more interesting, but I have never heard a word of scandal about Sir Herbert." She pulled a sad, mocking little face. "Rather to the contrary, he appears to be a brilliant surgeon but personally a boringly correct man, rather pompous, self-opinionated, socially, politically, and religiously orthodox."

She was watching Monk all the time. "I doubt if he ever had an original idea except in medicine, in which he is both innovative and courageous. It seems as if that has drained all his creative energies and attentions, and what is left is tedious to a degree." The laughter in her eyes was sharp and the interest in them more and more open, betraying that she did not believe for an instant that he fell into that category.

"Do you know him personally, Lady Ross Gilbert?" he asked, watching her face.

Again she shrugged, one shoulder a fraction higher than the other. "Only as business required, which is very little.

I have met Lady Stanhope socially, but not often." Her voice altered subtly, a very delicately implied contempt. "She is a very retiring person. She prefers to spend her time at home with her children—seven, I believe. But she always seemed most agreeable—not fashionable, you understand, but quite comely, very feminine, not in the least a strident or awkward creature." Her heavy eyelids lowered almost imperceptibly. "I daresay she is in every way an excellent wife. I have no reason to doubt it."

"And what of Nurse Barrymore?" he asked, again watching her face, but he saw no flicker in her expression, nothing to betray any emotion or knowledge that troubled her.

"I knew of her only the little I observed myself or what was reported to me by others. I have to confess, I never heard anything to her discredit." Her eyes searched his face. "I think, frankly, that she was just as tedious as he is. They were well matched."

"An interesting use of words, ma'am."

She laughed quite openly. "Unintentional, Mr. Monk. I had no deeper meaning in my mind."

"Do you believe she nourished daydreams about him?" he asked.

She looked up at the ceiling. "Heaven knows. I would have thought she would place them more interestingly—Dr. Beck, for a start. He is a man of feeling and humor, a little vain, and I would have thought of a more natural appetite." She gave a little laugh. "But then perhaps that was not what she wanted." She looked back at him again. "No, to be candid, Mr. Monk, I think she admired Sir Herbert intensely, as do we all, but on an impersonal level. To hear that it was a romantic vision surprises me. But then life is constantly surprising, don't you find?" Again the light was in her eyes and the lift, the sparkle that was almost an invitation, although whether to do more than admire her was not certain.

And that was all that he could learn from her. Not much use to Oliver Rathbone, but he reported it just the same.

* * *

274

With Kristian Beck he fared not much better, although the interview was completely different. He met him in his own home, by choice. Mrs. Beck was little in evidence, but her cold, precise nature was stamped on the unimaginative furnishings of her house, the rigidly correct placement of everything, the sterile bookshelves where nothing was out of place, either in the rows of books themselves or in their orthodox contents. Even the flowers in the vases were carefully arranged in formal proportions and stood stiffly to attention. The whole impression was clean, orderly, and forbidding. Monk never met the woman (apparently she was out performing some good work or other), but he could imagine her as keenly as if he had. She would have hair drawn back from an exactly central parting, eyebrows without flight or imagination, flat cheekbones, and careful passionless lips.

Whatever had made Beck choose such a woman? He was exactly the opposite; his face was full of humor and emotion and as sensuous a mouth as Monk had ever seen, and yet there was nothing coarse about it, nothing self-indulgent, rather the opposite. What mischance had brought these two together? That was almost certainly something he would never know. He thought with bitter self-mockery that perhaps Beck was as poor a judge of women as he himself. Maybe he had mistaken her passionless face for one of purity and refinement, her humorlessness for intelligence, even piety.

Kristian led him to his study, a room entirely different, where his own character held sway. Books were piled on shelves, books of all sorts, novels and poetry along with biography, history, philosophy, and medicine. The colors were rich, the curtains velvet, the fireplace faced with copper and the mantel displaying an idiosyncratic collection of ornaments. The icy Mrs. Beck had no place here. In fact, the room reminded Monk rather more of Callandra in its haphazard order, its richness and worth. He could picture her here, her sensitive, humorous face, her long nose, untidy hair, her unerring knowledge of what really mattered.

"What can I do to assist you, Mr. Monk?" Kristian was regarding him with puzzlement. "I really have no idea what happened, and the little I have learned as to why the police suspect Sir Herbert I find very hard to believe. At least if the newspaper reports are correct?"

"Largely," Monk replied, dragging his attention back to the case. "There is a collection of letters from Prudence Barrymore to her sister which suggests that she was deeply in love with Sir Herbert and that he had led her to suppose that he returned her feelings and would take steps to make marriage between them possible."

"But that's ridiculous," Kristian said with concern, silently indicating a chair for Monk to be seated. "What could he possibly do? He has an excellent wife and a large family—seven, I think. Of course he could have walked out on them, in theory, but in practice it would ruin him, a fact of which he cannot possibly have been unaware."

Monk accepted the invitation and sat down. The chair was extremely comfortable.

"Even if he did, it would not free him to marry Miss Barrymore," he pointed out. "No, I am aware of that, Dr. Beck. But I am interested to learn your opinion of both Sir Herbert and Miss Barrymore. You say you find all this hard to believe—do you believe it?"

Kristian sat opposite him, thinking for a moment before replying, his dark eyes on Monk's face.

"No—no, I don't think I do. Sir Herbert is essentially a very careful man, very ambitious, jealous for his reputation and his status in the medical community, both in Britain and abroad." He put the tips of his fingers together. He had beautiful hands, strong, broad palmed, smaller than Sir Herbert's. "To become involved in such a way with a nurse, however interesting or attractive," he went on, "would be foolish in the extreme. Sir Herbert is not an impulsive man, nor a man of physical or emotional appetite." He said it without expression, as if he neither admired nor despised such an absence. Looking at his face, Monk knew Dr. Beck was as different from Sir Herbert as it was possible for another clever and dedicated man to be, but he had no indication of Kristian's feelings.

"You used the words *intelligent* and *attractive* about Nurse Barrymore," he said curiously. "Did you find her so? I gathered from Lady Ross Gilbert that she was a trifle priggish, naive as to matters of love, and altogether not the sort of woman a man might find appealing."

Kristian laughed. "Yes—Berenice would see her in that light. Two such different women it would be hard to imagine. I doubt they could ever have understood each other."

"That is not an answer, Dr. Beck."

"No, it isn't." He seemed quite unoffended. "Yes, I thought Nurse Barrymore was most attractive, both as a person and, were I free to think so, as a woman. But then my taste is not usual, I confess. I like courage and humor, and I find intelligence stimulating." He crossed his legs and leaned back in the chair, regarding Monk with a smile. "It is, for me, extremely unprofitable to spend my time with a woman who has nothing to talk about but trivia. I dislike simpering and flirting, and I find agreement and obedience essentially very lonely things. If a woman says she agreed with you, whatever her own thoughts, in what sense do you have her true companionship at all? You may as well have a charming picture, because all you are receiving from her are your own ideas back again."

Monk thought of Hermione—charming, docile, pliable— and of Hester—opinionated, obstructive, passionate in her beliefs, full of courage, uncomfortable to be with (at times he disliked her more that anyone else he knew)—but real.

"Yes," he said reluctantly. "I take your point. Do you think it is likely that Sir Herbert also found her attractive?"

"Prudence Barrymore?" Kristian bit his lip thoughtfully. "I doubt it. I know he respected her professional abilities. We all did. But she occasionally challenged his opinions, and that incensed him. He did not accept that from his peers, let alone from a nurse—and a woman."

Monk frowned. "Might that have angered him enough to lash out at her for it?"

Kristian laughed. "Hardly. He was chief surgeon here. She was only a nurse. He had it eminently in his power to crush her without resort to anything so out of character, so dangerous to himself."

"Even if he had been wrong and she was right?" Monk pressed. "It would have become known to others."

Kristian's face suddenly became serious.

"Well, that would put a different complexion upon it, of course. He would not take that well at all. No man would."

"Might her medical knowledge have been sufficient for that to happen?" Monk asked.

Kristian shook his head slightly.

"I don't know. I suppose it is conceivable. She certainly knew a great deal, far more than any other nurse I have ever met, although the nurse who replaced her is extraordinarily good."

Monk felt a quick surge of satisfaction and was instantly discomfited by it.

"Enough?" he said a little more sharply than he had intended.

"Possibly," Kristian conceded. "But have you anything whatever to indicate that that is what happened? I thought he was arrested because of the letters?" He shook his head slightly. "And a woman in love does not show up a man's mistakes to the world. Just the opposite. Every woman I ever met defended a man to the end if she loved him, even if perhaps she should not have. No, Mr. Monk, that is not a viable theory. Anyway, from your initial remarks I gathered you were hired by Sir Herbert's barrister in order to help find evidence to acquit him. Did I misunderstand you?"

It was a polite way of asking if Monk had lied.

"No, Dr. Beck, you are perfectly correct," Monk answered, knowing he would understand the meaning behind the words as well. "I am testing the strength of the prosecution's case in order to be able to defend against it."

"How can I help you do that?" Kristian asked gravely. "I have naturally thought over the matter again and again, as

I imagine we all have. But I can think of nothing which will help or hurt him. Of course I shall testify to his excellent personal reputation and his high professional standing, if you wish it."

"I expect we shall," Monk accepted. "If I ask you here in private, Dr. Beck, will you tell me candidly if you believe him guilty?"

Kristian looked vaguely surprised.

"I will answer you equally candidly, sir. I believe it extremely unlikely. Nothing I have ever seen or heard of the man gives me to believe he would behave in such a violent, unself-disciplined, and overemotional manner."

"How long have you known him?"

"I have worked with him just a little less than eleven years."

"And you will swear to that?"

"I will."

Monk had to think about what the prosecution could draw out by skillful and devious questions. Now was the time to discover, not on the stand when it was too late. He pursued every idea he could think of, but all Kristian's answers were measured and uncritical. He rose half an hour later, thanked Kristian for his time and frankness, and took his leave.

It had been a curiously unsatisfactory interview. He should have been pleased. Kristian Beck had confirmed every aspect of Sir Herbert's character he had wished, and he was more than willing to testify. Why should Monk not be pleased?

If it were not Sir Herbert, then surely the other most obvious suspects were Geoffrey Taunton and Beck himself. Was he the charming, intelligent, only very faintly foreign man he seemed? Or was there something closed about him, something infinitely darker behind the exterior which even Monk found so pleasing?

He had no idea. His usual sense of judgment had left him.

* * *

Monk spoke to as many of Prudence's friends and colleagues as he could, but they were reluctant to see him and full of resentment. Young nurses glared at him defensively and answered with monosyllables when he asked if Prudence were romantic.

"No." It was as blunt as that.

"Did she ever speak of marriage?"

"No. I never heard her."

"Of leaving nursing and settling into a domestic life?" he pressed.

"Oh no—never. Not ever. She loved her job."

"Did you ever see her excited, flushed, extremely happy or sad for no reason you knew of?"

"No. She was always in control. She wasn't like you say at all." The answer was given with a flat stare, defiant and resentful.

"Did she ever exaggerate?" he said desperately. "Paint her achievements as more than they were, or glamorize the war in the Crimea?"

At last he provoked emotion, but it was not what he wanted.

"No she did not." The young woman's face flushed hot with anger. "It's downright wicked of you to say that! She always told the truth. And she never spoke about the Crimea at all, except to tell us about Miss Nightingale's ideas. She never praised herself at all. And I'll not listen to you say different! Not to defend that man who killed her, or anything else, I'll swear to that."

It was no help to him at all, and yet perversely he was pleased. He had had a long fruitless week, and had heard very little that was of use, and only precisely what he had foreseen. But no one had destroyed his picture of Prudence. He had found nothing that drew her as the emotional, blackmailing woman her letters suggested.

But what was the truth?

The last person he saw was Lady Stanhope. It was an emotionally charged meeting, as it was bound to be. Sir Herbert's arrest had devastated her. She required all the courage she could draw on to maintain a modicum of composure for her children's sake, but the marks of shock, sleeplessness, and much weeping were only too evident in her face. When he was shown in, Arthur, her eldest son, was at her elbow, his face white, his chin high and defiant.

"Good afternoon, Mr. Monk," Lady Stanhope said very quietly. She seemed at a loss to understand precisely who he was and why he had come. She blinked at him expectantly. She was seated on a carved, hard-backed chair, Arthur immediately behind her, and she did not rise when Monk came in.

"Good afternoon, Lady Stanhope," he replied. He must force himself to be gentle with her. Impatience would serve no one; it was a weakness, and he must look at it so. "Good afternoon, Mr. Stanhope," he added, acknowledging Arthur.

Arthur nodded. "Please be seated, Mr. Monk," he invited, rectifying his mother's omission. "What can we do for you, sir? As you may imagine, my mother is not seeing people unless it is absolutely necessary. This time is very difficult for us."

"Of course," Monk conceded, sitting in the offered chair. "I am assisting Mr. Rathbone in preparing a defense for your father, as I believe I wrote you."

"His defense is that he is innocent," Arthur interrupted. "The poor woman was obviously deluded. It happens to unmarried ladies of a certain age, I believe. They construct fantasies, daydreams about eminent people, men of position, dignity. It is usually simply sad and a little embarrassing. On this occasion it has proved tragic also."

With difficulty Monk suppressed the question that rose to his lips. Did this smooth-faced, rather complacent young man think of the death of Prudence Barrymore, or only of the charge against his father?

"That is one thing that is undeniable," he agreed aloud. "Nurse Barrymore is dead, and your father is in prison awaiting trial for murder."

Lady Stanhope gasped and the last vestige of color

drained from her cheeks. She clutched at Arthur's hand resting on her shoulder.

"Really, sir!" Arthur said furiously. "That was unnecessary! I would think you might have more sensitivity toward my mother's feelings. If you have some business with us, please conduct it as briefly and circumspectly as you can. Then leave us, for pity's sake."

Monk controlled himself with an effort. He could remember doing this before, sitting opposite stunned and frightened people who did not know what to say and could only sit mesmerized by their grief. He could see a quiet woman, an ordinary face devastated by tormenting loss, white hands clenched in her lap. She too had been unable to speak to him. He had been filled with a rage so vast the taste of it was still familiar in his mouth. But it had not been against her, for her he felt only a searing pity. But why? Why now, after all these years, did he remember that woman instead of all the others?

Nothing came, nothing at all, just the emotion filling his mind and making his body tense.

"What can we do?" Lady Stanhope asked again. "What can we say to help Herbert?"

Gradually, with uncharacteristic patience, he drew from them a picture of Sir Herbert as a quiet, very proper man with an ordinary domestic life, devoted to his family, predictable in all his personal tastes. His only appetite seemed to be for a glass of excellent whiskey every evening, and a fondness for good roast beef. He was a dutiful husband, an affectionate father.

The conversation was slow and tense. He explored every avenue he could think of to draw from either of them anything that would be of use to Rathbone, better than the predictable loyalty which he believed was quite literally the truth but not necessarily likely to influence a jury. What else could a wife say? And she was not a promising witness. She was too frightened to be coherent or convincing.

In spite of himself he was sorry for her.

He was about to leave when there was a knock at the

282

door. Without waiting for a reply, a young woman opened it and came in. She was slender—in fact, thin—and her face was so marked with illness and disappointment it was hard to tell her age, but he thought probably not more than twenty.

"Excuse my interruption," she began, but even before she spoke Monk was overcome by a wave of memory so vivid and so agonizing his present surroundings became invisible to him, Lady Stanhope and Arthur merely blurs on the edge of his vision. He knew what the old case was, violently and with sickening immediacy. A girl had been molested and murdered. He could still see her thin broken body and feel the rage inside himself, the confusion and the pain, the aching helplessness. That was why he had driven his constables so hard, worried and harassed his witnesses, why his contempt had scalded Runcorn without mercy or patience.

The horror was back inside him with all the freshness it had had when he was twenty. It did not excuse the way he had treated people, it did not undo anything, but it explained it. At least he had had a reason, a passion which was not centered upon himself. He was not merely cruel, arrogant, and ambitious. He had cared—furiously, tirelessly, single-mindedly.

He found himself smiling with relief, and yet there was a sickness in his stomach.

"Mr. Monk?" Lady Stanhope said nervously.

"Yes—yes, ma'am?"

"Are you going to be able to help my husband, Mr. Monk?"

"I believe so," he said firmly. "And I shall do everything within my power, I promise you."

"Thank you. I—we—are most grateful." She held Arthur's hand a little more tightly. "All of us."

9

THE TRIAL OF SIR HERBERT STANHOPE opened at the Old Bailey on the first Monday in August. It was a gray, sultry day with a hot wind out of the south and the smell of rain. Outside the crowds pressed forward, climbing up the steps, eager to claim the few public seats available. There was an air of excitement, whispering and pushing, an urgency. Newsboys shouted promises about exclusive revelations, prophesies of what was to come. The first few heavy drops of rain fell with a warm splatter on oblivious heads.

Inside the wood-paneled courtroom the jury sat in two rows, their backs to the high windows, faces toward the lawyers' tables, behind whom were the few public benches. To the jurors' right, twenty feet above the floor, was the dock, like a closed-in balcony, its hidden steps leading down to the cells. Opposite the dock was the witness box, like a pulpit. To reach it one crossed the open space of the floor and climbed the curving steps up, then stood isolated, facing the barristers and the public. Higher still, and behind the witness box, surrounded by magnificently carved panels and seated on plush, was the judge. He was robed in scarlet velvet and wigged in curled white horsehair.

The court had already been called to order. The jury was

empaneled and the charge had been read and answered. With immense dignity, head high and voice steady, Sir Herbert denied his guilt absolutely. Immediately there was a rustle of sympathy around the body of the court.

The judge, a man in his late forties with brilliant light gray eyes and a clean-boned, lean-cheeked face, flashed his glance around but refrained from speech. He was a hard man, young for such high office, but he owed no one favors and had no ambitions but the law. He was saved from ruthlessness by a sharp sense of humor, and redeemed by a love of classical literature and its soaring imagination, which he barely understood but knew he held to be of immense worth.

The prosecution was conducted by Wilberforce Lovat-Smith, one of the most gifted barristers of his generation and a man Rathbone knew well. He had faced him frequently across the floor of the court, and held him in high regard, and not a little liking. He was of barely average height, dark-complexioned with a sharp-featured face and heavy-lidded, surprisingly blue eyes. His appearance was not impressive. He looked rather more like an itinerant musician or player than a pillar of the establishment. His gown was a fraction too long for him, indifferently tailored, and his wig was not precisely straight. But Rathbone did not make the mistake of underestimating him.

The first witness to be called was Callandra Daviot. She walked across the space between the benches toward the witness stand with her back straight and her head high. But as she climbed the steps she steadied herself with her hand on the rail, and when she turned to Lovat-Smith her face was pale and she looked tired, as if she had not slept well for days, even weeks. It was apparent that either she was ill or she was carrying some well-nigh-intolerable burden.

Hester was not present; she was on duty at the hospital. Apart from the fact that financially she required the employment, both she and Monk believed she might still learn something useful there. It was a remote chance, but any chance at all was worth taking.

Monk was sitting in the center of the row toward the front, listening and watching every inflection and expression. He would be at hand if Rathbone wanted to pursue any new thread that should appear. He looked at Callandra and knew that something was deeply wrong. He stared at her for several minutes, until well into the beginning of her evidence, before he realized what troubled him about her appearance even more than the gauntness of her face. Her hair was totally, even beautifully tidy. It was quite out of character. The fact that she was in the witness box did not account for it. He had seen her at far more important and formal occasions, even dressed before departing to dine with ambassadors and royalty, still with wisps of hair curling wildly out of place. It touched him with an unanswerable unhappiness.

"They were quarreling about the fact that the laundry chute was apparently blocked?" Lovat-Smith was saying with affected surprise. There was total stillness in the courtroom, although everyone in it knew what was coming. The newspapers had screamed it in banner headlines at the time, and it was not a thing one forgot. Still the jurors leaned forward, listening to every word, eyes steady in concentration.

Mr. Justice Hardie smiled almost imperceptibly.

"Yes," Callandra was offering no more than exactly what she was asked for.

"Please continue, Lady Callandra," Lovat-Smith prompted. She was not a hostile witness, but she was not helpful either. A lesser man might have been impatient with her. Lovat-Smith was far too wise for that. The court sympathized with her, thinking the experience would have shocked any sensitive woman. The jurors were all men, naturally. Women were not considered capable of rational judgment sufficient to vote as part of the mass of the population. How could they possibly weigh the matter of a man's life or death as part of a mere twelve? And Lovat-Smith knew juries were ordinary men. That was both their strength and their weakness. They would presume Callandra was an average woman, susceptible, fragile, like all women. They had no idea she had both wit and strength far more than many of the soldiers her husband had treated when he was alive. Accordingly he was gentle and courteous.

"I regret having to ask you this, but would you recount for us what happened next, in your own words. Do not feel hurried. . . ."

The ghost of a smile crossed Callandra's mouth.

"You are very civil, sir. Of course. I shall tell you. Dr. Beck peered down the chute to see if he could discover what was blocking it, but he could not. We sent one of the nurses for a window pole to push down the chute and dislodge whatever it was. At that time . . ." She swallowed hard and continued in a hushed voice. "We assumed it was a tangle of sheets. Of course the window pole failed."

"Of course," Lovat-Smith agreed helpfully. "What did you do then, ma'am?"

"Someone, I forget which of the nurses, suggested we fetch one of the skivvies who was a child, and very small, and send her down the chute to clear it."

"Send the child down?" Lovat-Smith said very clearly. "At this time you were still of the belief it was linen blocking the way?"

There was a shiver of apprehension around the room. Rathbone pulled a face, but very discreetly, out of view of the jury. In the dock Sir Herbert sat expressionless. Judge Hardie drummed his fingers silently on the top of his bench.

Lovat-Smith saw it and understood. He invited Callandra to continue.

"Of course," she said quietly.

"Then what happened?"

"Dr. Beck and I went down to the laundry room to await the blockage."

"Why?"

"I beg your pardon?"

"Why did you go downstairs to the laundry room, ma'am?"

"I—I really don't remember. It seemed the natural thing to do at the time. I suppose to find out what it was, and see that the quarrel was resolved. That is why we intervened in the beginning, to resolve the quarrel."

"I see. Yes, quite natural. Will you please tell the court what occurred then?"

Callandra was very pale and seemed to require an effort to maintain her control. Lovat-Smith smiled at her encouragingly.

"After a moment or two there was a sort of noise. . . ." She drew in her breath, not looking at Lovat-Smith. "And a body came out of the chute and landed in the laundry basket below it."

She was prevented from continuing immediately by the rustles and murmurs of horror in the public gallery. Several of the jurors gasped and one reached for his handkerchief.

In the dock Sir Herbert winced very slightly, but his eyes remained steadily on Callandra.

"At first I thought it was the skivvy," she resumed. "Then an instant later a second body landed and scrambled to get out. It was then we looked at the first body and realized quite quickly that she was dead."

Again there was a gasp of indrawn breath around the room and a buzz of words, cut off instantly.

Rathbone glanced up at the dock. Even facial expressions could matter. He had known more than one prisoner to sway a jury against him by insolence. But he need not have worried. Sir Herbert was composed and grave, his face showing only sadness.

"I see." Lovat-Smith held up his hand very slightly. "How did you know this first body was dead, Lady Callandra? I know you have some medical experience; I believe your late husband was an army surgeon. Would you please just describe for us what the body was like." He smiled deprecatingly. "I apologize for asking you to relive what must be extremely distressing for you, but I assure you it is necessary for the jury, you understand?"

"It was the body of a young woman wearing a gray

nurse's dress." Callandra spoke quietly, but her voice was thick with emotion. "She was lying on her back in the basket, sort of folded, one leg up. No one who was not rendered senseless would have remained in such a position. When we looked at her more closely, her eyes were closed, her face ashen pale, and there were purple bruise marks on her throat. She was cold to the touch."

There was a long sigh from the public galleries and someone sniffed. Two jurors glanced at each other, and a third shook his head, his face very grave.

Rathbone sat motionless at his table.

"Just one question, Lady Callandra," Lovat-Smith said apologetically. "Did you know the young woman?"

"Yes." Callandra's face was white. "It was Prudence Barrymore."

"One of the hospital nurses?" Lovat-Smith stepped back a yard. "In fact, one of your very best nurses, I believe? Did she not serve in the Crimea with Florence Nightingale?"

Rathbone considered objecting that this was irrelevant: Lovat-Smith was playing for drama. But he would do his cause more harm than good by trying to deny Prudence Barrymore her moment of posthumous recognition, as Lovat-Smith would know; he could see it in his faintly cocky stance, as if Rathbone were no danger.

"A fine woman in every respect," Callandra said quietly. "I had the highest regard and affection for her."

Lovat-Smith inclined his head. "Thank you, ma'am. The court offers you its appreciation for what must have been a most difficult duty for you. Thank you, I have nothing further to ask you."

Judge Hardie leaned forward as Callandra moved fractionally.

"If you would remain, Lady Callandra, Mr. Rathbone may wish to speak."

Callandra flushed at her own foolishness, although she had not actually taken a step to leave.

Lovat-Smith returned to his table, and Rathbone rose, approaching the witness box and looking up at her. He was disturbed to see her so drawn.

"Good morning, Lady Callandra. My learned friend has concluded with your identification of the unfortunate dead woman. But perhaps you would tell the court what you did after ascertaining that she was beyond your help?"

"I—we—Dr. Beck remained with her"—Callandra stammered very slightly—"to see she was not touched, and I went to report the matter to Sir Herbert Stanhope, so that he might send for the police."

"Where did you find him?"

"In the theater—operating upon a patient."

"Can you recall his reaction when you informed him what had happened?"

Again faces turned toward the dock as people stared at Sir Herbert, curious and titillated by horror.

"Yes—he was shocked, of course. He told me to go to the police station and inform the police—when he realized it was a police matter."

"Oh? He did not realize it immediately?"

"Perhaps that was my fault," she acknowledged. "I may have told him in such a way he thought it was a natural death. There are frequently deaths in a hospital." ·

"Of course. Did he appear to you to be frightened or nervous?"

A ghost of bitter amusement passed over her face.

"No. He was perfectly calm. I believe he completed the operation."

"Successfully?" He had already ascertained that it was successfully, or he would not have asked. He could remember vividly asking Sir Herbert, and his candid, rather surprised reply.

"Yes." Callandra met his eyes and he knew she understood precisely.

"A man with a calm mind and a steady hand," he remarked. Again he was aware of the jury looking toward the dock.

Lovat-Smith rose to his feet.

290

"Yes, yes," Judge Hardie said, waving his hand. "Mr. Rathbone, please keep your observations till your summation. Lady Callandra was not present at the rest of the operation to pass judgment upon it. You have already elicited that the patient survived, which I imagine you knew? Yes— quite so. Please proceed."

"Thank you, my lord." Rathbone bowed almost imperceptibly. "Lady Callandra, we may assume that you did in fact inform the police. One Inspector Jeavis, I believe. Was that the end of your concern in the case?"

"I beg your pardon?" She blinked and her face became even paler, something like fear in her eyes and the quick tightening of her mouth.

"Was that the end of your concern in the case?" he repeated. "Did you take any further actions?"

"Yes—yes I did. . . ." She stopped.

"Indeed? And what were they?"

Again there was the rustle of movement in the court as silks and taffetas brushed against each other and were crushed as people leaned forward. On the jury benches all faces turned toward Callandra. Judge Hardie looked at her inquiringly.

"I—I employed a private agent with whom I am acquainted," she replied very quietly.

"Will you speak so the jury may hear you, if you please," Judge Hardie directed her.

She repeated it more distinctly, staring at Rathbone.

"Why did you do that, Lady Callandra? Did you not believe the police competent enough to handle the matter?" Out of the corner of his vision he saw Lovat-Smith stiffen and knew he had surprised him.

Callandra bit her lip. "I was not sure they would find the right solution. They do not always."

"Indeed they do not," Rathbone agreed. "Thank you, Lady Callandra. I have no further questions for you."

Before the judge could instruct her, Lovat-Smith rose to his feet again.

"Lady Callandra, do you believe they have found the correct answer in this instance?"

"Objection!" Rathbone said instantly. "Lady Callandra's opinion, for all her excellence, is neither professional nor relevant to these proceedings."

"Mr. Lovat-Smith," Judge Hardie said with a little shake of his head, "if that is all you have to say, Lady Callandra is excused, with the court's thanks."

Lovat-Smith sat down again, his mouth tight, avoiding Rathbone's glance.

Rathbone smiled, but with no satisfaction.

Lovat-Smith called Jeavis to the stand. He must have testified in court many times before, far more frequently than anyone else present, and yet he looked oddly out of place. His high, white collar seemed too tight for him, his sleeves an inch too short.

He gave evidence of the bare facts as he knew them, adding no emotion or opinion whatever. Even so, the jury drank in every word and only once or twice did any one of them look away from him and up at Sir Herbert in the dock.

Rathbone had debated with himself whether to cross-examine or not. He must not permit Lovat-Smith to goad him into making a mistake. There was nothing in Jeavis's evidence to challenge, nothing further to draw out.

"No questions, my lord," he said. He saw the flicker of amusement cross Lovat-Smith's face.

The next prosecution witness was the police surgeon, who testified as to the time and cause of death. It was a very formal affair and Rathbone had nothing to ask of him either. His attention wandered. First he studied the jurors one by one. They were still fresh-faced, concentration sharp, catching every word. After two or three days they would look quite different; their eyes would be tired, muscles cramped. They would begin to fidget and grow impatient. They would no longer watch whoever was speaking but would stare around, as he was doing now. And quite possibly they would already have made up their minds whether Sir Herbert was guilty or not.

Lastly before luncheon adjournment Lovat-Smith called Mrs. Flaherty. She mounted the witness box steps very carefully, face white with concentration, black skirts brushing against the railings on either side. She looked exactly like an elderly housekeeper in dusty bombazine. Rathbone almost expected to see a chain of keys hanging from her waist and an expense ledger in her hand.

She faced the court with offense and disapproval in every pinched line of her features. She was affronted at the necessity of attending such a place. All criminal proceedings were beneath the dignity of respectable people, and she had never expected in all her days to find herself in such a position.

Lovat-Smith was obviously amused by it. There was nothing but respect in his face, and his manners were flawless, but Rathbone knew him well enough to detect it in the angle of his shoulders, the gestures of his hands, even the way he walked across the polished boards of the floor toward the stand and looked up at her.

"Mrs. Flaherty," he began quietly. "You are a matron of the Royal Free Hospital, are you not?"

"I am," she said grimly. She seemed about to add something more, then closed her lips in a thin line.

"Just so," Lovat-Smith agreed. He had not been raised by a governess nor had he been in hospital. Efficient middle-aged ladies did not inspire in him the awe they did in many of his colleagues.

He had told Rathbone, in one of their rare moments of relaxation together, late at night over a bottle of wine, that he had gone to a charity school on the outskirts of the city before a patron, observing his intelligence, had paid for him to have extra tutelage.

Now Lovat-Smith looked up at Mrs. Flaherty blandly. "Would you be good enough, ma'am, to tell the court where you were from approximately six in the morning of the day Prudence Barrymore met her death until you heard that her body had been discovered? Thank you so much."

Grudgingly and in precise detail she told him what he wished. As a result of his frequently interposed questions, she also told the court the whereabouts of almost all the other nurses on duty that morning, and largely those of the chaplain and the dressers also.

Rathbone did not interrupt. There was no point of procedure he quarreled with, nor any matter of fact. It would have been foolish to draw attention to the weakness of his position by fighting when he could not win. Let the jury think he was holding his fire in the certainty that he had a fatal blow to deliver at some future time. He sat back in his chair a little, composing his face into an expression of calm interest, a very slight smile on his lips.

He noticed several jurors glancing at him and then at Lovat-Smith, and knew they were wondering when the real battle would begin. They also took furtive looks at Sir Herbert, high up in the dock. He was very pale, but if there was terror inside him, or the sick darkness of guilt, not a breath of it showed in his face.

Rathbone studied him discreetly as Lovat-Smith drew more fine details from Mrs. Flaherty. Sir Herbert was listening with careful attention, but there was no real interest in his face. He seemed quite relaxed, his back straight, his hands clasped in front of him on the railing. It was all familiar territory and he knew it did not matter to the core of the case. He had never contested his own presence in the hospital at the time, and Mrs. Flaherty excluded only the peripheral players who were never true suspects.

Judge Hardie adjourned the court, and as they were leaving Lovat-Smith fell in step beside Rathbone, his curiously light eyes glittering with amusement.

"Whatever made you take it up?" he said quietly, but the disbelief was rich in his voice.

"Take what up?" Rathbone looked straight ahead of him as if he had not heard.

"The case, man! You can't win!" Lovat-Smith watched his step. "Those letters are damning."

Rathbone turned and smiled at him, a sweet dazzling smile showing excellent teeth. He said nothing.

Lovat-Smith faltered so minutely only an expert eye could have seen it. Then the composure returned and his expression became smooth again.

"It might keep your pocket, but it won't do your reputation any good," he said with calm certainty. "No knighthood in this sort of thing, you know."

Rathbone smiled a little more widely to hide the fact that he feared Lovat-Smith was right.

The afternoon's testimony was in many ways predictable, and yet it left Rathbone feeling dissatisfied, as he told his father later that evening when he visited him at his home in Primrose Hill.

Henry Rathbone was a tall, rather stoop-shouldered, scholarly man with gentle blue eyes masking a brilliant intellect behind a benign air and a rich, occasionally erratic and irreverent sense of humor. Oliver was more deeply fond of him than he would have admitted, even to himself. These occasional quiet dinners were oases of personal pleasure in an ambitious and extremely busy life.

On this occasion he was troubled and Henry Rathbone was immediately aware of it, although he had begun with all the usual trivial talk about the weather, the roses, and the cricket score.

They were sitting together in the evening light after an excellent supper of crusty bread, pâté, and French cheese. They had finished a bottle of red wine; it was not of a particularly good year, but satisfaction lent to the tongue what the vintage did not.

"Did you make a tactical error?" Henry Rathbone asked eventually.

"What makes you ask that?" Oliver looked at him nervously.

"Your preoccupation," Henry replied. "If it had been

something you had foreseen you would not still be turning it over in your mind."

"I'm not sure," Oliver confirmed. "In fact, I am not sure how I should approach this altogether."

Henry waited.

Oliver outlined the case as he knew it so far. Henry listened in silence, leaning back in his chair, his legs crossed comfortably.

"What testimony have you heard so far?" he asked when Oliver finally came to an end.

"Just factual this morning. Callandra Daviot recounted how she found the body. The police and the surgeon gave the facts of death and the time and manner, nothing new or startling. Lovat-Smith played it for all the drama and sympathy he could, but that was to be expected."

Henry nodded.

"I suppose it was this afternoon," Oliver said thoughtfully. "The first witness after luncheon was the matron of the hospital—a tense, autocratic little woman who obviously resented being called at all. She made it quite obvious she disapproved of 'ladies' nursing, and even Crimean experience won no favor in her eyes. In fact, the contrary—it challenged her dominion."

"And the jury?" Henry asked.

Oliver smiled. "Disliked her," he said succinctly. "She cast doubt on Prudence's ability. Lovat-Smith endeavored to keep her quiet on that but she still created a bad impression."

"But . . ." Henry prompted.

Oliver gave a sharp laugh. "But she swore that Prudence pursued Sir Herbert, asked to work with him and spent far more time with him than any other nurse. She did admit, grudgingly, that she was the best nurse and that Sir Herbert asked for her."

"All of which you surely foresaw." Henry looked at him closely. "It doesn't sound sufficient to account for your feelings now."

Oliver sat in thought. Outside the evening breeze carried

the scent of late-blooming honeysuckle in through the open French windows and a flock of starlings massed against the pale sky, then swirled and settled again somewhere beyond the orchard.

"Are you afraid of losing?" Henry broke the silence. "You've lost before—and you will again, unless you prefer to take only certain cases, ones so safe they require only a conductor through the motions?"

"No, of course not!" Oliver said in deep disgust. He was not angry; the suggestion was too absurd.

"Are you afraid Sir Herbert is guilty?"

This time his answer was more considered. "No. No, I'm not. It's a difficult case, no real evidence, but I believe him. I know what it is like to have a young woman mistake admiration or gratitude for a romantic devotion. One has absolutely no idea—beyond perhaps a certain vanity—I will confess to that, reluctantly. And then suddenly there she is, all heaving bosom and melting eyes, flushed cheeks—and there you are, horrified, mouth dry, brain racing, and feeling both a victim and a cad, and wondering how on earth you can escape with both honor and some kind of dignity."

Henry was smiling so openly he was on the verge of laughter.

"It's not funny!" Oliver protested.

"Yes it is—it's delicious. My dear boy, your sartorial elegance, your beautiful diction, your sheer vanity, will one day get you into terrible trouble! What is this Sir Herbert like?"

"I am not vain!"

"Yes you are—but it is a small fault compared with many. And you have redeeming features. Tell me about Sir Herbert."

"He is not sartorially elegant," Oliver said a trifle waspishly. "He dresses expensively, but his taste is extremely mundane, and his figure and deportment are a trifle portly and lacking in grace. *Substantial* is the word I would choose."

"Which says more about your feeling for him than about the man himself," Henry observed. "Is he vain?"

"Yes. Intellectually vain. I think it very probable he did not even notice her except as an extremely efficient adjunct to his own skills. I would be very surprised if he even gave her emotions a thought. He expects admiration, and I have been led to believe he always gets it."

"But not guilty?" Henry wrinkled his brow. "What would he have to lose if she accused him of impropriety?"

"Not nearly as much as she. No one of any standing would believe her. And there is no evidence whatever except her word. His reputation is immaculate."

"Then what disturbs you? Your client is innocent and you have at least a fighting chance of clearing him."

Oliver did not answer. The light was fading a little in the sky, the color deepening as the shadows spread across the grass.

"Did you behave badly?"

"Yes. I don't know what else I could have done—but yes, I feel it was badly."

"What did you do?"

"I tore Barrymore to shreds—her father," Oliver answered quietly. "An honest, decent man devastated by grief for a daughter he adored, and I did everything I could to make him believe she was a daydreamer who fantasized about her abilities and then lied about them to others. I tried to show that she was not the heroine she seemed, but an unhappy woman who had failed in her dreams and created for herself an imaginary world where she was cleverer, braver, and more skilled than she was in truth." He drew in a deep breath. "I could see in his face I even made him doubt her. God, I loathed doing that! I don't think I have ever done anything for which I felt grubbier."

"Is it true?" Henry's voice was gentle.

"I don't know. It could be," Oliver said furiously. "That isn't the point! I put dirty, irreverent fingers over the man's dreams! I dragged out the most precious thing he had, held it up to the public, then smeared it all over with doubt and

ugliness. I could feel the crowd hating me—and the jury—
but not as much as I loathed myself." He laughed abruptly.
"I think only Monk equaled the hold of me as I was leaving and I thought he was going to strike me. He was white
with rage. Looking at his eyes, I was frightened of him."
He gave a shaky laugh as the shame of that moment on the
Old Bailey steps came back to him, the frustration and
the self-disgust. "I think if he could have got away with it,
he might have killed me for what I did to Barrymore—and
to Prudence's memory." He stopped, aching for some word
of denial, of comfort.

Henry looked at him with bright, sad eyes. There was
love in his face, the desire to protect, but not to excuse.

"Was it a legitimate question to raise?" he asked.

"Yes, of course it was. She was normally a highly intelligent woman, but there was nothing whatever to make anyone, even a fool, think that Sir Herbert would leave his
wife and seven children and ruin himself professionally, socially, and financially for her. It's preposterous."

"And what makes you think she believed he would?"

"The letters, damn it! And they are in her hand, there is
no question about that. The sister identified them."

"Then perhaps you do have a tormented woman with
two quite distinct sides to her nature—one rational, brave,
and efficient, the other quite devoid of judgment and even
of self-preservation?" Henry suggested.

"I suppose so."

"Then why do you blame yourself? What is it you have
done that is so wrong?"

"Shattered dreams—robbed Barrymore of his most precious belief—and perhaps a lot of others as well, certainly
Monk."

"Questioned it," Henry corrected. "Not robbed them—
not yet."

"Yes I have. I've made them doubt. It is tarnished. It
won't ever be the same again."

"What do you believe?"

Oliver thought for a long time. The starlings were quiet

at last. In the gathering dusk the perfume of the honeysuckle was even stronger.

"I believe there is something damned important that I don't know yet," he answered finally. "Not only don't I know it, I don't even know where to look."

"Then go with your beliefs," Henry advised, his voice comfortable and familiar in the near darkness. "If you don't have knowledge, it is all you can do."

The second day was occupied with Lovat-Smith's calling a tedious procession of hospital staff who all testified to Prudence's professional ability, and he was meticulous at no point to slight her. Once or twice he looked across at Rathbone and smiled, his gray eyes brilliant. He knew the precise values of all the emotions involved. It was pointless hoping he would make an error. One by one he elicited from them observations of Prudence's admiration for Sir Herbert, the inordinate number of times he chose her alone to work with him, their obvious ease with each other, and finally her apparent devotion to him.

Rathbone did what he could to mitigate the effect, pointing out that Prudence's feelings for Sir Herbert did not prove his feelings for her, and that he was not even aware that on her part it was more than professional, let alone that he had actively encouraged her. But he had an increasingly unpleasant certainty that he had lost their sympathy. Sir Herbert was not an easy man to defend; he did not naturally attract their liking. He appeared too calm, too much a man in command of his own destiny. He was accustomed to dealing with those who were desperately dependent upon him for the relief of bodily pain, even the continuance of their physical existence.

Rathbone wondered if he were frightened behind that masklike composure, if he understood how close he was to the hangman's noose and his own final pain. Was his mind racing, his imagination bringing out his body in cold sweat? Or did he simply believe such a thing could not happen?

Was it innocence which armored him against the reality of his danger?

What had really happened between himself and Prudence?

Rathbone went as far as he dared in trying to paint her as a woman with fantasies, romantic delusions, but he saw the faces of the jurors and felt the wave of dislike when he disparaged her, and knew he dared do little more than suggest, and leave the thought in their minds to germinate as the trial progressed. Henry's words kept coming back to him. *Go with your beliefs.*

But he should not have quarreled with Monk. That had been self-indulgent. He needed him desperately. The only way to save Sir Herbert from the gallows, never mind his reputation, was to find whoever did kill Prudence Barrymore. Even the escape of reasonable doubt was beginning to recede. Once he even heard a sharp note of panic in his own voice as he rose to cross-examine, and it brought him out in a sweat over his body. Lovat-Smith would not have missed it. He would know he was winning, as a dog on the chase scents the kill.

The third day was better. Lovat-Smith made his first tactical error. He called Mrs. Barrymore to the stand to testify to Prudence's spotless moral character. Presumably he had intended her to heighten the emotional pitch of sympathy for Prudence. Mrs. Barrymore was the bereaved mother, it was a natural thing to do, and in his position Rathbone would most certainly have done the same. He admitted as much to himself.

Nevertheless it proved a mistake.

Lovat-Smith approached her with deference and sympathy, but still all the cocky assurance in his stance that Rathbone had seen the previous day. He was winning, and he knew it. It was the sweeter for being against Oliver Rathbone.

"Mrs. Barrymore," he began with a slight inclination of his head, "I regret having to ask you to do this, painful as it must be for you, but I am sure you are as keen as the rest of us that justice should be done, for all our sakes."

She looked tired, her fair skin puffy around the eyes, but she was perfectly composed, dressed in total black, which became her fair coloring and delicate features.

"Of course," she agreed. "I shall do my best to answer you honestly."

"I am sure you will," Lovat-Smith said. Then, sensing the judge's impatience, he began. "Naturally you have known Prudence all her life, probably no one else knew her as well as you did. Was she a romantic, dreaming sort of girl, often falling in love?"

"Not at all," she said with wide-open eyes. "In fact, the very opposite. Her sister, Faith, would read novels and imagine herself the heroine. She would daydream of handsome young men, as most girls do. But Prudence was quite different. She seemed only concerned with study and learning more all the time. Not really healthy for a young girl." She looked puzzled, as if the anomaly still confused her.

"But surely she must have had girlhood romances?" Lovat-Smith pressed. "Hero worship, if you will, of young men from time to time?" But the knowledge of her answer was plain in his face, and in the assurance of his tone.

"No," Mrs. Barrymore insisted. "She never did. Even the new young curate, who was so very charming and attracted all the young ladies in the congregation, seemed to awaken no interest in Prudence at all." She shook her head a little, setting the black ribbons on her bonnet waving.

The jury members were listening to her intently, uncertain how much they believed her or what they felt, and the mixture of concentration and doubt was plain in their expressions.

Rathbone glanced quickly up at Sir Herbert. Oddly enough, he seemed uninterested, as if Prudence's early life were of no concern to him. Did he not understand the importance of its emotional value to the jury's grasp of her character? Did he not realize how much hinged upon what manner of woman she was—a disillusioned dreamer, an idealist, a noble and passionate woman wronged, a black-mailer?

"Was she an unemotional person?" Lovat-Smith asked, investing the question with an artificial surprise.

"Oh no, she felt things intensely," Mrs. Barrymore assured him. "Most intensely—so much so I feared she would make herself ill." She blinked several times and mastered herself only with great difficulty. "That seems so foolish now, doesn't it? It seems as if it has brought about her very death! I'm sorry, I find it most difficult to control my feelings." She shot a look of utter hatred at Sir Herbert across in the dock, and for the first time he looked distressed. He rose to his feet and leaned forward, but before he could do anything further one of the two jailers in the dock with him gripped his arms and pulled him back.

There was a gasp, a sigh around the court. One of the jurors said something which was inaudible. Judge Hardie opened his mouth, and then changed his mind and remained silent. Rathbone considered objecting and decided not to. It would only alienate the jury still further.

"Knowing her as you did, Mrs. Barrymore . . ." Lovat-Smith said it very gently, his voice almost a caress, and Rathbone felt the confidence in him as if it were a warm blanket over the skin. "Do you find it difficult to believe that in Sir Herbert Stanhope," Lovat-Smith went on, "Prudence at last found a man whom she could both love and admire with all her ardent, idealistic nature, and to whom she could give her total devotion?"

"Not at all," Mrs. Barrymore replied without hesitation. "He was exactly the sort of man to answer all her dreams. She would think him noble enough, dedicated enough and brilliant enough to be everything she could love with all her heart." At last the tears would not be controlled anymore, and she covered her face with her hands and silently wept.

Lovat-Smith stepped forward and reached high up with his arm to offer her his handkerchief.

She took it blindly, fumbling to grasp it from his hand. For once Lovat-Smith was lost for words. There seemed nothing to say that was not either trite or grossly inappropriate. He half nodded, a little awkwardly, knowing that she was not looking at him, and returned to his seat, waving his hand to indicate that Rathbone might now take his turn.

Rathbone rose and walked across to the center of the floor, acutely aware that every eye was on him. He could win or lose it all in the next few moments.

There was no sound except Mrs. Barrymore's gentle weeping.

Rathbone waited. He did not interrupt her. It was too great a risk. It might be viewed as sympathy; on the other hand, it might seem like indecent haste.

He ached to look around at the jury, and at Sir Herbert, but it would have betrayed his uncertainty, and Lovat-Smith would have understood it as a hunting animal scents weakness. Their rivalry was old and close. They knew each other too well for even a whisper of a mistake to go unnoticed.

Finally Mrs. Barrymore blew her nose very delicately, a restrained and genteel action, and yet remarkably effective. When she looked up her eyes were red, but the rest of her face was quite composed.

"I am very sorry," she said quietly. "I fear I am not as strong as I had imagined." Her eyes strayed upward for a moment to look at Sir Herbert on the far side of the court, and the loathing in her face was as implacable as that of any man she might have imagined to have the power she said she lacked.

"There is no need to apologize, ma'am," Rathbone assured her softly, but with that intense clarity of tone which he knew was audible even in the very back row of the public seats. "I am sure everyone here understands your grief and feels for you." There was nothing he could do to ameliorate her hatred. Better to ignore it and hope the jury had not seen.

"Thank you." She sniffed very slightly.

"Mrs. Barrymore," he began with the shadow of a smile, "I have only a few questions for you, and I will try to make them as brief as possible. As Mr. Lovat-Smith has already pointed out, you naturally knew your daughter as only a mother can. You were familiar with her love of medicine and the care of the sick and injured." He put his hands in his pockets and looked up at her. "Did you find it easy to believe that she actually performed operations herself?"

Anne Barrymore frowned, concentrating on what was obviously difficult for her.

"No, I am afraid I did not. It is something that has always puzzled me."

"Do you think that it is possible she exaggerated her own role a trifle in order to be—shall we say, closer to her ideal? Of more service to Sir Herbert Stanhope?"

Her face brightened. "Yes—yes, that would explain it. It is not really a natural thing for a woman to do, is it? But love is something we can all understand so easily."

"Of course it is," Rathbone agreed, although he found it increasingly hard to accept as the sole motive for anyone's actions, even a young woman. He questioned his own words as he said them. But this was not the time to be self-indulgent. All that mattered now was Sir Herbert, and showing the jury that he was as much a victim as Prudence Barrymore and that the affliction to him might yet prove as fatal. "And you do not find it difficult to believe that she wove all her hopes and dreams around Sir Herbert?"

She smiled sadly. "I am afraid it seems she was foolish, poor child. So very foolish." She shot a look of anger and frustration at Mr. Barrymore, sitting high in the public gallery, white-faced and unhappy. Then she turned back to Rathbone. "She had an excellent offer from a totally suitable young man at home, you know," she went on earnestly. "We could none of us understand why she did not accept him." Her brows drew down and she looked like a lost child herself. "A head full of absurd dreams. Quite impossible, and not to be desired anyway. It would never have made her happy." Suddenly her eyes filled with tears again. "And now it is all too late. Young people can be so wasteful of opportunity."

There was a deep murmur of sympathy around the room. Rathbone knew he was on the razor's edge. She had admitted Prudence created a fantasy for herself, that she misread reality; but her grief was also transparently genuine, and no honest person in the courtroom was untouched by it. Most had families of their own, a mother they could in their own minds put in her place, or a child they could imagine losing, as she had. If he were too tentative he would miss his chance and perhaps Sir Herbert would pay with his life. If he were too rough he would alienate the jury, and again Sir Herbert would bear the cost.

He must speak. The rustle of impatience was beginning; he could hear it around him.

"We all offer you not only our sympathy but our understanding, ma'am," he said clearly. "How many of us in our own youth have not let slip what would have been precious. Most of us do not pay so very dearly for our dreams or our misconceptions." He walked a few paces and turned, facing her from the other direction. "May I ask you one thing more? Do you find yourself able to believe that Prudence, in the ardor of her nature and her admiration of noble ideals and the healer's art, may have fallen in love with Sir Herbert Stanhope, and being a natural woman, have desired of him more than he was free to give her?"

He had his back to Sir Herbert, and was glad of it. He preferred not to see his client's face as he speculated on such emotions. If he had, his own thoughts might have intruded, his own anger and guilt.

"And that, as with so many of us," he continued, "the wish may have been father to the thought that in truth he returned her feelings, when in fact he felt for her only the respect and the regard due to a dedicated and courageous colleague with a skill far above that of her peers?"

"Yes," she said very quietly, blinking hard. "You have put it precisely. Foolish girl. If only she would have taken what was offered her and settled down like anyone else, she could have been so happy! I always said so—but she wouldn't listen. My husband"—she gulped—"encouraged

her. I'm sure he meant no harm, but he didn't understand!"
This time she did not look at the gallery.

"Thank you, Mrs. Barrymore," Rathbone said quickly,
wishing to leave the matter before she spoiled the effect. "I
have nothing further to ask you."

Lovat-Smith half rose to his feet, then changed his mind
and sat down again. She was confused and grief-stricken,
but she was also rooted in her convictions. He would not
compound his error.

After his quarrel with Rathbone on the steps of the court-
house two days previous, Monk had gone home in a furious
temper. It was not in the least alleviated by the fact that he
knew perfectly well that Rathbone was bound by his trust
to Sir Herbert, regardless of his opinion of Prudence
Barrymore. He was not free to divide his loyalties, and neither evidence nor emotion permitted him to swerve.

Still he hated him for what he had suggested of Prudence, generally because he had seen the faces of the jury
nodding, frowning, beginning to see her differently: less of
a disciple of the lady with the lamp, tending the sick and
desperate in dangerous foreign lands, and more as a fallible
young woman whose dreams overcame her good sense.

But more particularly, and at the root of his anger, was
the fact that it had woken the first stirrings of doubt in himself. The picture of her he had painted in his mind was now
already just so very slightly tarnished, and try as he might,
he could not clear it to the power and simplicity it had had
before. It did not matter whether she had loved Sir Herbert
Stanhope or not, was she deluded enough to have misread
him so entirely? And worse than that, had she really performed the medical feats she had claimed? Was she really
one of those sad but so understandable creatures who paint
on the gray world the colors of their dreams and then escape into parallel worlds of their own making, warping everything to fit?

He could understand that with a sudden sickening clarity.
How much of himself did he see only through the twisted

view of his own lack of memory? Was his ignorance of his past his own way of escaping what he could not bear? How much did he really want to remember?

To begin with he had searched with a passion. Then as he had learned more, and found so much that was harsh, ungenerous, and self-seeking, he had pursued it less and less. The whole incident of Hermione had been painful and humiliating. And he suspected also that much of Runcorn's bitterness lay at his door. The man was weak, that was his one flaw, but Monk had traded on it over the years. A better man might not have used it in that way. No wonder Runcorn savored his final triumph.

And even as he thought it, Monk understood enough of himself to know he would not let it rest. Half of him hoped Sir Herbert was not guilty and he could undercut Runcorn yet again.

In the morning he went back to the hospital and questioned the nurses and dressers once more about seeing a strange young man in the corridors the morning of Prudence's death. There was no doubt it had been Geoffrey Taunton. He had admitted as much himself. But perhaps someone had seen him later than he had said. Maybe someone had overheard an angry exchange, angry enough to end in violence. Perhaps someone had even seen Nanette Cuthbertson, or a woman they had not recognized who could have been her. She certainly had motive enough.

It took him the best part of the day. His temper was short and he could hear the rough edges to his voice, the menace and the sarcasm in his questions, even as he disliked them. But his rage against Rathbone, his impatience to find a thread, something to pursue, overrode his judgment and his better intentions.

By four o'clock all he had learned was that Geoffrey Taunton had been there, precisely as he already knew, and that he had been seen leaving in a red-faced and somewhat flustered state while Prudence was still very much alive. Whether he had then doubled back and found her again, to resume the quarrel, was unresolved. Certainly it was possible, but nothing suggested that it was so. In fact, nothing suggested he was of a nature or personality given to violence at all. Prudence's treatment of him would try the patience of almost any man.

About Nanette Cuthbertson he learned nothing conclusive at all. If she had worn a plain dress, such as nurses or domestics wear, she could have passed in and out again with no one giving her a second glance.

By late afternoon he had exhausted every avenue, and was disgusted with the case and with his own conduct of it. He had thoroughly frightened or offended at least a dozen people, and furthered his own interests hardly at all.

He left the hospital and went outside into the rapidly cooling streets amid the clatter and hiss of carriages, the sound of vendors' cries as costers' carts traveled by, peddlers called their wares, and men and women hurried to reach their destinations before the heavy skies opened up in a summer thunderstorm.

He stopped and bought a newspaper from a boy who was shouting: "Latest on trial o' Sir 'Erbert! Read all about it! Only a penny! Read the news 'ere!" But when Monk opened the page it was little enough: merely more questions and doubts about Prudence, which infuriated him.

There was one more place he could try. Nanette Cuthbertson had stayed overnight with friends only a few hundred yards away. It was possible they might know something, however trivial.

He was received very coolly by the butler; indeed, had he been able to refuse entirely without appearing to deny justice, Monk gathered he would have done so. The master of the house, one Roger Waldemar, was brief to the point of rudeness. His wife, however, was decidedly more civil, and Monk caught a gleam of admiration in her glance.

"My daughter and Miss Cuthbertson have been friends for many years." She looked at Monk with a smile in her eyes although her face was grave.

They were alone in her sitting room, all rose and gray, opening onto a tiny walled garden, private, ideal for

309

contemplation—or dalliance. Monk quashed his speculations as to what might have taken place there and returned his attention to his task.

"Indeed, you might say they had been from childhood," Mrs. Waldemar was saying. "But Miss Cuthbertson was with us at the ball all evening. Quite lovely she looked, and so full of spirits. She had a real fire in her eyes, if you know what I mean, Mr. Monk? Some women have a certain"—she shrugged suggestively—"vividness to them that others have not, regardless of circumstance."

Monk looked at her with an answering smile. "Of course I know, Mrs. Waldemar. It is something a man does not overlook, or forget." He allowed his glance to rest on her a fraction longer than necessary. He liked the taste of power, and one day he would push his own to find its limits, to know exactly how much he could do. He was certain it was far more than this very mild, implied flirtation.

She lowered her eyes, her fingers picking at the fabric of the sofa on which she sat. "And I believe she went out for a walk very early," she said clearly. "She was not at breakfast. However, I would not wish you to read anything unfortunate into that. I am sure she simply took a little exercise, perhaps to clear her head. I daresay she wished to think." She looked up at him through her lashes. "I should have in her position. And one must be alone and uninterrupted for such a thing."

"In her position?" Monk inquired, regarding her steadily.

She looked grave. She had very fine eyes, but she was not the type of woman that appealed to him. She was too willing, too obviously unsatisfied.

"I—I am not sure if this is discreet; it can hardly be relevant. . . ."

"If it is not relevant, ma'am, I shall immediately forget it," he promised, leaning an inch or two closer to her. "I can keep my own counsel."

"I am sure," she said slowly. "Well—for some time poor Nanette has been most fond of Geoffrey Taunton, whom you must know. And he has had eyes only for that unfortunate girl Prudence Barrymore. Well, lately young Martin Hereford, a most pleasing and totally acceptable young man . . ." She invested the words with a peculiar emphasis, conveying her boredom with everything so tediously expected. ". . . has paid considerable attention to Nanette," she concluded. "The night of the ball he made his admiration quite apparent. Such a nice young man. Far more suitable really than Geoffrey Taunton."

"Indeed?" Monk said with exactly the right mixture of skepticism, to entice her to explain, and encouragement, so she would not feel slighted. He kept his eyes on hers.

"Well . . ." She lifted one shoulder, her eyes bright. "Geoffrey Taunton can be very charming, and of course he has excellent means and a fine reputation. But there is more to consider than that."

He watched her intently, waiting for her to elaborate.

"He has a quite appalling temper," she said confidently. "He is utterly charming most of the time, of course. But if he is really thwarted, and cannot bear it, he quite simply loses all control. I have only seen him do it once, and over the silliest incident. It was a weekend in the country." She had Monk's attention and she knew it. She hesitated, savoring the moment.

He was becoming impatient. He could feel the ache in his muscles as he forced himself to sit, to smile at her, when he would like to have exploded in temper for her stupidity, her vacuous, meaningless flirting.

"A long weekend," she continued. "Actually, as I recall, it was from Thursday until Tuesday, or something like that. The men had been out shooting, I think, and we ladies had been sewing and gossiping all day, waiting for them to return. It was in the evening." She took a deep breath and stared around the room as if in an effort to recollect. "I think it was Sunday evening. We'd all been to church early, before breakfast, so they would have the whole day outside. The weather was glorious. Do you shoot, Mr. Monk?"

"No."

"You should. It's a very healthy pastime, you know."

He choked back the answer that came to his lips.

"I shall have to consider it, Mrs. Waldemar."

"They were playing billiards," she said, picking up the thread again. "Geoffrey had lost all evening to Archibald Purbright. He really is such a cad. Perhaps I shouldn't say that?" She looked at him inquiringly, her smile very close to a simper.

He knew what she wanted.

"I'm sure you shouldn't," he agreed with an effort. "But I shan't repeat it."

"Do you know him?"

"I don't think I care to, if he is a cad, as you say."

She laughed. "Oh dear. Still, I'm sure you will not repeat what I tell you?"

"Of course not. It shall be a confidence between us." He despised himself as he was doing it, and despised her the more. "What happened?"

"Oh, Archie was cheating, as usual, and Geoffrey finally lost his temper and said some perfectly terrible things. . . ."

Monk felt a rage of disappointment. Abuse, however virulent, was hardly akin to murder. Stupid woman! He could have hit her silly, smiling face.

"I see," he said with distinct chill. It was a relief not to have to pretend anymore.

"Oh no, you don't," she retorted urgently. "Geoffrey beat poor Archie over the head and shoulders with the billiard cue. He knocked him to the floor, and might have rendered him senseless had not Bertie and George pulled him off. It was really quite awful." There was a flush of excitement in her cheeks. "Archie was in bed for four days, and of course they had to send for the doctor. They told him Archie had fallen off his horse, but I don't think the doctor believed that for an instant. He was too discreet to say so, but I saw the look on his face. Archie said he'd sue, but he'd been cheating, and he knew we knew it, so naturally he didn't. But neither of them were invited again." She smiled up at him and shrugged her smooth shoulders. "So I daresay Nanette had a great deal to think about. After all, a temper

312

of that sort gives one cause for consideration, however charming a man may be otherwise, don't you agree?"

"I do indeed, Mrs. Waldemar," Monk said with sincerity. Suddenly she looked extremely different. She was not stupid; on the contrary, she was very perceptive. She did not prattle on; she recounted valuable and maybe extremely relevant information. He looked back at her with profound appreciation. "Thank you. Your excellent memory is most admirable and explains a great deal to me that had previously been beyond my understanding. No doubt Miss Cuthbertson was doing exactly as you say. Thank you so much for your time and courtesy." He rose to his feet, backing away from her.

"Not at all." She rose also, her skirts billowing around her with a soft sound of taffeta. "If I can be of any further assistance, please feel able to call upon me."

"Indeed I shall." And with such speed as grace allowed, he took his departure out into the darkening streets, the lamplighter passing on his way, one light glowing into life after another along the length of the pavement.

So Geoffrey had a violent temper, even murderous. His step lightened. It was a small thing so far, but definitely a break in the gloom around Sir Herbert Stanhope.

It did not explain Prudence's dreams or their reality, and that still burdened him, but it was a beginning.

And it would be an acute satisfaction to him to take it to Rathbone. It was something he had not found for himself, and Monk could imagine the look of surprise—and obligation—in Rathbone's clever, self-possessed face when he told him.

10

$A_{\text{S IT HAPPENED,}}$ Rathbone was too relieved to hear Monk's news of Geoffrey Taunton for his irritation to be more than momentary. There was a flash of anger at the smoothly complacent look on Monk's face, the tone of arrogant satisfaction in his voice, and then Rathbone's brain concentrated on what he would do with the knowledge, how best to use it.

When he went to see Sir Herbert briefly before the day's session began, he found him pensive, an underlying tension apparent in the nervous movement of his hands and the occasional gesture to adjust his collar or straighten his waistcoat. But he had sufficient control of himself not to ask how Rathbone thought the trial was progressing.

"I have a little news," Rathbone said immediately the jailer left them alone.

Sir Herbert's eyes widened and for a moment he held his breath. "Yes?" His voice was husky.

Rathbone felt guilty; what he thought was not enough for real hope. It would need all his skill to make it count.

"Monk has learned of a very unfortunate incident in Geoffrey Taunton's recent past," he said calmly. "A matter of catching an acquaintance cheating at billiards and becoming seriously violent. Apparently he attacked the man

314

and had to be hauled off him before he injured him, perhaps mortally." He was overstating the case a little, but Sir Herbert needed all the encouragement he could offer.

"He was in the hospital at the time she was killed," Sir Herbert said with a quick lift in his voice, his eyes alight. "And Heaven knows, he had motive enough. She must have confronted him—the stupid woman." He looked at Rathbone intently. "This is excellent! Why are you not better pleased? He is at least as good a suspect as I!"

"I am pleased," Rathbone said quietly. "But Geoffrey Taunton is not in the dock—not yet. I have a great deal to do yet before I can put him there. I just wished you to know: there is every hope, so keep your courage high."

Sir Herbert smiled. "Thank you—that is very honest of you. I appreciate you cannot say more. I have been in the same position with patients. I do understand."

As it chanced, Lovat-Smith unwittingly played into Rathbone's hands. His first witness of the day was Nanette Cuthbertson. She crossed the floor of the courtroom and mounted the steps to the witness stand gracefully, maneuvering her skirts up the narrow way with a single flick of her wrist. She turned at the top to face him, a calm smile on her face. She was dressed in dark brown, which was at once very sober and extremely flattering to her coloring and warm complexion. There was a murmur of appreciation around the crowd, and several people sat up a little straighter. One of the jurors nodded to himself, and another straightened his collar.

Their interest had been less sharp this morning. The revelations they had expected were not forthcoming. They had looked for their emotions to be torn one way and then another as piece after piece of evidence was revealed, while Sir Herbert appeared one moment guilty, the next innocent, and two giant protagonists battled each other across the courtroom floor.

Instead it had been a rather tedious procession of ordinary people offering their opinions that Prudence Barrymore was an excellent nurse, but not a great heroine, and that she had suffered the very ordinary feelings of many young women in that she had imagined a man to be in love with her, when in fact he was merely being civil. It was sad, even pathetic, but not the stuff of high drama. No one had yet offered a satisfactory alternative murderer, and yet quite clearly she had been murdered.

Now at last here was an interesting witness, a dashing and yet demure young woman. They craned forward, eager to see why she had been called.

"Miss Cuthbertson," Lovat-Smith began as soon as the necessary formalities had been completed. He knew the anticipation and the importance of keeping the emotion high. "You knew Prudence Barrymore from your childhood days together, did you not?"

"I did," Nanette replied candidly, her chin lifted, her eyes downcast.

"You knew her well?"

"Very well."

No one was bothering to look at Sir Herbert. They all stared at Nanette, waiting for the evidence for which she had been called.

Only Rathbone surreptitiously glanced sideways and up toward the dock. Sir Herbert was sitting well forward, peering at the witness stand in profound concentration. His face had a look on it almost of eagerness.

"Was she a romantic?" Lovat-Smith asked.

"No, not in the slightest." Nanette smiled ruefully. "She seemed of an extremely practical turn of mind. She took no trouble to be charming or to attract gentlemen." She covered her eyes, then looked up again. "I dislike speaking ill of one who is not here to answer for herself, but for the sake of preventing injustice, I must say what is true."

"Of course. I am sure we all understand," Lovat-Smith said a trifle sententiously. "Have you any knowledge of her ideas in the matter of love, Miss Cuthbertson? Young ladies sometimes confide in each other from time to time."

She looked suitably modest at mention of such a subject.

"Yes. I am afraid she would not look at anyone else but

316

Sir Herbert Stanhope. There were other, eminently suitable and quite dashing gentlemen who admired her, but she would have none of them. All the time she spoke only of Sir Herbert, his dedication, his skill, how he had helped her and shown her great care and attention." A frown crossed her face, as if what she was about to say both surprised and angered her, but never once did she lift her eyes to look at the dock. "She said over and over that she believed he was going to make all her dreams come true. She seemed to light up with excitement and a sort of inner life when she spoke his name."

Lovat-Smith stood in the very center of the floor, his gown less than immaculate. He had little of the grace of Rathbone, and yet he was so vibrant with suppressed energy that he commanded everyone's attention. Even Sir Herbert was temporarily forgotten.

"And did you gather, Miss Cuthbertson," he asked, "that she was in love with him and believed him to be in love with her, and that he would shortly make her his wife?"

"Of course," Nanette agreed, her eyes wide. "What other possible meaning could there have been?"

"Indeed, none that I know of," Lovat-Smith agreed. "Were you aware of the change in her beliefs, a time when she realized that Sir Herbert did not return her feelings after all?"

"No. No I was not."

"I see." Lovat-Smith walked away from the witness stand as if he were concluded. Then he turned on his heel and faced her again. "Miss Cuthbertson, was Prudence Barrymore a woman of determination and resolve? Had she great strength of will?"

"But of course," Nanette said vehemently. "How else would she have gone to the Crimea, of all places? I believe it was quite dreadful. Oh certainly, when she had set her heart upon something, she did not give up."

"Would she have given up her hope of marrying Sir Herbert without a struggle, in your estimation?"

Nanette answered before Judge Hardie could lean for-

317

ward and intervene, or Rathbone could voice his protest.
"Never!"

"Mr. Lovat-Smith," Hardie said gravely. "You are leading the witness, as you know full well."

"I apologize, my lord," Lovat-Smith said without a trace
of remorse. He shot a sideways glance at Rathbone, smiling. "Your witness, Mr. Rathbone."

"Thank you." Rathbone rose to his feet, smooth and
graceful. He walked over to the witness stand and looked
up at Nanette. "I regret this, ma'am, but there are many
questions I need to ask you." His voice was a beautiful instrument and he knew how to use it like a master. He was
at once polite, even deferential, and insidiously menacing.

Nanette looked down at him without any awareness of
what was to come, her eyes wide, her expression bland.

"I know it is your job, sir, and I am perfectly prepared."

One of the jurors smiled, another nodded in approval.
There was a murmur around the public benches.

"You knew Prudence Barrymore since childhood, and
knew her well," Rathbone began. "You told us that she
confided many of her inner feelings to you, which is quite
natural, of course." He smiled up at her and saw an answering flicker touch her lips only sufficient to be civil. She did
not like him because of who he represented. "You also
spoke of another admirer, whose attentions she rejected," he
continued. "Were you referring to Mr. Geoffrey Taunton?"

A pinkness colored her cheeks, but she kept her composure. She must have been aware that question would come.

"I was."

"You considered her foolish and unreasonable not to
have accepted him?"

Lovat-Smith rose to his feet. "We have already covered
that subject, my lord. The witness has said as much. I fear
in his desperation, my learned friend is wasting the court's
time."

Hardie looked at Rathbone inquiringly.

"Mr. Rathbone, have you some point, other than to give
yourself time?"

"Indeed I have, my lord," Rathbone replied.

"Then proceed to it," Hardie directed.

Rathbone inclined his head, then turned back to Nanette.

"You know Mr. Taunton well enough to judge that he is an admirable young man?"

The pink flushed her cheeks again. It was becoming, and possibly she knew it.

"I do."

"Indeed? You know of no reason why Prudence Barrymore should not have accepted him?"

"None whatever." This time there was some defiance in her voice and she lifted her chin a trifle higher. She was beginning to feel she had the measure of Rathbone. Even in the body of the court attention was waning. This was tedious, verging on pitiful. Sir Herbert in the dock lost his sharp interest and began to look anxious. Rathbone was achieving nothing. Only Lovat-Smith sat with a guarded expression on his face.

"Would you yourself accept him, were he to offer?" Rathbone asked mildly. "The question is hypothetical, of course," he added before Hardie could interrupt.

The blood burned up Nanette's cheeks. There was a hiss of breath around the room. One of the jurors in the back row cleared his throat noisily.

"I . . ." Nanette stammered awkwardly. She could not deny it, or she would effectively be refusing him, the last thing on earth she wished. "I—you . . ." She composed herself with difficulty. "You place me in an impossible position, sir!"

"I apologize," Rathbone said insincerely. "But Sir Herbert is also in an impossible position, ma'am, and one of considerably more peril to himself." He inclined his head a little. "I require you to answer, because if you would not accept Mr. Taunton, then that would indicate that you know of some reason why Prudence Barrymore also might not have accepted him. Which would mean her behavior was not so unreasonable, nor necessarily in any way connected with Sir Herbert, or any hopes she may have entertained regarding him. Do you see?"

"Yes," she conceded reluctantly. "Yes, I see."

He waited. At last the crowd on the public benches was caught. He could hear the rustle of taffeta and bombazine as they craned forward. They did not totally understand what was to come, but they knew drama when they smelled it, and they knew fear.

Nanette took a deep breath. "Yes—I would," she said in a strangled voice.

"Indeed." Rathbone nodded. "So I had been led to believe." He walked a pace or two, then turned to her again. "In fact, you are very fond of Mr. Taunton yourself, are you not? Sufficiently so to have marred your affection for Miss Barrymore when he persistently courted her in spite of her repeated refusal of his offers?"

There was a mutter of anger around the room. Several jurors shifted uncomfortably.

Nanette was truly appalled. The tide of scarlet ran right to the dark line of her hair, and she clung to the rail of the witness box as if to support herself. The rustle of embarrassment increased, but in no one did it exceed curiosity. No one looked away.

"If you suggest that I lie, sir, you are mistaken," Nanette said at length.

Rathbone was politeness itself.

"Not at all, Miss Cuthbertson. I suggest that your perception of the truth, like that of most of us in the grip of extreme emotion, is likely to be colored by our own imperatives. That is not to lie, simply to be mistaken."

She glared at him, confused and wretched, but not able to think of a retaliation.

But Rathbone knew the tone of drama would pass and reason reassert itself. He had achieved little to help Sir Herbert yet.

"You cared for him enough not to be dissuaded by his violent temper, Miss Cuthbertson?" he resumed.

Now suddenly she was pale.

"Violent temper?" she repeated. "That is nonsense, sir. Mr. Taunton is the gentlest of men."

But the crowd watching her intently had seen the difference between disbelief and shock. They knew from the tightness of her body beneath its fashionable gown and huge skirts that she was perfectly aware what Rathbone alluded to. Her confusion was to hide it, not to understand it.

"If I were to ask Mr. Archibald Purbright, would he agree with me?" Rathbone said smoothly. "I doubt Mrs. Waldemar would think so."

Lovat-Smith shot to his feet, his voice husky with assumed bewilderment.

"My lord, who is Archibald Purbright? My learned friend has made no previous mention of such a person. If he has evidence he must testify to it here, where the Crown may question him and weigh its validity. We cannot accept—"

"Yes, Mr. Lovat-Smith," Hardie interrupted him. "I am quite aware that Mr. Purbright has not been called." He turned to Rathbone, eyebrows raised inquiringly. "Perhaps you had better explain yourself?"

"I do not intend to call Mr. Purbright, my lord, unless Miss Cuthbertson should make it necessary." It was a bluff. He had no idea where to find Archibald Purbright.

Hardie turned to Nanette.

She stood stiffly, white-faced.

"It was a solitary incident, and some time ago." She almost choked on her words. "The man had been cheating. I regret having to say so, but it is true." She shot a look of loathing at Rathbone. "And Mrs. Waldemar would bear me out on that!"

The moment's tension evaporated. Lovat-Smith smiled.

"And Mr. Taunton was no doubt quite understandably extremely frustrated and felt a burning sense of injustice," Rathbone agreed. "As would we all. To have done your best, to feel you deserve to win because you are the better player, and to be constantly cheated out of your victory would be enough to try the temper of most of us."

He hesitated, taking a step or two casually and turning. "And in this instance, Mr. Taunton lashed out with such extreme violence that he was only prevented from doing Mr. Purbright a serious, perhaps fatal, injury by the overpowering strength of two of his friends."

Suddenly the tension was back again. Gasps of shock were clearly audible amid rustles of movement, scrapings of shoes as people sat sharply upright. In the dock Sir Herbert's lips curled in the very smallest smile. Even Hardie stiffened.

Lovat-Smith hid his surprise with difficulty. It was there on his face only for an instant, but Rathbone saw it. Their eyes met, then Rathbone looked back at Nanette.

"Do you not think it is possible, Miss Cuthbertson—indeed, do you not in your heart fear—that Mr. Taunton may have felt just the same sense of frustration and injustice with Miss Barrymore for persistently refusing him when she had no other admirer at hand, and no justifiable reason, in his view, for her actions?" His voice was calm, even solicitous. "Might he not have lashed out at her, if perhaps she were foolish enough to have mocked him or in some way slighted him to make her rejection plain? There were no friends to restrain him in the hospital corridor at that early hour of the morning. She was tired after a long night nursing the sick, and she would not expect violence—"

"No!" Nanette exploded furiously, leaning over the railing toward him, her face flushed again. "No! Never! It is quite monstrous to say such a thing! Sir Herbert Stanhope killed her"—she shot a look of loathing across at the dock and the jurors followed her eyes—"because she threatened to expose his affair with her," she said loudly. "We all know it. It wasn't Geoffrey. You are simply saying that because you are desperate to defend him." She directed another blazing glance at the dock, and even Sir Herbert seemed discomfited. "And you have nothing else," she accused him. "You are despicable, sir, to slander a good man for one miserable mistake."

"One miserable mistake is all it needs, ma'am," Rathbone said very levelly, his voice hushing the sudden murmur and movement in the room. "A strong man can strangle a woman to death in a very few moments." He held up his hands, fine, beautiful hands with long fingers. He made a quick, powerful wrenching movement with them, and heard a woman gasp and the rattle of taffeta as she collapsed somewhere behind him.

Nanette looked as if she too might faint.

Hardie banged sharply with his gavel, his face hard.

Lovat-Smith rose to his feet, and then subsided again.

Rathbone smiled. "Thank you, Miss Cuthbertson. I have nothing further to ask you."

Geoffrey Taunton was a different matter. Rathbone knew from Lovat-Smith's stance as he took the floor that he was in two minds as to whether he should have called Taunton at all. Should he leave bad alone rather than risk making it worse, or should he try to retrieve it with a bold attack? He was a brave man. He chose the latter, as Rathbone had been sure he would. Of course Geoffrey Taunton had been outside, as prospective witnesses always were, in case a previous testimony should color theirs, so he had no idea what had been said of him. Nor had he noticed Nanette Cuthbertson, now seated in the public gallery, her face tense, her body rigid as she strained to catch every word, at once dreading it, and yet unable to warn him in any way.

"Mr. Taunton," Lovat-Smith began, a note of confidence ringing in his voice to belie what Rathbone knew he felt. "You were well acquainted with Miss Barrymore and had been for many years," he went on. "Had you any reason to know her feelings for Sir Herbert Stanhope? I would ask you not to speculate, but to tell us only what you observed for yourself, or what she told you."

"Of course," Geoffrey agreed, smiling very slightly and perfectly confident. He was serenely unaware of the reason people were staring at him with such intensity, or why all the jurors looked but avoided his eyes. "Yes, I was aware for some years of her interest in medicine, and I was not surprised when she chose to go to the Crimea to help our wounded men in the hospital at Scutari." He rested his hands on the railing in front of him. He looked quite casual and fresh.

"However, I admit it took me aback when she insisted in pursuing the course of working in the Royal Free Hospital in London. She was no longer needed in the same way. There are hundreds of other women perfectly able and willing to do the sort of work in which she was involved, and it was totally unsuited to a woman of her birth and background."

"Did you point that out to her and try to dissuade her?" Lovat-Smith asked.

"I did more than that, I offered her marriage." There was only the faintest touch of pink in his cheeks. "However, she was set upon her course." His mouth tightened. "She had very unrealistic ideas about the practice of medicine, and I regret to say it of her, but she valued her own abilities quite out of proportion to any service she might have been able to perform. I think her experiences during the war gave her ideas that were impractical at home in peacetime. I believe she would have come to realize that, with good guidance."

"Your own guidance, Mr. Taunton?" Lovat-Smith said courteously, his blue eyes wide.

"And that of her mother, yes," Geoffrey agreed.

"But you had not yet succeeded?"

"No, I regret we had not."

"Do you have any knowledge as to why?"

"Yes I do. Sir Herbert Stanhope encouraged her." He shot a look of contempt at the dock.

Sir Herbert stared at him quite calmly, not a shadow of guilt or evasion in his face.

A juror smiled to himself. Rathbone saw it, and knew the elation of a small victory.

"Are you quite sure?" Lovat-Smith asked. "That seems an extraordinary thing to do. He, of all people, must surely have known that she had no abilities and no chance whatever of acquiring any beyond those of an ordinary nurse: to fetch and carry, to empty slops, prepare poultices, to change linen and bandages." He enumerated the points on his short strong hands, waving them with natural energy and expression. "To watch patients and call a doctor in case of distress, and to administer medicines as directed. What else could she conceivably do here in England? We have no field surgeries, no wagon loads of wounded."

"I have no idea," Geoffrey said with acute distaste twisting his features. "But she told me quite unequivocally that he had said there was a future for her, with advancement." Again the anger and disgust filled him as he glanced across at Sir Herbert.

This time Sir Herbert winced and shook his head a little, as if, even bound to silence, he could not bear to let it pass undenied.

"Did she speak of her personal feelings for Sir Herbert?" Lovat-Smith pursued.

"Yes. She admired him intensely and believed that all her future happiness lay with him. She told me so—in just those words."

Lovat-Smith affected surprise.

"Did you not attempt to disabuse her, Mr. Taunton? Surely you must have been aware that Sir Herbert Stanhope is a married man." He waved one black-clad arm toward the dock. "And could offer her nothing but a professional regard, and that only as a nurse, a position immeasurably inferior to his own. They were not even colleagues, in any equal sense of the term. What could she have hoped for?"

"I have no idea." He shook his head, his mouth twisted with anger and pain. "Nothing of any substance at all. He lied to her—that is the least of his offenses."

"Quite so," Lovat-Smith agreed sagely. "But that is for the jury to decide, Mr. Taunton. It would be improper for us to say more. Thank you, sir. If you will remain there, no doubt my learned friend will wish to question you." Then he stopped, turning on his heel and looking back at the witness stand. "Oh! While you are here, Mr. Taunton: were you in the hospital on the morning of Nurse Barrymore's death?" His voice was innocuous, as if the questions were merely by the way.

"Yes," Geoffrey said guardedly, his face pale and stiff.

Lovat-Smith inclined his head. "We have heard that you have a somewhat violent temper when you are provoked beyond endurance." He said it with a half smile, as if it were a foible, not a sin. "Did you quarrel with Prudence and lose control of yourself that morning?"

"No!" Geoffrey's hands were white-knuckled on the railing.

"You did not murder her?" Lovat-Smith added, eyebrows raised, his voice with a slight lift in it.

"No I did not!" Geoffrey was shaking, emotion naked in his face.

There was a ripple of sympathy from somewhere in the gallery, and from another quarter a hiss of disbelief.

Hardie lifted his gavel, then let it fall without sound.

Rathbone rose from his seat and replaced Lovat-Smith on the floor of the court. His eyes met Lovat-Smith's for an instant as they passed. He had lost the momentum, the brief ascendancy, and they both knew it.

He stared up at the witness stand.

"You tried to disabuse Prudence of this idea that her personal happiness lay with Sir Herbert Stanhope?" he asked mildly.

"Of course," Geoffrey replied. "It was absurd."

"Because Sir Herbert is already married?" He put his hands in his pockets and stood very casually.

"Naturally," Geoffrey replied. "There was no way whatsoever in which he could offer her anything honorable except a professional regard. And if she persisted in behaving as if there were more, then she would lose even that." His face tightened, showing his impatience with Rathbone for pursuing something so obvious, and so painful.

Rathbone frowned.

"Surely it was a remarkably foolish and self-destructive course of action for her to have taken? It could only bring embarrassment, unhappiness, and loss."

"Precisely," Geoffrey agreed with a bitter curl to his mouth. He was about to add something further when Rathbone interrupted him.

"You were very fond of Miss Barrymore, and had known her over a period of time. Indeed, you also knew her family. It must have distressed you to see her behaving in such a way?"

"Of course!" A flicker of anger crossed Geoffrey's face and he looked at Rathbone with mounting irritation.

"You could see danger, even tragedy, ahead for her?" Rathbone pursued.

"I could. And so it has transpired!"

There was a murmur around the room. They also were growing impatient.

Judge Hardie leaned forward to speak.

Rathbone ignored him and hastened on. He did not want to lose what little attention he had by being interrupted.

"You were distressed," he continued, his voice a little louder. "You had on several occasions asked Miss Barrymore to marry you, and she had refused you, apparently in the foolish belief that Sir Herbert had something he could offer her. Which, as you say, is patently absurd. You must have felt frustrated by her perversity. It was ridiculous, self-destructive, and quite unjust."

Geoffrey's fingers tightened again on the railing of the witness box and he leaned farther forward.

The creaking and rustling of fabric stopped as people realized what Rathbone was about to say.

"It would have made any man angry," Rathbone went on silkily. "Even a man with a less violent temper than yours. And yet you say you did not quarrel over it? It seems you do not have a violent temper after all. In fact, it seems as if you have no temper whatsoever. I can think of very few men, if any"—he pulled a very slight face, not quite of contempt—"who would not have felt their anger rise over such treatment."

The implication was obvious. His honor and his manhood were in question.

There was not a sound in the room except the scrape of Lovat-Smith's chair as he moved to rise, then changed his mind.

Geoffrey swallowed. "Of course I was angry," he said in a choked voice. "But I did not quarrel violently. I am not a violent man."

Rathbone opened his eyes very wide. There was total silence in the room except for Lovat-Smith letting out his breath very slowly.

"Well of course violence is all relative," Rathbone said smoothly. "But I would have thought your attack upon Mr. Archibald Purbright, because he cheated you at a game of billiards—frustrating, of course, but hardly momentous—that was violent, was it not? If your friends had not restrained you, you would have done the man a near-fatal injury."

Geoffrey was ashen, shock draining him.

Rathbone gave him no time.

"Did you not lose your temper similarly with Miss Barrymore when she behaved with such foolishness and refused you yet again? Was that really so much less infuriating to you than losing a game of billiards to a man everyone knew was cheating anyway?"

Geoffrey opened his mouth but no coherent sound came.

"No." Rathbone smiled. "You do not have to answer that! I quite see that it is unfair to ask you. The jury will come to their own decisions. Thank you, Mr. Taunton. I have no further questions."

Lovat-Smith rose, his eyes bright, his voice sharp and clear.

"You do not have to answer it again, Mr. Taunton," he said bitterly. "But you may if you chose to. Did you murder Miss Barrymore?"

"No! No I did not!" Geoffrey found speech at last. "I was angry, but I did her no harm whatsoever! For God's sake." He glared across at the desk. "Stanhope killed her. Isn't it obvious?"

Involuntarily everyone, even Hardie, looked at Sir Herbert. For the first time Sir Herbert looked profoundly uncomfortable, but he did not avert his eyes, nor did he blush. He looked back at Geoffrey Taunton with an expression which seemed more like frustration and embarrassment than guilt.

Rathbone felt a surge of admiration for him, and in that moment a renewed dedication to seeing him acquitted.

"To some of us." Lovat-Smith smiled patiently. "But not all—not yet. Thank you, Mr. Taunton. That is all. You may be excused."

Geoffrey Taunton climbed down the steps slowly, as if he were still uncertain if he should, or could add something more. Then finally he realized the opportunity had slipped, if it was ever there, and he covered the few yards of the floor to the public benches in a dozen strides.

The first witness of the afternoon was Berenice Ross Gilbert. Her very appearance caused a stir even before she said anything at all. She was calm, supremely assured, and dressed magnificently. It was a somber occasion, but she did not choose black, which would have been in poor taste since she was mourning no one. Instead she wore a jacket of the deepest plum shot with charcoal gray, and a huge skirt of a shade similar but a fraction darker. It was wildly flattering to her coloring and her age, and gave her an air both distinguished and dramatic. Rathbone could hear the intake of breath as she appeared, and then the hush of expectancy as Lovat-Smith rose to begin his questions. Surely such a woman must have something of great import to say.

"Lady Ross Gilbert," Lovat-Smith began. He did not know how to be deferential—something in his character mocked the very idea—but there was respect in his voice, whether for her or for the situation. "You are on the Board of Governors of the hospital. Do you spend a considerable time there?"

"I do." Her voice was vibrant and very clear. "I am not there every day, but three or four in the week. There is a good deal to be done."

"I am sure. Most admirable. Without the generous gift of

329

service of people like yourself, such places would be in a parlous state," Lovat-Smith acknowledged, although whether that was true was debatable. He spent no further effort on the thought. "Did you see Prudence Barrymore often?"

"Of course. The moral welfare and the standards and duties of nurses were a matter I was frequently asked to address. I saw poor Prudence on almost every occasion I was there." She looked at him and smiled, waiting for the next obvious question.

"Were you aware that she worked very frequently with Sir Herbert Stanhope?"

"Of course." There were the beginnings of regret in her voice. "To begin with I assumed it was merely coincidence, because she was an excellent nurse."

"And later?" Lovat-Smith prompted.

She lifted one shoulder in an eloquent posture. "Later I was forced to realize that she was devoted to him."

"Do you mean more than could be accounted by the duties that would fall to her because of her skill?" Lovat-Smith phrased the question carefully, avoiding any slip that would allow Rathbone to object.

"Indeed," Berenice said with a modest share of reluctance. "It became obvious that her admiration for him was intense. He is a fine surgeon, as we all know, but Prudence's devotion to him, the extra duties she performed of her own volition, made it unmistakable that her feelings were more than merely professional, no matter how dedicated and conscientious."

"Did you see evidence that she was in love with Sir Herbert?" Lovat-Smith asked it with a gentle, unassuming voice, but his words carried to the very back of the room in the total silence.

"Her eyes lit at mention of him, her skin glowed, she gained an extra, inward energy." Berenice smiled and pulled a slightly rueful face. "I can think of no other explanation when a woman behaves so."

"Nor I," Lovat-Smith admitted. "Given the moral welfare of nurses was your concern, Lady Ross Gilbert, did you address her on the subject?"

"No," she said slowly, as if still giving the matter thought. "To be frank I never saw evidence that her morality was in jeopardy. To fall in love is part of the human condition." She looked quizzically beyond Lovat-Smith to the public benches. "If it is misplaced, and hopeless of any satisfactory conclusion, it is sometimes safer for the morals than if it is returned." She hesitated, affecting discomfort. "Of course at that time I had no idea the whole affair would end as it has."

Not once had she looked at Sir Herbert opposite in the dock, although his eyes never left her face.

"You say that Prudence's love was misplaced." Lovat-Smith was not yet finished. "Do you mean by that that Sir Herbert did not return her feelings?"

Berenice hesitated, but it appeared it was a pause to find exactly the right words rather than because she was uncertain of her belief.

"I am less skilled at reading the emotions of men than of women, you understand. . . ."

There was a murmur around the room, whether of belief or doubt it was impossible to say. A juror nodded sagely.

Rathbone had the distinct impression she was savoring the moment of drama and her power to hold and control her audience.

Lovat-Smith did not interrupt.

"He asked for her on every occasion he required a skilled nurse," she said slowly, each word falling distinctly into the bated hush. "He worked closely with her over long hours, and at times without any other person present." She spoke without ever looking across at him, her eyes fixed on Lovat-Smith.

"Perhaps he was unaware of her personal emotions toward him?" Lovat-Smith suggested without a shred of conviction. "Is he a foolish man, in your experience?"

"Of course not! But—"

"Of course not," he agreed, cutting her off before she

331

could add her explanation. "Therefore you did not consider it necessary to warn him?"

"I never thought of it," she confessed with irritation. "It is not my place to make suggestions on the lives of surgeons, and I did not think I could tell him anything of which he was not already perfectly aware and would deal with appropriately. Looking back now I can see that I was—"

"Thank you," he interrupted. "Thank you, Lady Ross Gilbert. That is all I have to ask you. But my learned friend . . . may." He left it a delicate suggestion that Rathbone's cause was broken, and he might already have surrendered to the inevitable.

And indeed Rathbone was feeling acutely unhappy. She had undone a great deal, if not all, of the good he had accomplished with Nanette and with Geoffrey Taunton. At best all he had raised was a reasonable doubt. Now even that seemed to be slipping away. The case was hardly an ornament to his career, and it was looking increasingly as if it might not even save Sir Herbert's life, let alone his reputation.

He faced Berenice Ross Gilbert with an air of casual confidence he did not feel. Deliberately he stood at ease. The jury must believe he had some tremendous revelation in hand, some twist or barb that would at a stroke destroy Lovat-Smith's case.

"Lady Ross Gilbert," he began with a charming smile. "Prudence Barrymore was an excellent nurse, was she not? With far above the skills and abilities of the average?"

"Most certainly," she agreed. "She had considerable actual medical knowledge, I believe."

"And she was diligent in her duties?"

"Surely you must know this?"

"I do." Rathbone nodded. "It has already been testified to by several people. Why does it surprise you, then, that Sir Herbert should have chosen her to work with him in a large number of his surgical cases? Would that not be in the interest of his patients?"

"Yes—of course it would."

"You testified that you observed in Prudence the very recognizable signs of a woman in love. Did you observe any of these signs in Sir Herbert, when in Prudence's presence, or anticipating it?"

"No I did not," she replied without hesitation.

"Did you observe any change in his manner toward her, any departure from that which would be totally proper and usual between a dedicated surgeon and his best and most responsible nurse?"

She considered only a moment before replying. For the first time she looked across at Sir Herbert, just a glance, and away again.

"No—he was always as usual," she said to Rathbone. "Correct, dedicated to his work, and with little attention to people other than the patients, and of course the teaching of student doctors."

Rathbone smiled at her. He knew his smile was beautiful.

"I imagine men have been in love with you, possibly many men?"

She shrugged very slightly, a delicate gesture of amusement and concurrence.

"Had Sir Herbert treated you as he treated Prudence Barrymore, would you have supposed that he was in love with you? Or that he considered abandoning his wife and family, his home and reputation, in order to ask you to marry him?"

Her face lit with amusement.

"Good Heavens, no! It would be totally absurd. Of course not."

"Then for Prudence to imagine that he was in love with her was unrealistic, was it not? It was the belief of a woman who could not tell her dreams from reality?"

A shadow crossed her face, but it was impossible to read it.

"Yes—yes it was."

He had to press home the point.

"You said she had some medical skill, ma'am. Do you

have any evidence that it was surgical skill of a degree where she was capable of performing amputations herself, unaided and successfully? Was she indeed not a mere nurse, but a surgeon?"

There was an unhappy murmur around the room and a confusion of emotions.

Berenice's eyebrows shot up.

"Good Heavens. Of course not! If you forgive me, Mr. Rathbone, you have no knowledge whatever of the medical world if you can ask such a question. A woman surgeon is absurd."

"Then in that respect also, she had lost the ability to distinguish between daydreams and reality?"

"If that is what she said, then most certainly she had. She was a nurse, a very good one, but certainly not a doctor of any sort. Poor creature, the war must have unhinged her. Perhaps we are at fault if we did not see it." She looked suitably remorseful.

"Perhaps the hardships she endured and the suffering she saw unbalanced her mind," Rathbone agreed. "And her wish to be able to help led her to imagine she could. We may never know." He shook his head. "It is a tragedy that such a fine and compassionate woman, with so intense a desire to heal, should have been strained beyond the point she could endure with safety to her own nature; and above all that she should end her life by such a means." He said that for the jury, not that it had any relevance to the evidence, but it was imperative to keep their sympathy. He had destroyed Prudence's reputation as a heroine; he must not take from her even the role of honorable victim.

Lovat-Smith's last witness was Monk.

He climbed the steps of the witness box stone-faced and turned to the court coldly. As before, he had caught snatches of what Rathbone had drawn from Berenice Ross Gilbert from those who were coming and going from the courtroom: press reporters, clerks, idlers. He was furious even before the first question.

"Mr. Monk," Lovat-Smith began carefully. He knew he

had a hostile witness, but he also knew his evidence was incontestable. "You are no longer with the police force but undertake private inquiries, is that correct?"

"It is."

"Were you employed to inquire into the murder of Prudence Barrymore?"

"I was." Monk was not going to volunteer anything. Far from it losing the public's interest, they sensed antagonism and sat a little more upright in order not to miss a word or a look.

"By whom? Miss Barrymore's family?"

"By Lady Callandra Daviot."

In the dock Sir Herbert sat forward, his expression suddenly tense, a small vertical line between his brows.

"Was it in that capacity that you attended the funeral of Miss Barrymore?" Lovat-Smith pursued.

"No," Monk said tersely.

If Monk had hoped to disconcert Lovat-Smith, he succeeded only slightly. Some instinct, or some steel in Monk's face, warned him not to ask what his reason had been. He could not guarantee the answer. "But you were there?" he said instead, sidestepping the issue.

"I was."

"And Miss Barrymore's family knew your connection with the case?"

"Yes."

There was not a sound in the room now. Something of the rage in Monk, some power in his face, held the attention without a whisper or a movement.

"Did Miss Barrymore's sister, Mrs. Faith Barker, offer you some letters?" Lovat-Smith asked.

"Yes."

Lovat-Smith kept his evenness of expression and voice with difficulty.

"And you accepted them. What were they, Mr. Monk?"

"Letters from Prudence Barrymore to her sister," Monk replied. "In a form close to a diary, and written almost every day for the last three and a half months of her life."

"Did you read them?"

"Naturally."

Lovat-Smith produced a sheaf of papers and handed them up to Monk.

"Are these the letters Mrs. Barker gave you?"

Monk looked at them, although there was no need. He knew them immediately.

"They are."

"Would you read to the court the first one I have marked with a red ribbon, if you please?"

Obediently, in a tight hard voice, Monk read:

"My dearest Faith,

"What a marvelous day I have had! Sir Herbert performed splendidly. I could not take my eyes from his hands. Such skill is a thing of beauty in itself. And his explanations are so lucid I had not the slightest difficulty in following him and appreciating every point.

"He has said such things to me, I am singing inside with the sheer happiness of it. All my dreams hang in the balance, and he has it all in his power. I never thought I should find anyone with the courage. Faith, he truly is a wonderful man—a visionary—a hero in the best sense—not rushing around conquering other peoples who should be left alone, or battling to discover the source of some river or other—but crusading here at home for the great principles which will help tens of thousands. I cannot tell you how happy and privileged I am that he has chosen me!

"Until next time, your loving sister,

Prudence."

"And the second one I have marked, if you will?" Lovat-Smith continued.

Again Monk read, and then looked up, no emotion in his eyes or his features. Only Rathbone knew him well enough to be aware of the revulsion inside him for the intrusion into the innermost thoughts of a woman he admired.

The room was in silence, every ear strained. The jury stared at Sir Herbert with undisguised distaste.

"Are the others in a similar vein, Mr. Monk?" Lovat-Smith asked.

"Some are," Monk replied. "Some are not."

"Finally, Mr. Monk, would you read the letter I have marked with a yellow ribbon."

In a low hard voice, Monk read:

"Dear Faith,
   "Just a note. I feel too devastated to write more, and so weary I could sleep with no desire to wake. It was all a sham. I can scarcely believe it even now, when he has told me face to face. Sir Herbert has betrayed me completely. It was all a lie—he only wished to use me—all his promises meant nothing. But I shall not let it rest at that. I have power, and I shall use it!

Prudence."

There was a sigh of breath, a rustle as heads turned from Monk to stare up at the dock. Sir Herbert looked strained; his face showed the lines of tiredness and confusion. He did not look frightened so much as lost in a nightmare which made no sense to him. His eyes rested on Rathbone with something close to desperation.

Lovat-Smith hesitated, looking at Monk for several moments, then decided against asking him anything further. Again, he was not sufficiently certain of the answer.

"Thank you," he said, looking toward Rathbone.

Rathbone racked his brains for something to say to mitigate what they had all just heard. He did not need to see Sir Herbert's white face as at last fear overtook the benign puzzlement he had shown so long. Whether he understood the letters or not, he was not naive enough to miss their impact on the jury.

Rathbone forced himself not to look at the jurors, but he knew from the nature of the silence, the reflected light on the pallor of their faces as they turned sideways to look up at the dock, that there was condemnation already in their minds.

What could he ask Monk? What could he possibly say to mitigate this? Nothing whatever came to him. He did not even trust Monk. Might his anger against Sir Herbert for having betrayed Prudence, however unintentionally, blind him now to any kinder interpretation? Even if it did not, what was his opinion worth?

"Mr. Rathbone?" Judge Hardie looked at him with pursed lips.

"I have no questions of this witness, thank you, my lord."

"That is the case for the prosecution, if you please, my lord," Lovat-Smith said with a faint, complacent smile.

"In that case, since it is growing late we will adjourn, and the defense may begin its case tomorrow."

Callandra had not remained in court after her testimony. Part of her wished to. She hoped desperately that Sir Herbert was guilty and would be proved so beyond any doubt whatsoever, reasonable or unreasonable. The terror inside her that it had been Kristian was like a physical pain filling her body. During the day she sought every possible duty to absorb her time and deny her mind the opportunity to return to gnaw at the anxiety, turn over the arguments again and again, trying uselessly to find the solution she wanted.

At night she fell into bed, believing herself exhausted, but after an hour or so of sleep she woke, filled with dread, and the slow hours of the morning found her tossing and turning, longing for sleep, afraid of dreams, and even more afraid of waking.

She wanted to see Kristian, and yet she did not know what to say to him. She had seen him so often in the hospital, shared all kinds of crises in other peoples' lives—and deaths—and yet she was now achingly aware how little she knew of him beyond the life of healing, labor, comfort, and loss. Of course she knew he was married, and that his wife was a chilly remote woman with whom he shared little tenderness or laughter, and none of the work into which he poured so much passion, none of the precious things of humor and understanding, small personal likes and dislikes such as the love of flowers, voices singing, the play of light on grass, early morning.

But how much else was there unknown to her? Sometimes in the long hours when they had sat, talking far longer than there was any need, he had told her of his youth, his struggle in his native Bohemia, the joy he had felt as the miraculous workings of the human physiology had been revealed in his studies. He had spoken of the people he had known and with whom he had shared all manner of experiences. They had laughed together, sat in sudden sweet melancholy remembering past losses, made bearable in the certain knowledge that the other understood.

In time she had told him of her husband, how fiercely alive he had been, full of hot temper, arbitrary opinions, sudden insights, uproarious wit, and such a wild vigor for life.

But what of Kristian's present? All he had shared with her stopped fifteen or twenty years ago, as if the years from then until now were lost, not to be spoken of. When had the idealism of his youth been soured? When had he first betrayed the best in himself and then tarnished everything else by performing abortions? Did he really need more money so desperately?

No. That was unfair. She was doing it again, torturing herself by beginning that dreadful train of thought that led her eventually to Prudence Barrymore, and murder. The man she knew could not have done that. Everything she knew of him could not be an illusion. Perhaps what she had seen that day had not been what she thought? Maybe Marianne Gillespie had been suffering some complication? After all, the child within her was the result of rape. Perhaps she had been injured internally in some way, and Kristian had been repairing it—and not destroying the child at all.

Of course. That was a very possible solution. She must find out—and set all her fears at rest forever.

But how? If she were to ask him she would have to admit she had interrupted—and he would know she had suspected and indeed believed the worst.

And why should he tell her the truth? She could hardly ask him to prove it. But the very act of asking would damage forever the closeness they shared—and however fragile that was, however without hope of ever being more, it was unreasonably precious to her.

But the fear inside her, the sick doubt, was ruining it anyway. She could not meet his eyes or speak to him naturally as she used to. All the old ease, the trust, and the laughter were gone.

She must see him. Win or lose, she must know.

The opportunity came the day Lovat-Smith concluded his case. She had been discussing a pauper who had just been admitted and had persuaded the governors that the man was deserving and in great need. Kristian Beck was the ideal person to treat him. The case was too complex for the student doctors, the other surgeons were fully occupied, and of course Sir Herbert was absent for an unforeseeable time—perhaps forever.

She knew Kristian was in his rooms from Mrs. Flaherty. She went to his door and knocked, her heart beating so violently she imagined her whole body shook. Her mouth was dry. She knew she would stumble when she spoke.

She heard his voice invite her to enter, and suddenly she wanted to run, but her legs would not move.

He called again.

This time she pushed the door and went in.

His face lit with pleasure as soon as he saw her and he rose from his seat behind the table.

"Callandra! Come in—come in! I have hardly seen you for days." His eyes narrowed a little as he looked at her more closely. There was nothing critical in him, just a gentleness that sent her senses lurching with the power of her own feelings. "You look tired, my dear. Are you not well?"

It was on her lips to tell him the truth, as she always had, most particularly to him, but it was the perfect excuse to evade.

"Not perhaps as I would like to be. But it is of no importance." Her words came in a rush, her tongue fumbling. "I certainly don't need a doctor. It will pass."

"Are you sure?" He looked anxious. "If you'd prefer not to see me, then ask Allington. He is a good man, and here today."

"If it persists, I will," she lied. "But I have come about a man admitted today who most certainly does need your help." And she described the patient in detail, hearing her own voice going on and on as if it were someone else's.

After several moments he held up his hand.

"I understand—I will see him. There is no need to persuade me." Again he looked at her closely. "Is something troubling you, my dear? You are not at all yourself. Have we not trusted one another sufficiently that you can allow me to help?"

It was an open invitation, and she knew that by refusing she would not only close the door and make it harder to open again next time, but she would hurt him. His emotion was there in his eyes, and it should have made her heart sing.

Now she felt choked with unshed tears. All the loneliness of an uncounted span, long before her husband had died, times when he was brisk, full of his own concerns—not unkind, simply unable to bridge a gulf of difference between them—all the hunger for intimacy of the heart was wide and vulnerable within her.

"It's only the wretched business of the nurse," she said, looking down at the floor. "And the trial. I don't know what to think, and I am allowing it to trouble me more than I should . . . I am sorry. Please forgive me for burdening everyone else with it when we all have sufficient to bear for ourselves."

"Is that all?" he said curiously, his voice lifted a little in question.

"I was fond of her," she replied, looking up at him be-

341

cause that at least was totally true. "And she reminded me of a certain young woman I care about even more. I am just tired. I will be much better tomorrow." And she forced herself to smile, even though she felt it must look ghastly.

He smiled back, a sad, gentle look, and she was not sure whether he had believed anything she had said. One thing was certain, she could not possibly ask him about Marianne Gillespie. She could not bear to hear the answer.

She rose to her feet, backing toward the door.

"Thank you very much for accepting Mr. Burke. I was sure you would." And she reached for the door handle, gave him another brief, sickly smile, and escaped.

Sir Herbert turned the moment Rathbone came in the cell door. Seen from the floor of the courtroom at all but a few moments, he had looked well in command of himself, but closer to, in the hard daylight of the single, high window, he was haggard. The flesh of his face was puffy except around the eyes, where the shadows were dark, as if he had slept only fitfully and without ease. He was used to decisions of life or death, he was intimately acquainted with all the physical frailty of man and the extremity of pain and death. But he was also used to being in command; the one who took the actions, or refrained; the one who made the judgments on which someone else's fate was balanced. This time he was helpless. It was Rathbone who had control, not he, and it frightened him. It was in his eyes, in the way he moved his head, something even in the smell of the room.

Rathbone was used to reassuring people without actually promising anything. It was part of his profession. With Sir Herbert it was more difficult than usual. The accepted phrases and manners were ones with which he was only too familiar himself. And the cause for fear was real.

"It is not going well—is it?" Sir Herbert said without prevarication, his eyes intent on Rathbone's face. There was both hope and fear in him.

"It is early yet." Rathbone moderated, but he would not

lie. "But it is true that we have so far made no serious inroads into his case."

"He cannot prove I killed her." There was the very faintest note of panic in Sir Herbert's voice. They both heard it. Sir Herbert blushed. "I didn't. This business of having a romantic liaison with her is preposterous. If you'd known the woman you would never have entertained the idea. She simply wasn't—wasn't remotely of that turn of mind. I don't know how to make it plainer."

"Can you think of another explanation of her letters?" Rathbone asked with no real hope.

"No! I can't. That is what is so frightening! It is like an absurd nightmare." His voice was rising with fear, growing sharper. Looking at his face, his eyes, Rathbone believed him entirely. He had spent years refining his judgment, staking his professional reputation upon it. Sir Herbert Stanhope was telling the truth. He had no idea what Prudence Barrymore had meant, and it was his very confusion and ignorance which frightened him most, the complete loss of reality, events he could neither understand nor control sweeping him along and threatening to carry him all the way to destruction.

"Could it be some sort of malicious joke?" Rathbone asked desperately. "People write strange things in their diaries. Could she be using your name to protect someone else?"

Sir Herbert looked startled, then a flicker of hope brightened his face. "I suppose it is conceivable, yes. But I have no idea whom. I wish to God I had! But why would she do such a thing? She was only writing to her sister. She cannot have expected the letters ever to be public."

"Her sister's husband, perhaps?" Rathbone suggested, knowing it was foolish even as the words were out.

"An affair with her sister's husband?" Sir Herbert was both shocked and skeptical.

"No," Rathbone replied patiently. "It is possible her sister's husband might read the letters. It is not unknown for a man to read his wife's letters."

"Oh!" Sir Herbert's face cleared. "Yes of course. That would be perfectly natural. I have done that from time to time myself. Yes—that is an explanation. Now you must find who the man is that she means. What about that man Monk? Can't he find him?" Then the moment's ease slipped away from him. "But there is so little time. Can you ask for an adjournment, a continuance, or whatever it is called?"

Rathbone did not answer.

"It gives me much more ammunition with which to question Mrs. Barker," he replied instead, then remembered with a chill that it was Faith Barker who had offered the letters to Monk in the conviction they would hang Sir Herbert. Whatever Prudence had meant, her sister was unaware of any secret the letters contained. He struggled to keep his disillusion from his face, and knew he failed.

"There is an explanation," Sir Herbert said desperately, his fists clenched, his powerful jaw gritted tight. "God damn it—I never had the slightest personal interest in the woman! Nor did I ever say anything which could . . ." Suddenly sheer, blind horror filled him. "Oh God!" He stared at Rathbone, terror in his eyes.

Rathbone waited, teetering on the edge of hope.

Sir Herbert swallowed. He tried to speak, but his lips were dry. He tried again.

"I praised her work! I praised it a great deal. Do you think she could have misinterpreted that as admiration for her person? I praised her often!" There was a fine sweat of fear on his lip and brow. "She was the finest nurse I ever had. She was intelligent, quick to learn, precise to obey, and yet not without initiative. She was always immaculately clean. She never complained of long hours, and she fought like a tiger to save a life." His eyes were fixed on Rathbone's. "But I swear before God, I never meant anything personal by my praise for her—simply what I said. No more, never more!" He put his head in his hands. "God preserve me from working with young women—young women of good family who expect and desire suitors."

Rathbone had a very powerful fear that he was going to get his wish—and be preserved from working with anyone at all—although he doubted God had anything to do with it.

"I will do everything I can," he said with a voice far firmer and more confident than he felt. "Keep your spirits high. There is very much more than a reasonable doubt, and your own manner is one of our strongest assets. Geoffrey Taunton is by no means clear, nor Miss Cuthbertson. And there are other possibilities also—Kristian Beck, for one."

"Yes." Sir Herbert rose slowly, forcing himself to regain his composure. Years of ruthless self-discipline finally conquered his inner panic. "But reasonable doubt. Dear Heaven—that would ruin my career!"

"It does not have to be forever," Rathbone said with complete honesty. "If you are acquitted, the case will remain open. It may be a very short time, a few weeks, before they find the true killer."

But they both knew that even reasonable doubt had still to be fought for to save Sir Herbert from the gallows—and they had only a few days left.

Rathbone held out his hand. It was a gesture of faith. Sir Herbert shook it, holding on longer than was customary, as if it were a lifeline. He forced a smile which had more courage in it than confidence.

Rathbone left with a greater determination to fight than he could recall in years.

After his testimony Monk left the court, his stomach churning and his whole body clenched with anger. He did not even know against whom to direct it, and that compounded the pain inside him. Had Prudence really been so blind? He did not wish to think of her as fallible to such a monstrous degree. It was so far from the woman for whom he had felt such grief at the crowded funeral in the church at Hanwell. She had been brave, and noble, and he had felt a cleanness inside from having known of her. He had understood her dreams, and her fierce struggle, and the price she had paid for them. Something in him felt at one with her.

And yet he was so flawed himself in his judgment or he would never have loved Hermione. And the very word *love* seemed inappropriate when he thought of the emotion he had felt, the turmoil, the need, the loneliness. It was not for any real woman, it was for what he had imagined her to be, a dream figure who would fill all his own emptinesses, a woman of tenderness and purity, a woman who both loved and needed him. He had never looked at the reality—a woman afraid of the heights and the depths of feeling, a small, craven woman who hugged her safety to her and was content to stand on the edge of all the heat of the battle.

How could Monk, of all people, condemn Prudence Barrymore for misjudgment?

And yet it still hurt. He strode across Newgate Street regardless of horses shying and drivers shouting at him and a light gig veering out of his way. He was nearly run down by a black landau; the footman riding at the side let fly at Monk a string of language that caused even the coachman to sit a little more upright in surprise.

Without making any deliberate decision, Monk found himself going in the general direction of the hospital, and after twenty minutes' swift walking, he hailed a hansom and completed the rest of the journey. He did not even know if Hester was on duty or in the nurses' dormitory catching some well-needed sleep, and he was honest enough to admit he did not care. She was the only person to whom he could confide the confusion and power of his feelings.

As it chanced, she had just fallen asleep after a long day's duty beginning before seven, but he knew where the nurses' dormitory was and he strode in with an air of such authority that no one stopped or questioned him until he was at the entrance doorway. Then a large nurse with ginger hair and arms like a navvy stood square in the middle, staring at him grimly.

"I need to see Miss Latterly in a matter of urgency," he

said, glaring back at her. "Someone's life may depend on the matter." That was a lie, and he uttered it without a flicker.

"Oh yeah? Whose? Yours?"

He wondered what her regard for Sir Herbert Stanhope had been.

"None of your affair," he said tartly. "I've just come from the Old Bailey, and I have business here. Now out of my way, and fetch Miss Latterly for me."

"I don't care if yer've come from 'Ell on a broomstick, yer not comin' in 'ere." She folded her massive arms. "I'll go an' tell 'er as yer 'ere if yer tell me who yer are. She can come and see yer if she feels like it."

"Monk."

"Never!" she said in disbelief, looking him up and down.

"That's my name, not my calling, you fool!" he snapped. "Now tell Hester I'm here."

She snorted loudly, but she obeyed, and about three minutes later Hester herself came out of the dormitory looking tired, very hastily dressed, and her hair over her shoulder in a long brown braid. He had never seen it down before, and it startled him. She looked quite different, younger and more vulnerable. He had a twinge of guilt for having woken her on what was essentially a selfish errand. In all probability it would make no difference at all to the fate of Sir Herbert Stanhope whether he spoke to her this evening or not.

"What happened?" she said immediately, still too full of exhaustion and sleep to have thought of all the possibilities fear could suggest.

"Nothing in particular," he said, taking her arm to lead her away from the dormitory door. "I don't even know if it is going well or badly. I shouldn't have come, but there was no one else I really wished to speak to. Lovat-Smith has finished his case, and I wouldn't care to be in Stanhope's shoes. But then Geoffrey Taunton comes out of it badly too. He has a vile temper, and a record of violence. He was in

347

the hospital at the time—but it's Stanhope in the dock, and nothing so far is strong enough to change their places."

They were in front of one of the few windows in the corridor and the late afternoon sun shone in a haze of dusty light over them and in a pool on the floor around their feet.

"Has Oliver any evidence to bring, do you know?" She was too tired to pretend formality where Rathbone was concerned.

"No I don't. I'm afraid I was short with him. His defense so far is to make Prudence look a fool." There was pain and anger still tight inside him.

"If she thought Sir Herbert Stanhope would marry her, she was a fool," Hester said, but with such sadness in her voice he could not be angry with her for it.

"He also suggested that she exaggerated her own medical abilities," he went on. "And her stories of having performed surgery in the field were fairy tales."

She turned and stared at him, confusion turning to anger.

"That is not so! She had as good a knowledge of amputation as most of the surgeons, and she had the courage and the speed. I'll testify. I'll swear to that, and they won't shake me, because I know it for myself."

"You can't," he answered, the flat feeling of defeat betrayed in his tone, even his stance.

"I damned well can!" she retorted furiously. "And let go of my arm! I can stand up perfectly well by myself! I'm tired, not ill."

He kept hold of her, out of perversity.

"You can't testify, because Lovat-Smith's case is concluded," he said through clenched teeth. "And Rathbone certainly won't call you. That she was accurate and realistic is not what he wants to hear. It will hang Sir Herbert."

"Maybe he should be hanged," she said sharply, then immediately regretted it. "I don't mean that. I mean maybe he did kill her. First I thought he did, then I didn't, now I don't know what I think anymore."

"Rathbone still seems convinced he didn't, and I must admit, looking at the man's face in the dock, I find it hard to believe he did. There doesn't seem any reason—not if you think about it intelligently. And he will be an excellent witness. Every time Prudence's infatuation with him is mentioned, a look of total incredulity crosses his face."

She gazed at him, meeting his eyes with searching candor.

"You believe him, don't you?" she concluded.

"Yes—it galls me to concede it, but I do."

"We will still have to come up with some better evidence as to who did it, or he is going to hang," she argued, but now there was pity in her, and determination.

He knew it of old, and the memory of it, once so passionately on his behalf, sent a thrill of warmth through him.

"I know," he said grimly. "And we will have to do it quickly. I've exhausted all I can think of with Geoffrey Taunton. I'd better follow what I can with Dr. Beck. Haven't you learned anything more about him?"

"No." She turned away, her face sad and vulnerable. The light caught her cheekbones and accentuated the tiredness around her eyes. He did not know what hurt her; she had not shared it with him. It pained him sharply and unexpectedly that she had excluded him. He was angry that he wanted to spare her the burden of searching as well as her nursing duties, and angriest of all that it upset him so much. It should not have. It was absurd—and weak.

"Well, what are you doing here?" he demanded harshly. "In all this time surely you have done more than fetch and carry the slops and wind bandages? For God's sake, think!"

"Next time you haven't a case, you try nursing," she snapped back. "See if you can do it all—and detect at the same time. You're no earthly use to anybody except as a detective—and what have you found out?"

"That Geoffrey Taunton has a violent temper, that Nanette Cuthbertson was here in London and had every reason to hate Prudence, and that her hands are strong enough to control a horse many a man couldn't," he said instantly.

349

"We. knew that ages ago." She turned away. "It's helpful—but it's not enough."

"That is why I've come, you fool. If it were enough, I wouldn't need to."

"I thought you came to complain. . . ."

"I am complaining. Don't you listen at all?" He knew he was being totally unfair, and he went on anyway. "What about the other nurses? Some of them must have hated her. She was arrogant, arbitrary, and opinionated. Some of them look big enough to pull a dray, never mind strangle a woman."

"She wasn't as arrogant as you think . . ." she began.

He laughed abruptly. "Not perhaps by your standards—but I was thinking of theirs."

"You haven't the first idea what their standards are," she said with contempt. "You don't murder somebody because they irritate you now and then."

"Plenty of people have been murdered because they constantly nag, bully, insult, and generally abuse people," he contradicted her. "It only takes one moment when the temper snaps because someone cannot endure any more." He felt a sudden very sharp anxiety, almost a premonition of loss. "That's why you should be careful, Hester."

She looked at him in total amazement, then she began to laugh. At first it was only a little giggle, then it swelled into a delirious, hilarious surge.

For an instant his temper flared, then he realized how much he would rather not quarrel with her. But he refused to laugh as well. He merely waited with a look of resigned patience.

Eventually she rubbed her eyes with the heel of her hand, most inelegantly, and stopped laughing. She sniffed.

"I shall be careful," she promised. "Thank you for your concern."

He drew breath to say something sharp, then changed his mind.

"We never looked very carefully into Kristian Beck. I still don't know what Prudence was going to tell the authorities when he begged her not to." A new thought occurred to him, which he should have seen before. "I wonder what particular authority she had in mind? The governors—or Sir Herbert? Rathbone could ask Sir Herbert."

Hester said nothing. Again the look of weariness crossed her face.

"Go back to sleep," he said gently, instinctively putting his hand on her shoulder. "I'll go and see Rathbone. I expect we've got a few days yet. We may find something."

She smiled doubtfully, but there was a warmth in it, a sharing of all the understanding and the emotions that needed no words, past experiences that had marked them with the same pains and the same fears for the present. She reached out and touched his face momentarily with her fingertips, then turned and walked back into the dormitory.

He had very little hope Sir Herbert would know anything about Kristian Beck, or he would surely have said so before now. It was conceivable he might tell them which authority something ought to be reported to, the chairman of the Board of Governors, perhaps? Altogether the case looked grim. It would rest in Rathbone's skill and the jury's mood and temper. Hester had been little help. And yet he felt a curious sense of happiness inside, as if he had never been less alone in his life.

At the earliest opportunity the following day Hester changed her duties with another nurse and went to see Edith Sobell and Major Tiplady. They greeted her with great pleasure and some excitement.

"We were going to send a message to you," the major said earnestly, assisting her to a chintz-covered chair as if she had been an elderly invalid. "We have news for you."

"I am afraid it is not going to please you," Edith added, sitting in the chair opposite, her face earnest. "I'm so sorry."

Hester was confused. "You found nothing?" That was hardly news sufficient to send a message.

"We found something." Now the major also looked confused, but his questioning look was directed at Edith. Hester only peripherally noticed the depth of affection in it.

"I know that is what she asked," Edith said patiently. "But she likes Dr. Beck." She turned back to Hester. "You will not wish to know that twice in the past he has been accused of mishandling cases of young women who died. Both times the parents were sure there was nothing very wrong with them, and Dr. Beck performed operations which were quite unnecessary, and so badly that they bled to death. The fathers both sued, but neither won. The proof was not sufficient."

Hester felt sick. "Where? Where did this happen? Surely not since he's been with the Royal Free Hospital?"

"No," Edith agreed, her curious face with its aquiline nose and wry, gentle mouth full of sadness. "The first was in the north, in Alnwick, right up near the Scottish border; the second was in Somerset. I wish I had something better to tell you."

"Are you sure it was he?" It was a foolish question, but she was fighting for any rescue at all. Callandra filled her mind.

"Can there be two surgeons from Bohemia named Kristian Beck?" Edith said quietly.

The major was looking at Hester with anxiety. He did not know why it hurt her so much, but he was painfully aware that it did.

"How did you find out?" Hester asked. It did not affect the reality of it, but even to question it somehow put off the finality of acceptance.

"I have become friends with the librarian at one of the newspaper offices," Edith replied. "It is her task to care for all the back copies. She has been most helpful with checking some of the details of events referred to in the major's memoirs, so I asked her in this as well."

"I see." There seemed nothing else she could pursue. That was the missing element, the thing Prudence was going to tell the authorities—only Beck had killed her before she could.

Then another thought occurred to her, even uglier. Was it possible Callandra already knew? Was that why she had looked so haggard lately? She was racked with fear—and her own guilt in concealing it.

Edith and the major were both looking at her, their faces crumpled with concern. Her thoughts must be so transparent. But there was nothing she could say without betraying Callandra.

"How are the memoirs going?" she asked, forcing a smile and a look of interest which would have been genuine at any other time.

"Ah, we are nearly finished," Edith replied, her face filled with light again. "We have written all his experiences in India, and such things in Africa you wouldn't dream of. It was quite the most exciting thing I have ever heard in my life. You must read them when we have finished. . . ." Then something of the light drained away as the inevitable conclusion occurred to all of them. Edith had been unable to leave the home which stifled her, the parents who felt her early widowhood meant that she should spend the rest of her life as if she were a single woman, dependent upon her father's bounty financially, and socially upon her mother's whim. She had had one chance at marriage, and that was all any woman was entitled to. Her family had done its duty in obtaining one husband for her; her misfortune that he had died young was one she shared with a great many others. She should accept it gracefully. The tragedy of her brother's death had opened up ugliness from the past which was far from healed yet, and perhaps never would be. The thought of returning to live in Carlyon House again was one which darkened even the brilliance of this summer day.

"I shall look forward to it," Hester said quietly. She turned to the major. "When do you expect to publish?"

He looked so deep in anxiety and concentration she was surprised when he answered her.

"Oh—I think . . ." Then he closed his eyes and took a deep breath. He let it out slowly. His face was very pink. "I was going to say there is much work to be done, but that

353

is not true. Edith has been so efficient there is really very little. But I am not sure if I can find a publisher willing to take it, or if I may have to pay to have it done." He stopped abruptly.

He took another deep breath, his face even pinker, and turned to Edith with fierce concentration. "Edith, I find the thought of concluding the work, and your leaving, quite intolerable. I thought it was writing about India and Africa which was giving me such pleasure and such inner peace, but it is not. It is sharing it with you, and having you here every day. I never imagined I should find a woman's company so extremely . . . comfortable. I always considered them alien creatures, either formidable, like governesses and nurses, or totally trivial and far more frightening, like ladies who flirt. But you are the most . . . agreeable person I have ever known." His face was now quite scarlet, his blue eyes very bright. "I should be desperately lonely if you were to leave, and the happiest man alive if you were to remain—as my wife. If I presume, I apologize—but I have to ask. I love you so very dearly." He stopped, overcome by his own audacity, but his eyes never left her face.

Edith looked down at the floor, blushing deeply; she was smiling, not with embarrassment but with happiness.

"My dear Hercules," she said very gently. "I cannot think of anything in the world I should like so much."

Hester rose to her feet, kissed Edith gently on the cheek, then kissed the major in exactly the same way, and tiptoed outside into the sun to walk back toward more suitable transport to the Old Bailey and Oliver Rathbone.

11

BEFORE HE COULD BEGIN the case for the defense, Rathbone went to see Sir Herbert again to brief him now that he would be called to the witness stand.

It was not a meeting he looked forward to. Sir Herbert was far too intelligent a man not to realize how slender his chances were, how much depended on emotion, prejudices, sympathies; certainly intangibles that Rathbone was well skilled in handling, but frail threads from which to dangle a man's life. Evidence was unarguable. Even the most perverse jury seldom went against it.

However, he found Sir Herbert in a far more optimistic mood than he had feared. He was freshly washed and shaved and dressed in clean clothes. Except for the shadows around his eyes and a certain knack of twisting his fingers, he might have been about to set off for the hospital and his own professional rounds.

"Good morning, Rathbone," he said as soon as the cell door was closed. "This morning is our turn. How do you propose to begin? It seems to me that Lovat-Smith has far from a perfect case. He has not proved it was me. Nor can he ever; and he has certainly not proved it was not Taunton or Beck, or even Miss Cuthbertson, let alone anyone else. What is your plan of action?" He might have been discussing an interesting medical operation in which he had no personal stake, except for a certain tightness in the muscles of his neck and an awkwardness in his shoulders.

Rathbone did not argue with anything he had said, even though he doubted it had the importance Sir Herbert attached to it. Quite apart from any motives of compassion, for all practical reasons it was most important that Sir Herbert should maintain his appearance of calm and assurance. Fear would convey itself to the jury, and they might very easily equate fear with guilt. Why should an innocent man be afraid of their judgment?

"I shall call you to the stand first," he said aloud, forcing himself to smile as if he had every confidence. "I shall give you the opportunity to deny having had any personal relationship with Prudence at all, and of course to deny having killed her. I would also like to be able to mention one or two specific incidents which she may have misunderstood." He watched Sir Herbert closely. "Simply to say in a general way that she daydreamed or twisted reality will not do."

"I have been trying to remember," Sir Herbert protested earnestly, his narrow eyes on Rathbone's. "But for Heaven's sake I can't remember trivial comments passed in the course of business! I can't remember being more than civil to her. Of course I passed the odd word of praise—she more than warranted it. She was a damned good nurse."

Rathbone remained silent, pulling a very slight face.

"Good God man!" Sir Herbert exploded, turning on his heel as if he would pace, but the walls of the cell confined him, bringing him up sharply. "Can you remember every casual word you pass to your clerks and juniors? It is just my misfortune I work largely with women. Perhaps one shouldn't?" His tone was suddenly savage. "But nursing is a job best done by women, and I daresay we could not find reliable men willing and able to do it." His voice rose a tone, and then another, and through long experience Rathbone knew it was panic just below the surface, every now and again jutting through the thin skin of control. He had seen it so often before, and as always he felt a stab of pity and another heavy drag of the weight of his own responsibility.

He put his hands in his pockets and stood a trifle more casually.

"I strongly advise you not to say anything of that sort on the stand. Remember that the jurors are ordinary people, and almost certainly hold medicine in some awe, and very little understanding. And after Miss Nightingale, who is a national heroine, whatever you think of her, her nurses are heroines also. Don't appear to criticize Prudence, even obliquely. That is the most important single piece of advice I can give you. If you do, you can resign yourself to conviction."

Sir Herbert stared at him, his bright intelligent eyes very clear. "Of course," he said quietly. "Yes, of course I understand that."

"And answer only what I ask you, add nothing whatever. Is that absolutely clear?"

"Yes—yes, of course, if you say so."

"And don't underestimate Lovat-Smith. He may look like a traveling actor, but he is one of the best lawyers in England. Don't let him goad you into saying more than you have to in order to answer the question exactly. He'll flatter you, make you angry, challenge you intellectually if he thinks it will make you forget yourself. Your impression on the jury is the most important weapon you have. He knows that as well as I do."

Sir Herbert looked pale, a furrow of anxiety sharp between his brows. He stared at Rathbone as if weighing him for some inner judgment.

"I shall be careful," he said at last. "Thank you for your counsel."

Rathbone straightened up and held out his hand.

"Don't worry. This is the darkest hour. From now on it is our turn, and unless we make some foolish mistake, we will carry the day."

Sir Herbert grasped his hand and held it hard.

"Thank you. I have every confidence in you. And I shall

357

obey your instructions precisely." He let go and stepped back, a very slight smile touching his lips.

As on every day so far, the court was packed with spectators and journalists, and this morning there was an air of expectancy among them and something not unlike hope. The defense was about to begin, there might at last be disclosures, drama, even evidence toward another murderer. Everyone's eyes were to the front, the noise was not talking but the myriad tiny rustles and creaks of movement as one fabric rubbed against another, whalebone shifted pressure, and the leather soles of boots scraped on the floor.

Rathbone was not as well prepared as he would have liked, but there was no more time. He must look as if he not only knew Sir Herbert was innocent but also who was guilty. He was acutely aware of the eyes of every juror intent upon him; every movement was watched, every inflection of his voice measured.

"My lord, gentlemen of the jury," he began with a very slight smile. "I am sure you will appreciate it is much easier for the prosecution to prove that a man is guilty of a crime than for the defense to prove he is not. Unless, of course, you can prove that someone else is. And unfortunately I cannot do that—so far. Although it is always possible something may emerge during the evidence yet to come."

The whisper of excitement was audible, even the hasty scratching of pencil on paper.

"Even so," he continued, "the prosecution has failed to demonstrate that Sir Herbert Stanhope killed Prudence Barrymore, only that he could have. As could many others: Geoffrey Taunton, Nanette Cuthbertson, Dr. Beck are only some. The main thrust of his argument"—he indicated Lovat-Smith with a casual gesture—"is that Sir Herbert had a powerful motive, as evidenced by Prudence's own letters to her sister, Faith Barker."

His smile broadened a fraction and he looked squarely at the jury.

"However, I will show you that those letters are open to a quite different interpretation, one which leaves Sir Herbert no more culpable than any other man might be in his position and with his skills, his personal modesty, and the other urgent and powerful calls upon his attention."

There was more fidgeting on the public benches. A fat woman in the gallery leaned forward and stared at Sir Herbert in the dock.

Before Hardie could become restive, Rathbone proceeded to the point.

"I shall now call my first witness, Sir Herbert Stanhope himself."

It took several moments for Sir Herbert to disappear from the dock down the stairs and reappear in the body of the court. Leaving his escort of jailers behind, he crossed the floor to mount the steps to the witness stand, walking very uprightly, an immaculately dressed and dignified figure. All the time there was a hush in the room as if everyone had held their breath. The only sound was the scratching of pencils on paper as the journalists sought to catch the mood in words.

As soon as Sir Herbert reached the top of the steps and turned there was a ripple of movement as a hundred heads craned forward to look at him, and everyone shifted very slightly in their seats. He stood square-shouldered, head high, but Rathbone watching him felt it was assurance, not arrogance. He glanced at the jury's faces and saw interest and a flash of reluctant respect.

The clerk swore him in, and Rathbone moved to the center of the floor and began.

"Sir Herbert, you have been chief surgeon at the Royal Free Hospital for approximately the last seven years. During that time you must have been assisted by many nurses, probably even hundreds, would you say?"

Sir Herbert's slight eyebrows rose in surprise.

"I never thought of counting," he said frankly. "But, yes, I suppose so."

"Of very varying degrees of skill and dedication?"

359

"I am afraid that is true." Sir Herbert's mouth curled almost imperceptibly in wry, self-mocking amusement.

"When did you first meet Prudence Barrymore?"

Sir Herbert concentrated in thought for a moment. The court was utterly silent, every eye in the room upon his face. There was no hostility in the jurors' total attention, only a keen awaiting.

"It must have been in July of 1856," he replied. "I cannot be more exact than that, I am afraid." He drew breath as if to add something, then changed his mind.

Rathbone noted it with inner satisfaction. He was going to obey. Thank God for that! He affected innocence. "Do you recall the arrival of all the new nurses, Sir Herbert?"

"No, of course not. There are scores of them. Er ..." Then again he stopped. A bitter amusement stirred Rathbone. Sir Herbert was obeying him so very precisely; it was a betrayal of the depth of the fear he was concealing. Rathbone judged he was not a man who obeyed others easily.

"And why did you note Miss Barrymore in particular?" he asked.

"Because she was a Crimean nurse," Sir Herbert replied. "A gentlewoman who had dedicated herself to the care of the sick, at some considerable cost to herself, even risk of her own life. She did not come because she required to earn her living but because she wished to nurse."

Rathbone was aware of a low murmur of agreement from the crowd and the open expressions of approval on the jurors' faces.

"And was she as skilled and dedicated as you had hoped?"

"More so," Sir Herbert replied, keeping his eyes on Rathbone's face. He stood a little forward in the box, his hands on the rails, arms straight. It was an attitude of concentration and even a certain humility. If Rathbone had schooled him he could not have done better. "She was tireless in her duties," he added. "Never late, never absent without cause. Her memory was phenomenal and she learned with remarkable rapidity. And no one ever had cause to question her total morality in any area whatsoever. She was altogether an excellent woman."

"And handsome?" Rathbone asked with a slight smile.

Sir Herbert's eyes opened wider in surprise. He had obviously not expected the question, or thought of an answer beforehand.

"Yes—yes I suppose she was. I am afraid I notice such things less than most men. In such circumstances I am more interested in a woman's skills." He glanced at the jury in half apology. "When you are dealing with the very ill, a pretty face is little help. I do recall she had very fine hands indeed." He did not look down at his own beautiful hands resting on the witness box railing.

"She was very skilled?" Rathbone repeated.

"I have said so."

"Enough to perform a surgical operation herself?"

Sir Herbert looked startled, opened his mouth as if to speak, then stopped.

"Sir Herbert?" Rathbone prompted.

"She was an excellent nurse," he said earnestly. "But not a doctor! You have to understand, the difference is enormous. It is an uncrossable gulf." He shook his head. "She had no formal training. She knew only what she learned by experience and observation on the battlefield and in the hospital at Scutari." He leaned a trifle farther forward, his face creased with concentration. "You have to understand the difference between such haphazardly gained knowledge, unorganized, without reference to cause and effect, to alternatives, possible complication—without knowledge of anatomy, pharmacology, the experience and case notes of other doctors—and the years of formal training and practice and the whole body of lateral and supplementary learning such education provides." Again he shook his head, more vehemently this time. "No, Mr. Rathbone, she was an excellent nurse, I have never known better—but she was most certainly not a doctor. And to tell you the truth"—he faced Rathbone squarely, his eyes brilliantly direct—"I believe that the tales we have heard of her performing operations in the field of battle did not come in that form from her. She was not an arrogant woman, nor untruthful. I believe she must have been misunderstood, and possibly even misquoted."

There were quite audible murmurs of approval from the body of the court, several people nodded and glanced at neighbors, and on the jury benches two members actually smiled.

It had been a brilliant move emotionally, but tactically it made Rathbone's next question more difficult to frame. He debated whether to delay it, and decided it would be seen as evasive.

"Sir Herbert . . ." He walked a couple of steps closer to the witness box and looked up. "The prosecution's evidence against you was a number of letters from Prudence Barrymore to her sister in which she writes of her profound feelings toward you, and the belief that you returned those feelings and would shortly make her the happiest of women. Is this a realistic view, a practical and honest one? These are her own words, and not misquoted."

Sir Herbert shook his head, his face creased with confusion.

"I simply cannot understand it," he said ruefully. "I swear before God, I have never given her the slightest cause to think I held her in that kind of regard, and I have spent hours, days, trying to think of anything I could have said or done that could give her such an impression, and I honestly can think of nothing."

He shook his head again, biting his lip. "Perhaps I am casual in manner, and may have allowed myself to speak informally to those with whom I work, but I truly cannot see how any person would have interpreted my remarks as statements of personal affection. I simply spoke to a trusted colleague in whom I had the utmost confidence." He hesitated. Several jurors nodded in sympathy and understanding. From their faces it seemed they too had had such experiences. It was all eminently reasonable. A look of profound regret transformed his features.

"Perhaps I was remiss?" he said gravely. "I am not a romantic man. I have been happily married for over twenty years to the only woman whom I have ever regarded in that light." He smiled self-consciously.

Above in the gallery women nudged each other understandingly.

"She would tell you I have little imagination in that region of my life," Sir Herbert continued. "As you may see, I am not a handsome or dashing figure. I have never been the subject of the romantic attentions of young ladies. There are far more . . ." He hesitated, searching for the right word. "More charming and likely men for such a role. We have a number of medical students, gifted, young, good-looking, and with fine futures ahead of them. And of course there are other senior doctors as well, with greater gifts than mine in charm and appealing manner. Quite frankly, it never occurred to me that anyone might view me in that light."

Rathbone adopted a sympathetic stance, although Sir Herbert was doing so well he hardly needed help.

"Did Miss Barrymore never say anything which struck you as more than usually admiring, nothing personal rather than professional?" he asked. "I imagine you are used to the very considerable respect of your staff and the gratitude of your patients, but please think carefully, with the wisdom of hindsight."

Sir Herbert shrugged and smiled candidly and apologetically.

"Believe me, Mr. Rathbone, I have tried, but on every occasion on which I spent time, admittedly a great deal of time, with Nurse Barrymore, my mind was on the medical case with which we were engaged. I never saw her in any other connection." He drew his brows together in an effort of concentration.

"I thought of her with respect, with trust, with the utmost confidence in her dedication and her ability, but I did not think of her personally." He looked down. "It seems I was grievously in the wrong in that, which I profoundly regret. I have daughters of my own, as you no doubt know, but my profession has kept me so fully occupied that their upbringing has been largely left to their mother. I do not really know the ways of young women as well as I might, as well as many men whose personal lives allow them more time in their homes and with their families than does mine."

There was a whisper and rustle of sympathy around the court.

"It is a price I do not pay willingly." He bit his lip. "And it seems perhaps it may have been responsible for a tragic misunderstanding by Nurse Barrymore. I—I cannot think of any specific remarks I may have made. I really thought only of our patients, but this I do know." His voice dropped and became hard and intense. "I at no time whatever entertained any romantic notions about Miss Barrymore, or said or did anything whatever that was improper or could be construed by an unbiased person to be an advance or expression of romantic intent. Of that I am as certain as I am that I stand here before you in this courtroom."

It was superb. Rathbone himself could not have written anything better.

"Thank you, Sir Herbert. You have explained this tragic situation in a manner I believe we can all understand." He looked at the jury with a rueful gesture. "I myself have experienced embarrassing encounters, and I daresay the gentlemen of the jury may have also. The dreams and priorities in life of young women are at times different from ours, and perhaps we are dangerously, even tragically, insensitive to them." He turned back to the witness stand. "Please remain where you are. I have no doubt my learned friend will have questions to ask you."

He smiled at Lovat-Smith as he walked back to the table and resumed his seat.

Lovat-Smith stood up and straightened his gown before moving across to the center of the floor. He did not look to right or left, but directly up at Sir Herbert.

"In your own words, Sir Herbert, you are not a ladies' man, is that correct?" His voice was courteous, even smooth. There was no hint of panic or defeat in it, just a deference toward a man held in public esteem.

Rathbone knew he was acting. Lovat-Smith was as well aware as he himself how excellent Sir Herbert's testimony had been. All the same his confidence gave Rathbone a twinge of unease.

"No," Sir Herbert said carefully, "I am not."

Rathbone shut his eyes. Please Heaven Sir Herbert would remember his advice now. Say nothing more! Rathbone said over and over to himself. Add nothing. Offer nothing. Don't be led by him. He is your enemy.

"But you must have some considerable familiarity with the ways of women . . ." Lovat-Smith said, raising his eyebrows and opening his light blue eyes very wide.

Sir Herbert said nothing.

Rathbone breathed out a sigh of relief.

"You are married, and have been for many years," Lovat-Smith pointed out. "Indeed you have a large family, including three daughters. You do yourself an injustice, sir. I have it on excellent authority that your family life is most contented and well ordered, and you are an excellent husband and father."

"Thank you," Sir Herbert said graciously.

Lovat-Smith's face tightened. There was a faint titter somewhere in the body of the court, instantly suppressed.

"It was not intended as a compliment, sir," Lovat-Smith said sharply. Then he hurried on before there was more laughter. "It was to point out that you are not as unacquainted with the ways of women as you would have us believe. Your relationship with your wife is excellent, you say, and I have no reason to doubt it. At least it is undeniably long and intimate."

Again a titter of amusement came from the crowd, but it was brief and stifled almost immediately. Sympathy was with Sir Herbert; Lovat-Smith realized it and would not make that mistake again.

"Surely you cannot expect me to believe you are an innocent in the nature and affections of women, in the way which they take flattery or attention?"

Now Sir Herbert had no one to guide him as Rathbone had done. He was alone, facing the enemy. Rathbone gritted his teeth.

Sir Herbert remained silent for several minutes.

Hardie looked at him inquiringly.

Lovat-Smith smiled.

"I do not think," Sir Herbert answered at last, lifting his eyes and looking squarely at Lovat-Smith, "that you can reasonably liken my relationship with my wife to that with my nurses, even the very best of them, which undoubtedly Miss Barrymore was. My wife knows me and does not misinterpret what I say. I do not have to be watchful that she has read me aright. And my relationship with my daughters is hardly of the nature we are discussing. It does not enter into it." He stopped abruptly and stared at Lovat-Smith.

Again jurors nodded, understanding plain in their faces.

Lovat-Smith shifted the line of his attack slightly.

"Was Miss Barrymore the only young woman of good birth with whom you have worked, Sir Herbert?"

Sir Herbert smiled. "It is only very recently that such young women have taken an interest in nursing, sir. In fact, it is since Miss Nightingale's work in the Crimea has become so famous that other young women desired to emulate her. And of course there are those who served with her, such as Miss Barrymore, and my present most excellent nurse, Miss Latterly. Previously to that, the only women of gentle birth who had any business in the hospital—one could not call it work in the same sense—were those who served in the Board of Governors, such as Lady Ross Gilbert and Lady Callandra Daviot. And they are not romantically impressionable young ladies."

Rathbone breathed out a sigh of relief. He had negotiated it superbly. He had even avoided saying offensively that Berenice and Callandra were not young.

Lovat-Smith accepted rebuff gracefully and tried again.

"Do I understand correctly, Sir Herbert, that you are very used to admiration?"

Sir Herbert hesitated. "I would prefer to say 'respect,' " he said, deflecting the obvious vanity.

"I daresay." Lovat-Smith smiled at him, showing sharp, even teeth. "But admiration is what I meant. Do not your students admire you intensely?"

"You were better to ask them, sir."

"Oh come now!" Lovat-Smith's smile widened. "No false modesty, please. This is not a withdrawing room where pretty manners are required." His voice hardened suddenly. "You are a man accustomed to inordinate admiration, to people hanging upon your every word. The court will find it difficult to believe you are not well used to telling the difference between overenthusiasm, sycophancy, and an emotional regard which is personal, and therefore uniquely dangerous."

"Student doctors are all young men," Sir Herbert answered with a frown of confusion. "The question of romance does not arise."

Two or three of the jurors smiled.

"And nurses?" Lovat-Smith pursued, eyes wide, voice soft.

"Forgive me for being somewhat blunt," Sir Herbert said patiently. "But I thought we had already covered that. Until very recently they have not been of a social class where a personal relationship could be considered."

Lovat-Smith did not look in the least disconcerted. He smiled very slightly, again showing his teeth. "And your patients, Sir Herbert? Were they also all men, all elderly, or all of a social class too low to be considered?"

A slow flush spread up Sir Herbert's cheeks.

"Of course not," he said very quietly. "But the gratitude and dependence of a patient are quite different. One knows to accept it as related to one's skills, to the patient's natural fear and pain, and not as a personal emotion. Its intensity is transient, even if the gratitude remains. Most men of

367

medicine experience such feelings and know them for what they are. To mistake them for love would be quite foolish."

Fine, Rathbone thought. Now stop, for Heaven's sake! Don't spoil it by going on.

Sir Herbert opened his mouth and then, as if silently hearing Rathbone's thoughts, closed it again.

Lovat-Smith stood in the center of the floor, staring up at the witness box, his head a little to one side. "So in spite of your experience with your wife, your daughters, your grateful and dependent patients, you were still taken totally by surprise when Prudence Barrymore expressed her love and devotion toward you? It must have been an alarming and embarrassing experience for you—a happily married man as you are!"

But Sir Herbert was not so easily tripped.

"She did not express it, sir," he replied levelly. "She never said or did anything which would lead me to suppose her regard for me was more than professional. When her letters were read to me it was the first I knew of it."

"Indeed?" Lovat-Smith said with heavy disbelief, giving a little shake of his head. "Do you seriously expect the jury to believe that?" He indicated them with one hand. "They are all intelligent, experienced men. I think they would find it hard to imagine themselves so . . . naive." He turned from the witness stand and walked back to his table.

"I hope they will," Sir Herbert said quietly, leaning forward over the railing with hands clasping it. "It is the truth. Perhaps I was remiss, perhaps I did not look at her as a young and romantic woman, simply as a professional upon whom I relied. And that may be a sin—for which I shall feel an eternal regret. But it is not a cause to commit murder!"

There was a brief murmur of applause from the court. Someone called out, "Hear, hear!" and Judge Hardie glanced at them. One of the jurors smiled and nodded.

"Do you wish to reexamine your witness, Mr. Rathbone?" Hardie asked.

"No thank you, my lord," Rathbone declined graciously.

Hardie excused Sir Herbert, who walked with dignity, head high, back to his place in the dock.

Rathbone called a succession of Sir Herbert's professional colleagues. He did not ask them as much as he had originally intended; Sir Herbert's impression upon the court in general had been too powerful for him to want to smother it with evidence which now seemed largely extraneous. He asked them briefly for their estimation of Sir Herbert as a colleague and each replied unhesitatingly of his great skill and dedication. He asked of his personal moral reputation and they spoke equally plainly that he was beyond reproach.

Lovat-Smith did not bother to pursue them. He made something of a show of boredom, looking at the ceiling while Rathbone was speaking, and when it was his own turn, waiting several seconds before he began. He did not exactly say that their loyalty was totally predictable—and meaningless—but he implied it. It was a ploy to bore the jury and make them forget this impression of Sir Herbert, and Rathbone knew it. He could see from the jurors' faces that they were still completely in sympathy with Sir Herbert, and further laboring of the point risked insulting their intelligence and losing their attention. He thanked the doctor at that moment on the stand and excused him, sending a message that no further colleagues would be required—except Kristian Beck.

It would have been a startling omission had he not called him, but apart from that, he wished to sow in the jurors' minds the strong possibility that it had been Beck himself who had murdered Prudence.

Kristian took the stand without the slightest idea of what awaited him. Rathbone had told him only that he would be called to witness to Sir Herbert's character.

"Dr. Beck, you are a physician and surgeon, are you not?"

"I am." Kristian looked faintly surprised. It was hardly necessary for the validity of his testimony.

"And you have practiced in several places, including

369

your native Bohemia?" He wanted to establish in the jurors' minds Beck's foreignness, his very differentness from the essentially English, familiar Sir Herbert. It was a task he disliked, but the shadow of the noose forms strange patterns on the mind.

"Yes," Kristian agreed again.

"But you have worked with Sir Herbert Stanhope for more than ten or eleven years, is that correct?"

"About that," Kristian agreed. His accent was almost indiscernible, merely a pleasant clarity to certain vowels. "Of course we seldom actually work together, since we are in the same field, but I know his reputation, both personal and professional, and I see him frequently." His expression was open and candid, his intention to help obvious.

"I understand," Rathbone conceded. "I did not mean to imply that you worked side by side. What is Sir Herbert's personal reputation, Dr. Beck?"

A flash of amusement crossed Kristian's face, but there was no malice in it.

"He is regarded as pompous, a little overbearing, justifiably proud of his abilities and his achievements, an excellent teacher, and a man of total moral integrity." He smiled at Rathbone. "Naturally he is joked about by his juniors, and guyed occasionally—I think that is the word—as we all are. But I have never heard even the most irresponsible suggest his behavior toward women was other than totally correct."

"It has been suggested that he was somewhat naive concerning women." Rathbone lifted his voice questioningly. "Especially young women. Is that your observation, Dr. Beck?"

"I would have chosen the word *uninterested*," Kristian replied. "But I suppose *naive* would do. It is not something to which I previously gave any thought. But if you wish me to say that I find it extremely difficult to believe that he had any romantic interest in Nurse Barrymore, or that he would be unaware of any such feeling she might have had for him, then I can do so very easily. I find it harder to believe that Nurse Barrymore cherished a secret passion for Sir Herbert." A pucker of doubt crossed his face, and he stared at Rathbone very directly.

"You find that hard to believe, Dr. Beck?" Rathbone said very clearly.

"I do."

"Do you consider yourself a naive or unworldly man?"

Kristian's mouth curled into faint self-mockery. "No—no, I don't."

"Then if you find it surprising and hard to accept, is it hard to believe that Sir Herbert was also quite unaware of it?" Rathbone could not keep the ring of triumph out of his voice, although he tried.

Kristian looked rueful, and in spite of what Rathbone had said, surprised.

"No—no, that would seem to follow inevitably."

Rathbone thought of all the suspicions of Kristian Beck that Monk had raised to him: the quarrel overheard with Prudence, the possibilities of blackmail, the fact that Kristian Beck had been in the hospital all the night of Prudence's death, that his own patient had died when he had been expected to recover—but it was all suspicion, dark thoughts, no more. There was no proof, no hard evidence of anything. If he raised it now he might direct the jury's thoughts toward Beck as a suspect. On the other hand, he might only alienate them and betray his own desperation. It would look ugly. At the moment he had their sympathy, and that might just be enough to win the verdict. Sir Herbert's life could rest on this decision.

Should he accuse Beck? He looked at his interesting, curious face with its sensuous mouth and marvelous eyes. There was too much intelligence in it—too much humor; it was a risk he dare not take. As it was, he was winning. He knew it—and Lovat-Smith knew it.

"Thank you, Dr. Beck," he said aloud. "That is all."

Lovat-Smith rose immediately and strode toward the center of the floor.

"Dr. Beck, you are a busy surgeon and physician, are you not?"

"Yes," Kristian agreed, puckering his brows.

"Do you spend much of your time considering the possible romances within the hospital, and whether one person or another may be aware of such feelings?"

"No," Kristian confessed.

"Do you spend any time at all so involved?" Lovat-Smith pressed.

But Kristian was not so easily circumvented.

"It does not require thought, Mr. Lovat-Smith. It is a matter of simple observation one cannot avoid. I am sure you are aware of your colleagues, even when your mind is upon your profession."

This was so patently true that Lovat-Smith could not deny it. He hesitated a moment as if some argument were on the tip of his tongue, then abandoned it.

"None of them is accused of murder, Dr. Beck," he said with a gesture of resignation and vague half-rueful amusement. "That is all I have to ask you, thank you."

Hardie glanced at Rathbone.

Rathbone shook his head.

Kristian Beck left the witness stand and disappeared into the body of the court, leaving Rathbone uncertain whether he had just had a fortunate escape from making a fool of himself, or if he had just missed a profound opportunity he would not get again.

Lovat-Smith looked across at him, the light catching in his brilliant eyes, making his expression unreadable.

The following day Rathbone called Lady Stanhope, not that he expected her evidence to add anything of substance. Certainly she knew no facts germane to the case, but her presence would counter the emotional impact made by Mrs. Barrymore. Lady Stanhope also stood to lose not only her husband to a ghastly death, but her family to scandal and shame—and in all probability her home to a sudden and almost certainly permanent poverty and isolation.

She mounted the stand with a little assistance from the clerk and faced Rathbone nervously. She was very pale and seemed to keep her posture only with difficulty. But she did stop and quite deliberately look up and across at her husband in the dock, meet his eyes, and smile.

Sir Herbert blinked, gave an answering smile, and then looked away. One could only guess his emotions.

Rathbone waited, giving the jury time to observe and remember, then he stepped forward and spoke to her courteously, very gently.

"Lady Stanhope, I apologize for having to call you to testify at what must be a most distressing time for you, but I am sure you would wish to do everything possible to assist your husband to prove his innocence."

She swallowed, staring at him.

"Of course. Anything . . ." She stopped, obviously also remembering his instruction not to say more than she was asked for.

He smiled at her. "Thank you. I don't have a great deal to ask you, simply a little about Sir Herbert and your knowledge of his life and his character."

She looked at him blankly, not knowing what to say.

This was going to be extremely difficult. He must steer a course between catering to her so much he learned nothing and being so forceful he frightened her into incoherence. He had thought when he had originally spoken to her that she would be an excellent witness, now he was wondering if he had made an error in calling her. But if he had not, her absence would have been noticed and wondered upon.

"Lady Stanhope, how long have you been married to Sir Herbert?"

"Twenty-three years," she replied.

"And you have children?"

"Yes, we have seven children, three daughters and four sons." She was beginning to gain a little more confidence. She was on familiar ground.

"Remember you are on oath, Lady Stanhope," he warned

373

gently, not for her but to draw the jury's attention, "and must answer honestly, even if it is painful to you. Have you ever had cause to doubt Sir Herbert's complete loyalty to you during that time?"

She looked a little taken aback, even though he had previously ascertained that her answer would be in the negative or he would not have asked.

"No, most certainly not!" She flushed faintly and looked down at her hands. "I'm sorry, that was insensitive of me. I am quite aware that many women are not so fortunate. But no, he has never given me cause for distress or anxiety in that way." She took a breath and smiled very slightly, looking at Rathbone. "You must understand, he is devoted to his profession. He is not a great deal interested in personal affection of that sort. He loves his family, he likes to be comfortable with people, to be able, if you understand what I mean, to take them for granted." She smiled apologetically, looking steadily at Rathbone and keeping her eyes from everyone else. "I suppose you might say that is lazy, in a sort of way, but he puts all his energy into his work. He has saved the lives of so many people—and surely that is more important than making polite conversation, flattering people and playing little games of etiquette and manners? Isn't it?" She was asking him for reassurance, and already he was conscious of the sounds of sympathy and agreement from the crowd, little murmurs, shiftings and nods, matters of affirmation.

"Yes, Lady Stanhope, I believe it is," he said gently. "And I am sure there are many thousands of people who will agree with you. I don't think I have anything further to ask you, but my learned friend may. Please would you remain there, just in case."

He walked slowly back to his seat, meeting Lovat-Smith's glance as he did so, and knowing his opponent was weighing up what he might gain or lose by questioning Lady Stanhope. She had the jury's sympathy. If he appeared to embarrass or fluster her he might jeopardize his own position, even if he discredited her testimony. How much of the jurors' verdict would rest on fact, how much on anticipation, emotion, prejudice, whom they believed or liked, and whom they did not?

Lovat-Smith rose and approached the witness stand with a smile. He did not know how to be humble, but he understood charm perfectly.

"Lady Stanhope, I also have very little to ask you and shall not keep you long. Have you ever been to the Royal Free Hospital?"

She looked surprised. "No—no I have never had the need, fortunately. All my confinements have been at home, and I have never required an operation."

"I was thinking rather more of a social visit, ma'am, not as a patient. Perhaps out of interest in your husband's profession?"

"Oh no, no, I don't think that would be at all necessary, and really not suitable, you know?" She shook her head, biting her lip. "My place is in the home, with my family. My husband's place of work is not—not appropriate . . ." She stopped, uncertain what else to add.

In the gallery two elderly women glanced at each other and nodded approvingly.

"I see." Lovat-Smith turned a little sideways, glancing at the jury, then back at Lady Stanhope. "Did you ever meet Nurse Prudence Barrymore?"

"No." Again she was surprised. "No, of course not."

"Do you know anything about the way in which a skilled nurse normally works with a surgeon caring for a patient?"

"No." She shook her head, frowning with confusion. "I have no idea. It is—it is not anything that occurs to me. I care for my house and my children."

"Of course, and most commendable," Lovat-Smith agreed with a nod of his head. "That is your vocation and your skill."

"Yes."

"Then you really are not in a position to say whether your husband's relationship with Miss Barrymore was unusual, or personal, or whether it was not—are you?"

375

"Well—I . . ." She looked unhappy. "I—I don't know."

"There is no reason why you should, ma'am," Lovat-Smith said quietly. "Neither would any other lady in your position. Thank you. That is all I have to ask you."

A look of relief crossed her face, and she glanced up at Sir Herbert. He smiled at her briefly.

Rathbone rose again.

"Lady Stanhope, as my learned friend has pointed out, you know nothing about the hospital or its routines and practices. But you do know your husband and his personality, and you have for nearly a quarter of a century?"

She looked relieved. "Yes, yes I do."

"And he is a good, loyal, and affectionate husband and father, but dedicated to his career, not socially skilled, not a ladies' man, not sensitive or aware of the emotions and daydreams of young women?"

She smiled a little ruefully, looked up at the dock as if uncertain, apology plain in her face. "No sir, not at all, I am afraid."

A shadow of relief, almost satisfaction, touched Sir Herbert. It was a complex emotional expression, and the jury noticed it with approval.

"Thank you, Lady Stanhope," Rathbone said with rising confidence. "Thank you very much. That is all."

Rathbone's last witness was Faith Barker, Prudence's sister, recalled now for the defense. When he had first spoken to her she had been utterly convinced that Sir Herbert was guilty. He had murdered her sister, and for her that was a crime for which there was no forgiveness. But Rathbone had spoken to her at length, and finally she had made pronounced concessions. She was still uncertain, and there was no mercy in her for Sir Herbert, but on one point at least she was adamant, and he felt the risk of what else she might say was worth it.

She took the stand with her head high, face pale, and marked with the depth of grief. Her anger also was unmistakable, and she shot Sir Herbert in the dock opposite her a look of unsuppressed loathing. The jury saw it and were

376

distinctly uncomfortable; one man coughed and covered his mouth in a gesture of embarrassment. Rathbone saw it with a rising heart. They believed Sir Herbert; Faith Barker's grief made them uncomfortable. Lovat-Smith saw it also. His jaw tightened and he pursed his lips.

"Mrs. Barker," Rathbone began clearly and very politely. "I know that you are here at least in part against your will. However, I must direct you to exercise all your fairness of mind, that integrity which I am sure you have in common with your sister, and answer my questions only with what is asked. Do not offer your own opinions or emotions. At such a time they cannot but be profound and full of pain. We sympathize with you, but we sympathize also with Lady Stanhope and her family, and all other people this tragedy has touched."

"I understand you, Mr. Rathbone," she replied stiffly. "I shall not speak out of malice, I swear to you."

"Thank you. I am sure you will not. Now please, if you would consider this matter of your sister's regard for Sir Herbert and what you know of her character. What we have heard of her from witnesses of very different natures, and different circumstances in which they knew her, all paints the picture of a woman of compassion and integrity. We have not heard from anyone of a single cruel or selfish act on her part. Does that sound like the sister you knew?"

"Certainly," Faith agreed without hesitation.

"An excellent woman?" Rathbone added.

"Yes."

"Without fault?" He raised his eyebrows.

"No, of course not." She dismissed the idea with a faint smile. "None of us is without fault."

"Without being disloyal, I am sure you can tell us in which general area her flaws lay?"

Lovat-Smith rose to his feet. "Really, my lord, this is hardly enlightening, and surely not relevant? Let the poor woman rest in as much peace as is possible, considering the manner of her death."

Hardie looked at Rathbone.

"Is this as totally pointless and tasteless as it seems, Mr. Rathbone?" he said with disapproval sharp in his lean face.

"No, my lord," Rathbone assured him. "I have a very definite purpose in asking Mrs. Barker such a question. The prosecution's charge against Sir Herbert rests on certain assumptions about Miss Barrymore's character. I must have the latitude to explore them if I am to serve him fairly."

"Then arrive at your point, Mr. Rathbone," Hardie instructed, his expression easing only slightly.

Rathbone turned to the witness stand.

"Mrs. Barker?"

She took a deep breath. "She was a little brusque at times. She did not suffer fools graciously, and since she was of extraordinary intelligence, to her there were many who fell into that category. Do you need more?"

"If there is more?"

"She was very brave, both physically and morally. She had no time for cowards. She could be hasty in her judgment."

"She was ambitious?" he asked.

"I do not see that as a flaw." She looked at him with undisguised dislike.

"Nor I, ma'am. It was merely a question. Was she ruthless in reaching after her ambitions, regardless of the cost or consequences to others?"

"If you mean was she cruel or dishonest, no, never. She did not expect or wish to gain her desires at someone else's expense."

"Have you ever known her to force or coerce anyone into a gesture or act they did not wish?"

"No, I have not!"

"Or to use privileged knowledge to exert pressure upon people?"

A look of anger crossed Faith Barker's face.

"That would be blackmail, sir, and in every way despicable. I resent profoundly that you should mention such a sinful act in the same breath with Prudence's name. If you had known her, you would realize how totally abhorrent

378

and ridiculous such a suggestion is." Again she stared, tight-faced and implacable, at Sir Herbert, then at the jury.

"No. She despised moral cowardice, deceit, or anything of that nature," she continued. "She would consider anything gained by such means to be tainted beyond any value it might once have had." She glared at Rathbone, then at the jury. "And if you imagine she would have blackmailed Sir Herbert in order to make him marry her, that is the most ridiculous thing of all. What woman of any honor or integrity whatever would wish for a husband in such circumstances? Life with him would be insupportable. It would be a living hell."

"Yes, Mrs. Barker," Rathbone agreed with a soft, satisfied smile. "I imagine it would be. And I am sure Prudence was not only too honorable to use such a method, but also too intelligent to imagine it could possibly bring her anything but lifelong misery. Thank you for your candor. I have no further questions for you. Perhaps my learned friend has?" He looked at Lovat-Smith with a smile.

Lovat-Smith's answering smile was bright, showing all his teeth, and probably only Rathbone knew it was empty of feeling.

"Oh certainly I have." He rose to his feet and advanced toward the stand. "Mrs. Barker, did your sister write home to you of her adventures and experiences while she was in the Crimea?"

"Yes, of course she did, although I did not receive all her letters. I know that because she would occasionally make reference to things she had said on certain occasions, and I knew nothing of them." She looked puzzled, as if she did not comprehend the reason for his inquiry. Even Hardie seemed dubious.

"But you did receive a considerable number of her letters?" Lovat-Smith pressed.

"Yes."

"Sufficient to have formed a picture of her experiences, her part in the nursing, and how it affected her?"

379

"I believe so." Still Faith Barker did not grasp his purpose.

"Then you will have a fairly vivid understanding of her character?"

"I think I have already said so, to Mr. Rathbone," she replied, her brow puckered.

"Indeed—so you have." Lovat-Smith took a pace or two and stopped again, facing her. "She must have been a very remarkable woman; it cannot have been easy even to reach the Crimea in time of war, let alone to master such a calling. Were there not difficulties in her path?"

"Of course," she agreed with something close to a laugh.

"You are amused, Mrs. Barker," he observed. "Is my question absurd?"

"Frankly, sir, yes it is. I do not mean to be offensive, but even to ask it, you cannot have the least idea of what obstacles there are to a young single woman of good family traveling alone to the Crimea on a troopship to begin nursing soldiers. Everyone was against it, except Papa, and even he was dubious. Had it been anyone other than Prudence, I think he would have forbidden it outright."

Rathbone stiffened. Somewhere in the back of his head there was an urgent warning, like a needle pricking him. He rose to his feet.

"My lord, we have already established that Prudence Barrymore was a remarkable woman. This seems to be irrelevant and wasting the court's time. If my learned friend had wished to have Mrs. Barker testify on the subject, he had ample opportunity when she was his witness."

Hardie turned to Lovat-Smith.

"I have to agree, Mr. Lovat-Smith. This is wasting time and serves no purpose. If you have questions to ask this witness in cross-examination, then please do so. Otherwise allow the defense to proceed."

Lovat-Smith smiled. This time it was with genuine pleasure.

"Oh it is relevant, my lord. It has immediate relevance to my learned friend's last questions to Mrs. Barker, regarding her sister's character and the extreme unlikelihood of her resorting to coercion"—his smile widened—"or not!"

"Then get to your point, Mr. Lovat-Smith," Hardie directed.

"Yes, my lord."

Rathbone's heart sank. He knew now what Lovat-Smith was going to do.

And he was not mistaken. Lovat-Smith looked up at Faith Barker again.

"Mrs. Barker, your sister must have been a woman who was capable of overcoming great obstacles, of disregarding other peoples' objections when she felt passionately about a subject; when it was something she wished intensely, it seems nothing stood in her way."

There was a sighing of breath around the room. Someone broke a pencil.

Faith Barker was pale. Now she also understood his purpose.

"Yes—but—"

"Yes will do," Lovat-Smith interrupted. "And your mother: did she approve of this adventure of hers? Was she not worried for her safety? There must have been remarkable physical danger: wreck at sea, injury from cargo, horses, not to mentioned frightened and possibly rough soldiers separated from their own women, going to a battle from which they might not return? And that even before she reached the Crimea!"

"It is not necessarily—"

"I am not speaking of the reality, Mrs. Barker!" Lovat-Smith interrupted. "I am speaking of your mother's perceptions of it. Was she not concerned for Prudence? Even terrified for her?"

"She was afraid—yes."

"And was she also afraid of what she might experience when close to the battlefield—or in the hospital itself? What if the Russians had prevailed? What would have happened to Prudence then?"

A ghost of a smile crossed Faith Barker's face.

"I don't think Mama ever considered the possibility of the Russians prevailing," she said quietly. "Mama believes we are invincible."

There was a murmur of amusement around the room, even an answering smile on Hardie's face, but it died away instantly.

Lovat-Smith bit his lip. "Possibly," he said with a little shake of his head. "Possibly. A nice thought, but perhaps not very realistic."

"You asked for her feelings, sir, not the reality of it."

There was another titter of laughter, vanishing into silence like a stone dropped into still water.

"Nevertheless," Lovat-Smith took up the thread again, "was your mother not gravely worried for her, even frightened?"

"Yes."

"And you yourself? Were you not frightened for her? Did you not lie awake visualizing what might happen to her, dreading the unknown?"

"Yes."

"Your distress did not deter her?"

"No," she said, for the first time a marked reluctance in her voice.

Lovat-Smith's eyes widened. "So physical obstacles, personal danger, even extreme danger, official objections and difficulties, her family's fear and anxiety and emotional pain, none of these deterred her? She would seem to have a ruthless streak in her, would she not?"

Faith Barker hesitated.

There was a fidgeting in the crowd, an unhappy restlessness.

"Mrs. Barker?" Lovat-Smith prompted.

"I don't care for the word *ruthless*."

"It is not always an attractive quality, Mrs. Barker," he agreed. "And that same strength and drive which took her to the Crimea, against all odds, and preserved her there amidst fearful carnage, daily seeing the death of fine brave men, may in peacetime have become something less easy to understand or admire."

"But I—"

"Of course." Again he interrupted her before she could speak. "She was your sister. You do not wish to think such things of her. But I find it unanswerable nevertheless. Thank you. I have no further questions."

Rathbone rose again. There was total silence in the court. Even on the public benches no one moved. There was no rustle of fabric, no squeak of boots, no scratching of pencils.

"Mrs. Barker, Prudence went to the Crimea regardless of your mother's anxieties, or yours. You have not made it plain whether she forced or coerced you in any way, or simply told you, quite pleasantly, that she wished to do this and would not be dissuaded."

"Oh the latter, sir, quite definitely," Faith said quickly. "We had no power to prevent her anyway."

"Did she try to persuade you of her reasons?"

"Yes, of course she did—she believed it was the right thing to do. She wished to give her life in service to the sick and injured. The cost to herself was of no account." Suddenly grief filled her face again. "She frequently said that she would rather die in the course of doing something fine than live to be eighty doing nothing but being comfortable—and dying of uselessness inside."

"That does not sound particularly ruthless to me," Rathbone said very gently. "Tell me, Mrs. Barker, do you believe it is within the nature of the woman, and even my learned friend agrees you knew her well, to have attempted to blackmail a man into marrying her?"

"It is quite impossible," she said vehemently. "It is not only of a meanness and small-mindedness totally at odds with all her character—it is also quite stupid. And whatever you believe of her, no one has suggested she was that."

"No one indeed," Rathbone agreed. "Thank you, Mrs. Barker. That is all."

Judge Hardie leaned forward.

"It is growing late, Mr. Rathbone. We will hear your final arguments on Monday. Court is adjourned."

All around the room there was a sigh of tension released, the sound of fabric whispering as people relaxed, and then immediately after a scramble as journalists struggled to be the first out, free to head for the street and the hasty ride to their newspapers.

Oliver Rathbone was unaware of it, but Hester had been in the court for the last three hours of the afternoon, and had heard Faith Barker's testimony both as to the letters she had received and her beliefs as to Prudence's character and personality. When Judge Hardie adjourned the court, she half hoped to speak to Rathbone, but he disappeared into one of the many offices, and since she had nothing in particular to say to him, she felt it would be foolish to wait.

She was leaving, her thoughts turning over and over what she had heard, her own impressions of the jurors' moods, of Sir Herbert Stanhope, and of Lovat-Smith. She felt elated. Of course nothing could possibly be certain until the verdict was in, but she was almost certain that Rathbone had won. The only unfortunate aspect was that they were still as far from discovering who really had murdered Prudence. And that reawoke the sick ache inside that perhaps it had been Kristian Beck. She had never fully investigated what had happened the night before Prudence's death. Kristian's patient had died unexpectedly, that was all she knew. He had been distressed; was he also guilty of some negligence—or worse? And had Prudence known that? And uglier and more painful, did Callandra know it now?

She was outside on the flight of wide stone steps down to the street when she saw Faith Barker coming toward her, her face furrowed in concentration, her expression still one of confusion and unhappiness.

Hester stepped forward.

"Mrs. Barker . . ."

Faith froze. "I have nothing to say. Please leave me alone."

It took Hester a moment to realize what manner of person Faith Barker had supposed her to be.

"I am a Crimean nurse," she said immediately, cutting across all the explanations. "I knew Prudence—not well, but I worked with her on the battlefield." She saw Faith Barker's start of surprise and then the sudden emotion flooding through her, the hope and the pain.

"I certainly knew her well enough to be completely sure that she would never have blackmailed Sir Herbert, or anyone else, into marriage," Hester hurried on. "Actually, what I find hardest to believe is that she wished to get married at all. She seemed to me to be utterly devoted to medicine, and marriage and family were the last things she wished for. She refused Geoffrey Taunton, of whom I believe she was really quite fond."

Faith stared at her.

"Were you?" she said at last, her eyes clouded with concentration, as if she had some Gordian knot of ideas to untangle. "Really?"

"In the Crimea? Yes."

Faith stood motionless. Around them in the afternoon sun people stood arguing, passing the news and opinions in heated voices. Newsboys shouted the latest word from Parliament, India, China, the Court, society, cricket, and international affairs. Two men quarreled over a hansom, a pie seller cried his wares, and a woman called out after an errant child.

Faith was still staring at Hester as if she would absorb and memorize every detail of her.

"Why did you go to the Crimea?" she said at last. "Oh, I realize it is an impertinent question, and I beg your pardon. I don't think I can explain it to you but I desperately need to know—because I need to understand Prudence, and I don't. I always loved her. She was magnificent, so full of energy and ideas."

She smiled and she was close to tears. "She was three years older than I. As a child I adored her. She was like a magical creature to me—so full of passion and nobility. I al-

385

ways imagined she would marry someone very dashing—a hero of some sort. Only a hero would be good enough for Prudence." A young man in a top hat bumped into her, apologized, and hurried on, but she seemed oblivious of him. "But then she didn't seem to want to marry anyone at all." She smiled ruefully. "I used to dream all sorts of things too—but I knew they were dreams. I never really thought I would sail up the Nile to find its source, or convert heathens in Africa, or anything like that. I knew if I were fortunate I should find a really honorable man I could be fond of and trust, and marry him, and raise children."

An errand boy with a message in his hand asked them directions, listened to what they said, then went on his way uncertainly.

"I was about sixteen before I realized Prudence really meant to make her dreams come true," Faith continued as if there had been no interruption.

"To nurse the sick," Hester put in. "Or specifically to go to some place like the Crimea—a battlefield?"

"Well really to be a doctor," Faith answered. "But of course that is not possible." She smiled at the memory. "She used to be so angry she was a woman. She wished she could have been a man so she could do all these things. But of course that is pointless, and Prudence never wasted time on pointless emotions or regrets. She accepted it." She sniffed in an effort to retain her control. "I just—I just cannot see her jeopardizing all her ideals to try to force a man like Sir Herbert into marrying her. I mean—what could she gain by it, even if he agreed? It's so stupid! What happened to her, Miss ..." She stopped, her face full of pain and confusion.

"Latterly," Hester supplied. "I don't know what happened to her—but I won't rest until I do. Someone murdered her—and if it wasn't Sir Herbert, then it was someone else."

"I want to know who," Faith said very intently. "But more than that, I have to know why. This doesn't make any sense. ..."

"You mean the Prudence you knew would not have behaved as she seems to have?" Hester asked.

"Exactly. That is exactly it. Do you understand?"

"No—if only we had access to those letters. We could read them again and see if there is anything in them at all to explain when and why she changed so completely!"

"Oh they don't have them all," Faith said quickly. "I only gave them the ones that referred most specifically to Sir Herbert and her feelings for him. There are plenty of others."

Hester clasped her arm, forgetting all propriety and the fact that they had known each other barely ten minutes.

"You have them! With you in London?"

"Certainly. They are not on my person, of course—but in my lodgings. Would you care to come with me and see them?"

"Yes—yes I certainly would—if you would permit it?" Hester agreed so quickly there was no courtesy or decorum in it, but such things were utterly trivial now. "May I come immediately?"

"Of course," Faith agreed. "We shall require to take a hansom. It is some little distance away."

Hester turned on her heel and plunged toward the curb, pushing her way past men arguing and women exchanging news, and calling out at the top of her voice, "Hansom! Cabby? Over here, if you please!"

Faith Barker's lodgings were cramped and more than a trifle worn, but scrupulously clean, and the landlady seemed quite agreeable to serving two for supper.

After the barest accommodation to civility, Faith fetched the rest of Prudence's letters and Hester settled herself on the single overstuffed sofa and began to read.

Most of the detail was interesting to her as a nurse. There were clinical notes on a variety of cases, and as she read them she was struck with the quality of Prudence's medical knowledge. It was far more profound than her own, which until now she had considered rather good.

The words were familiar, the patterns of speech reminded her of Prudence so sharply she could almost hear them spoken in her voice.

She remembered the nurses lying in narrow cots by candlelight, huddled in gray blankets, talking to each other, sharing the emotions that were too terrible to bear alone. It was a time which had burned away her innocence and forged her into the woman she was—and Prudence had indelibly been part of that, and so part of her life ever afterwards.

But as far as indication of a change in her ideals or her personality, Prudence's letters offered nothing whatsoever.

Reference to Sir Herbert Stanhope was of a very objective nature, entirely to do with his medical skills. Several times she praised him, but it was for his courage in adapting new techniques, for his diagnostic perception, or for the clarity with which he instructed his students. Then she praised his generosity in sharing his knowledge with her. Conceivably it might have sounded like praise for the man, and a warmer feeling than professional gratitude, but to Hester, who found the medical details both comprehensible and interesting, it was Prudence's enthusiasm for the increase in her own knowledge that came through, and she would have felt the same for any surgeon who treated her so. The man himself was incidental.

In every paragraph her love of medicine shone through, her excitement at its achievements, her boundless hope for its possibilities in the future. People were there to be helped; she cared about their pain and their fear—but always it was medicine itself which quickened her heart and lifted her soul.

"She should really have been a doctor," Hester said again, smiling at her own memories. "She would have been so gifted!"

"That is why being so desperate to marry just isn't like her," Faith replied. "If it had been to be accepted into medical training, I would have believed it. I think she would have done anything for that. Although it was impossible—of course. I know that. No school anywhere takes women."

"I wonder if they ever would . . ." Hester said very slowly. "If an important enough surgeon—say, someone like Sir Herbert—were to recommend it?"

"Never!" Faith denied it even while the thought lit her eyes.

"Are you sure?" Hester said urgently, leaning forward. "Are you sure Prudence might not have believed they would?"

"You mean that was what she was trying to force Sir Herbert to do?" Faith's eyes widened in dawning belief. "Nothing at all to do with marriage, but to help her receive medical training—not as a nurse but as a doctor? Yes—yes—that is possible. That would be Prudence. She would do that." Her face was twisted with emotion. "But how? Sir Herbert would laugh at her and tell her not to be so absurd."

"I don't know how," Hester confessed. "But that is something she would do—isn't it?"

"Yes—yes she would."

Hester bent to the letters again, reading them in a new light—understanding why the operations were so detailed, every procedure, every patient's reaction noted so precisely.

She read several more letters describing operations written out in technical detail. Faith sat silently, waiting.

Then quite suddenly Hester froze. She had read three operations for which the procedure was exactly the same. There was no diagnosis mentioned, no disease, no symptoms of pain or dysfunction at all. She went back and reread them very carefully. All three patients were women.

Then she knew what had caught her attention: they were three abortions—not because the mother's life was endangered, simply because for whatever personal reason she did not wish to bear the child. In each case Prudence had used exactly the same wording and recording of it—like a ritual.

Hester raced through the rest of the letters, coming closer to the present. She found seven more operations detailed in

389

exactly the same way, word for word, and each time the patient's initials were given but not her name, and no physical description. That also was different from all other cases she had written up: in others she had described the patient in some detail, often with personal opinion added—such as: "an attractive woman" or "an overbearing man."

There was one obvious conclusion: Prudence knew of these operations, but she had not attended them herself. She had been told only sufficient to nurse them for the first few hours afterwards. She was keeping her notes for some other reason.

Blackmail! It was a cold, sick thought—but it was inescapable. This was her hold over Sir Herbert. This was why Sir Herbert had murdered her. She had tried to use her power, had tried once too hard, and he had stretched out his strong beautiful hands and put them around her neck—and tightened his hold until there was no breath in her!

Hester sat still in the small room with the light fading outside. She was suddenly completely cold, as if she had swallowed ice. No wonder he had looked dumbfounded when he had been accused of having an affair with Prudence. How ridiculously, absurdly far from the truth.

She had wanted him to help her study medicine, and had used her knowledge of his illegal operations to try to force him—and paid for it with her life.

She looked up at Faith.

Faith was watching her, her eyes intent on Hester's face. "You know," she said simply. "What is it?"

Carefully and in detail Hester explained what she knew. Faith sat ashen-faced, her eyes dark with horror.

"What are you going to do?" she said when Hester finished.

"Go to Oliver Rathbone and tell him," Hester answered.

"But he is defending Sir Herbert!" Faith was aghast. "He is on Sir Herbert's side. Why don't you go to Mr. Lovat-Smith?"

"With what?" Hester demanded. "This is not proof. We understand this only because we knew Prudence. Anyway,

390

Lovat-Smith's case is closed. This isn't a new witness, or new evidence—it is only a new understanding of what the court has already heard. No, I'll go to Oliver. He may know what to do—please God!"

"He'll get away with it," Faith said desperately. "Do you—do you really think we are right?"

"Yes, I do. But I'm going to Oliver tonight. I suppose we could be mistaken—but . . . no—we are not. We are right." She was on her feet, scrambling to pick up her wrap, chosen during the warmth of the day and too thin for the chiller evening air.

"You can't go alone," Faith protested. "Where does he live?"

"Yes I can. This is no occasion for propriety. I must find a hansom. There is no time to lose. Thank you so much for letting me have these. I'll return them, I promise." And without waiting any longer she stuffed the letters in her rather large bag, hugged Faith Barker, and bolted out of the sitting room down the stairs and out into the cool, bustling street.

"I suppose so," Rathbone said dubiously, holding the sheaf of letters in his hand. "But medical school? A woman! Can she really have imagined that was possible?"

"Why not?" Hester said furiously. "She had all the skill and the brains, and a great deal more experience than most students when they start. In fact, than most when they finish!"

"But then . . ." he began, then met her eyes and stopped. Possibly he thought better of his argument, or more likely he saw the expression on her face and decided discretion was the better part of valor.

"Yes?" she demanded. "But what?"

"But did she have the intellectual stamina and the physical stomach to carry it through," he finished, looking at her warily.

"Oh I doubt that!" Her voice was scalding with sarcasm. "She was only a mere woman, after all. She managed to study on her own in the British Museum library, get out to the Crimea and survive there, on the battlefield and in the hospital. She remained and worked amid the carnage and mutilation, epidemic disease, filth, vermin, exhaustion, hunger, freezing cold, and obstructive army authority. I doubt she could manage a medical course at a university!"

"All right," he conceded. "It was a foolish thing to have said. I beg your pardon. But you are looking at it from her point of view. I am trying to see it, however mistaken they are, from that of the authorities who would—or would not—have allowed her in. And honestly, however unjust, I believe there is no chance whatsoever that they would."

"They might have," she said passionately, "if Sir Herbert had argued for her."

"We'll never know." He pursed his lips. "But it does shed a different light on it. It explains how he had no idea why she appeared to be in love with him." He frowned. "It also means he was less than honest with me. He must have known what she referred to."

"Less than honest!" she exploded, waving her hands in the air.

"Well, he should have told me he gave her some hope, however false, of being admitted to study medicine," he replied reasonably. "But perhaps he thought the jury would be less likely to believe that." He looked confused. "Which would make less of a motive for him. It is curious. I don't understand it."

"Dear God! I do!" She almost choked over the words. She wanted to shake him till his teeth rattled. "I read the rest of the letters myself—carefully. I know what they mean. I know what hold she had over him! He was performing abortions, and she had detailed notes of them— names of the patients and days, treatments—everything! He killed her, Oliver. He's guilty!"

He held out his hand, his face pale.

She pulled the letters out of her bag and gave them to him.

"It's not proof," she conceded. "If it had been, I'd have

given them to Lovat-Smith. But once you know what it means, you understand it—and what must have happened. Faith Barker knows it's true. The chance to study and qualify properly is the only thing Prudence would have cared about enough to use her knowledge like that."

Without answering he read silently all the letters she had given him. It was nearly ten minutes before he looked up.

"You're right," he agreed. "It isn't proof."

"But he did it! He murdered her."

"Yes—I agree."

"What are you going to do?" she demanded furiously.

"I don't know."

"But you know he's guilty!"

"Yes . . . yes I do. But I am his advocate."

"But—" She stopped. There was finality in his face, and she accepted it, even though she did not understand. She nodded. "Yes—all right."

He smiled at her bleakly. "Thank you. Now I wish to think."

He called her a hansom, handed her up into it, and she rode home in wordless turmoil.

As Rathbone came into the cell Sir Herbert rose from the chair where he had been sitting. He looked calm, as if he had slept well and expected the day to bring him vindication at last. He looked at Rathbone apparently without seeing the total change in his manner.

"I have reread Prudence's letters," Rathbone said without waiting for him to speak. His voice sounded brittle and sharp.

Sir Herbert heard the tone in it and his eyes narrowed. "Indeed? Does that have significance?"

"They have also been read by someone who knew Prudence Barrymore and herself had nursing experience."

Sir Herbert's expression did not alter, nor did he say anything.

"She writes in very precise detail of a series of operations you performed on women, mostly young women. It is apparent from what she wrote that those operations were abortions."

Sir Herbert's eyebrows rose.

"Precisely," he agreed. "But Prudence never attended any of them except before and afterwards. I performed the actual surgery with the assistance of nurses who had not sufficient knowledge to have any idea of what I was doing. I told them it was for tumors—and they knew no differently. Prudence's writings of her opinions are proof of nothing at all."

"But she knew it," Rathbone said harshly. "And that was the pressure she exerted over you: not for marriage—she would probably not have married you if you had begged her—but for your professional weight behind her application to attend a medical school."

"That was absurd." Sir Herbert dismissed the very idea with a wave of his hand. "No woman has ever studied medicine. She was a good nurse, but she could never have been more. Women are not suitable." He smiled at the idea, derision plain in his face. "It requires a man's intellectual fortitude and physical stamina—not to mention emotional balance."

"And moral integrity—you missed that," Rathbone said with scalding sarcasm. "Was that when you killed her—when she threatened to expose you for performing illegal operations if you did not at least put in a recommendation for her?"

"Yes," Sir Herbert said with total candor, meeting Rathbone's eyes. "She would have done it. She would have ruined me. I was not going to permit that."

Rathbone stared at him. The man was actually smiling.

"There is nothing you can do about it," Sir Herbert said very calmly. "You cannot say anything, and you cannot withdraw from the case. It would prejudice my defense totally. You would be disbarred, and they would probably declare a mistrial anyway. You still would not succeed."

He was right, and Rathbone knew it—and looking at Sir

Herbert's smooth, comfortable face, he knew he knew it also.

"You are a brilliant barrister." Sir Herbert smiled quite openly. He put his hands in his pockets. "You have defended me almost certainly successfully. You do not need to do anything more now except give a closing speech—which you will do perfectly, because you cannot do anything else. I know the law, Mr. Rathbone."

"Possibly," Rathbone said between his teeth. "But you do not know *me*, Sir Herbert." He looked at him with a hatred so intense his stomach ached, his breath was tight in his chest, and his jaw throbbed with a pain where he had clenched it. "But the trial is not over yet." And without waiting for Sir Herbert to do or say anything else, to give any instructions, he turned on his heel and marched out.

12

THEY STOOD in Rathbone's office in the early morning sun, Rathbone white-faced, Hester filled with confusion and despair, Monk incredulous with fury.

"Damn it, don't stand there!" Monk exploded. "What are you going to do? He's guilty!"

"I know he's guilty," Rathbone said between his teeth. "But he's also right—there is nothing I can do. The letters are not proof, and anyway, we've already read them into evidence once, we can't go back now and try to tell the court they mean something else. It's only Hester's interpretation. It's the right one—but I can't repeat anything Sir Herbert said to me in confidence—even if I didn't care about being disbarred, which I do! They'd declare a mistrial anyway."

"But there must be something," Hester protested, desperately clenching her fists, her body rigid. "Even the law can't just let that happen."

"If you can think of anything," Rathbone said with a bitter smile, "so help me God, I'll do it. Apart from the monumental injustice of it, I can't think when I have hated a man so much." He closed his eyes, the muscles in his cheeks and jaws tight. "He stood there with that bloody smile on his face—he knows I have to defend him, and he was laughing at me!"

Hester stared at him helplessly.

"I beg your pardon." He apologized automatically for his language. She dismissed it with an impatient gesture. It was totally unimportant.

Monk was lost in concentration, not seeing the room around them but something far in his inner mind.

On the mahogany mantel the clock ticked the seconds by. The sun shone in a bright pool on the polished floor between the window and the edge of the carpet. Beyond in the street someone hailed a cab. There were no clerks or juniors in the office yet.

Monk shifted position.

"What?" Hester and Rathbone demanded in unison.

"Stanhope was performing abortions," Monk said slowly.

"No proof," Rathbone said, dismissing it. "Different nurse each time, and always women too ignorant to know how to do anything but pass him the instruments he pointed at and clean up after him. They would accept that the operation was whatever he told them—removal of a tumor seems most obvious."

"How do you know?"

"Because he told me. He is perfectly open about it, because he knows I can't testify to it!"

"His word," Monk pointed out dryly. "But that isn't the point."

"It is," Rathbone contradicted. "Apart from the fact that we don't know which nurses—and God knows, there are enough ignorant ones in the hospital. They won't testify, and the court wouldn't believe them above Sir Herbert even if they would. Can you imagine one of them, ignorant, frightened, sullen, probably dirty and not necessarily sober." His face twisted with a bitter, furious smile. "I would rip her apart in moments."

He assumed a stance at once graceful and satirical. "Now, Mrs. Moggs—how do you know that this operation was an abortion and not the removal of a tumor, as the em-

397

inent surgeon, Sir Herbert Stanhope, has sworn? What did you see—precisely?" He raised his eyebrows. "And what is your medical expertise for saying such a thing? I beg your pardon, where did you say you trained? How long had you been on duty? All night? Doing what? Oh yes—emptying the slop pail, sweeping the floor, stoking the fire. Are these your usual duties, Mrs. Moggs? Yes I see. How many glasses of porter? The difference between a large tumor and a six-week fetus? I don't know. Neither do you? Thank you, Mrs. Moggs—that will be all."

Monk drew in his breath to speak, but Rathbone cut him off.

"And you have absolutely no chance at all of getting the patients to testify. Even if you could find them, which you can't. They would simply support Sir Herbert and say it was a tumor." He shook his head in tightly controlled fury. "Anyway it is all immaterial! We can't call them. And Lovat-Smith doesn't know anything about it! And his case is closed. He can't reopen it at this point without an exceptional reason."

Monk looked bleak.

"I know all that. I wasn't thinking of the women. Of course they won't testify. But how did they know that Sir Herbert would perform abortions?"

"What?"

"How did—" Monk began.

"Yes! Yes I heard you!" Rathbone cut across him again. "Yes, that is certainly an excellent question, but I don't see how the answer could help us, even if we knew it. It is not a thing one advertises. It must be word of mouth in some way." He turned to Hester. "Where does one go if one wishes to obtain an abortion?"

"I don't know," she said indignantly. Then, the moment after, she frowned. "But perhaps we could find out?"

"Don't bother." Rathbone dismissed it with a sharp return of misery. "Even if you found out, with proof, we couldn't call a witness, nor could we tell Lovat-Smith. Our hands are tied."

Monk stood near the window, the clarity of the sunlight only emphasizing the hard lines of his face, the smooth skin over his cheeks, and the power of his nose and mouth.

"Maybe," he conceded. "But it won't stop me looking. He killed her, and I'm going to see that sod hang for it if I can." And without waiting to see what either of them thought, he turned on his heel and went out, leaving the door swinging behind him.

Rathbone looked at Hester standing in the center of the floor.

"I don't know what I'm going to do," she said quietly. "But I'm going to do something. What *you* must do"—she smiled very slightly to soften the arrogance of what she was saying—"is keep the trial going as long as you can."

"How?" His eyebrows shot up. "I've finished!"

"I don't know! Call more character witnesses to say what a fine man he is."

"I don't need them," he protested.

"I know you don't. Call them anyway." She waved a hand wildly. "Do something, anything—just don't let the jury bring in a verdict yet."

"There's no point—"

"Do it!" she exploded, her voice tight with fury and exasperation. "Just don't give up."

He smiled very slightly, merely a touch at the corners of his lips, but there was a shining admiration in his eyes, even if there was no hope at all.

"For a while," he conceded. "But there isn't any point."

Callandra knew how the trial was progressing. She had been there on that last afternoon, and she saw Sir Herbert's face, and the way he stood in the dock, calm-eyed and straight-backed, and she saw that the jurors were quite happy to look at him. There was not one who avoided his glance or whose cheeks colored when he looked toward them. It was plain they believed him not guilty.

So someone else was—someone else had murdered Prudence Barrymore.

Kristian Beck? Because he performed abortions and she knew it, and had threatened to tell the authorities?

The thought was so sickening she could no longer keep it at the back of her mind. It poisoned everything. She tossed and turned in bed until long after midnight, then finally sat up hunched over with her hands around her knees, trying to find the courage to force the issue at last. She visualized facing him, telling him what she had seen. Over and over again she worded it and reworded it to find a way that sounded bearable. None did.

She played in her mind all the possible answers he might give. He might simply lie—and she would know it was a lie and be heartsick. The hot tears filled her eyes and her throat at the thought of it. Or he might confess it and make some pathetic, self-serving excuse. And that would be almost worse. She thrust that thought away without finishing it.

She was cold; she sat shivering on the bed with the covers tangled uselessly beside her.

Or he might be angry and tell her to mind her own business, order her to get out. It might be a quarrel she could never heal—perhaps never really want to. That would be horrible—but better than either of the other two. It would be violent, ugly, but at least there would be a certain kind of honestly in it.

Or there was a last possibility: that he would give her some explanation of what she had seen which was not abortion at all but some other operation—perhaps trying to save Marianne after a back-street butchery? That would be the best of all and he would have kept it secret for her sake.

But was that really possible? Was she not deluding herself? And if he did tell her such a thing, would she believe it? Or would it simply return her to where she was now—full of doubt and fear, and with the awful suspicion of a crime far worse.

She bent her head to her knees and sat crumpled without knowledge of time.

Gradually she came to an understanding that was inescapable. She must face him and live with whatever followed. There was no other course which was tolerable.

"Come in."
She pushed the door open firmly and entered. She was shaking, and there was no strength in her limbs, but neither was there indecision, that had been resolved and there was no thought of escape now.

Kristian was sitting at his desk. He rose as soon as he saw her, a smile of pleasure on his face in spite of very obvious tiredness. Was that the sleeplessness of guilt? She swallowed, and her breath caught in her throat, almost choking her.

"Callandra? Are you all right?" He pulled out the other chair for her and held it while she sat down. She had intended to stand, but found herself accepting, perhaps because it put off the moment fractionally.

"No." She launched into the attack without prevarication as he returned to his own seat. "I am extremely worried, and I have decided to consult you about it at last. I cannot evade it any longer."

The blood drained from his face, leaving him ashen. The dark circles around his eyes stood out like bruises. His voice when he spoke was very quiet and the strain was naked in it.

"Tell me."
This was even worse than she had thought. He looked so stricken, like a man facing sentence.

"You look very tired . . ." she began, then was furious with herself. It was a stupid observation, and pointless.

The sad ghost of a smile touched his mouth.
"Sir Herbert has been absent some time. I am doing what I can to care for his patients, but with them as well as my own it is hard." He shook his head minutely. "But that is unimportant. Tell me what you can of your health. What pain do you have? What signs that disturb you?"

How stupid of her. Of course he was tired—he must be exhausted, trying to do Sir Herbert's job as well as his own.

She had not even thought of that. Neither had any of the other governors, so far as she knew. What a group of incompetents they were! All they had spoken of when they met was the hospital's reputation.

And he had assumed she was ill—naturally. Why else would she consult him with trembling body and husky voice?

"I am not ill," she said, meeting his eyes with apology and pain. "I am troubled by fear and conscience." At last it was said, and it was the truth, no evasions. She loved him. It eased her to admit it in words, without evasion at last. She stared at his face with all its intelligence, passion, humor, and sensuality. Whatever he had done, that could not suddenly be torn out. If it came out at all, it would leave a raw wound, like the roots of a giant tree ripping out of the soil, upheaving all the land around it.

"By what?" he asked, staring at her. "Do you know something about Prudence Barrymore's death?"

"I don't think so—I hope not. . . ."

"Then what?"

This was the moment.

"A short while ago," she began, "I accidentally intruded on you while you were performing an operation. You did not see or hear me, and I left without speaking." He was watching her with a small pucker of concern between his brows. "I recognized the patient," she went on. "It was Marianne Gillespie, and I fear that the operation was to abort the child she was carrying." She did not need to go on. She knew from his face, the total lack of surprise or horror in it, that it was true. She tried to numb herself so she would not feel the pain inside. She must distance herself from him, realize that she could not love a man who had done such things, not possibly. This abominable hurt would not last!

"Yes it was," he said, and there was neither guilt nor fear in his eyes. "She was with child as a result of rape by her brother-in-law. She was in the very early stages, less than six weeks." He looked sad and tired, and there was fear of

402

hurt in his face, but not shame. "I have performed abortions on several occasions before," he said quietly, "when I have been consulted early enough, in the first eight or ten weeks, and the child is a result of violence or the woman is very young indeed, sometimes even less than twelve years old—or if she is in such a state of ill health that to bear the child would, in my judgment, cost her her own life. Not in any other circumstances and not ever for payment." She wanted to interrupt him and say something, but her throat was too tight, her lips stiff. "I am sorry if that is abhorrent to you." A ghost of a smile touched his mouth. "Very sorry indeed. You must know how deeply I care for you, although it has never been right that I should tell you, since I am not free to offer you anything honorable—but whatever you feel about it, I have thought long and deeply. I have even prayed." Again the self-mocking humor flashed and disappeared. "And I believe it to be right—acceptable before God. I believe in those cases a woman has the right to choose. I cannot change that, even for you."

Now she was terrified for him. He would be caught, and that would mean professional ruin and imprisonment. She was aching inside with the tension of fear.

"Victoria Stanhope," she said huskily, her heart full of memories of a girl in a pink dress, her face drawn, her eyes full of hope, and then despair. She had to know this one last thing, and then dismiss it forever. "Did you operate on her?"

His face shadowed with grief.

"No. I would have, since the child was the result of both incest and seduction—her brother Arthur, God help him—but she was only four months from term. It was too late. There was nothing I could do. I wish there had been."

Suddenly the whole picture was different. It was not abortion for money but an attempt to help some of the weakest and most desperate people to cope with a situation beyond their bearing. Should he have? Or was it still a sin?

Surely not? Surely it was compassion—and wisdom?

She stared at him, unable to grasp the joy of it, the im-

403

measurable relief that washed over her. Her eyes were prickling with tears and her voice was trapped somewhere in her throat.

"Callandra?" he said gently.

She smiled, a ridiculous, radiant smile, meeting his eyes with such intensity it was like a physical touch.

Very slowly he began to smile too. He reached out his hand across the desktop and took hers. If it occurred to him that she had thought also that he had killed Prudence, he did not say so. Nor did he ask her why she had not told the police. She would have told him it was because she loved him fiercely, unwillingly and painfully, but it was far better for all that such things be unsaid. It was known between them, and understood, with all the other impossibilities which did not need words now.

For several minutes they sat in silence, hands clasped, staring across the desk and smiling.

Rathbone entered court in a white-hot anger. Lovat-Smith sat somberly at his table, knowing he had lost. He looked up at Rathbone without interest, then saw his expression and stiffened. He glanced up at the dock. Sir Herbert was standing with a faint smile on his lips and an air of calm confidence, nothing so vulgar or ill-judged as jubilation, but unmistakable nonetheless.

"Mr. Rathbone?" Judge Hardie looked at him questioningly. "Are you ready to present your closing argument?"

Rathbone forced his voice to sound as level as he could.

"No, my lord. If it please the court, I have one or two further witnesses I should like to call."

Hardie looked surprised, and Lovat-Smith's eyes widened. There was a faint rustle around the public benches. Several of the jurors frowned.

"If you think it necessary, Mr. Rathbone," Hardie said doubtfully.

"I do, my lord," Rathbone replied. "To do my client complete justice." As he said it he glanced up at the dock and saw Sir Herbert's smile fade just a fraction and a tiny furrow mark his brows. But it did not last. The smile reappeared; he met Rathbone's eyes with confidence and a brilliance which only the two of them knew was contempt.

Lovat-Smith looked curious, shifting his glance from Rathbone to the dock and back again, sitting up a little straighter at his table.

"I would like to call Dr. James Cantrell," Rathbone said clearly.

"Call Dr. James Cantrell," the usher repeated in a loud voice.

After several seconds he duly appeared, young, thin, his chin and throat spotted with blood where he had cut himself shaving in his nervousness. He was a student doctor and his career hung in the balance. He was sworn in and Rathbone began to ask him long, detailed questions about Sir Herbert's immaculate professional behavior.

The jury was bored, Hardie was growing irritated, and Lovat-Smith was quite candidly interested. The smile never faltered on Sir Herbert's face.

Rathbone struggled on, feeling more and more absurd—and hopeless—but he would give Monk all the time he could.

Hester had arranged with another nurse to take care of her duties for a few hours, promising to return the favor in due course at double the hours. She met Monk at his lodgings at six in the morning. Every minute must be made use of. Already the sun was high, and they did not know how long Rathbone could give them.

"Where shall we begin?" she asked. "I have been thinking, and I confess I do not feel nearly as optimistic as I did before."

"I was never optimistic," he said savagely. "I'm just certain I'm not going to let that bastard walk away." He smiled at her bleakly, but there was something in it which was not warmth—he was too angry for that—but even deeper. It was total trust, the certainty that she understood and, without explanation, shared his feeling. "He didn't advertise and he didn't tout for business. Somewhere there is a man or woman who did that for him. He will not have accepted women without money, so that means society—old or new—"

"Probably old," she interrupted wryly. "Trade, which is new society, comes from the genteel upper working classes with social ambitions—like Runcorn. Their morals are usually very strict. It's the older money, which is sure of itself, which flouts convention and is more likely to need abortions—or to feel unable to cope with above a certain number of children."

"Poor women are even less able to manage," Monk said with a frown.

"Of course," she agreed. "But can you see them affording Sir Herbert's prices? They'll go to the women in the back streets, or try to do it themselves."

A look of irritation crossed his face—at his own stupidity, not hers. He stood by the mantel shelf, his foot on the fender.

"So how would a society lady find herself an abortionist?" he demanded.

"Word of mouth, I suppose," she said thoughtfully. "But who would she dare ask?"

He remained silent, watching her and waiting.

She continued, thinking aloud. "Someone her husband would not know—or her father, if she is unmarried—or possibly her mother also. Where does she go alone without causing comment?" She sat down in the high chair and rested her chin on her hands. "Her dressmaker—her milliner," she answered herself. "She might trust a friend, but unlikely. It is the sort of thing you don't want your friends to know—it is their opinion you are guarding against."

"Then those are the people we must try," he said swiftly. "But what can I do? I'm not standing here waiting for you!"

"You are trying the milliners and dressmakers," she replied with decision, rising to her feet. "I am going to try the hospital. Someone there must know. He was assisted, even if it was by a different nurse each time. If I read Prudence's

406

letters again for dates and names"—she straightened her
skirts—"I may be able to trace it back to particular people.
She left initials. One of them may be prepared to testify as
to the middle man . . . or woman."

"You can't do that—it's too dangerous," he said instantly.
"Besides, they won't tell you anything."

She looked at him with disgust. "I'm not going to ask
them outright, for Heaven's sake. And we haven't got time
to be squeamish. Oliver will be able to protract the trial not
more than another day or two at the very best."

Protests rose to his lips and died unspoken.

"What time do milliners open?" he asked. "And what in
God's name am I going to go into a milliner's for?"

"Hats," she said bluntly, clasping her reticule, ready to
leave.

He glared at her.

"For your sister, your mother, your aunt. Anybody you
like."

"And what am I going to do with two dozen women's
hats? And if you give me an impertinent answer . . ."

"You don't have to buy any! Just say you will consider
it and then . . ." She stopped.

"Ask if they can guide me to a good abortionist," he finished.

She raised her chin sharply.

"Something like that."

He gave her a filthy look, then opened the door for her
to leave. It was now quarter to seven. On the step she
turned to meet his eyes in a long, steady gaze, then smiled
a little, just turning up the corners of her mouth. It was a
gesture of courage rather than humor or hope.

He watched her leave without the sense of despair he
ought to have felt, considering how totally absurd their venture was.

His first attempt was ghastly. The establishment opened
for business at ten o'clock, although the flowermakers,
stitchers, ribboners, and pressers had been there since

407

seven. A middle-aged woman with a hard, watchful face welcomed him in and inquired if she might be of service.

He asked to see a hat suitable for his sister, avoiding looking at the displays of any manner of hats in straw, felt, linen, feather, flowers, ribbons, and lace stacked in several corners of the room and along shelves to the sides.

With a supercilious air she asked him to describe his sister and the type of occasion for which the hat was required.

He made an attempt to tell her of Beth's features and general aspect.

"Her coloring, sir," she said with ill-concealed weariness. "Is she dark like yourself, or fair? Does she have large eyes? Is she tall or small?"

He seized on something definite, cursing Hester for having sent him on this idiot's venture.

"Light brown hair, large blue eyes," he replied hastily. "About your height."

"And the occasion, sir?"

"Church."

"I see. Would that be a London church, sir, or somewhere in the country?"

"Country." Did his Northumbrian heritage show so transparently? Even after his years of careful diction to eradicate it? Why had he not said London: it would have been so much easier, and it did not matter. He was not going to buy a hat anyway.

"I see. Perhaps you would care to look at a few of these?" She led him to several very plain shapes in straw and fabric. "We can, of course trim them as you please," she added, seeing the look on his face.

The color rose up his cheeks. He felt like a complete fool. Again he cursed Hester. Nothing except his rage against Sir Herbert would have kept him here. "What about something in blue?"

"If you like," she said with disapproval. "Rather obvious, don't you think? What about green and white?" She picked up a bunch of artificial daisies and held them against a pale green straw bonnet with a green ribbon, and suddenly the effect was so fresh and dainty it took him back with a jolt of memory to childhood days in the summer fields with Beth as a little girl.

"That's lovely," he said involuntarily.

"I'll have it delivered," she said immediately. "It will be ready by tomorrow evening. Miss Liversedge will see to the details. You may settle the account with her."

And five minutes later Monk found himself in the street, having purchased a bonnet for Beth and wondering how on earth he would post it to Northumberland for her. He swore profoundly. The bonnet would have suited Hester, but he certainly was not going to give it to her—of all people.

The next shop was less expensive, busier, and his by now blazing temper saw him through the difficulty of actually expressing approval of any particular bonnet.

He could not waste all day looking at hats. He must broach the subject of his call, however difficult.

"Actually the lady in question is with child," he said abruptly.

"So she will shortly be remaining at home for some time," the assistant observed, thinking of the practicalities. "The hat will be worn only for a few months, or even weeks?"

He pulled a face.

"Unless she is able to . . ." He stopped, shrugged slightly.

The woman was most perceptive. "She already has a large family?" she suggested.

"Indeed."

"Unfortunate. I assume, sir, that she is not—happy—with the event?"

"Not happy at all," he agreed. "In fact, it may well jeopardize her health. There is a limit. . . ." He looked away and spoke very quietly. "I believe if she knew how to—take steps . . ."

"Could she afford . . . assistance?" the woman inquired, also very quietly.

He turned to face her. "Oh yes . . . if it were anything within reason."

The woman disappeared and returned several moments later with a piece of paper folded over to conceal the writing on it.

"Give her this," she offered.

"Thank you. I will." He hesitated.

She smiled. "Have her tell them who gave you the address. That will be sufficient."

"I see. Thank you."

Before he went to the address she had given him, which was in one of the back streets off the Whitechapel Road, he walked some distance in that general direction, thinking long and carefully about the story he would present. It crossed his mind with some humor that he should take Hester and say that she was the lady in need of help. But dearly as he would have liked to do that—the poetic justice of it would have been sweet—she was too importantly occupied as she was at the hospital.

He could no longer pretend to be going for a sister. The abortionist would expect the woman herself; it was not something which could be done at one removed. The only case where she might accept a man making the inquiries would be if the woman were too young to come in person until the last moment—or too important to risk being seen unnecessarily. Yes—that was an excellent idea! He would say he was inquiring for a lady—someone who would not commit herself until she knew it was safe.

He hailed a cab, gave the driver directions to the Whitechapel Road, and sat back, rehearsing what he would say.

It was a long journey. The horse was tired and the cabby sullen. They seemed to stop every few yards and the air was loud with the shouts of other frustrated drivers. Peddlers and costers called their wares, the driver of a dray misjudged a corner and knocked over a stall, and there was a brief and vicious fight, ending with bloody noses and a lot of blasphemous language. A drunken coachman ran straight over a junction at something close to a gallop, and several other horses either shied or bolted. Monk's own hansom had gone a full block before the driver managed to bring it under control again.

Monk alighted onto the Whitechapel Road, paid the driver, who by now was in an unspeakable temper, then began walking toward the address he had been given at the milliner's shop.

At first he thought he had made a mistake. It was a butcher's. There were pies and strings of sausages in the window. If he were right, someone had a macabre sense of humor—or none at all.

Three thin children in dirty clothes stood on the pavement watching him. They were all white-faced. One, about ten or eleven years old, had broken front teeth. A dog with mange in its fur crept around the corner and went in the doorway.

After a moment's hesitation Monk went in after it.

Inside was hot and dim, little light getting through the grimy windows—the smoke of countless factory chimneys and domestic fires had grayed them over the months, and the summer thunderstorms had done nothing to help. The air was heavy and smelled stale and rancid. A large fly buzzed lazily and settled on the counter. The young woman apparently awaiting customers picked up an old newspaper and slammed it down, killing the fly instantly.

"Gotcher!" she said with satisfaction. "What can I do for yer?" she asked Monk cheerfully. "We got fresh mutton, rabbit pie, pigs' trotters, calves'-foot jellies, brawn, best in the East End, and tripes, sheeps' brains, pigs' liver, and sausages o' course! What yer want then?"

"Sausages look good," he lied. "But what I really want is to see Mrs. Anderson. Is this the right address?"

"That depends," she said guardedly. "There are lots of Mrs. Andersons. What did yer want 'er for?"

"She was recommended to me by a lady who sells hats. . . ."

"Was she now." She looked him up and down. "I can't think what for."

411

"For a lady of my acquaintance who would rather not be seen in this neighborhood until it is absolutely necessary."

"So she sent you, did she?" She smiled with a mixture of satisfaction, amusement, and contempt. "Well, maybe Mrs. Anderson'll see you an' maybe not. I'll ask 'er." And she turned and walked slowly toward the back of the room and through a paint-peeled door.

Monk waited. Another fly came in and buzzed lazily around, settling on the blood-spotted counter.

The woman came back and wordlessly held the door open. Monk accepted the invitation and went through. The room beyond was a large kitchen opening onto a yard with coal scuttles, bins overflowing with rubbish, several broken boxes, and a cracked sink full of rainwater. A tomcat slunk across the yard, his body low like a leopard's, a dead rat in his mouth.

Inside the kitchen was chaotic. Bloodstained linen filled one of the two stone sinks by the wall to the right, and the thick, warm smell of blood hung in the air. To the left was a wooden dresser with plates, bowls, knives, scissors, and skewers heaped haphazardly on it. Several bottles of gin lay around, some open, some still sealed.

In the center of the room was a wooden table, dark with repeated soaking of blood. Dried blood made black lines in the cracks and there were splashes of it on the floor. A girl with an ashen face sat in a rocking chair, hugging herself and weeping.

Two dogs lay by the dead ashes of the fire. One scratched itself, grunting with each movement of its leg.

Mrs. Anderson was a large woman with sleeves rolled up to show immense forearms. Her fingernails were chipped and dark with immovable dirt.

" 'Allo," she said cheerfully, pushing her fair gold hair out of her eyes. She cannot have been more than thirty-five at the most. "Need a spot of 'elp do yer, dearie? Well there ain't nothin' I can do for yer, now is there? She'll 'ave to come in 'ere 'erself, sooner or later. 'Ow far gorn is she?"

Monk felt a wave of anger so violent it actually nauseated him. He was forced to breathe deeply for several seconds to regain his composure. With a flood of memory so vivid the sounds and smells returned to him, the thick sweetness of blood, the sounds of a girl whimpering in pain and terror, rats' feet scuttering across a stained floor. He had been in back-street abortionists like this before, God knew how many times, or whether in connection with some woman bled to death, poisoned by septicemia, or simply the knowledge of the crime and the extortionate money.

And yet he also knew of the white-faced women, exhausted by bearing child after child, unable to feed them, selling them as babies for a few shillings to pay for food for the rest.

He wanted to smash something, hurl it to pieces and hear the splintering and cracking as it shattered, but after the instant satisfaction everything else would be the same. If he could weep perhaps he could ease the weight which was choking inside him.

"Well?" the woman said wearily. "Are yer gonna tell me or not? I can't do nothing for 'er if yer just stand there like an idiot! 'Ow far gorn is she? Or doncher know?"

"Four months," Monk blurted.

The woman shook her head. "Left it a bit, ain't yer? Still . . . I spec' I can do summink. Gets dangerous, but I s'pose 'avin it'd be worse."

The girl in the chair whimpered softly, bright blood seeping into the blanket around her and dripping through its thin folds onto the floor. Monk pulled his wits together. He was here for a purpose. Indulgence in his own emotions would solve nothing and not help convict Herbert Stanhope.

"Here?" he asked, although he knew the answer.

"No—out in the street," she said sarcastically. "Of course 'ere, yer fool! Where d'yer think? I don't go to people's houses. If yer want summink fancy yer'll 'ave to see if yer can bribe some surgeon—although I dunno where yer'll find one. It's an 'anging crime, or it used ter be. Now it's just jail—and ruin."

"You don't seem worried," he retorted.

413

"I'm safe enough," she said with dry humor. "Them as comes ter me is desperate, or they wouldn't be 'ere. And I don't charge too much. The fact they're 'ere makes 'em as guilty as me. Anyway, it's a public service as I give—'oo 'round here is gonna turn me in?" She gestured to indicate the whole street and its environs. "Even the rozzers don't bother me if I keep discreet, like. An' I do. So you mind 'ow yer go. I wouldn't wancher ter 'ave an accident. . . ." Her face was still smiling, but her eyes were hard, and the threat was unmistakable.

"How do I find one of these surgeons that do abortions?" he asked, watching her intently. "The lady I'm asking for can afford to pay."

"Not sure as I'd tell yer if I knew—which I don't. Ladies as can pay that sort 'ave their own ways o' findin' 'em."

"I see." He believed her. He had no reason except instinct, but for once, even with thought, he had confidence in his own judgment. This sickening rage was familiar, and the helplessness. He could see in his mind confused and bitter widowers, frightened at being faced suddenly with looking after a dozen children by themselves, not knowing, not understanding what had happened or why. Their wives had faced the growing burden of incessant childbearing without speaking of it. They had gone to the abortionist secretly and alone. They had bled to death without even sharing the reason; it was private, shameful, women's business. The husband had never stretched his imagination beyond his own physical pleasures. Children were a natural thing—and what women were made for. Now he was bereaved, frightened, angry, and totally bemused.

And Monk could see just as clearly young girls, not yet sixteen, ashen-faced, sick with fear of the abortionist and her instruments, her gin bottle, and the shame of it, just like the girl in the chair now; and yet knowing even this was still better than the ruin of becoming a fallen woman. And what waited for a bastard child of a destitute mother? Death was better—death before birth, in some filthy back kitchen with a woman who smiled at you, was gentle according to

414

her abilities, took all the money you could scrape together, and kept her mouth shut. He wished so fiercely it hurt him that he could do something for this child here now, weeping quietly and bleeding. But what was there?

"I'll try to find a surgeon," Monk said with ironic honesty.

"Please yerself," the woman answered, apparently without rancor. "But yer lady friend won't thank yer if yer spread it all over the city among 'er fine friends. Keepin' it quiet is wot it's all for, in'it?"

"I'll be discreet," Monk answered, suddenly longing to be outside this place. It seemed to him as if the very walls were as soaked with pain as the linens and the table were with blood. Even the Whitechapel Road with its grime and poverty would be better than this. It choked him and felt thick in his nostrils and he could taste it at the back of his throat. "Thank you." It was a ridiculous thing to say to her; it was merely a way of closing the encounter. He turned on his heel and flung the door open, strode through the butcher's shop and outside into the street, taking in long gasps of air. Leaden with the smells of smoke and drains as it was, it was still infinitely better than that abominable kitchen.

He would go on looking, but first he must get out of Whitechapel altogether. There was no point in looking to the back-street abortionists, thank God. Stanhope would never have trusted his business to them: they would betray him as quickly as thought—he took some of their best paying customers. He would be a fool to lay his life in their hands. The opportunities to blackmail for half his profit were too rich to pass up—half or more! He would have to look higher in society, if he could think of a way.

There was no time for subtlety. Maybe there was only a day, two at the most.

Callandra! She might know something, and there was no better person to ask. It would mean telling her that Sir Herbert was guilty, and how they knew, but there was no time or opportunity to ask Rathbone's permission. He had told Monk because Monk was his employee in this case, and bound by the same rules of confidentiality. Callandra was not. But that was a nicety Monk did not give a damn about. Sir Herbert could complain from the gallows steps!

It was late when Monk delivered his news, after six in the evening.

Callandra was horrified when the full impact struck her of what he had said. He had left with what little advice she could give, his face pale and set in an expression which frightened her. Now she was alone in her comfortable room lit by the fading sun, with a dark weight of knowledge. A week ago it would have made her heart sing, simply with the sheer certainty that Kristian was not guilty of Prudence's death. Now all she could think of was that Sir Herbert would almost certainly walk free—and more oppressive yet, of the pain that hung over Lady Stanhope, a new grief which she must face. Whether she would ever know that Sir Herbert was guilty of murder, Callandra could only guess, probably not. But she must be told that her eldest son had been the father of Victoria's aborted child. The act of incest was not often a sole event. Her other daughters stood in danger of the same crippling tragedy.

There was no way to ease the telling, nothing Callandra could think of or imagine which would make it bearable. And there was no point in sitting here in her soft chair amid the bowls of flowers and the books and cushions, the cats asleep in the sun and the dog looking at her hopefully with one eye, in case she should decide to walk.

She rose and went to the hall, calling for the butler and the footman. She would take the carriage to Lady Stanhope's house now. It was an uncivil time for calling, and it was unlikely Lady Stanhope was receiving visitors in the circumstances anyway, but she was prepared to force the issue if that was necessary. She was wearing a very simple afternoon dress, fashionable two years ago, and it did not occur to her to change.

She rode in the carriage deep in thought, and was startled to be told she had arrived. She instructed the coachman to

416

wait, alighted without assistance, and went straight to the front door. It was handsome, discreet, speaking of a great deal of money. She noted it absently, aware with bitterness that Sir Herbert would keep all this, probably even with his reputation little damaged. It gave her no satisfaction that his personal life would be scarred forever. All her thoughts were filled with the pain she was about to inflict upon his wife.

She rang the bell, and it was answered by a footman. Perhaps in these anguished times the women were being kept in the rear of the house. It might be deemed better for a man to deal with the curious and tasteless who might call.

"Yes ma'am?" he said guardedly.

"Lady Callandra Daviot," Callandra said briskly, passing him her card. "I have a matter of extreme urgency to discuss with Lady Stanhope, and I regret it cannot wait until a more fortunate time. Will you inform her that I am here." It was an order, not a question.

"Certainly ma'am," he replied stiffly, taking the card without reading it. "But Lady Stanhope is not receiving at present."

"This is not a social call," Callandra replied. "It is a matter of medical emergency."

"Is—is Sir Herbert ill?" The man's face paled.

"Not so far as I am aware."

He hesitated, in spite of experience, uncertain what best to do. Then he met her eyes; something in him recognized power and authority and a strength of will which would not be overridden or gainsaid.

"Yes, ma'am. If you would be good enough to wait in the morning room." He opened the door wider to allow her in, and then showed her to a very formal room, at present devoid of flowers and bleak in its sense of being unused. It was like a house in mourning.

Philomena Stanhope came after only a few moments, looking pinched and anxious. She regarded Callandra without apparent recognition. Society had never meant anything to her, and the hospital was only a place where her husband

417

worked. Callandra was touched by pity for the ruinous disillusion she was about to inflict on her. Her comfortable family and home were about to be ripped apart.

"Lady Callandra?" Philomena said questioningly. "My footman says you have some news for me."

"I am afraid I have. I profoundly regret it, but further tragedy may occur if I do not."

Philomena remained standing, her face even paler.

"What is it?" She was so shaken already that the rules of etiquette were totally ignored. This was in a way worse than death. Death was expected, and there were procedures to follow; whatever the grief, one knew what to do. And death visited all households; there was no shame or peculiarity about it. "What has happened?"

"It is not a simple thing to tell," Callandra replied. "I should prefer to do so seated." She was about to add that it would be easier, but the words were absurd. Nothing could make this easier.

Philomena remained where she was. "Please tell me what has happened, Lady Callandra."

"Nothing new has happened. It is simply knowledge of old sins and sadness which must be known in order to prevent them happening again."

"To whom?"

Callandra took a breath. This was every bit as painful as she had foreseen—perhaps even worse.

"To your children, Lady Stanhope."

"My children?" There was no real alarm in her, only disbelief. "What have my children to do with this—this ordeal? And what can you possibly know about it?"

"I am one of the governors of the Royal Free Hospital," Callandra replied, sitting down, whether Philomena chose to or not. "Your daughter Victoria consulted a surgeon there some time ago, when she first knew she was with child."

Philomena was very pale, but she kept her composure and she did not sit down.

"Indeed? I did not know that, but it does not seem to me

to be of importance now. Unless—unless you are saying that it was he who marred her?"

"No—it was not." Thank God she could say that. "Her pregnancy was too far advanced. He refused to operate."

"Then I cannot see how raising the matter now can serve any purpose whatsoever, except to open old wounds."

"Lady Stanhope . . ." Callandra hated this. She could feel her stomach clenching so hard her whole body hurt. "Lady Stanhope—do you know who was the father of Victoria's child?"

Philomena's voice was strangled. "That is hardly your concern, Lady Callandra."

"You do know!"

"I do not. Nothing I could say would persuade her to tell me. The very fact that I pressed her seemed to drive her to such terror and despair I feared she would take her own life if I continued."

"Please sit down."

Philomena obeyed, not because Callandra asked her but because her legs threatened to give way if she did not. She stared at Callandra as at a snake about to strike.

"She did tell the surgeon," Callandra went on, hearing her own voice in the still room with its dead atmosphere and loathing it. "Because it was one of the circumstances in which he might have considered the operation, had he been consulted sooner."

"I don't understand—Victoria was in excellent health—then . . ."

"But the child was a result of incest. The father was her brother Arthur."

Philomena tried to speak. Her mouth opened, but no sound came. She was so pale Callandra was afraid she was going to faint, even sitting as she was.

"I wish I could have spared you," she said quietly. "But you have other daughters. For their sakes I had to inform you. I wish it were not so."

Still Philomena seemed paralyzed.

Callandra leaned forward and took one of her hands. It

419

was cold to the touch, and stiff. Then she rose and pulled the bell sharply and stood facing the door.

As soon as a maid appeared she sent her for brandy and then a hot, sweet tisane.

The maid hesitated.

"Don't stand there, girl," Callandra said sharply. "Tell the butler to bring the brandy and then fetch the tisane. Hurry yourself!"

"Arthur," Philomena said suddenly in a harsh voice thick with anguish. "Dear God! If only I'd known! If she'd told me!" Slowly she bent forward, her body shuddering with terrible dry sobs and long cries, straining for breath.

Callandra did not even look to see if the maid had gone or not. She knelt and put her arms around the agonized woman and held her close while she shook with a storm of weeping.

The butler brought the brandy, stood helpless and anguished with uncertainty and embarrassment, then put the tray down and left.

Eventually Philomena's strength was spent and she clung to Callandra in motionless exhaustion.

Gently Callandra eased her back into the chair and fetched the brandy, holding it to her lips.

Philomena sipped it, choked, then drank the rest.

"You don't understand," she said at last, her eyes redrimmed, her face smeared with the signs of weeping. "I could have saved her. I knew where to find a woman who could have got her a proper abortion, a woman who knows where to find a real surgeon who would do it—for sufficient money. If she had felt she could trust me, I would have taken her to that man in time. When she got there herself—it was too late."

"You—" Callandra could hardly believe it. "You knew how to find such a woman?"

Philomena misunderstood her emotion. She colored deeply. "I—I have seven children. I . . ."

Callandra grasped her hand and held it. "I understand," she said immediately.

"I didn't go." Philomena's eyes opened wide. "She would not refer me. She—she herself—gave me . . ." She faltered to a stop, unable to say the words.

"But she knew how to find him?" Callandra pressed, the irony bitter inside her.

"Yes." Philomena sobbed again. "God forgive me—I could have helped Victoria. Why didn't she trust me? Why? I loved her so much! I didn't condemn her—what did I fail to do that she . . ." Again the tears filled her eyes and she looked at Callandra desperately, as if she could find some answer that somehow, anyhow, would take away the appalling pain that overwhelmed her.

Callandra said the only thing that came into her mind.

"Perhaps she was ashamed because it was Arthur. And you don't know what he said to her. She may have felt she must defend him from anyone's knowing, even you—or perhaps you most of all because of the distress it would cause you. One thing I am sure of: she would not wish you to bear the burden of guilt for it now. Has she ever reproached you?"

"No."

"Then be assured she does not hold you responsible."

Philomena's face filled with self-disgust. "Whether she does or not, I am to blame. I am her mother. I should have prevented it in the first place—and when it did happen, I should have helped her."

"Who would you have gone to?" She made it sound casual, almost unimportant, but her breath rasped in her throat as she waited for the answer.

"Berenice Ross Gilbert," Philomena replied. "She knows how to obtain safe abortions. She knows of a surgeon who will do it."

"Berenice Ross Gilbert. I see." Callandra tried to hide her amazement and almost succeeded; there was only a lift at the end of her words, a half squeak.

"It makes no difference now," Philomena said immediately. "It is all done. Victoria is ruined—far worse than if she had had the child!"

421

"Perhaps." Callandra could not deny it. "You must send Arthur away to university, or military college, or anything to keep him from the house. Your other daughters must be protected. And you had better make sure none of them is— well, if they are, I will find you a surgeon who will perform the operation without charge, and immediately."

Philomena stared at her. There was nothing else to say. She was numb, wretched, weak with pain and bewilderment.

There was a knock on the door and it opened a crack. The maid put her head around, eyes wide and filled with alarm.

"Bring in the tisane," Callandra ordered. "Put it down there and then leave Lady Stanhope for a while. There are to be no callers admitted."

"Yes ma'am. No ma'am." She obeyed and withdrew.

Callandra remained with Philomena Stanhope for a further half hour, until she was sure she was capable of retaining her composure and beginning to face the dreadful task ahead of her, then she excused herself and left, going outside into the warm dusk to where her carriage still awaited her. She gave the coachman instructions to take her to Fitzroy Street, and Monk's lodgings.

Hester began immediately upon the same task of finding the link between Sir Herbert and his patients that Monk had done. For her it was far easier. She could deduce from Prudence's notes which nurses had assisted him, and even though the notes went back to shortly after Prudence's arrival at the hospital, most of the nurses were still here and not difficult to encounter.

She met one rolling bandages, a second sweeping the floor, a third preparing poultices. The fourth she found carrying two heavy pails of slops.

"Let me help you," she offered uncharacteristically.

"Why?" the woman said with suspicion. It was not a job people took up voluntarily.

"Because I'd rather carry one for you than have to mop

up behind you if you spill it," Hester said with something less than the truth. The task would not have been hers.

The woman was not going to argue herself out of help with a distasteful job. She passed over the heavier of the two pails immediately.

By now Hester had worked out a plan of action. It was not likely to make her popular, and would almost certainly make working in the Royal Free Hospital impossible once the nurses spoke to each other and realized what she was doing, but she would worry about that after Sir Herbert was convicted. For now her anger overrode all such practical considerations.

"Do you think he did it?" she said casually.

"What?"

"Do you think he did it?" she repeated, walking side by side down the corridor with the pails.

" 'Oo did wot?" the woman said irritably. "Are you talking about the treasurer groping after Mary Higgins again? 'Oo knows? And 'oo cares? She asked for it anyway—stupid cow!"

"Actually I meant Sir Herbert," Hester explained. "Do you think he killed Barrymore? The papers say the trial will end soon, then I suppose he'll be back here. I wonder if he'll have changed?"

"Not 'im. Snooty sod. It'll still be 'Fetch this'—'Gimme that'—'Stand 'ere'—'Stand there'—'Empty this'—'Roll up the bandages and pass me the knife.' "

"You worked with him, didn't you?"

"Me? Gor! I just empty slops and sweep floors!" she said with disgust.

"Yes, you did! You assisted him with an operation! I heard you did it very well! July last year—woman with a tumor in her stomach."

"Oh ... yeah! An' in October—but never again after that. Not good enough—me!" She hawked and spat viciously.

"So who is good enough, then?" Hester said, investing

her voice with a suitable contempt. "Doesn't sound like anything very special to me."

"Dora Parsons," the woman replied grudgingly. "Used 'er 'alf the time, 'e did. An' yer right—it weren't nothin' special. Just 'anding 'im knives an' towels an' such. Any fool could've done it. Dunno why 'e picked Dora special. She didn't know nothin'. No better than I am!"

"And no prettier either," Hester said with a smile.

The woman stared at her, then suddenly burst into a loud, cackling laugh.

"Yer a caution, you are! Never know what yer'll say next! Don't you never say that to ol' Cod Face, or she'll 'ave yer up before Lady Almighty for immorality. Although God knows if 'e fancied Dora Parsons 'e'd not be safe wi' the pigs." And she laughed even louder and longer, till the tears ran down her roughened cheeks. Hester emptied the pail and left her still chuckling to herself.

Dora Parsons. That was what Hester had wanted, although she wished it had been anyone else. So Sir Herbert had still lied to Rathbone—he had used one nurse more than the others. Why? And why Dora? For more complicated operations, or ones performed later in the pregnancy, when it was more likely the nurse would know what the operation was? More important patients—perhaps ladies of good family, or maybe women who were terrified for their reputations? It looked as if he trusted Dora—and that raised more questions.

The only way to answer them was to find Dora herself.

That she accomplished after dark when she was so weary all she longed for was to sit down and relieve the ache in her back and her legs. She was carrying blood-soaked bandages down to the stove to burn them (they were beyond any laundress to reclaim), and she met Dora coming up the stairs, a pile of sheets on her arms. She carried the weight of them as if they were merely handkerchiefs.

Hester could not afford to wait for a better time or to get up her courage and prepare. She stopped in the middle of the stairs, under the lamp, blocking Dora's way, trying to look as if she had done it unintentionally.

"I have a friend who is attending the trial," she said, not as casually as she had wished.

"Wot?"

"Sir Herbert," she replied. "It's nearly over. They'll probably bring in the verdict in the next day or two."

Dora's face was guarded. "Oh yeah?"

"At the moment it looks as if they'll find him not guilty." Hester watched her minutely.

She was rewarded. An expression of relief lit Dora's eyes and something inside her relaxed. "Oh yeah?" she said again.

"The trouble is," Hester went on, still blocking the way. "Nobody knows who did kill Prudence. So the case will still be open."

"So what if it is? It weren't you an' it weren't me. An' looks as if it weren't Sir 'Erbert."

"Do you think it was?"

" 'Oo—me? No, I don't reckon as't was." There was a fierceness in her voice, as if she had suddenly forgotten to be so careful.

Hester frowned. "Not even if she knew about the abortions? Which she did. She could have made things pretty hard for him if she threatened to go to the law."

Dora was tense again, her huge body balanced carefully as if to make some sudden move, if she could only decide what. She stared at Hester, hovering between confidence in her and total enmity.

A prickle of sharp physical fear tightened Hester's body, making her gulp for breath. They were alone on the steps, the only light the small oases of the gas lamps at top and bottom and the one under which they stood. The dark well of the stairs yawned below and the shadows of the landing above.

She plunged on.

"I don't know what proof she had. I don't know if she was even there—"

425

"She weren't." Dora cut across her with finality.

"Wasn't she?"

"No—'cos I know 'oo were. 'E wouldn't be daft enough ter have 'er in. She knew too much." Her big face puckered. "Damn near as good as a doctor 'erself, she were. Knew more than any of them student doctors. She'd never 'ave believed they was operations for tumors and the like."

"But you knew! Did the other nurses?"

"No—wouldn't know stones from a broken leg, most of 'em." There was contempt in her tone as well as a mild tolerance.

Hester forced herself to smile, although she felt it was a sickly gesture, more a baring of the teeth. She tried to invest her voice with respect.

"Sir Herbert must have trusted you very deeply."

Pride lit Dora's eyes. "Yeah—'e does. An'e's right. I'd never betray 'im."

Hester stared at her. It was not only pride in her eyes, it was a burning idealism, a devotion and a passionate respect. It transformed her features from their habitual ugliness into something that had its own kind of beauty.

"He must know how much you respect him for it," Hester said chokingly. A flood of emotion shook her. She had wept more tears than she could remember over dead women who had not the strength left to fight disease and loss of blood because their bodies were exhausted with bearing child after child. She had seen the hopelessness in their eyes, the weariness, the fear for babies they knew they could not cherish. And she had seen the tiny, starving creatures come into the world ill before they started, sprung from an exhausted womb.

In the pool of light on the stairs Dora Parsons was waiting, watching her.

And neither could Hester forget Prudence Barrymore, her eagerness and her passion to heal, her burning vitality.

"You're right," she said aloud in the silence. "Some women need a far better help than the law lets us give

426

them. You have to admire a man who risks his honor, and his freedom, to do something about it."

Dora relaxed, the ease washing through her visibly. Slowly she smiled.

Hester clenched her fists in the folds of her skirts.

"If only he did it for the poor, instead of rich women who have simply lost their virtue and didn't want to face the shame and ruin of an illegitimate child."

Dora's eyes were like black holes in her head.

Hester felt the stab of fear again. Had she gone too far?

" 'E didn't do that," Dora said slowly. " 'E did poor women, sick women . . . them as couldn't take no more."

"He did rich women," Hester repeated gravely, in little more than a whisper, her hand on the stair rail as if it were some kind of safety. "And he took a lot of money for it." She did not know if that was true or not—but she had known Prudence. Prudence would not have betrayed him for doing what Dora believed. And Sir Herbert had killed her. . . .

" 'E didn't." Dora's voice was plaintive, her face beginning to crumple like a child's. " 'E didn't take no money at all." But already the doubt was there.

"Yes he did," Hester repeated. "That's why Prudence threatened him."

"Yer lyin'," Dora said simply and with total conviction. "I knew her too, an' she'd never 'ave forced 'im into marryin' 'er. That don't make no sense at all. She never loved 'im. She'd no time for men. She wanted to be a doctor, Gawd 'elp 'er! She'd no chance—no woman 'as, 'owever good she is. If you'd really knew 'er, you'd never 'ave said anything so daft."

"I know she didn't want to marry him," Hester agreed. "She wanted him to help her get admittance to a medical school!"

Slowly a terrible understanding filled Dora's face. The light, the element of beauty, left it and was replaced by an agony of disillusion—and then hatred, burning, implacable, corroding hatred.

" 'E used me," she said with total comprehension.

Hester nodded. "And Prudence," she added. "He used her too."

Dora's face puckered. "Yer said 'e's goin' t' get orf?" she asked in a low, grating voice.

"Looks like it at the moment."

"If 'e does, I'll kill 'im meself!"

Looking into her eyes, Hester believed her. The pain she felt would not let her forget. Her idealism had been betrayed, the only thing that had made her precious, given her dignity and belief, had been destroyed. He had mocked the very best in her. She was an ugly woman, coarse and unloved, and she knew it. She had had one value in her own eyes, and now it was gone. Perhaps to have robbed her of it was a sin like murder too.

"You can do better than that," Hester said without thinking, putting her hand on Dora's great arm, and with a shock feeling the power of the rocklike muscle. She swallowed her fear. "You can get him hanged," she urged. "That would be a much more exquisite death—and he would know it was you who did it. If you kill him, he will be a martyr. The world will think he was innocent, and you guilty. And *you* might hang! My way you'll be a heroine— and he'll be ruined!"

" 'Ow?" Dora said simply.

"Tell me all you know."

"They won't believe me. Not against 'im!" Again the rage suffused her face. "Yer dreamin'. No—my way's better. It's sure. Yours ain't."

"It could be," Hester insisted. "You must know something of value."

"Like what? They in't goin' ter believe me. I'm nobody." There was a wealth of bitterness in her last words, as if all the abyss of worthlessness had conquered her and she saw the light fading out of her reach with utter certainty.

"What about all the patients?" Hester said desperately. "How did they know to come to him? It isn't something he would tell people."

" 'Course not! But I dunno 'oo got 'em fer 'im."

"Are you sure? Think hard! Maybe you saw something or heard something. How long has he been doing it?"

"Oh, years! Ever since 'e did it for Lady Ross Gilbert. She were the first." Her face lit with sudden, harsh amusement, as if she had not even heard Hester's sudden, indrawn breath. "What a thing that were. She were well on—five months or more, and in such a state—beside herself she were. She'd just come back in a boat from the Indies—that would be why she was so far gorn." She let out a low rumble of laughter, her face twisted in a sneer of contempt. "Black, it were—poor little sod! I saw it plain—like a real baby. Arms an' legs an' 'ead an' all." Tears filled her eyes and her face was soft and sad with memory. "Fair made me sick to see it took away like that. But black as yer 'at it'd 'ave been. No wonder she din't want it! 'Er 'usband'd 'ave turned her out, and all London'd 'ave thrown up their 'ands in 'orror in public—and laughed theirselves sick be'ind their doors arterwards."

Hester too was amazed and sick and grieved for a helpless life, unwanted and disposed of before it began.

Without any explanation she knew Dora's contempt was not that the child was black but that Berenice had got rid of it for that reason, and it was mixed with her sense of loss for what was so plainly a human being on the brink of form and life. Anger was the only way she knew to defuse the horror and the pity. She had no children herself, and probably never would have. What emotions must have racked her to see the growing infant, so nearly complete, and dispose of it like a tumor into the rubbish. For a few moments she and Dora shared a feeling as totally as if their paths through life had been matched step for step.

"But I dunno 'oo sends women to 'im," Dora said angrily, breaking the mood. "Maybe if you can find some of them, they'll tell yer, but don't count on it! They in't goin' ter say anything." Now she was twisted with anger again. "You put 'em in court an' they'll lie their 'eads off before they'll admit they done such a thing. Poor women might not—but the rich ones will. Poor women's afraid o' 'avin more kids they can't feed. Rich ones is afraid 'o the shame."

Hester did not bother arguing that rich women could be just as physically exhausted by confinement after confinement. Every woman gives birth in the same way—all the money on earth cannot alter the work of the body, the pain or the dangers, the tearing, the bleeding, the risk of fever or blood poisoning. That surely is the one place where all women are equal. But this was not the time to say so.

"See what you can remember," she argued. "I will reread all Prudence's notes again, just in case there is anything else there."

"You won't get nowhere." There were hopelessness back in Dora's voice and in her face. " 'E'll get off—and I'll kill 'im, the same as 'e killed 'er. I might 'ang fer it—but I'll go gladly if I'm sure 'e's in 'Ell too." And with that she pushed her way past Hester, tears suddenly spilling over her eyes and coursing down her ugly face.

Monk was elated when Hester brought him her news. It was the solution. He knew precisely what to do. Without hesitation he went to Berenice Ross Gilbert's home and commanded the reluctant footman to let him in. He accepted no protests as to the hour, which was approaching. midnight. This was an emergency. It mattered not a jot that Lady Ross Gilbert had retired for the night. She must be awakened. Perhaps it was something in his bearing, an innate ruthlessness, but after only a moment's hesitation the footman obeyed.

Monk waited in the withdrawing room, an elegant expensive room with French furniture, gilded wood, and brocade curtains. How much of it had been paid for by desperate women? He had no time even to look at it now. He stood in the center facing the double doors, waiting for her.

She threw them open and came in, smiling, dressed in a magnificent aquamarine robe which billowed around her.

She looked like a medieval queen: all she lacked was a circlet over her long, bright hair.

"How perfectly extraordinary, Mr. Monk," she said with complete composure. There was nothing but curiosity in her face. "What on earth can have happened that brings you here at this time of night? Do tell me!" She regarded him with undisguised interest, looking him up and down, her eyes at last resting on his face.

"The trial will probably finish tomorrow," he answered, his voice hard and clear, his diction exaggeratedly perfect. "Sir Herbert will be acquitted."

Her eyebrows rose even higher. "Don't say you have come here in the middle of the night to tell me that? I expected it—but regardless, when it happens will be quite soon enough." There was still amusement and question in her face. She did not entirely believe he was so absurd. She was waiting for his real reason for coming.

"He is guilty," he said harshly.

"Indeed?" She came farther in and closed the doors behind her. She was a remarkably handsome woman in a unique way. The whole room was filled with her presence, and he had a powerful feeling that she knew it. "That is only your own opinion, Mr. Monk. If you had proof you would be at Mr. Lovat-Smith's house, telling him, not here doing . . ." She hesitated. "Whatever it is you are doing? You have not so far explained yourself. . . ."

"I don't have proof," he answered. "But you do."

"I do?" Her voice rose in sheer amazement. "My dear man, you are talking the most arrant rubbish. I have nothing of the kind."

"Yes you do." He remained staring at her, meeting her eyes and holding them. Gradually she recognized the power in him, and the implacable intent. The amusement died out of her face.

"You are mistaken," she said softly. "I do not." She turned away and began fiddling idly with an ornament on the marble-topped table. "The whole idea of her wishing to marry him is utterly foolish. Mr. Rathbone has demonstrated that."

"Of course it is," he agreed, watching her long fingers caress the porcelain of the figurine. "She was using her knowledge to try to get him to help her gain admittance to a medical school."

"That is preposterous," she said, still not looking at him. "No school would take a woman. He must have told her that."

"I imagine he did, but not until after he had used her skills to the full, had her work long hours unrewarded, and given her hope. Then, when she became impatient and wanted a commitment, he killed her."

She put the ornament down and turned to face him. The humor was back in her eyes.

"All he had to do was tell her it was hopeless," she answered. "Why on earth would he kill her? You are being ridiculous, Mr. Monk."

"Because she threatened to tell the authorities he was performing abortions—for money," he replied, his voice tight with rage. "Unnecessary abortions to save rich women the embarrassment of children they did not want."

He saw the blood drain from her cheeks, but her expression did not alter.

"If you can prove that, what are you doing here telling me, Mr. Monk? It is a very serious charge—in fact, he would be imprisoned for it. But without proof, what you say is slander."

"You know it is true—because you procure his patients for him," he said.

"Do I?" Her eyes widened and there was a smile on her lips, but it was fixed, and already there was something dead in it. "That too is slanderous, Mr. Monk."

"You knew he performed abortions, and you could testify of it," he said very levelly. "Your word would not be slander, because you have all the facts, dates, names, details."

"Even if I had such knowledge"—she was gazing at him without a flicker, her eyes boring into his—"surely you

432

would not expect me to condemn myself by saying so? Why on earth should I?"

He smiled too, a slow showing of the teeth.

"Because if you do not, I shall make it known to all the right people in society—a whisper, a laugh, a word hushed as you approach—that you were his first patient. . . ."

Her face did not alter. She was not frightened.

"When you came back from the Indies," he went on relentlessly. "And that your child was negroid."

All the color fled from her skin and he heard the gasp of her indrawn breath and then a choking in her throat.

"Is that slanderous too, Lady Ross Gilbert?" he said between his teeth. "Take me to court and sue me! I know the nurse who put the child into the rubbish and threw it away."

She gave a harsh cry which was strangled in her throat before it was out.

"On the other hand," he went on, "should you testify against Sir Herbert, that you referred desperate women to him, whom you could name did not discretion prevent you, and upon whom he performed abortions, then I shall forget I ever knew of such a thing—and you will never hear from me, or from the nurse, again."

"Won't I?" she said with desperate, vicious disbelief. "And what is to stop you coming back again and again—for money, or whatever it is you want?"

"Madam," he said icily, "apart from your testimony, you have nothing I want."

She reached forward and slapped him as hard as she could.

He almost lost his balance from the force of it, and his cheek burned where her open hand had struck him, but he smiled very slowly.

"I am sorry if that disappoints you," he said softly. "Be in court tomorrow. Mr. Rathbone will call you—for the defense, of course. How you manage to impart your information is up to you." And with a very slight bow he walked

433

past her to the door, through the hallway, and out into the street.

The trial was all but over. The jury was bored. They had already reached their verdict in their own minds and could not understand why Rathbone was calling more witnesses to testify to what everyone already believed. Sir Herbert was a paragon of professional virtue and a tediously correct man in his personal and domestic life. Lovat-Smith was openly irritated. The public was restless. For the first time since the trial began, there were even empty seats in the gallery.

Judge Hardie leaned forward, his face creased with impatience.

"Mr. Rathbone, the court is always inclined to give whatever leniency it can to an accused man, but you appear to be wasting our time. Your witnesses are all saying the same thing, and the prosecution has not contested it. Is it really necessary to continue?"

"No, my lord," Rathbone conceded with a smile. As soon as he spoke the quality of suppressed excitement in his voice caused a ripple of movement in the room, a shifting, a straightening as the tension sharpened again. "I have only one more witness, whom I trust will complete my case."

"Then call him, Mr. Rathbone, and proceed," Hardie said sharply.

"I beg leave to recall Lady Berenice Ross Gilbert," Rathbone said loudly.

Lovat-Smith frowned and leaned forward.

Sir Herbert was still smiling in the dock. Only the faintest shadow crossed his eyes.

"Lady Berenice Ross Gilbert!" the clerk called out, and the cry was taken up and echoed into the hallway.

She came in white-faced, her head held high, and she looked neither to right nor left as she crossed the floor to the witness stand, climbed the steps, and turned to face Rathbone. Just once she glanced across at the dock, but her

434

expression was unreadable. If she had noticed Philomena Stanhope on the gallery public benches, she gave no indication.

She was reminded that she was still under oath.

"I am aware of that," she said. "I have no intention to tell other than the truth!"

"You are the last witness I am calling to testify to the character and qualities of the man the prosecution has accused." Rathbone walked into the center of the floor gracefully, elegantly, and stood for an instant smiling up at the dock. He met Sir Herbert's eyes, and Sir Herbert saw for an instant that there was triumph in him, that the anger was gone, and his own composure flickered for a second. Then the certainty returned, and he smiled back.

"Lady Ross Gilbert"—Rathbone looked back at her— "you have served excellently on the Board of Governors of the hospital for some time. Have you been acquainted with Sir Herbert during all these years?"

"Naturally."

"Only professionally, or do you know him personally as well?"

"Slightly. He does not mix in society very much. I imagine he is too fully occupied with the practice of his art."

"So we have heard," Rathbone agreed. "I believe one of your duties as a governor is to make sure that the morals of the nurses employed there are above reproach."

Hardie sighed impatiently. One of the jurors had his eyes closed.

"That would be impossible," Berenice said with a curl of contempt. "All I can do is see that their behavior is acceptable while actually in the hospital premises."

There was a titter of amusement around the room. The juror opened his eyes again.

Judge Hardie leaned forward.

"Mr. Rathbone, you are covering ground which is already exceedingly well trodden. If you have a point, come to it!"

"Yes, my lord. I apologize. Lady Ross Gilbert, have you

at any time in your dealings with the nurses had one of them make a complaint of any sort against Sir Herbert?"

"No. I think I said that before." She was frowning, beginning to look anxious.

"To your knowledge his relationships with women have always been strictly professional?"

"Yes."

"Morally without blemish?" he insisted.

"Well . . ." A flicker of surprise crossed her face, and then sudden perception.

Hardie frowned, looking at her.

In the dock Sir Herbert's certainly wavered.

"Have they, or have they not, Lady Ross Gilbert?" Rathbone demanded, an edge of keenness to his voice.

"That depends upon your interpretation of morality," she replied. Never once did she glance toward Monk on the public benches, or Hester beside him.

Everyone was listening now, straining not to miss a word or an inflection.

"In what category of morality do you find the question difficult to answer?" Hardie asked her, twisting sideways to face her. "Remember you are on oath, madam."

Rathbone made a last attempt to save his own reputation.

"Are you saying he had an affair with someone, Lady Ross Gilbert?" He invested the tone with surprise and disbelief.

Someone in the gallery coughed and was instantly hissed into silence.

"No," Berenice answered.

"Then what are you saying?" Hardie looked confused. "Please make yourself plain!"

Now there was total silence in the room. Every face was turned toward her. Rathbone did not dare to interrupt again in case she lost the opportunity. He might not be able to offer her another.

Still she hesitated.

Sir Herbert leaned over the edge of the dock railing, his face tight, the first flicker of real fear touching him.

436

"Have you some charge of immorality to bring against Sir Herbert?" Rathbone heard his voice rising with pretended outrage. "You had better make it, madam, or cease these insinuations!"

"I am on oath," she said very quietly, looking at no one. "I know that he performed abortions upon many women, at a price. I know it for a fact, because I was the person who referred them to him for help."

There was utter, prickling soundlessness. No one moved. There was not even a sigh of breath.

Rathbone did not dare look up at the dock. He pretended disbelief.

"What?"

"I was the person who referred them to him for help," she repeated slowly and very clearly. "I suppose you would have to say that is immoral. It might be questionable, done for charity—but for payment . . ." She let the words hang in the air.

Hardie was staring at Berenice.

"This is of the utmost seriousness, Lady Ross Gilbert. Do you have any conception of the meaning of what you have just said?"

"I believe so."

"And yet when you came in the witness stand before, you said nothing of this!"

"I did not need to. I was not asked."

His eyes narrowed. "Are you telling us, madam, that you are so naive that you had no idea of the importance of this evidence?"

"It did not seem to be relevant," she replied, her voice trembling a little. "The prosecution charged that Nurse Barrymore had tried to force Sir Herbert into marrying her. I know that was absurd. She would never have done anything of the sort. Nor would he have behaved in such a way. I knew it then, and I know it now."

In the dock Sir Herbert was ashen, looking desperately at Rathbone.

Hardie pursed his lips.

437

Lovat-Smith stared from Hardie to Berenice, then to Rathbone. He still was not totally sure what was happening.

Rathbone clenched his fists so tightly his nails bit into his flesh. It was slipping away again. He was guilty of murder. And he could not be tried for it twice.

He strode forward a couple of paces.

"Ah! Then you are not for an instant suggesting that Prudence Barrymore knew of this and was blackmailing Sir Herbert? You are not saying that—are you!" It was a challenge, hard and defiant.

Lovat-Smith rose very slightly to his feet, still confused.

"My lord, would you please instruct my learned friend to allow the witness to answer for herself and to not interpret for her what she has, or has not, said?"

Rathbone could hardly endure the tension. He dared not interrupt again. He must not be seen to condemn his own client. He turned to Berenice. Please God she would take her opportunity!

"Lady Ross Gilbert?" Hardie prompted.

"I—I don't recall the question," she said wretchedly.

Rathbone answered before Hardie could reword it and make it innocuous.

"You are not saying that Prudence Barrymore was blackmailing Sir Herbert, are you?" he demanded, his voice louder and sharper than he had intended.

"Yes," she said quietly. "Yes, she was blackmailing him."

"But," Rathbone protested, as if horror-stricken, "but you said—why, for God's sake? You said yourself she had no wish whatever to marry him!"

Berenice stared at him with unmitigated hatred.

"She wanted him to help her gain medical training. I know that from deduction—not observation. You cannot charge me with concealing it."

"Ch—charge you?" Rathbone stammered.

"For God's sake!" She leaned over the witness stand railing, her face twisted with fury. "You know he killed her!

You just have to go through this charade because you are supposed to defend him. Get on with it! Get it done!"

Rathbone turned to her very slightly, then away again to look up at Sir Herbert in the dock.

His face was gray, his mouth slack with disbelief, his eyes bright with sick panic.

There was only the faintest, thinnest flicker of hope. Very slowly he turned from Rathbone to the jury. He looked at one, then another, then another, right to the last. Then he knew it was defeat . . . final and absolute.

There was silence in the room. Not even a pencil moved.

Philomena Stanhope looked up at the dock steadily, and there was something in her face very close to pity.

Lovat-Smith held out his hand to Rathbone, his face burning with admiration.

In the public benches Hester turned to Monk, afraid of the triumph she would see in his eyes. But it was not there. It was not a victory they had achieved, only the conclusion of a tragedy, and some measure of justice, at least for Prudence Barrymore and those who had loved her.

Available now in bookstores
everywhere!

SINS OF THE WOLF

by Anne Perry

A Victorian mystery featuring Inspector
William Monk.

Published in hardcover by
Fawcett Columbine.
Read on for a compelling excerpt from
SINS OF THE WOLF . . .

H*ESTER'S FIRST FEELING* was one of profound loss. Long ago she might have had an initial moment of rejecting the fact altogether, refusing to believe Mary was dead, but she had seen too much death not to recognize it, even when it was completely without warning. Last night Mary had seemed in excellent health and buoyant spirits, and yet she must have died quite early in the night. Her body was cold to the touch, and such stiffness took from four to six hours to achieve.

Hester pulled the blanket up over her, gently covering her face, and then stood back. The train was moving more slowly now, and there were houses in the gray, early morning beyond the rain-streaked windows.

Then the next emotion came: guilt. Mary had been her patient, entrusted to her care, and after only a few hours she was dead. Why? What had she done so badly? What had she bungled, or forgotten, that Mary had died without even a sound, no cry, no gasp, no struggle for breath? Or perhaps there had been, only Hester had been too soundly asleep to hear, and the clatter of the train had masked it.

She could not just continue to stand there, staring at the motionless form under the rug. She must tell the authorities, beginning with the conductor and the guard. Then of course

443

when they reached the station there would be the station-master, and possibly the police. After that, infinitely worse, she would have to tell Griselda Murdoch. The thought of that made her feel a little sick.

Better begin. Standing there would not help anything, and the contemplation of it was only adding to the hurt. Feeling numb she went to the compartment entranceway, in her awkwardness banging her elbow on the wooden partition. She was cold and stiff with tension. It hurt more than it would have normally, but she had no time for pain. Which way to go? Either. It made no difference. Just do something, don't stand undecided. She went left, towards the front of the train.

"Conductor! Conductor! Where are you?"

A military man with a mustache peered around a corner and stared at her. He drew breath to speak, but she had rushed on.

"Conductor!"

A very thin woman with gray hair looked at her sharply.

"Goodness, girl, whatever is the matter? Must you make so much noise?"

"Have you seen the conductor?" Hester demanded breathlessly.

"No I haven't. But for heaven's sake lower your voice." And without further comment she withdrew into her compartment.

"Can I help you, miss?"

She spun around. It was the conductor at last, his bland face unsuspecting of the trouble she was about to impart. Perhaps he was used to hysterical female passengers. She made an effort to keep her voice calm and under some control.

"I am afraid something very serious has happened. . . ." Why was she shaking so much? She had seen hundreds of dead bodies before.

"Yes, miss. What would that be?" He was still quite unmoved, merely politely interested.

444

"I am afraid Mrs. Farraline, the lady with whom I was traveling, has died in the night."

"Probably just asleep, miss. Some folk sleep very deep—"

"I'm a nurse!" Hester snapped at him, her voice rising sharply. "I know death when I see it!"

This time he looked thoroughly disconcerted. "Oh dear. You quite sure? Elderly lady, is she? Heart, I suppose. Took bad, was she? Ye should'a' called me then, you know." He looked at her critically.

At another time Hester might have asked him what he could have done, but she was too distressed to argue.

"No—no, she made no sound in the night. I just found her when I went to rouse her now." Her voice was wavering again, and her lips almost too stiff to form the words. "I don't know—what happened. I suppose it was her heart. She was taking medicine for it."

"She had forgot to take it, did she?" He looked at her dubiously.

"No of course she didn't! I gave it to her myself. Hadn't you better report it to the guard?"

"All in good time, miss. Ye'd better take me to your compartment and we'll have a look. Maybe she's only poorly?" But his voice held little hope and he was only staving off the moment of acknowledgment.

Obediently Hester turned and led the way back, stopping at the entrance and allowing him to go in. He pulled the blanket back from the face and looked at Mary for only an instant before replacing it and stepping out again hastily.

"Yes, miss. Afraid you're right. Poor lady's passed over. I'll go and tell the guard. You stay 'ere, and don't touch anything, understand?"

"Yes."

"Good. Maybe you'd better sit down. We don't want you fainting or anything."

Hester was about to tell him she didn't faint, and then changed her mind. Her knees were weak and she would be very glad to sit down again.

445

The compartment was cold and, in spite of the rattle and jolt of the train, seemed oddly silent. Mary lay on the seat opposite, no longer in the comfortable position in which she had gone to sleep, but half turned over as Hester had left her, and the conductor had seen her upturned face. It was ridiculous to think of comfort, but Hester had to restrain herself from going and trying to ease her back to a more natural position. She had liked Mary, right from the moment they had met. She had a vitality and candor which were uniquely appealing, and had already awoken in Hester something close to affection.

Her thoughts were interrupted by the arrival of the guard. He was a small man with a heavy mustache and lugubrious eyes. There was a smudge of snuff on the front of his uniform jacket.

"Sad business," he said dolefully. "Very sad. Fine lady, no doubt. Still, nothing to be done now to 'elp 'er, poor soul. Where was you takin' 'er?"

"To meet her daughter and son-in-law," Hester replied. "They will be at the station. . . ."

"Oh dear, oh dear. Well, nothing else for it." He shook his head. "We'll let all the other passengers get orff, and we'll send for the stationmaster. No doubt 'e'll find this daughter. What's 'er name? D'ye know 'er name, miss?"

"Mrs. Griselda Murdoch. Her husband is Mr. Connal Murdoch."

"Very good. Well, I'm afraid the train is full, so I can't offer you another compartment to sit in, I'm sorry. But we'll be in London in another few moments. You just try to stay calm." He turned to the conductor. "You got something as you can give this young lady, medicinal, like?"

The conductor's bushy eyebrows shot up.

"Are you asking me if I got strong drink on me person, sir?"

"Of course I in't," the guard said smoothly. "That'd be agin company policy. But I just thought as yer might 'ave had summink medicinal on yer, against the cold, or shock, or summink. For passengers, and the like."

446

"Well . . ." The conductor looked at Hester's wan face. "Well, I suppose I might be able to find something—like . . ."

"Good. You go and look, Jake, an' if you can, you give this poor soul a nip, right?"

"Yes sir! Right!"

And he was as good as his word. Having "found" the forbidden brandy, he gave Hester a brimming capful and then left her again, muttering unintelligibly about duty. It was a further quarter of an hour, during which she was shivering cold and feeling increasingly apprehensive, before the stationmaster appeared in the compartment entranceway. He had a bland, curious face, auburn hair and, at the present moment, a severe cold in the head.

"Now then, miss," he said, and sneezed violently. "You'd better tell us exactly what happened to the poor lady. Who is she? And for that matter, who are you?"

"Her name is Mrs. Mary Farraline, from Edinburgh," Hester replied. "I am Hester Latterly, employed to accompany her from Edinburgh to London in order to give her her medicine and see that she was comfortable." It sounded hollow now, even absurd.

"I see. What was the medicine for, miss?"

"A heart ailment, I believe. I was not told any details of her condition, only that the medicine must be given to her regularly, how much, and at what time."

"And did you give it to her, miss?" He regarded her under his eyebrows. "Ye'r sure you did?"

"Yes, absolutely sure." She rose to her feet and pulled down the medicine cabinet, opened it, and showed him the empty vials.

"There's two gone," the stationmaster observed.

"That's right. I gave her one last night, at about a quarter to eleven, the other they must have used in the morning."

"But you only joined the train yesterday evenin'," the conductor pointed out, peering over the stationmaster's shoulder. " 'Ad to 'ave. It don't start till evenin'."

"I know that," Hester said patiently. "Perhaps they were short of medicine, or the maid was lazy, and this was already made up, ready to use. I don't know. But I gave her the second one, out of this vial." She pointed to the second one in its bed. "Last night."

"And how was she then, miss? Poorly?"

"No—no she seemed very well," Hester said honestly.

"I see. Well, we'd best put a guard on duty 'ere to see she in't"—he hesitated—"in't disturbed, and you'd better come and find the poor lady's daughter who's come to meet her, poor soul." The stationmaster frowned, still staring at Hester. "You sure she didn't call out in the night? You were here, I take it—all night?"

"Yes I was," Hester said stiffly.

He hesitated again, then sneezed fiercely and was obliged to blow his nose. He looked at her carefully for several minutes, regarding her straight-backed very slender figure, and making some estimate of her age, and decided she was probably telling the truth. It was not a flattering conclusion.

"I don't know Mr. and Mrs. Murdoch," Hester said quietly. "You will have to make some sort of announcement in order to find them."

"We'll take care of all that sort of thing. Now you just compose yourself, miss, and come and tell these poor souls that their mother has passed over." He looked at her narrowly. "Are you going to be able to do that, miss?"

"Yes—yes certainly I am. Thank you for your concern."

She followed after the stationmaster as he backed out of the entrance and led the way to the carriage door. He turned and assisted her to alight onto the platform. The outside air was sharp and cold on her face, smelling of steam and soot and the grime of thousands of dirty feet. A chill wind whistled along the platform, in spite of the roof overhead, and the noise of trollies, boot heels, banging doors and voices echoed up into the vast overhead span. She followed the stationmaster jostling through the thinning crowd as they reached the steps to his office.

"Are they . . . here?" she asked, suddenly finding her throat tight.

"Yes, miss. Weren't 'ard to find. Young lady and gentleman looking to that train. Only 'ad to ask."

"Has anyone told them yet?"

"No, miss. Thought it better to learn that from you, seein' as you know the family, and o' course knew the lady herself."

"Oh."

The stationmaster opened the door and stood back. Hester went straight in.

The first person she saw was a young woman with fair auburn hair, waved like Eilish's, but much duller in color, sandy rather than burning autumnal. Her face was oval, her features good, but lacking both the passion and the beauty of her sister. Compared with anyone else, she would have been handsome enough, in a quiet, very seemly sort of way, but having met Eilish, Hester could only see her as a shadow, a pale reflection. Perhaps in time, when her present condition had run its term and she was no longer plagued by anxieties, she could be more like Oonagh, have more vivacity and confidence in her.

But it was the man beside her who spoke. He was three or four inches taller than she, his face bony, with hooded eyes and a habit of pursing his lips, which drew attention to his well-shaped mouth.

"You are the nurse employed to accompany Mrs. Farraline on the train?" he demanded. "Good. Perhaps you can tell us what this is all about? Where is Mrs. Farraline? Why have we been kept waiting here?"

Hester met his eyes for a moment in acknowledgment that she had heard him, then turned to Griselda.

"I am Hester Latterly. I was employed to accompany Mrs. Farraline. I am deeply sorry to have to bring you very bad news. She was in excellent spirits last evening, and seemed to be quite well, but she passed away in her sleep, during the night. I think she could not have suffered, because she did not cry out. . . ."

449

Griselda stared at her as if she had not comprehended a word she had heard.

"Mother?" She shook her head. "I don't know what you are saying. She was coming down to London to tell me—I don't know what. But she said it would all be all right! She said so! She promised me." She turned helplessly to her husband.

He ignored her and stared at Hester.

"What are you saying? That is not an explanation of anything. If Mrs. Farraline was in perfect health yesterday evening, she wouldn't simply have"—he looked for the right euphemism—"have passed over—without . . . For heaven's sake, I thought you were a nurse. What is the point of having a nurse to come with her if this is what happens? You are worse than useless!"

"Come now, sir," the stationmaster said reasonably. "If the good lady was getting on in years, and had a bad heart, she could have gone any time. It's something to be grateful for, she didn't suffer."

"Didn't suffer, man? She's dead!" Murdoch exploded.

Griselda covered her face and collapsed backwards onto the wooden chair behind her.

"She can't be gone," she wailed. "She was going to tell me . . . I can't bear this! She promised!"

Murdoch looked at her, his face filled with confusion, anger and helplessness. He seized on the refuge offered him.

"Come now, my dear. There is some truth in what the stationmaster says. It was extraordinarily sudden, but we must be grateful that she did not suffer. At least it appears so."

Griselda looked at him with horror in her wide eyes. "But she didn't—I mean, there wasn't even a letter. It is vitally important. She would never have . . . Oh this is terrible." She covered her face again and began to weep.

Murdoch looked at the stationmaster, ignoring Hester.

"You must understand, my wife was devoted to her mother. This has been a great shock to her."

"Yes sir, only natural," the stationmaster agreed. " 'Course it is. Would to anyone, especially a young lady o' sensibility."

Griselda rose to her feet suddenly. "Let me see her!" she demanded, pushing her way forward.

"Now really, my dear," Murdoch protested, grasping her shoulders. "That would do no good at all and you must rest. Think of your condition. . . ."

"But I must!" She fought free of him and confronted Hester, her face so pale the dusting of freckles across her cheeks stood out like dirty marks. Her eyes were wild and staring. "What did she say to you?" she demanded. "She must have told you something! Something about her purpose in coming here—something about me! Didn't she?"

"Only that she was coming to reassure you that you had no cause for anxiety," Hester said gently. "She was quite definite about that. You need have no anxiety at all."

"But why?" Griselda said furiously, her hands held up as if she would grasp Hester and shake her if she had dared. "Are you sure? She might not have meant it! She could have been simply— I don't know—being kind."

"I don't think so," Hester replied quite frankly. "From what I saw of Mrs. Farraline, she did not speak idly in order to set someone's mind at rest; if what she had said was not completely true, she need not have mentioned it at all. Of course it is extremely difficult for you at such a dreadful time, but I should try to believe that you really do have no cause for concern."

"Would you?" Griselda said eagerly. "Do you think so, Miss . . ."

"Latterly. Yes I do."

"Come, my dear," Connal said soothingly. "This is really not important now. We have arrangements to make. And you must write to your family in Edinburgh. There is a great deal to take care of."

Griselda turned to him as if he had been speaking a foreign language.

"What?"

"Don't worry yourself. I shall attend to it all. I shall write this morning, a full letter with all that we know. If I post it today, it will go on the night train, and they will receive it in Edinburgh tomorrow morning. I will assume then that it was very quiet and she almost certainly felt nothing." He shook his head a little. "Now, my dear, this has been a terrible day for you. I shall take you home where Mama can care for you." His voice held a sudden relief at having thought of the ideal way of releasing himself from a situation beyond his ability. "You really must consider your . . . health, my dear. You should rest. There is nothing you can do here, I assure you."

"That's right, ma'am," the stationmaster said quickly. "You go with your husband. 'E is absolutely right, ma'am."

Griselda hesitated, shot another anguished look at Hester, then succumbed to a superior force.

Hester watched her go with relief, and a sharp, sad memory of Mary saying how unnecessarily Griselda worried. She could almost hear Mary's voice in her head, and the very humor in it. Perhaps she should have said more to comfort her. She had seemed more devastated by the lack of reassurance over her child than by her mother's death. But perhaps that was the easier of the two emotions to face. Where some people retreated into anger, and she had seen that often enough, Griselda was grasping on to fear. Being with child, especially a first, could cause all kinds of strange turmoils in the mind, feelings that would not normally be so close to the surface.

But Griselda was gone, and there was nothing she could add now. Perhaps in time Murdoch would think of the right things to say or do.

It was nearly another hour of questions and repeated futile answers before Hester was permitted to leave the station. She had recounted to every appropriate authority the exact instructions she had been given in Edinburgh, how Mary had seemed during the evening, that she had made no complaint whatever of illness, on the contrary, she had seemed in unusually good spirits. No, Hester had heard nothing unusual in the night, the sound of the wheels on the track had obliterated almost everything else anyway. Yes, without question she had given Mrs. Farraline her medicine, one vial as instructed. The other vial had already been empty.

No, she did not know the cause of Mrs. Farraline's death. She assumed it was the heart complaint from which she suffered. No, she had not been told the history of the illness. She was not nursing her, simply accompanying her and making sure she did not forget her medicine or take a double dose. Could she have done so? No, she had not opened the case herself, it was exactly where Hester had put it. Besides which, Mary was not absentminded, nor approaching senility.

At last, feeling numb with sadness, Hester was permitted to leave, and made her way to the street, where she hailed a hansom cab and gave the driver Callandra Daviot's address. She did not even consider whether it was a courteous thing to turn up in the middle of the morning, unannounced and in a state of distress. Her desire to be warm and safe, and to hear a familiar voice, was so intense it drove out normal thoughts of decorum. Not that Callandra was someone who cared much for such things, but eccentricity was not the same as lack of consideration.

It was a gray day, with gusts of rain on the wind, but she was unaware of her surroundings. Grimy streets and soot-stained walls and wet pavements gave way to more gracious squares, falling leaves and splashes of autumn color, but they did not intrude into her consciousness.

" 'Ere y'are, miss," the driver said at last, peering down at her through the peephole.

"What?" she said abruptly.

"We're 'ere, miss. Ye goin' ter get out, or d'yer wanner stay sitting in 'ere? I'll 'ave ter charge yer. I got me livin' ter make."

"No of course I don't want to stay in here," she said crossly, scrambling to open the door with one hand and grasp her bag with the other. She alighted awkwardly and, setting her bag on the pavement, paid him and bade him a good day. As the horse moved off, and the rain increased in strength, making broad puddles where the stones were uneven, she picked up the bag again and climbed the steps to the front door. Please heaven Callandra was at home, and not out engaged in one of her many interests. She had refused to think of that before, because she did not want to face the possibility, but now it seemed so likely she even hesitated on the step, and stood undecided in the rain, her feet wet, her skirts becoming sodden where they brushed the stones.

There was nothing to lose now. She pulled the bell knob and waited.

ANNE PERRY

Published by Fawcett and Ivy Books.
Available in your local bookstore.